"A masterful storyteller."
— Catherine Anderson, *New York Times* bestselling
author of *Walking on Air*

"Compelling and beautifully written."
— Debbie Macomber, #1 *New York Times* bestselling
author of *Mr. Miracle*

"Thomas knocks it out of the park . . . Intense and beautiful."
— *Publishers Weekly*

Marie Force

"Marie Force makes you believe in the power of true love
and happily ever after."
— Carly Phillips, *New York Times* bestselling
author of *Dare to Touch*

"Genuine and passionate."   — *Publishers Weekly*

"Draws you in, and never lets you go."
— *Guilty Pleasures Book Reviews*

Shirley Jump

"Inviting, intriguing, heart-tugging, and splendid."
— *USA Today*

continued . . .

ASK ME WHY

Jodi Thomas
Marie Force
Shirley Jump
Virginia Kantra

JOVE BOOKS, NEW YORK

JOVE

An imprint of Penguin Random House LLC
375 Hudson Street, New York, New York 10014

ASK ME WHY

A Jove Book / published by arrangement with the authors

ISBN: 978-0-515-15538-9

PUBLISHING HISTORY
Jove mass-market edition / July 2015

PRINTED IN THE UNITED STATES OF AMERICA

10 9 8 7 6 5 4 3 2 1

Cover art by Jim Griffin.
Cover design by George Long.
Text design by Kelly Lipovich.

Penguin
Random
House

CONTENTS

MIDNIGHT BET

Jodi Thomas

ONE

Matheson Ranch
July 6, 2014

RICK MATHESON DROPPED off the side of the wide porch
of his cousin's home and walked toward a stand of cottonwood
trees that were old when he'd played among their low branches
as a kid twenty years ago.

Summer Sundays in the South, he thought. Everyone still
dressed in their church best and stuffed themselves on a potluck
meal that was better than any restaurant could serve. He heard
laughter from the under-forty crowd scattered in folding chairs
on the front lawn and porch. They were supposed to be watching the little Mathesons play in the afternoon shade, but the kids
pretty much ran free-range on the wide lawn.

The half-dozen teenagers who usually had the babysitting job
were over in the corral saddling a few of Hank's horses so they
could ride. In an hour the shade in the canyon behind his head-
quarters would be perfect for an afternoon gallop.

Mathesons lived on farms and ranches for fifty miles around
Harmony, Texas. A few, like Rick, even lived in town, but he
knew all considered this old place the family home. It wasn't the

original homestead. That had burned down generations ago. But
Hank Matheson's ranch had been built on the first small acreage
the family settled on. It was home base. Rick had grown up
chasing fireflies in the front yard and racing his cousins on
horseback across the open land. At thirty, he'd always thought
he'd be married by now and have joined the kid watchers on the
porch.

Only life and his apparently dangerous career choice had
derailed his plan.

He looked back at his family and swore he could feel his
heart turning to lead. He was in trouble this time, bad trouble,
and he had to keep it from them for as long as possible.

Rick was four years out of law school and, for the second
time, someone wanted to kill him. He had no proof, just a feeling.
Hang-ups on his phone. His old office had been broken into
twice. A car, with the brights on, almost ran him off the road last
week. Trouble was stalking him.

When revenge came after him this time, murder might suc-
ceed. If Rick told his family, they'd protect him, but he couldn't
allow that. One of them might get caught in the cross fire. So he
had to go on living his life exactly as always and pretend a storm
wasn't blowing full out toward him.

Rick tried to shake his mood. Maybe he was overreacting?
Hell, maybe he should change careers. Being a lawyer didn't
seem to be working out. He thought of himself as good-looking;
he came from an upstanding family, was well educated, and had
all his own teeth. But the last woman he'd asked out had simply
smiled and said that she didn't date lawyers.

Maybe he should have made an objection to her rejection,
but he hadn't been that into her to start with. She'd simply been
someone he might go to dinner with, or maybe they would even-
tually move into a casual relationship. He didn't see love and
offspring with the lawyer-hater, or with any woman he met. He
didn't see passion either, which bothered him. He was working
far too hard. Monks had more social life than he did.

Rick turned and walked back toward the house. When he
stepped inside the kitchen door, he heard his old Aunt Fat telling
one of her favorite stories to his second cousin's new bride.

"There's an old bridge near downtown that runs across a
dried-up creek bed where water used to flow wild." Aunt Fat, like

the teacher she'd been for forty years, paused, making sure she had everyone's attention. "The bridge doesn't look like much now, it being old and all, but there's a legend about the spot. Word is, if a couple kiss while standing in the exact middle of the bridge, they'll never stop loving each other."

The bride winked at her new husband and he nodded. Everyone in the kitchen laughed, knowing exactly where the newlyweds would be heading as soon as the family dinner broke up.

Rick smiled. Aunt Fat had told that story for as long as he could remember, and it always had the same effect on brides.

"You all right, Rick?" his mother asked as he passed her. She was one of those magic moms who could look at any one of her children and know their mood or temperature or if they needed to eat something.

"I'm fine, Mom," he lied. "I just got a lot of work waiting for me at the office. I think I'll head on in."

"You work too hard, Rick." She patted his back. "You're just like your father was." When her arm circled around his waist, she added, "And you need to eat something. You're thin as a fence post."

"I know," he answered, "but the work has to get done. I forget to eat." He'd moved into a bigger office last month and hadn't had time to unpack before he went to work. Now he felt like a prisoner, barred in by boxes every time he showed up at the office. "I really need to leave," he said, knowing he'd have to say it at least one more time before he made it out the door.

Only tonight his mother surprised him. She simply kissed his cheek and whispered, "Offer Lizzie a ride back to town. She wrecked another car."

Rick might be tapping thirty, but he knew a direct order from his mother when he heard it.

Looking over her head, he spotted Lizzie, dressed like a hooker in mourning. Black fishnet hose. Black, almost see-through dress with one shoulder cut out to show off her tattoo. Platform sandals that could have doubled as stilts. The only color she wore lately was the green streaks in her hair. Elizabeth Lee Matheson. The only nut to ever fall off the Matheson tree. She'd gotten every wild, weird gene in the family, and she'd always been a bother. She was a few years younger than he, so he'd had to play with her when none of the other cousins would, and teach her to ride when she didn't want to learn, and drive her to high school when she wrecked three cars her sophomore year. Her hardship license was hard on cars.

Rick could continue, but the list was too long and too painful. He didn't bother to argue with his mom now. "Sure. Glad to drive her home," he lied again.

Walking over to the long bar that separated the kitchen from the den, Rick tapped Lizzie on her bare shoulder. "You about ready to go, Lizzie Lee? I could give you a lift."

She looked up from trying to pop the top on her latest beer. "I'm so-o-o-o-o ready to leave." As always, she'd brought a six-pack to the potluck and had drunk most of it herself.

Rick helped her off the stool, thinking that the high-heeled shoes almost made her normal size. With a woman who didn't tip five feet or a hundred pounds, four or five beers must make her dead drunk.

Lizzie waved good-night to everyone while he tugged her around the crowd. Almost every family gathering, someone had to take her home, and this must be his time.

He poured her into his new car and prayed she wouldn't throw up on the way to town.

"Hey, Ricky, you want to stop for a drink on the way home?" She giggled. "Oh, it's Sunday, I forgot. Every place is closed. Guess you'll just have to give me a rain check."

"I couldn't tonight anyway, Lizzie. I have work to do at my office." Another thing he hated about Lizzie, she called him Ricky when she'd been drinking. No one called him Ricky. Plus, if his dating life wasn't already dead, showing up with his wacky cousin in public would probably do the trick. She seemed to always say the wrong thing in a crowd or accidentally spill something. But his cousin had one flaw that was his favorite, if anyone can have a favorite flaw, and that was the way she always mixed up people's names. She called his cousin Hank "Hunk" and the preacher's second wife Two instead of Lou. Since the Leary twins' birth, she'd called them "Pete and Repeat."

"Could we stop at the bridge Aunt Fat was talking about?"

"No," he answered, starting the engine.

"I'd really like to see it. A legend in Harmony. Too bad my parents hadn't kissed on the bridge. I think my dad took every deployment he could sign up for to get away from Mom. My first memories are of them yelling in the middle of the night."

He drove under the ranch arch and headed toward Harmony on the Farm to Market Road everyone called Lone Oak Road. "All right. We'll stop. Five minutes."

She leaned back and closed her eyes. "Thanks for offering to take me home. You're the only one in the family I can stand to talk to or who wants to talk to me."

Rick tossed his jacket over her bare shoulder and cranked up the air-conditioning, even though the afternoon hadn't reached ninety degrees. Maybe the circulation would help clear her perfume from the air. "You're not so bad, Lizzie." In truth, she'd had it rough. Her dad had been in the Navy. When he was listed as missing in action, her mother couldn't stand the pressure and had sent Lizzie, who was about eight years old then, to live with her Matheson grandmother. He'd heard her mother had cracked up completely when her husband was moved from "missing" to "killed in action." Granny always said Lizzie's mother "just went to sleep," but Rick thought a bottle of pills might have helped the process. Anyway, Granny and Little Lizzie grieved, and the money they inherited from her parents helped keep food on the table.

Granny loved Lizzie, but she never let the girl out of her sight. Rick remembered Granny even made Lizzie go everywhere with her. Quilting. Widows Sunday class. She had to sit in the beauty shop while Granny got her hair curled and sprayed every week. Rick remembered Lizzie called her grandmother's Sunday school class the "Nearest to Heaven" class and the all-day quilting bees "Stitch and Complain."

From grade school on, she'd never fit in. Somewhere in middle school, she'd given up trying. Lizzie seemed to go out of her way to be unique. Half her outfits looked like they'd been on the Halloween closeout special rack. Granny always told people Lizzie simply marched to a different drummer, but if so, Rick had never heard the beat.

"The whole family just tolerates me, and I feel the same way about them," Lizzie said as she fought with her seat belt. "They're all nice folks, but I feel like I've been assigned to the wrong family, you know?"

He didn't know, but he answered, "They all love you,

honey." Lies were starting to dribble out of his mouth. At this rate, he'd need a bib before long.

"That must be why they all want to change me into someone else. I swear if they thought they could get away with it, half of them would vote to have me stretched so I'd at least look more Matheson." She ducked her head down in his coat like a turtle retreating into a shell. "I just want to find my people, you know? Somewhere, someplace probably far away, there are people just like me waiting supper, wondering where I am."

"Right," Rick answered, thinking that if anyone ever found that place, it would take about a second to collect the money to send her there.

Ten minutes later, they pulled up to the bridge and climbed out of the car. She leaned against the fender, pulling his jacket around her as if it were cold. "I'm never going to fall in love," she whispered. "This is probably the one time I'll ever stand on this bridge, and I'm here with my cousin."

He agreed. "I almost fell once. Met a woman I thought was perfect, but it turned out she didn't want commitment; she only wanted my body."

"Yeah, I played that game a few times in high school."

Rick didn't comment that he'd heard all about it from some of his friends.

She straightened. "I think I'd better head home. I don't feel so good. Beer and pot roast seem to be fighting in my stomach."

He reached for the handle on his side as she did the same.

Something sounding very much like a shot whistled through the still air. Rick ducked inside his car as if the glass would somehow protect him.

Lizzie, with less skill, did the same. As she leaned out to close the door on her side, his coat tumbled off her shoulders and into the dirt. She reached down, grabbed it and tugged it over her.

For a few heartbeats they were both silent, listening for another shot.

Without a word to Lizzie, he gunned the engine and threw the car into Drive. They flew off the bridge and headed toward Lizzie's place on the other side of town.

Rick's mind raced. The shot could be another attempt on his life? One of these days whoever was out there wanting him dead might get lucky.

Lizzie didn't say a word as he drove down sleepy streets, past the tiny mall, then bounced over railroad tracks. Nothing much had been built beyond the tracks in fifty years. A few grain elevators spotted the horizon. A dozen houses were scattered out along the winding road, not close enough to be considered in the town or far apart enough to be called "in the country." Half a mile farther, Lizzie's house hid behind one of the town's veterinary clinics. Corrals and trailers scattered around the vet's office almost hid her place from view.

Rick bumped along a dirt lane to her property as he circled a corral to get to her house. An adobe fence, overgrown with morning glories, separated her land from the vet's. Rick didn't breathe until he neared her back door.

"You really should get this road paved, Lizzie. One day a car is going to disappear in a rut."

"Why, if it rains, I can park in Dr. McCall's lot. He doesn't mind, and there's a path from my front door to his place." She stepped out as if there were nothing else to talk about and tossed his coat back to him.

"Thanks," she called without looking back.

"You're welcome," he answered too low for her to hear.

Rick tried to decide if, in her world, gunfire didn't seem strange or if she was too drunk to have noticed.

Watching her hug herself and stagger toward the porch, he wondered if she was really that drunk or if the ridiculous shoes simply weren't made for cobblestones. He didn't care. All he wanted to do was drop her off and head back to his office. The federal prosecutor had asked for his help on an old case, and Rick had a feeling that somewhere in his files might be the clue needed to send a really bad guy to jail. Only problem was, he had to get to it before the bad guys got to him.

He'd call the sheriff and tell her about the shot, if it was a shot. Then he'd be careful about standing around looking like an easy target. The idea of someone following him didn't make sense. Harmony was a small town; folks still noticed strangers and license plates that weren't local. If the shot had been directed at him, it was probably meant to scare him off, and the guy just caught a lucky chance when Rick was dumb enough to stop on the bridge.

Lizzie had almost made it to her home, but she missed a step two feet from the porch and sank her high heels into the mud. Shaking off mud, she climbed onto the first step and turned to wave good-bye. As if just remembering what had happened, she yelled back to him, "You going to call that gunfire in?"

He shook his head. "Probably only a backfire."

"Want to tell me why that might not be the truth?" She glanced at him with those big eyes of hers. "You know, Ricky, if you ever need me, I'll come running."

"No. Don't worry about me, Lizzie Lee." The last thing he wanted to do was talk with her about his problems. Shifting the car into Reverse, he offered a quick wave.

As he drove away, he remembered the veterinarian who had built the clinic had once owned her house. Years ago, the clinic, Lizzie's house, and the small shop across the road had all been one property. The last vet had lived in the house, run the clinic, and rented out the shop. Now Lizzie owned the house and the shop, where she did pet grooming on Wednesdays and Fridays. Who knows what she did the other days, but he didn't want her worrying about him.

Rick thought about asking where the new vet lived, but he really didn't care. With no pets, he wasn't likely to use either of their services. "Good night, Lizzie," he yelled as he glanced back and saw her entering her house.

He tossed his jacket into the backseat knowing that it would need cleaning. Between her perfume and her dropping it on the bridge, he doubted he could wear it now.

Rick couldn't help wondering just how few friends she must have if she counted him among them. He thought of yelling, "Don't call me Ricky, and for God's sake, please don't ever try to save me," but she was already inside.

Rick laughed. The last person on this planet he'd ever call for help was his nutty cousin.

Two

A LITTLE AFTER dark, Lizzie tapped on the door of the veterinarian's office. The entrance had been designed to look like a barn door four years ago when Dr. McCall moved to town, bought the practice, and remodeled.

Four years and everyone still called him the new vet, she thought. He wasn't new or fresh out of school. He'd been practicing in San Antonio for a few years before he came to Harmony. Someone said the doc mentioned wanting to move to West Texas after he lost his wife. No one wanted to pry and ask whether she left him or died, but Dr. McCall seemed to have given up on people in general. A kind of sadness hung over his broad shoulders. If his wife had left him, she'd left him broken.

Though still in his thirties, he was grumpy and never bothered with idle conversation, but Lizzie accepted him, just as she guessed he did her. Dr. McCall might not like people, but he cared about animals, including her cats, although he mostly handled large stock at the clinic. Their usual interaction, if he noticed her passing his place, was little more than a nod. The other vet had handed out advice about everything in life. Dr. McCall simply talked to the patient on his examining table and barely noticed her.

Sometimes when she was grooming a dog or cat in her tiny pet salon across the road from him, she would notice something wrong with her client and run to his office. He always took the time to examine her animal while his waited. The horses never seemed to mind. He'd explain to her what she needed to tell the pet's owner, and he never charged her for the advice.

Dr. McCall might not be friendly, but he wasn't unkind, and in Lizzie's world that counted.

On the third knock the porch light came on, and the doc opened the door.

"Evening, Elizabeth, you got a problem with Sam or Molly?" He leaned down, not looking at her face but searching for a carrier.

Lizzie tried to smile. He always said her name as if that day he'd read it on the mailbox for the first time, even though they'd lived next to each other for years.

The doctor was a mixture of the actor Jake Gyllenhaal—add a few years—and Sam Elliot—take away thirty years. Cute in a roughed-up, uncared for kind of way. He always wore worn jeans, boots, and a sweater from September to March. In summers he switched into short-sleeve knit shirts, but Lizzie suspected there was a sweater hiding a few feet away in the closet. Guessing, she'd say he could have been handsome if he tried, which he didn't. But, with just enough gray in his shaggy hair to look sexy and with his clothes always wrinkled, he'd somehow managed to stay off the available bachelor list in town. She had the feeling he always talked down to people and up to animals.

Pulling the raincoat around her, she whispered, "May I come in, Doc? I have a medical question."

He stepped back. "Of course, Elizabeth, if it's something that can't wait until tomorrow morning. The fellows and I were just sitting down to watch a movie."

As she passed him, the doc poked his head outside and glanced at the cloudy sky, then looked back at her raincoat.

She walked into his wide foyer and waited, not sure which door to take. His quarters were on one side of the long, narrow building and his office on the other. She wasn't surprised to see two dogs waiting at his open apartment door as if they were his assistants. The smell of popcorn drifted from his place.

Doc shooed the curious dogs back as he closed the door. "Go on, boys, eat your supper without me. I'm needed in the office."

She waited as he opened the door on the other side. There was no reception area, just a large room with equipment lining the walls and three doors opening out to an arena where larger animals could be brought up to a stall/examining room. As always, the place was clean but cluttered with supplies and books.

The doc offered her a chair as he leaned on an old desk that had to have survived several vets. "How may I help you?" he asked as he shoved shaggy hair back with one rake of his big hand.

Lizzie slowly pulled open her coat. "I need to know what to do about this. I can't seem to stop the bleeding."

For a moment, he froze as if he couldn't make sense of what he saw, then he knelt in front of her chair hesitantly. His chocolate eyes were wide with concern. "Elizabeth, you're bleeding."

She tried to smile. "Thanks for confirming my diagnosis, but that's not the question."

His almost-bushy eyebrows wrinkled. "You've got to go to the hospital. I can't treat you."

When she just stared at him, he seemed to understand that she didn't consider that an option. Slowly lifting her off the chair, he set her on the desk. "I'll get something to help stop the bleeding then I'm driving you to the hospital."

While he collected supplies, she shook her head. "I'm not going anywhere. I'll treat myself. I just need you to tell me how."

He shook his head as he cleared the desk and spread out a clean sheet. With one twist he rolled a fresh towel to use for a pillow.

She lay down on her unharmed side and tugged up the T-shirt she'd switched into when her cousin brought her home. Half the white cotton was already covered in blood.

He pulled the raincoat away from her side and pushed the shirt up past her bra. An inch of flesh had been ripped away halfway between her bra and the low-cut waist of her jeans.

"It's just a scratch." She closed her eyes almost believing her own lie. "I don't want anyone to know. I could have doctored it at my place, but I had a little problem."

Doc McCall put gauze over the place where blood seemed

to be dripping out of an opening in her side the size of a dime and planted her hand over it. "Press," he ordered as he rolled up his sleeves and washed his hands. "If it's only a scratch, I guess I could patch you up. Not as a doctor, of course, but as a friend."

"Thanks. It's a hard place to clean up, and I'm still too drunk to have a steady hand."

"Been at your Sunday family dinner again?" he asked as he worked.

She tried to smile. "You know me well." Six months ago she'd taken out all his trash cans trying to park, and three months ago she'd locked herself out after one of the Sunday dinner binges.

Doc pulled up the chair and sat so he was eye level with the wound. Carefully he began cleaning blood away. "How'd you hurt yourself, Lizzie? Fall into that wild flower bed of yours and puncture yourself?"

His hands were warm on her skin as he cleaned.

"I didn't do anything, Doc. I was just standing on that old bridge downtown and all at once I felt something hit me. It came out of nowhere." She fought back tears and gripped his shoulder. He felt solid as a rock, and right now she needed something or someone to hold on to. The room was starting to circle around her. "I didn't know if I could dig the bullet out myself, so I came here." She let out a low cry as the cotton passed over the wound.

"You've been shot!" Suddenly the always-stone-faced doctor sounded very young. His hand brushed her hair away from her face as he looked at her, really looked at her. "Elizabeth." He forced calm into his words, but she saw fear and worry in his face. "You were shot?"

"It was an accident." She couldn't tell him that the bullet was meant for Rick Matheson. She didn't know that for sure. "A stray bullet I'm guessing. If I go to the hospital, I'll have to fill out forms and answer questions." She almost added that it would somehow turn into being all her fault and, by the end of the day, people would be speculating that she probably shot herself.

He pressed his palm over the wound gently, his long fingers brushing her skin from the underside of her breast to her waist as if he thought the touch necessary. "I can't treat you. It's against the law."

"You'd take care of me if I were an animal."

McCall shook his head, silently telling her that there was no use in arguing.

"I'll do it myself, then." She tried to rise. "I'm not going to the hospital. I'll do it alone if you won't help." Tears were rolling down her cheeks. This had been a crazy idea, coming here, asking a man she didn't even know by his first name for help. Thinking he'd show her the same kindness he'd show an animal. Of course, he couldn't help her.

"I'll drive you to the hospital." He tried again, his hands holding her still.

"No." She shook her head. "I told you, I'm not going. I'm sorry I bothered you. I can do this alone." It felt as if every troubled time in her life she'd always walked alone. People were nice, but never wanted to be real friends. Family, teachers, everyone seemed to believe she'd do best left to herself. Just add being shot and surviving to the list.

He kept his hand on her side as she sat up. She saw the panic in his eyes and almost felt sorry for him. He hadn't volunteered to help; he'd been drafted.

"But—" he began.

"No buts. I don't have to seek medical attention, and I doubt anyone would consider this a life-threatening situation. If you can't help me, and you won't tell me what to do, I'll figure it out. I'm sure I can Google instructions on how to remove a bullet."

McCall still didn't turn her loose. "All right," he reluctantly agreed. "Let me take a look at it. Maybe all it needs is just a dressing."

They both knew it would require more.

She leaned back on the sheet now spotted with blood, and he began. After a few minutes, he whispered, "I can see the bullet. It didn't go in far. You're going to need something for the pain, only guessing from your breath, you've already fairly self-medicated."

"No. Nothing for the pain. Just do it." Lizzie closed her eyes so hard, tears flowed out in tiny rivers.

Doc pulled clean towels from a shelf and placed them on either side of her, bookending her small frame. As he worked, his gloved hand stroked her gently, keeping her calm with his touch. "It's not as bad as it could have been. The bullet skirted

along just under the skin, scraping off enough hide to bleed." His
hand spread out over her middle. "You're going to be just fine,
but you'll have a scar."

Lizzie tried to smile as she realized she'd stepped up in the
world. Doc was treating her like an animal. The pain sobered
her, and his gentle touch soothed her. She didn't make a sound
as he worked, but her fingers dug into his shoulder as if it were
a lifeline.

When he placed butterfly stitches over her wound and ban-
daged it, she relaxed, knowing this latest crisis was almost over.
The reluctant doctor had made that possible even if he didn't
care for people. He'd smiled when he thought she'd brought one
of her cats, but he hadn't smiled since.

"I've got antibiotics in my purse. The emergency room gave
them to me last month when I stepped on a nail while trying to
clean out a clogged gutter. I also had a tetanus shot, so I'm covered there." Nerves made her ramble. "I still can't figure out how
the nails got on my roof. I clean that gutter almost every time it
rains, and I never saw nails sticking up before, but last month I
must have found a dozen at the gutter's edge. It's a wonder I
didn't tumble off the roof in pain."

He nodded, only half-listening as he examined his work.
"Tug off that bloody shirt, and I'll loan you another."

When she groaned as she lifted her arm, he did the job for
her. Then he just stood in front of her, staring.

"What's wrong?" she asked, fearing that she might be turning green or already bleeding through the bandage.

His frown deepened, and she swore she saw a blush.

"My patients usually don't wear bras," he said, "or look so
hairless."

She glanced down at the lacy underwear that hid little. "I'm
not your patient, remember. I'm sure this isn't the first time
you've seen a woman in her underwear."

"It's been a long while," he confessed with a shy smile.

She pushed off the desk and wavered as she stood.

Without a word, he picked her up and carried her across the
foyer to his apartment. He set her down in front of what had to
be the bathroom door. "If you think you're strong enough to
wash up, I'll get you one of my shirts to wear. I'd like you to stay
a while to make sure you're all right."

Nodding her head as if it were missing a few screws, she disappeared into the bathroom. Just like the main room they'd passed, the bathroom was decorated totally in brown and cream. Cream walls and fixtures, brown towels. She'd seen truck-stop restrooms with more colorful décor. After washing her face and making sure she was no longer bleeding, she felt much better.

Slowly she walked down the hallway to the living area they'd passed on the way in. He offered her a seat on his brown leather couch. When she sat, he handed her a tan blanket and soup in a big mug.

Lizzie smiled. "My granny used to always give me soup late at night."

"I figured it was the least I could do when a friend dropped by to ask questions."

She saw his reasoning and fell easily into the lie. "Thanks for answering my questions." She didn't mention that he'd forgotten the shirt he'd offered to lend her. Since his patients usually didn't wear clothes, maybe having her without a top didn't seem so strange. In truth, she'd never been modest. When she was a kid, living with just her grandmother, Lizzie had once declared that she would eat breakfast only in the nude. Her grandmother hadn't argued; she'd just waited a week for a cold spell to blow in, then opened all the windows at dawn.

Lizzie gave up breakfast in the nude. She smiled into her cup of soup as the doc fussed over her like Granny used to do.

"No problem," he said as if needing to talk. "Glad I could loan you a few supplies." He looked down as she leaned back against the couch. For a moment, he just studied her bra, or maybe what he could see through it, and then he jumped into action. "The shirt, I forgot the shirt."

As he ran out of the room, she giggled. He'd finally noticed her breasts. She almost wished she'd stripped the bra off earlier along with that terrible black dress, but then the doc might have fainted if he saw what she always thought was her best feature.

He came back with a flannel shirt. His eyes never left hers as he handed it over and disappeared into the kitchen. A few moments later he returned with his own cup of soup and a bag of Oreos. With the dogs taking up all the space in the middle of the couch, Lizzie ate in comfortable silence. She wasn't surprised when he ate only the center of one Oreo and fed the outer cookies to the dogs.

"Isn't chocolate bad for dogs?" she asked between spoonfuls of soup.

He nodded. "Both my houseguests are over a hundred in human years and still healthy. I figure they should live a little now and then. Half an Oreo won't hurt them."

She decided she liked the doc. He didn't ask questions, and he didn't look at her like she might be from another planet. In her book, that made him her best friend.

"Anything else you need?" he said as he stood holding an empty glass of milk. "We've got popcorn for the movie."

She shook her head, fighting down the urge to laugh.

The dogs jumped off the couch, planning to follow him to the kitchen for any leftovers. His words were almost lost in the tapping of their feet on the wooden floor. "You're welcome to stay a while," he said as he disappeared into the kitchen. "The boys and I never have company."

Lizzie knew she was stepping out of the socially acceptable behavior her granny always claimed she'd never learned. But she didn't care. Between the drinking and the fright and the pain, she simply didn't care.

When he returned with a bowl of popcorn and two bottled Cokes, she looked into his kind brown eyes and said exactly what was on her mind. "Would you hold me for a while, Doc? I've had quite a night."

Without a word he set down the popcorn and drinks. The room was growing darker and the Western was starting, but no one noticed. He lowered next to her on the old couch that smelled a little like wet dog hair and lifted her legs across his, then pulled her into a gentle hug.

When she rested her head on his shoulder, it felt so right, so safe, so warm.

She fell asleep as his hands brushed over her, almost as if he were petting her. Between reality and dreams, she thought she heard him whisper against her ear, "I'll hold you as long as you like, Elizabeth."

THREE

AFTER RICK MATHESON let Lizzie out at her place, he went straight to his office on the third floor of the courthouse. He knew the sheriff, Alex Matheson, a relative by marriage, would still be at the family dinner. Rick decided reporting the shooting could wait an hour. He'd feel like a fool for calling to report a shot when it could have been a firecracker left over from the Fourth or a car backfiring. Surely if it had been real gunfire, people would have reported it already.

Besides, if someone was trying to kill him, they couldn't have had a better shot at him than when he stood in the middle of the bridge. He took little comfort in knowing, if he'd really been a target, the hired gun was pitiful at his chosen profession.

Rick decided he was being paranoid. A few years ago he'd thought someone was trying to kill him, and his relatives had talked a federal marshal into watching over him. She'd been great at her job, saved his life more than once, but she'd stolen his heart.

The local crazy guy had tried to make Rick's life miserable because he thought Rick was after his longtime secret love. When Marshal Trace Adams came in to protect him, Rick fell hard for her. After a few days, the guy causing trouble was caught, and Trace said she had to leave. Rick had gone to

Chicago twice looking for her. He'd tried calling, e-mailing, even writing to her in care of the marshal's office. Nothing. She'd simply disappeared out of his life.

Trace Adams had vanished, leaving everything he thought they had between them unsettled. She hadn't broken his heart; she'd taken it with her, leaving him bitter.

He still played the role of the happy, easygoing guy he'd always been, but he no longer felt it. The only drug he'd found that kept his mind off of her was work. He'd made good money the past few years. Bought a new car, a town house in a nice part of Harmony, even owned half a dozen suits, but none of it mattered. If she'd left his broken heart, it might have mended. But she hadn't, and wherever she was tonight, his heart was still there with her.

Rick swore over the sorry case of his love life as he unlocked his office door. He made a pot of coffee and sat down at his desk. If no one called, he could get a good four hours of work in before midnight.

As he opened his e-mail, he decided to send Trace a note. Now and then he did that, knowing the address he had for her was probably dead. But somehow it gave him the feeling that a thread still stretched between them.

Got shot at tonight. Thought of you. R

Before he thought better of it, he pushed Send, then flipped over to his files and began piecing together details that might help a lawyer in Dallas with his federal case. The bad guy they were looking into, Max Dewy, was a real piece of work. Not only was he laundering money for arms dealers, he also ran an investment scheme on some of the locals in Harmony and worked for some lowlifes moving drugs. One fed had told Rick that every time they turned over a criminal rock in West Texas, Max Dewy's picture was under it. The question wasn't "if" he was going to prison but "for what."

Rick liked the idea of helping put a real scumbag behind bars. Most of his cases were small-time. Divorces, wills, drunk drivers, and shoplifters. Every case he won seemed to end with someone yelling a threat at him. He wouldn't be surprised if there wasn't a website for people who hated him.

An hour later he was deep into the search when an e-mail popped up on the corner of his screen.

Are you all right? T

Rick stared at it for a moment. He didn't recognize the mix of numbers and letters that made up the e-mail address, but he knew who it was from. Trace.

Angry that she could care about him, keep up with him, answer him, and he had no idea where she was, he typed:

If you want to know, come to Harmony. I dare you.

He leaned back in his chair. The work was forgotten. The night was lost to all but memories of her. He closed his eyes and let the thoughts pound him like hail in a spring storm. No matter how badly it hurt, he had to watch, had to feel, had to remember.

She'd been the wildest, sexiest woman he'd ever seen. He'd been hurt from a fall that had been no accident. She'd watched over him, fought with him, guarded him, and made a kind of wild love with him that even his dreams couldn't have imagined.

There had been women before her. Easy, gentle, loving women he'd had short affairs with or fun-loving one-night stands. But there was no one after Trace. He told himself the passion they'd shared would fade, and he'd barely remember her one day.

But that never happened.

After a while he'd tried to convince himself he would forget her. She'd told him from the first that she didn't want ties. Only every other woman he tried to go out with couldn't measure up to Trace.

Rick realized that if a shot had hit him dead center in the chest tonight, it wouldn't have killed him. The bullet would have simply passed through the empty hole she'd left.

He closed up his office and turned out the lights a little after midnight. As he walked to the elevator, he tried to picture her somewhere in an empty office or apartment, maybe thinking of him. She'd broken the silence between them tonight. That was a good thing, but he held out no hope that it would lead anywhere. She was a big-city marshal who fought crime, and he was nothing but a small-town lawyer. He didn't think he could live in her world, and she didn't want to live in his.

No match. No future. No heart. *Three strikes, you're out,* he thought.

When he reached the parking lot, rain had started falling as it had the midnight before. The whole town seemed to sleep under a foggy blanket. Lights all blinked yellow as he drove the dark streets. Rick wondered if there was another soul on earth who was as lonely as he was tonight. He'd lived with the condition for so long, the cure would probably kill him. If he had any sense, he would have moved on, found another, gotten on with his life.

Laughing, he decided maybe Lizzie wasn't the only nut to fall off the family tree. If everyone knew his story, they would think he was just as mixed up. She lived with her flaws on the outside, her seams and scars showing as if she'd put her clothes on inside out. All his flaws were on the inside, buried so no one could see, but he was just as broken.

As he pulled into the underground parking beneath his condo, he decided Lizzie must see clearer than he did. That's why she thought they were alike. Maybe they should be friends. Taking his offbeat cousin out to dinner made more sense than trying to date someone. At least with Lizzie, they could laugh about their relatives. Besides, Lizzie would probably insist on buying every other meal. Her grandmother had left her comfortable, much to the other grandchildren's distress.

Rick didn't know Lizzie's two older first cousins on her mother's side. Apparently Lizzie's mother and Granny's older daughter never got along. When Lizzie's mother and father died, the big sister refused to take Lizzie in, leaving Granny the burden. Lizzie's aunt Alice thought her sister's only child should go to a children's home or into the welfare system. When Granny didn't see it her way, Alice swore she'd never come home again and she didn't, not even when Granny grew ill and Lizzie quit high school to take care of her. Two years later, when Granny died, Alice still didn't return to Harmony or offer to help Lizzie.

At twenty, after passing her GED, Lizzie sold the house she'd inherited and left for college. She'd also inherited all of Granny's small savings and oil rights to the land her grandparents bought after World War II but had never got around to farming. Oil lease checks had evidently been deposited in an account for Lizzie for years.

Word was Aunt Alice called every lawyer for a hundred miles around to try to fight the will, but none would take her case. Granny had been in her right mind when she signed the papers, and Lizzie was an adult when she inherited. Rick never heard whether Alice had tried to contact Lizzie directly, but he doubted she would have taken her aunt's call.

Rick almost laughed aloud as he grabbed his jacket from the backseat of his car and took the stairs two at a time to his place. He and Lizzie could keep each other company. They were both alone and probably always would be.

He didn't bother to turn on the lights as he walked through his apartment to the bedroom. If he had flipped the switch, it would only depress him. In the year he'd lived here, he hadn't hung a picture or bought any furniture for the living room. His kitchen looked like the recycling center for fast-food containers. Dropping the jacket in an already full basket of dirty clothes, he thought maybe tomorrow he'd make a list of all the things, other than work, that he needed to do. Laundry, buy food, invite his cousin to lunch.

In the dark, he stripped off his clothes and climbed into bed. His sheets felt cold against the damp night. He was so tired, he barely noticed the open window that faced the lights of downtown.

Stretching out, he tried to calm his breathing and think of anything except Trace. If she was on his mind when he fell asleep, he'd dream of her, and come morning he'd miss her even more than usual. Sometimes, deep down, he hated her for not stopping him from loving her. She had known she wasn't going to stay around.

A shadow moved across the window. The fuzzy yellow lights outside blinked as if turning off and on.

Rick opened his eyes wider. The feeling that someone was in the room hit him as fact. "Trace," he whispered, as if wishing for someone could make them appear.

"Yes," she answered calmly, as though she'd only been a room away all these months.

Rick's body came full awake. She was here. She was in his room. She had to be. Either that or he'd finally gone mad.

"Come over here," he ordered, wondering if dreams followed directions.

A shadow moved closer. Her lean athletic form was outlined for a moment, and he could almost feel his hand sliding over her. He could smell leather. She'd ridden in on her motorcycle just as she had once before.

"Trace," he whispered again as he shoved the covers aside and put his feet on the floor. Before he could stand, she moved in front of him, her leg touching his knee.

"Let me see where you're hurt."

Rick stood, closing the distance between them, daring her to back down.

He wasn't surprised when she didn't. Digging his hand into her damp hair, he pulled her toward him for a kiss.

She jerked away so suddenly, he didn't have time to react. "I said where are you shot, Matheson?"

"I'm not hurt." He caught her wrist as she reached for the lamp beside the bed.

"Don't lie to me, Rick. I saw the blood all over the inside of the coat you dropped coming in."

He released her hand and reached for his pants. "I was shot at, but not hit." Facts flooded his memory as he pieced the scene on the bridge together. "My cousin Lizzie had been wearing my coat. She must be hurt. She must have been too drunk to realize it."

Trace flipped on the light.

He could almost feel her gaze examining him as he pulled on his jeans and shirt. "I gave her a ride home. She borrowed my coat. Oh, God, she's shot."

With his back to Trace he watched her through the mirror's reflection. Her whole body seemed to relax. No matter how angry she sounded or how mad she was at him, one fact was clear: She still cared about him.

Rick told himself he didn't care. He couldn't love a woman who could walk out on him so easily or come back looking so angry. If he had been shot and bled to death, she'd probably yell at his lifeless body.

"I've got to go check on her," he said as he shoved his feet into loafers. "You coming?"

When she didn't answer, he turned and walked out without looking back. If she followed, he'd deal with it. If she didn't, he'd handle that as well. Nothing Trace Adams did was under his control.

He walked down the stairs. No footsteps followed, but he wasn't surprised she sat waiting in his car when he got to the underground parking. She'd probably used the same window to leave that she used to enter. He had no idea how she got into the secure underground parking area, and she probably wouldn't tell him if he asked.

Backing out of his spot, he glanced at her profile. She was as beautiful as ever and just as deadly. A federal marshal who could easily kill him in a dozen ways right now. Maybe that was what fascinated him so. Trace didn't need him. Hell, half the time she didn't even act like she liked him.

"What brings you back to Harmony, Trace? And don't bother to say me."

She was silent for so long he decided she didn't plan to answer. Then, her words sounded tired, almost washed away in the rainy night. "I was following a lead on another case that went dead. I was on my way back home when I got your e-mail and decided Harmony wasn't that far out of my way."

He read what she didn't say. "You were going to check on me tonight and then leave." A chill seeped deep into him. "You hadn't planned on my being awake."

Silence was her answer.

He drove through the midnight streets silver with rain. "You've checked up on me before." It wasn't a question. All the times he thought he could still smell her, or thought he saw a shadow that looked like her, came tumbling back.

"I hate you," he said calmly.

"I know," she answered as if they were talking about the weather and not their lives. "I can live with that as long as you're safe."

He slowed to turn onto the dirt road next to the veterinary clinic. "I don't need you watching over me." Rick, who rarely got irritated, much less mad, was furious. He thought about swearing or yelling at her or even hitting her. Only he'd never been one to swear or yell, and if he hit Trace, she'd probably strike back and kill him with one punch to the throat. Then his mother would dig him up and double murder him for hitting a lady.

He saw no winner in this battle, so he concentrated on where he might be needed. "I'm checking on my cousin, and then we're going to have a talk. If you're going to break into my room at night, I want you in my bed."

He climbed out of the car and slammed the door a heart-beat later than she did.

She frowned across the hood at him. "Fine."

"Really?" All the anger vanished. "Really?" He smiled. "We'll talk about this later and work out the details."

"Fine," she repeated with only slightly less fury in her voice. "Only first we have to know why someone is trying to kill you *again*."

"Agreed," he said as he moved toward the walkway to his cousin's house.

Neither seemed to care that they were getting wet from a misty rain, but Rick did notice that the muddy road he'd maneu-vered several hours ago when he brought Lizzie home was turn-ing into a river. He had to know Lizzie was all right, and then he planned to have a long talk with Trace. Someone was shooting at him, his cousin might be hurt, and the security system he'd paid for at his place didn't work. But on the bright side, he thought he could hear his heart beating again.

FOUR

RICK BANGED ON the door of his cousin's adobe house. The place was so overgrown with flowers and ivy, he feared nature might take it back before fall froze out the Jack-and-the-beanstalk look. Though this house Lizzie had bought when she came home from college was nicer, with foot-thick walls that could withstand any tornado and a low fence tiled as if it belonged in Santa Fe, it still reminded him of Lizzie's grandmother's place. Granny's house had been a cheap wood-frame place, poorly built in the forties, but she'd always had flowers, even in the cracks of the walk.

"It's almost one in the morning, Matheson." Trace simply stated the fact. She'd made no attempt to stop him. "If she's drunk, she might not even hear you banging loud enough to wake any neighbors within a mile."

"I don't care." He started pounding as if nailing each of his words to the door. "I'm going to keep it up until she answers if it takes all night." He stopped long enough to swear, then continued, "It's my fault she's wounded. Someone's probably trying to kill me. I'm the one digging into old cases. I'm the . . ."

The lock clicked. Someone from inside turned the knob and the door opened.

"Thank God, Lizzie," he said as he shoved his way in. "I thought . . ."

Trace Adams stared up at him. Somehow she'd got inside. She'd let him in like she wasn't the burglar. *And* she was the one smiling at him as if she'd just discovered an idiot on Lizzie's porch.

"How'd you get in?" he snapped. "Oh, never mind." He could feel the night breeze from the window off the front porch. "Why didn't you say something? If I'd known you were busy breaking in, I might have counseled you against it."

"I saw it more as saving the door. I tried to talk, but you seemed so determined. My dad always said never interfere with a man on a mission."

Rick frowned. "That the same Dad who named you Trace after trace evidence?"

"Yep." She flipped on the hallway light. "No one's in the house, Matheson. I don't know where your cousin is, but she's not home."

He stood in the center of the entry, realizing he could see into all four rooms. They were big and airy with bookshelves lining every wall and color exploding everywhere. Painting supplies were scattered over old coffee tables like colorful Easter eggs, and well-worn easels accented every corner.

"I had time to look around while you were pounding." Trace leaned against one of the shelves.

"What'd you learn?"

"Looks like all she paints is animals."

"I didn't know that piece of worthless information." He fought down his anger and frustration by baiting Trace. "Wonder how she started?" he said without any hint of surprise. Nothing Lizzie did would surprise him.

"Probably with kittens." Trace's slow smile drew him, and he forgot what they were talking about.

This sexy woman before him in her black leather and long midnight braid blinded him with her beauty. Maybe once in a lifetime a man meets his fantasy. He'd been attracted to other women, could've even loved them, but he'd found only one woman who was exactly what he dreamed of holding. Trace was that for him. He didn't care that they'd just broken into a house or that someone was trying to shoot him; all he wanted to do was touch her, hold her, make sure she was finally real and not just left over from a great dream.

Trace obviously read his mind. She moved out of his reach as she continued their pointless conversation. "Maybe she'll give you a picture if we ever find this cousin. Which we're never going to do if you don't concentrate. Do all lawyers have the attention span of rabbits, or were you just the top of the class? You've got a cousin probably bleeding. Forget the cat paintings and the break-in and get in the game, Matheson."

Choking her came to mind, but then there was the fact that she'd kill him before she even worried about air.

Loving and hating were two sides of the same coin spinning in his mind. Like an out-of-control fire, she would burn him he knew, but he couldn't help moving closer. If he took in the full beauty of her much longer, it would only make the memories more painful when she walked away. And she would walk away. That just seemed to be what she did.

He must have blinked. Trace had vanished while he was thinking. If he ever did get her in bed again, he planned to tie her down or, better yet, tie himself to her. Then when she disappeared, he'd be dragged along for the ride.

It took him a few minutes to find Trace in the bathroom. She was holding the black dress Lizzie had worn to the family dinner. "Blood," Trace whispered as she moved her hand over the dark material that now looked wet. "Maybe she went to the hospital?"

Rick shook his head. "No car. That's why the family usually drives her. Lizzie shouldn't even have a learner's permit when she's sober. She replaces cars like some women do shoes. Once I found her wandering around the mall parking lot because she'd forgotten what kind of car she'd bought the day before."

Trace lifted her hand, now red with blood.

"What do we do?" he asked.

"We step outside and widen the search." Trace moved past him to the porch. "Without a car, she must have walked to a neighbor's house or called someone to drive her to the hospital."

As he followed the marshal off the porch, lights came on at the veterinary clinic, flooding the corrals and parking lot fifty yards away. It took Rick a minute to make out the broad-shouldered vet standing at his back door. What looked like a shotgun rested at the ready over one arm.

Rick wished he'd wake up from this nightmare. Things had been going downhill since he'd rolled out of bed this morning. He'd been late to church, he couldn't remember one word of the sermon, the family dinner was so boring he wanted to forget it altogether, then being shot at on the bridge and having Trace come back just to yell at him.

He should have kissed Trace first thing when he saw her—before even letting her ask questions. Now, the way his luck was running tonight, the vet would shoot him, and Trace would shoot the vet for shooting him, and his wounded cousin would bleed to death in one of the flower beds. Any way he looked at this, Rick decided he was destined to be the most-talked-about Matheson in history.

"Dr. McCall!" Rick yelled waving his arms hoping not to be ID'd as the target. "Sorry we woke you. I'm looking for my cousin. I'm worried she may be hurt."

The doc didn't move, but Rick's petite cousin came around the big guy and leaned into the vet like she was comfortable there. "I'm fine, Rick. You didn't wake us. We were just watching the midnight Western."

Dr. McCall set the rifle down just inside the door and put his arm over Lizzie's shoulders as if the rainy night was too cold for her. "Come on over, Matheson. I'll put on some coffee," he said none-too-politely. "After all the banging you did, none of us are going to get any more sleep tonight."

Lizzie laughed, turning her face against the vet's chest. "I thought all the noise was thunder. If the dogs hadn't started barking, we might not have gone to check."

Rick started walking toward the clinic trying to keep his mumbling to himself. He couldn't believe he'd been worrying about poor Lizzie Lee being all alone when she was cuddling up to Dr. McCall. Rick had no idea where *his* date for the evening disaster party had disappeared. Keeping up with Trace was like taking the measurements of smoke.

A dog shot past the vet and ran directly toward a huge tree at the property line of Lizzie's house. The animal went nuts barking.

McCall lifted his rifle and took a few steps toward the tree. "We've had coyotes before, but usually in the winter. If an animal is treed, it could be a big cat come to bother the stock.

They've been known to travel the canyon at night and can smell out wounded animals." Halfway to the tree, he slapped his hand against his leg twice and the dog settled.

Rick walked near enough that he didn't have to yell. "It's not coyotes, Doc, or a cat. You mind if I bring a date for coffee?" He raised his hand toward the tree.

Trace dropped gracefully to the ground and looped her arm in his as if they'd just been out for a stroll when she'd decided to climb a tree.

The vet must have seen some strange things in his life because having a woman in leather drop out of a tree didn't even earn a raised eyebrow. But, come to think of it, he had lived next to Lizzie for four years. He'd known her to have birthday parties for her cats.

The sudden brush of Trace's body against his almost took Rick to his knees. He considered making up a lie for the vet, but with her so close he didn't have enough blood left in his brain to think. Maybe he should just stick with the truth. Since it looked like Lizzie was wearing one of the doc's shirts, Rick guessed the man already knew that she'd been shot tonight. The only question left was why.

When Rick reached the door, he introduced Trace as a federal marshal, then he hugged Lizzie. He could feel the bandage on her side. "Are you all right, Cousin?"

"I'm fine. It was just a scratch." She smiled at him, really smiled. Something he hadn't seen her do in years.

Rick saw a light in her green eyes that he'd never seen before. Maybe for the first time, Lizzie was happy, and he had a feeling it had nothing to do with being shot. When the backyard lights sparkled in the green streaks of her hair, Rick didn't even mind. *Lizzie looks pretty,* he thought, *really pretty.*

The four of them sat down at the doc's kitchen table and went through every fact. Trace asked most of the questions. Rick didn't miss how McCall brushed his hand over Lizzie's when his cousin told about how much it had hurt and how she hadn't wanted to tell anyone.

"There are too many questions I don't have answers for." Lizzie didn't have to mention the times she'd been hurt or wrecked her car and half the town whispered that it might be a suicide attempt. "I don't want folks jumping to the wrong conclusion. It was just a stray shot, right?" Her big eyes moved from one to the other of them; she wanted her theory to be true.

"Maybe," Rick finally said, but he had the feeling neither the doc nor the marshal bought into the idea.

When the coffeepot was empty, Rick stood and offered his hand to Trace. He wasn't surprised when she didn't take it. First, she didn't need help, and second, she didn't seem like the hand-holding type.

She did say she would check things out to see if she could learn anything about the one shot. Maybe someone spotted a stranger in town. Maybe they'd get lucky and find a shell casing, but everyone knew the odds were against them.

Dr. McCall and Lizzie walked them to the front door, and McCall promised he'd keep an eye on Lizzie. Which Rick didn't think would be much trouble, because his cousin didn't look like she was going anywhere.

Leaning down to Lizzie, Rick kissed her cheek for the first time ever. "I'm sorry I got you involved in this."

"It could have been just a stray shot," she said for the third time. "Don't make trouble out of an accident."

Rick nodded.

Trace didn't say anything when he opened the car door and waited for her to climb in. She slid into the seat without looking up at him, and he fought the urge to touch her. She'd haunted every dream he'd had since the day she rode away more than two years ago. Her absence had changed him, hardened him, but not for one moment had he stopped wanting her, loving her.

He half-expected her to jump from the car and vanish again, but she simply leaned back and closed her eyes. When he pulled into his parking spot and cut the engine, he turned toward her. His mind told him she was here next to him. He could see her, feel her, hear her breathing, but still a part of him couldn't believe it. He'd wanted her near for so long.

Her eyes were still closed, but he knew she wasn't asleep. Slowly he leaned over and brushed his lips over hers as he whispered, "Come up with me, Trace. We'll sleep after we make love." He didn't give her time to argue; his mouth closed down on hers in the kind of wild kiss he knew she loved.

After one long kiss, she broke free, bolted out of the car and ran for the stairs. He was right behind her.

A few steps from his door she stopped so suddenly, he bumped into her. Turning, she fisted his jacket and slammed him against the door. Leaning into him, she took back the kiss he'd just given her. Her body pinned him, and he made no move to escape or fight off her attack.

When she pulled away to breathe, he unlocked the door. She walked past him as if in control, but one brush of his hand over her hip made her shake with need.

He closed the door. "It's about time you came back to me, Trace." He moved behind her, slowly pulling her to him. His hands moved over the leather of her jacket, learning every curve as he'd once known. He began undressing her, knowing that she could easily stop him if she had any objections.

"You want this?" he asked as her skin replaced leather beneath his touch.

Something in Trace broke, as if she'd fought loving him since the day they'd met and could no longer hold the line.

"Yes," she whispered as she turned in his arms and tugged at his clothes, suddenly wanting to be closer to him.

They didn't have time to talk or question what they were doing. Sparks ignited a fire in both, and they had to feel the heat.

Rick didn't think, he barely took time to breathe. All he wanted to do was press her against him, and she had the same passion.

They rocked the bed with their lovemaking. There was nothing gentle or hesitant in their mating. The need was too great. The longing sharpened by a never-ending satisfaction he knew would fill them both. If he made love to her every day, every night of his life, he'd never have enough. And deep down he knew she felt the same. As wrong as they were for each other, one thing was right between them—no, not just right: perfect.

When their passion was spent, they started again as soon as their breathing slowed. The second mating was loving, tender, pure slow delight. For two people who hardly knew how to talk to each other, neither could get enough.

Finally they lay as close as their bodies could get, satisfied, exhausted.

Rick wrapped his arm around her, holding her so near, their hearts sounded in rhythm. They didn't talk. There was nothing left to say. They'd admitted everything in their actions. Slowly she relaxed and slept. He wondered how many hours she'd been up, how many days she'd been on the road . . . It didn't matter. She was here now. She was with him and he'd hold her for as long as she'd let him.

He kissed her cheek, loving every inch of her, wishing he had the energy to make love to her while she slept. "I love you, Trace," he whispered against her hair. "I always will." His hand moved along her damp body, memorizing these few moments, the pace of her breath, the taste of her lips, and the hum of her low moan of pleasure, even in sleep. He loved her all the way to the core of his soul.

Though he doubted she'd ever say the words to him, he knew she felt the same. She'd rushed to him when she thought he was hurt. He'd seen the worry, the caring in her. Trace might live for her job. She might have to always be in control. But she'd let down her guard with him long enough to love him.

She could deny it all she wanted, but he knew she cared about him. His beautiful warrior would protect him with her life, and he'd do the same for her.

At dawn, he reached to pull her closer and felt only the sheet. She'd gone. Vanished without a good-bye. He knew he should be angry, and he would be in days to come, but all Rick could do for now was lie very still and remember their night.

FIVE

LIZZIE RETURNED TO the doc's warm apartment after her cousin and the marshal left. Dr. McCall walked silently beside her. He seemed so tall now that they were standing. When she'd been cuddled next to him, she hadn't really noticed how much bigger he was than her. Now they no longer seemed to fit. At Lizzie's five feet, anyone over six feet was tall. But Dr. McCall was more the tree level now that they were so close.

She'd never thought of herself as having a type of man, but someone like the doc wouldn't be in the running. He would more likely make the good-friend category. They shared a love for animals, so that was a good base. He wasn't noisy and never had wild parties; he could help her with her pets and even give her advice on bullet wounds. Cuddling with him had been nice, but now it was about time to move to the "let's just be friends" category before either of them became foolish enough to think there could be more.

It was late, but she was in no hurry to go back to her place. The way he'd held her, all protected and warm, made her wish they could go back to the couch and hold each other for just a few minutes more. Only affection wasn't something she'd ever known to come in quantity.

She realized she didn't even know his first name. Everyone just called him Doc, or McCall. Someone said he was a widower, but there were no pictures of his life before Harmony, so it was hard to tell. Maybe he was divorced. Wouldn't a man who lost his wife keep her picture?

The rooms he lived in were as bare as those in a cheap hotel. Everything that wasn't wood was brown. As far as she knew, he never traveled or joined any clubs or churches. He simply worked. His old pickup was either parked in his lot out front or flying down a back road to check on some rancher's stock.

There was nothing exciting or even mildly interesting about McCall, she decided, except one observation: He loved animals as much as she did. She had seen him kneeling by a mare once, fighting to save mother and colt. He cared.

"I guess I should be going." She helped him pick up coffee cups off his little dining table.

"I'll walk you home," he said. "If you like, old Scotty can stay with you. He'll bark if anyone comes near your house, so he's good to have around on a night like this."

She wasn't worried. No one uninvited had ever come near her house. Most of her Matheson relatives hadn't even seen the inside, and she didn't even know what her mother's relatives looked like.

Her pet grooming salon was in an old converted beauty shop across the road from the vet's office. The Matheson relatives who did stop by usually visited her there. Two of her favorite great-aunts came every Wednesday with a bag of hamburgers and fries. She'd learned never to book a twelve o'clock appointment and to have the iced tea ready. They'd huddle around the break-room table and talk like they hadn't seen her in months.

"Thanks for helping me out tonight, Doc." She moved outside, feeling the cold more than she had earlier. If she'd been brave, she would have begged to stay longer.

He followed her out to the long porch that wrapped around three sides of his offices. The two old dogs tagged along behind him. When he jumped off the porch, he turned to face her. Now that he was three steps below her, she was finally at eye level with the man. Both smiled.

"You've got pretty eyes," he whispered.

"So do you." She giggled, thinking her aunt Fat would say he had bedroom eyes if she saw him in this moonlight.

Without a word they walked the path. The lights around his business and her front-porch light offered just enough glow to see the way. All the world seemed fussy in the damp night.

"When it rains, I don't mind you parking in my lot," he finally broke the silence. "I've got plenty of room, and I'd hate you getting stuck in the mud in that trail you call a road."

"Thanks, but I don't know when I'll get another car. Since I totaled the last one, I don't feel much like going shopping. Usually one of my relatives calls me and offers to sell me his old car. They all know my record. I seem to be where Mathesons send their vehicles to die."

He laughed. "You're not so bad. I heard the last car got hit in the parking lot."

She shrugged. "That's right. I wasn't even in it. Guess I should have parked between the lines, though."

"And the one before that someone said you wrecked on an icy road."

She nodded, guessing he heard a great deal about her problems while he circled the relatives' ranches. Suddenly Lizzie wanted to change the subject.

"Why didn't you buy my place when you bought the clinic?" She'd always wanted to ask him. After all, the old vet had built the business and then the home to live in. Some old-timers said the former vet's wife had tried her hand at running a beauty shop across the street, but it never took off. It only made sense that the property would have sold as one place.

"I didn't have the money," he answered honestly. "The offices were already under the same roof as the clinic. They had a little kitchen and bathroom, so I figured I'd just live there. I really didn't have any use for your house or the shop. I wouldn't have minded having the land around, though. I understand you bought the pastures on either side of me."

She shrugged as she realized her property almost surrounded his. "If you ever need to put an animal in those pastures, I wouldn't mind. I'll trade you for the parking space if I ever get another car."

He leaned low and nodded, as if scaling the deal as they

crossed the boundary line between their places. The old tree Trace had fallen from shadowed the path. He took her hand in his. "I wouldn't want you to fall, Elizabeth," he said softly. "That wound could start bleeding again. It might seem small now that it's stitched up, but you need to be careful."

Lizzie almost giggled again. In his way, he was taking care of her, and no one had taken care of her in so many years.

When they were past the shadow, he squeezed her fingers before letting go. "If you want, I could check the wound for you tomorrow. I've got to spend most of the day out on farms, but I should be in by seven."

She thought about saying that she could take care of herself, but she liked being around him. Better yet, she had the feeling he liked being around her. "How about you come to dinner tomorrow? Then after supper you can check me out."

He didn't answer, but slowed. After a moment, he whispered, "Elizabeth, your front door is wide open. Did you leave it that way?"

"Never," she said so low the wind stole her answer.

They both slowed. Reason told her Rick might have opened it, but how? It always locked automatically when she stepped out. She'd grown up with only a curtain for a door at Granny's. Then in the dorm she'd had roommates who always invaded her space. When she moved to Harmony, she loved the idea of having her own place with locks on the doors.

As a kid she'd carried her grandmother's front-door key on a chain and continued with a dorm key for four years. Even now, with the door wide open, she reached for the key about her neck.

"How about I go in with you?" McCall whispered as if he might frighten a burglar and somehow protect her.

She nodded and let him go in first. Two steps behind him, she turned on the lights as they moved from room to room. All looked as she had left it. The big kitchen lined with appliances she'd bought online, the living room with its long wall of windows on one side and bookshelves on the other. Her paintings and supplies were scattered about in a colorful mess. They passed into the roomy bedroom she loved, with her desk tucked between wide windows facing the sunrise.

"Looks all right," he said when all the lights were on. "Do you notice anything missing?"

She laughed. "Someone could take a truckful and I probably wouldn't notice."

He slowly turned as if just now really seeing the room. "Your world is so colorful. It's like visiting an art gallery." He picked up one of the paintings. "I saw this cat once. It looks like the old tom you brought over one day for me to take a look at."

Lizzie nodded. "Hershel died. That's why I painted him." She didn't want to tell the doctor more. He'd only join all the folks who thought she was strange. But she didn't want to lie either, so she took a chance that he might understand. "I used to give the paintings to the pet owners. I thought they'd like them. The first one said it was creepy, and she hadn't liked the pet anyway— she'd just got stuck with him. The second told me I had no right to paint her precious without permission.

"So now I just paint the ones I want to remember. Sometimes I really believe that animals understand us far more than we understand them."

McCall nodded. "Folks are funny about their animals. I knew this owner who taught his little colt to rear up and put his front legs on the man's shoulder. It looked cute when the horse was small, but a few months later I heard the colt had knocked all the rancher's teeth out with the trick. The rancher sold the horse off the next week like the accident was his fault. Unfair."

"I know what you mean. One of my ladies comes in once a month for me to cut her dog's hair just like hers. She even dyed her hair the same color as her pet and swears that they plan to be buried together."

McCall laughed. "Wonder if anyone asked the dog's opinion?"

He lifted his hand and gently brushed over the streaks of green in her hair. "Why?" he asked simply.

For a moment she thought of acting like she had no idea what he was talking about, but the truth won out. "I'm afraid of fading away. Sometimes I feel like no one sees me. Maybe if I stand out, people will remember I was here."

"I see you, Elizabeth. I always have. It doesn't matter what color is in your hair or what you wear." He grinned. "Sometimes just watching you walk across my lot on your way to your shop makes me smile. In a small way, you add color to my world."

Looking up into his eyes she realized that maybe he was

trying just as hard to fade away, become invisible, as she was trying to be seen. Before she could say anything, his dogs discovered her cats and a wild chase ensued.

The war finally ended when her tabby, Molly, swung one blow and sent both dogs running.

While she held her fat cat, the doc examined both his dogs' noses. He scolded them for chasing the cat; Lizzie told her cat to be nice, but it was obvious none of the animals were listening.

Lizzie had always believed that if cats could talk, they'd be cussing most of the time, and dogs, no matter what trouble they got into, always managed to have a "Who, me?" look about them.

She and McCall let the animals go, determined to watch them. "I guess I'd better say good-night, Elizabeth." He looked toward the windows but didn't move. "Sun's coming up."

"It's been a long night, but I'm not tired. If I had a car, I'd run into Harmony and have breakfast at the diner."

He faced her. "Mind riding in an old pickup? We could be sitting at the diner in ten minutes."

She grabbed her jacket by the door. "I guess that means we'll have to walk the path again." Before she could think to stop herself, she added, "Will you still hold my hand when we go by the tree, Doc?"

His face looked deadly serious when he said, "I'd be happy to."

Her cheeks warmed. That she'd asked sounded childish, but he hadn't seemed to mind. As they walked back, she was quiet, thinking it would take her half an hour to explain how little she knew about men or dating or even being friends. Rick, her cousin, was probably the only man she felt comfortable with, and they never talked about anything important.

As he'd promised, he took her hand at the tree and didn't turn loose until they reached his old pickup.

When they got to the Blue Moon Diner, it was just opening, so they had their pick of booths. Lizzie pointed to one in the middle, and he headed toward one at the back corner. Laughing, they settled on a table halfway between.

She was always comfortable in the old diner because breakfast is one meal you can eat out alone and not feel so lonely. At least once a week she'd eat breakfast out—when she had a car and the weather wasn't too bad. She'd buy a paper and read as she downed her pancakes. No one bothered her.

Only this morning was different. She wasn't alone.

This morning she was eating with Dr. McCall. After they ordered, he talked about his work and she asked questions. They discovered he loved dogs and horses best. She loved cats and little dogs. They both hated bats, snakes, and rats.

When they finished breakfast, the morning crowds were filling up the booths. A few waved at the doc, and one of Lizzie's cousins, who worked at the bank, gave her a slight nod.

The excitement of the night faded, and the real world set in as they drove home. She wasn't some wounded princess, and the doc wasn't her knight. They were just two neighbors who had had breakfast together. The shooting, the cuddling, the breakfast conversation would fade, and everything would go back like it was.

Only as she climbed into the doctor's pickup, she began to think. The shot had been real. Someone almost killed her. Maybe they'd been aiming at Rick or maybe she'd been the target.

Lizzie couldn't shake the feeling that no matter what she'd said to Rick, the bullet hadn't been a stray shot, an accident. He might feel as if he'd put her in danger because someone was after him, but she suspected the opposite. Maybe she was the one with an enemy?

She had to face facts.

Trouble wasn't hunting him; a killer was hunting her. In the past year she'd gotten two letters after she'd had accidents. At first she'd thought it only a cruel joke, but now she feared someone might really wish her dead.

One accident she'd had on a rainy road. She'd heard some folks had hinted that it might have been an attempt at suicide. The wreck had left her shaken and bruised. The note arrived two days later in the mail. It was printed in pencil and said simply, *Maybe you'll have better luck with killing yourself next time.*

Lizzie thought the note mean-spirited and cruel, but she told no one about it.

Then last month when she stepped on a nail and fell off her roof, another letter came. Typed this time. This one said, *Fall on your head next time and finish the job right.*

After that, Lizzie quit opening any mail that didn't have a return address. She wouldn't even return the call when her aunt

Alice left a message saying that it was time they got together because, after all, they were family.

Lizzie thought the notes were pranks, a cruel joke someone had decided to play. Maybe the same someone had cut her phone line at the shop last spring, and two weeks ago that someone might have cut her screen at the shop, just enough to push the water hose in. She'd walked into a flooded shop. If the breaker hadn't been thrown, she might have been electrocuted when she turned on the lights.

Lizzie had fixed the problems without telling anyone.

What bothered her even more than the letters or the pranks was not knowing who was doing them. It could be anyone. She first thought of cousins on her mother's side, who hated her for inheriting the money Granny left. Only her aunt had left that message trying to patch things up. Then she considered it might be a Matheson who thought she had embarrassed them one time too many. That side of the family was so normal, and, if not kind, all were at least tolerant of her.

Who knows? Maybe someone hated her in school. She was always the odd one who never fit in, who always ruined the curve in grading, the one who accidentally leaked any secret she heard to the wrong person. Maybe someone in her class cracked up and wanted to start his serial-killing spree with her.

The doc pulled her back from worrying as he parked in front of the clinic. "You're awful quiet, Elizabeth. Lack of sleep finally catching up to you?"

"No, I'm fine." She glanced over at his kind face. "Would you mind if I went with you today on your house calls, or barn calls, or whatever you call them? I could help."

He seemed to understand. "I wouldn't mind at all. I'd be happy to have the company."

"Thanks," she whispered, lowering her head. It wasn't that she was afraid to be alone, she told herself. She just needed time to think. All her life she had never worried so much about doing what was proper; she just worried about not doing something wrong. When she'd finally grown up, she thought everything would be all right if she just lived alone.

Only trouble seemed to have found her anyway.

Six

RICK TOOK HIS time getting dressed as he slowly relived every minute of his night with Trace. She'd felt so good in his arms, in his bed. With her, he believed he just might be a great lover. Only problem was no one would ever know, because he couldn't imagine loving anyone but Trace.

They fit together so perfectly. They were wild hungry animals leaving bruises one minute, and the next, loving so tenderly he felt he breathed her into his entire body. He hadn't asked her if she'd taken another lover in the months they'd been apart. He knew she hadn't. Just like him, she was starving, demanding, on fire. She'd wanted him with every part of her being, just as he'd wanted her.

Strangely, the fact that she hadn't said good-bye gave him hope. She was still around, and he had no choice but to wait until she appeared again. If she believed someone was stalking him, planning to kill him, she'd be watching over him from somewhere in the shadows. His own private, long-legged, beautiful guardian angel.

When he climbed into his car, a text blinked on his cell phone.

One word. Midnight. He didn't recognize the number, but

he pressed return and punched: I dare you to come back for more.

He pressed Send and smiled. Trace wasn't gone. They'd have another night.

He didn't bother to search the corners of the parking garage or study the people in other cars. She was out there. He knew it, but he wouldn't see her until midnight. An endless day lay ahead, which offered him hours to think about the pleasure to come. He'd make love to her again, wild and free, as if for the first time, or maybe the last time.

He stopped for coffee at the diner, bought a paper in the bookstore, climbed the stairs to his office on the third floor of the courthouse, and adjusted his chair. Fifteen minutes later he was sound asleep.

Finally, the sound of someone pounding on his door woke him. Rick stood, trying to shake off sleep before he made it to the lock. The sunshine that had been sparkling across his floor was gone, so he guessed he'd been asleep for hours. It had to be near noon.

His cousin's wife, Alex, the sheriff of Harmony, stood waiting, none too patiently as he unlocked the door. She didn't say a word, just walked in, turned, and glared at him.

"What?" he snapped. Alex tended to frown when she was unhappy with him, which was most of the time. The sheriff was only kin by marriage, but she'd been big-sistering him since he'd hung up a shingle and started practicing law.

"Why didn't you let me know Marshal Trace Adams was in town? She charged into my office three hours ago and the dust hasn't settled since."

"What do I look like? Instagram? Maybe she just came in to see me."

Alex rolled her eyes. "She thinks your life is in danger. That's why she's back."

He guessed the fact that he'd slept with Trace couldn't look more obvious. "You've talked to Trace this morning then." It really wasn't a question. Of course she'd been filled in on the shot that hit Lizzie. If she hadn't, Trace wouldn't be in town, and Alex wouldn't be in his office.

Sheriff Matheson grinned. "I saw her. She looked just like

you, exhausted with a permanent smile stuck on her face. Let me give you some advice, Rick. When you sleep with a woman, take some time out and sleep."

Great, Rick thought, now the whole family would know his business. He hated small towns. And relatives. And coffee that hadn't kept him awake. Coughing, he muttered, "I think I'm coming down with a cold. Maybe you should go."

She walked past him and sat in the chair in front of his desk. "I'm not going back to the office. Trace is there going through files and hinting that I'm not doing my duty. Half the deputies are afraid of her, and the other half are following her around like lost puppies."

"What duty are you supposed to be doing?" Rick wasn't interested, but Alex didn't appear to be leaving.

"The one of taking care of you. She thinks someone's out to kill you, and she's mad at me for not already solving the case. Which is hard to do, counselor, when no one reports being shot at."

He circled the desk and dropped into his napping chair. "It was just one shot. Probably a stray bullet. Lizzie said it just scratched her. You can ask her."

Alex leaned forward. Her long catlike movements reminded him a little of Trace. They were both tall and slim and beautiful enough to have been models, if they hadn't picked fighting bad guys for a living.

"I would ask Lizzie, but she's not at home or at her workplace. Don't you think it's a little strange that she's disappeared when she doesn't even have a car?" Alex frowned as she confessed. "I even broke into her house to make sure she wasn't in there dead."

"I've done that," Rick admitted. "Did you check with the vet who lives in front of her place? Maybe he'd know where she's gone."

"I didn't know they were friends." Alex looked surprised. "I did see a note on his door saying anyone with an emergency should call his cell. He jotted down something about visiting a few ranches and being at the rodeo arena around five when the rough stock came in."

"Rough stock?" Rick couldn't remember much about the

rodeo. He'd played football all the way through high school and college. Jocks and cowboys usually only met in the emergency room.

Alex, with a brother who'd been a real rodeo star, knew all about it. "Rough stock is the bulls and horses that are provided for the guys to ride. They're raised to be in the game. If the doc's checking out the stock, he's in for a hard afternoon."

Rick really didn't want a lecture on rodeo problems. In truth, he'd like to get back to his dream, but Alex wasn't here to gripe about Trace or look for Lizzie. She had something else on her mind—he'd bet on it. "Say what you came to say, Alex. I know you didn't walk over here just to wake me up so you could give out advice on my love life."

She leaned back in her chair again and steepled her fingers. "Did it ever cross that thick Matheson skull of yours, Rick, that maybe, just maybe, you weren't the target last night? Maybe whoever was shooting hit what he aimed at?"

Rick came wide awake. "Why would anyone want to hurt Lizzie? She does dress like she's trying out for a part in *Sweeney Todd* and her hair changes color regularly, but she's a kind person. Word is she doesn't charge near enough for the grooming and does all the pound dogs free to help them get adopted. Who would want to hurt her?"

"I know. It didn't make sense to me at first. I agree that she's kind. The family might not have said much to her, but we all admired her for taking care of her grandmother. She gave up two years of her life to stay home and be a nurse. That's why I want to get to the bottom of this fast, before someone tries again."

Rick leaned closer. The sheriff had his full attention.

Alex pulled out three letters from a folder she carried. "Six days ago, Davidson called me over to the post office and said Lizzie had opened a P.O. box and asked if he would cancel all delivery to her house."

"Lots of folks do that." Rick picked up a pen and began jotting down notes. If this was going anywhere, he wanted to have the facts right.

"He said she'd come by about once a week to clear the mostly junk mail out of her box. Then last week she just came in, stopped at the trash, and tossed all the mail she'd pulled from her box. He claimed, near as he could tell, she didn't look at a single letter."

"Maybe she pays her bills online." Rick used reason. "I wouldn't think she'd get many letters. Everyone she cares about lives around here. She was probably just tossing junk mail."

Alex didn't look happy. "Davidson pulled three letters she'd gotten out of the trash. It's not illegal to look at mail tossed in a public trash." Alex placed the letters on the desk.

"None have return addresses, but the postmark came out of the Dallas area."

"That's not much to go on," he said. "I assume you opened them."

Nodding, Alex pulled the single sheet of paper out of the first envelope. "It's not exactly a threat on her life, but it is close. We've already run tests on them. Only one had a fingerprint on it, and that belonged to Davidson."

Rick took the note: *No one knows how long they have to live. Like daughter, like mother. Maybe it is your turn to go to sleep.*

Silently, he glanced at the second and third. *Enjoy your last summer, Lizzie. It's time to finish what you started that night in the dorm room.* The last said simply, *There is nowhere to run. Think about how peaceful pills would be. You already have them with you.*

Alex just stared at the letters. "I checked the records. Her mother committed suicide the year after Lizzie's father was killed by a land mine."

"Someone wants her dead," Rick said, stating the obvious. Inside he felt sorry for not spending more time with her. Lizzie was different, but no one really believed she was insane.

"Someone who knows her," Alex added. "I called the college she went to, and after a little digging, found a dorm mother who remembered her. She said she had a serious injury her freshman year. Lizzie claimed it was an accident. She'd been trying to hang a curtain across her part of the room and slipped off a chair. One of the cords wrapped around her neck. The room-mates told everyone that she'd been depressed and they'd heard her crying. That had to be soon after her grandmother died, I'm guessing. The dorm mother said a report was filed and they called a few relatives. The next thing she knew, Lizzie showed up with a tattoo of ivy running from her shoulder to her neck. It covered up any scar the cord would have left."

"Any of the Mathesons know about the accident?"

"No, I called Aunt Fat and Aunt Pat. They would know if anyone would. They were close to her grandmother and still go visit with Lizzie. Aunt Pat said she'd never heard of such a thing, but she did know that Lizzie took pills to get to sleep. She told them once that she'd had nightmares all her life."

"What about the other side of her family? Her mother had a sister. Maybe that was 'the family' the dorm mother said was notified. I heard Lizzie say once that her granny had two other grandchildren who never visited."

"It took about five minutes to trace that." Alex folded up the letters as if she couldn't tolerate looking at them. "Lizzie's mother died shortly after Lizzie came to live in Harmony with her granny. Evidently, according to Aunt Fat, Granny and her other daughter had a falling-out over Granny taking Lizzie in. No one has heard or seen the daughter or anyone in her family for almost twenty years. Aunt Fat said she thought the daughter had two children, boys. Last name, Rogers. As far as anyone knows, they've made no effort to ever contact Lizzie."

Rick stood and began to pace. "I've heard from a few old lawyers that Granny's other daughter tried to fight the will after Granny died, but it was solid."

"I've heard that, too." Worry wrinkled Alex's forehead.

"How can I help?" Rick wanted in on this hunt. "We'll turn this town upside down until we find Lizzie, but that still leaves us with no clue as to who is sending the notes."

"That's where you come in. If we can locate Granny's will, we might find a lead."

Rick didn't think so, but he went downstairs to the county clerk's office. Fifteen minutes later he found the clue he'd feared. According to the will, after Lizzie's death the oil rights to the land her grandparents owned would pass to Granny's other grandchildren, two men who'd be in their thirties.

He looked up at Alex. "We've found motive. Now all we have to find is the Rogers boys."

Alex shook her head. "You find Lizzie. It's going to take me a while to find the right two men in Texas when their names are Fred and John Rogers."

"How many do you think there are?"

"Hundreds, but the only two I'm worried about are the two that are in my town. I know nothing about them except that one is armed." Alex looked straight at Rick. "Get your marshal over here. She'll have resources we could use that might make this go much faster."

He pulled out his phone as Trace stepped around the open door.

Rick couldn't hide his smile. She looked great, as always. He wondered if the sight of her would ever be common enough that his heart didn't stop every time he saw her. "There's my marshal, my lady," he said, loving that she didn't deny it as she joined the group.

SEVEN

DUST COVERED LIZZIE from head to toe. Her white tennis shoes with rhinestones on them were so brown they didn't even sparkle. Lizzie looked up and smiled at McCall. She'd never had so much fun in her life.

"You're doing great, partner," he said. "You almost caught that one."

Lizzie knew she was no good at rounding up calves, but she didn't care and she had a feeling McCall didn't either. They might be working in a dusty corral with half-wild cattle, but Lizzie grinned like she'd been dancing at a grand ball in glass slippers. She was helping him, or at least trying her best to. Having someone to talk to while he worked was as rare for him as it was for her.

Looking down, she giggled. A grand ball indeed. They were standing in a pen with mud and manure all over the ground. He'd been doctoring stock for an hour. Only with her at one hundred pounds trying to control a month-old calf, it seemed an even game. Sometimes she won. Sometimes the calf knocked her down and ran.

At first when he'd laughed it sounded like a cough, but as the day passed she liked to think that the doc was learning how to laugh all over again. She didn't even mind that he called her "partner" sometimes, like they were a team.

As he vaccinated the last calf, he handed her one of the medicine bags and gripped her arm to make sure she made it out of the corral without falling down again. "We got one more stop, then we'll head home. If I can take a rain check on that dinner you offered to cook, I'll buy you supper in town tonight. Where would you like to eat?"

She hadn't had anything since breakfast at dawn. "Anywhere that brings the food to the pickup. I'm too hungry to take the time to clean up."

He took both medical bags as they left the pen and crossed them over his shoulder as if they weighed nothing.

She slipped her hand around his arm and walked through tall grass toward the truck.

He slowed to her pace and leaned close. "I'm starving. Fast food sounds great."

She patted his dirty shirt. "I'm thinking if you get any more dirt layered on, you could be your own dust devil." When he slapped his jeans and dust flew, she added, "I've had a ball, Doc. It's been a wonderful day."

Now they were out of range of the other cowhands helping with the branding, McCall asked, "How's that wound on your side?"

"It's fine," she lied. "I haven't felt it all day." Twice she'd winced when it pulled, and she knew that a few of the butterfly stitches he'd put on were loose. She just hoped it wouldn't bleed through on his shirt that she'd worn all day with the shirttail tied around her waist. If McCall had seen the blood, he would've made her stop.

He opened the pickup door and shoved the bags toward the middle of the seat, then helped her in. "I promised I'd check out the stock coming in for the rodeo before dark, then it's off to the nearest hamburger joint that delivers food to the pickup."

As they drove back to town, he mostly answered questions. She'd discovered a whole new world and wanted to know all about it. She learned that no two days as a vet were the same. He told her about how great it feels to see a newborn colt stand for the first time and how when he had to put an animal down, he always prayed they were heading to a special heaven.

Lizzie saw McCall's gentle kindness and understood. He wasn't a man used to talking, but as the day wore on, she noticed he liked to touch her. First he'd help her up or offer her a steady brace of his hand along her back, but as time passed she found he often communicated with a pat or by brushing close. Even now, as they rode side by side, his hand, leaning across the bags, rested easy next to her leg.

When she slid her fingers beneath his hand, he lifted her hand and moved it to his leg, then slowly spread her fingers out. She smiled, too shy to look at him. He kept his eyes on the road, but she knew he was smiling also.

When he pulled into the rodeo grounds at the edge of town, he said, "How about you sit this one out, Elizabeth? Just relax. I won't be long."

Lizzie didn't want to miss anything, but exhaustion and lack of sleep were getting the better of her. With the window down, the afternoon breeze was just right for a nap. "All right, but if you need me, I'll come running."

He brushed his hand along her shoulder. "You've been great today. Rest up or we'll both sleep through the Western tonight."

She made no comment as he climbed out and headed toward the corrals at the far end of the small arena. She couldn't have said a word without crying. He talked about watching the Western tonight, like they'd done it a million times. Closing her eyes, she let herself hope. All her life she'd been one of those people trying to have fun but never quite making it. She was always the person at the party who never really had a group to laugh with, and when she tried too hard, it only made her awkwardness worse. Today, she hadn't tried at all to fit in. She'd been her uncoordinated self, and he'd liked her just fine.

She closed her eyes thinking of how she'd curl up against his side tonight.

A pickup pulled up next to her, but she barely opened her eyes. Lizzie was too busy reliving the perfect day and dreaming of being next to him for a Western. Maybe she'd spread her hand out over his leg again. She would like the feel of his muscles beneath the rough fabric of his jeans.

As she drifted off to sleep, she was aware of the dirt parking lot filling up. Horses were being unloaded. Men were talking. Somewhere in the distance, a crew was testing the mics. The rodeo wouldn't start until seven thirty, but hundreds of things had to be ready.

"You Lizzie?" A voice invaded her sleep.

She opened one eye and saw a short man in a cowboy hat standing at the driver's-side window. "Yes," she said, trying to see his face in the shadow of the big hat.

He nodded and turned toward the arena. "Doc says you're needed in the holding corral. Just follow the chute at the back gate and you'll find it."

Lizzie scrambled. "Does he need the medical bag?"

No answer. The stranger was gone.

She ran across the parking lot, the bag banging against her leg. At the back of the arena was a gate that led off into an even smaller chute tunneling around smaller stalls. Without hesitation, she ran in. The ground was soft, cut up by hooves and still muddy from the rain. Shadows were long across the high wood fences. She couldn't see the back corral, but it had to be in front of her.

Suddenly she heard the click of the gate she'd just closed behind her, and then the thunder of hooves rolled toward her down the chute.

Lizzie turned. Bulls. Huge horned bulls were coming after her.

For a few steps she tried to run, but the muddy ground was too slippery. Considering that she couldn't see the end ahead, instinct told her the bulls would reach her before she could get into the holding corral. Even if she did make it, she'd still be trapped with the bulls.

Holding to the bag, she tried to climb the fence. One board, another. More stitches at her side jerked free as she pulled herself up with one arm. She couldn't lose the doc's bag. She couldn't go fast with only one arm.

She heard the bulls coming closer. Too fast. As she turned, she saw them ten feet away and knew she was out of time. Even if she made it one more step, she'd still be scraped off the fence by their huge heads and horns.

Closing her eyes, she lifted the doc's bag and tossed it over the fence. The bag would be safe, and if she was lucky she would survive with only a few broken bones.

As she gulped in her last breath, someone grabbed her from

above and jerked her up just as the bulls hit the fence where she'd been. The force of their attack was so hard that it felt like the ground shook, and for a second, Lizzie thought she was flying, out of control.

One arm went around her as they tumbled to the packed dirt outside the chute. Lizzie lay very still on her stomach, slowly breathing in the air she had thought she'd never live to take.

When she looked at the man crumbled beside her, she smiled. "Hi, cousin."

"Are you all right?" Rick stood slowly as if testing for broken bones. "You almost frightened me to death. I saw you running from the pickup, but I couldn't catch you. When you disappeared into that chute, I knew there was going to be trouble the minute the men started herding stock in behind you."

She took his offered help and stood. "Thanks for the hand up," she said, guessing they both knew Rick had just saved her life.

He dusted off. "Anytime. The world would be a much darker place without you around."

"Thanks," she said. "That's the nicest thing you've ever said to me."

Rick put his arm around her. "Come on, Lizzie, the sheriff wants to talk to you."

"You told her about the shooting?"

"Not me. Everybody knows Alex has radio waves instead of brain waves. She knows everything going on in this town."

They stepped into the now-empty arena before McCall caught up to them. He'd been in the barn and heard the cattle being moved but never dreamed Lizzie was in danger. She tried to explain everything to him, and then she had to explain it all to Alex. Everyone started asking questions at once. Did she hear anything before the gate opened? Did she see anyone?

When McCall circled her waist to offer comfort and felt blood coming from her side, he ordered everyone to stop talking. He lifted her and carried her to his pickup.

"If you all have any more questions, you can find us at the hospital," McCall said simply.

No one argued.

While he drove, Lizzie pressed close to him. After he shifted gears, he put his hand across her legs. "We're going to the hospital, Elizabeth, and this time I won't listen to any argument."

She didn't care. She was hurting all over. "I'm sorry about your bag. I had to toss it over. I'm sorry about your shirt. I'll try to get the blood out when . . ."

"I don't care about the bag or the shirt," he snapped. "All I care about is you."

Tears cleaned two streaks down her face.

She didn't want him to say anything more. If he did, she'd lose what little control she had left. Later when she was cleaned up and patched up and more in control, she'd ask him to say the words again. *All I care about is you.* No one had ever said those words to her.

In only minutes, he lifted her out of the pickup and carried her into the hospital. Emergency room staff came running to help. Apparently the sheriff had called in to alert them.

When he stepped back a few feet to give them room to work, McCall announced he wasn't leaving. No one bothered to argue with the vet. They just walked around the tree of a man like he'd been planted there all his life.

Lizzie drifted off. The pain dulled, and it almost felt as if someone kept tickling her side, trying to keep her awake. The air around her smelled of cleaning materials, and the lights above her kept growing too bright, then too dim.

When she awoke, she felt no pain, and the sheriff had replaced the doc at the foot of her bed. "Where's McCall?" Lizzie whispered.

"He's gone to clean up. He told me not to leave your side until he got back." Alex smiled and brushed her service weapon. "I don't think he would have left you in my care if I weren't armed."

"I'm all right." Lizzie tried to make her voice stronger. "I just pulled a few of the butterfly stitches loose."

The sheriff stepped closer. "Lizzie, I don't know if you're clear enough to understand, but the fall did do some damage to that injured side, only that's not why I'm here. You'll heal, but you're not out of danger. We think the gate being opened and the bulls being driven in after you was not an accident. We believe it was an attempt on your life, just like the shot was Sunday night."

Lizzie started to ask why anyone would want to kill her. She didn't matter to anyone. But that wasn't true.

She mattered to McCall.

Closing her eyes, she tried to make sense of what the sheriff was trying to tell her, but sleep claimed her before her brain could clear enough to think. When she woke some time later, McCall was standing at the foot of the bed.

"I want to go back to your place," she whispered with a smile. "We're missing the Western."

He grinned. "They're keeping you here tonight, partner. Mind if I spend the night with you?" He nodded toward a recliner beside her bed. "When I refused to leave while you were sleeping, one of the staff brought that in."

"The sheriff said"—she couldn't finish. Maybe it wasn't true. Maybe she'd dreamed that the sheriff thought someone was trying to kill her.

"I know what the sheriff said." He moved his hand gently along her arm. "Rick filled me in."

"If it's true, you'd be safer if you left."

McCall shook his head. "I'm not leaving this hospital until you're with me."

Some men might have said more, but for Lizzie, he'd said enough.

EIGHT

RICK AND TRACE stood just outside Lizzie's hospital room, listening to Lizzie and her vet talking quietly.

Rick felt like he'd run a marathon. First, trying to find his cousin in the tunnel of boards she'd disappeared into at the rodeo arena. And then flying down the road to the hospital behind an old pickup he couldn't seem to catch up to, even in his sports car. Trace had been right beside him all the way, telling him to hurry. Telling him how to drive.

He tried to relax now that all was quiet. His cousin was safe. They all were safe. He glanced in at the big vet standing close to his cousin's bed. "I think those two may be falling in love," Rick whispered to himself.

"Sounds sappy." Trace folded her arms when Rick offered to hold her hand. "Don't get all mushy on me, Matheson."

Rick raised an eyebrow. "Don't you believe in love?"

She shook her head. "Lust maybe, but not love."

"You think that's all it is between us? Lust? Animal attraction? Nothing more?"

"Probably." She rolled against the wall and bumped her shoulder with his. "Sparks fly. That's all. That's enough. What else do people like us need?"

Rick thought about telling her that he felt used, but if he did, she might stop. Either way he figured he was heading for a heart attack. "It's not that way with me, Trace. It's more. It's deeper. I need you around, not just your body. I need you."

She looked like she didn't believe him. "So you'd still be attracted to me if we didn't have sex?"

"Of course." Why else was he thinking of her every waking hour? Why else would he hope every phone call was Trace? Hell, sometimes he half-wished trouble would come back to Harmony just so she would drop in to check on him.

The elevator door opened, and the deputy assigned to Lizzie's room for the night walked out. He had a stack of newspapers, a cup of coffee, and a folding chair. "I'm here, folks. You can go home now." When they both frowned, he added, "I won't leave this door, I swear."

Rick and Trace walked to the elevator in silence. She stepped in and pushed the button for the first floor. They stood inches apart as the door closed, then she turned toward him. "I say you're wrong, Matheson. If we're not all about sex, then prove it. Let's go back to your place and sleep, just sleep. No touching, no playing around."

He smiled. "You know you couldn't keep your hands off me."

"I can. You'll be the one to break, proving my point. I'm betting you crack before midnight."

As they walked to the car he glanced at the tower clock. "One hour, I can make that." All day they'd had the attempt on Lizzie's life to talk about, but now she was safe. "All right, I'll take your bet, but no teasing. No dirty talk. No touching me in foreplay."

"Foreplay. I didn't think you knew what that was, counselor."

"You know what I mean."

"All right, I agree. No talking sex, no foreplay, no touching." She waited until they climbed in his car before adding, "So what do we do?"

"We talk."

"About what? My work? Your work? I don't have a family, and I've already met more of yours than I want to know."

"We talk about stuff. Like hobbies and dreams and our childhood." Rick tried to think of something, anything.

"I don't have hobbies, and my dreams are usually about you and involve sex, and that subject is off the table." She stretched.

He forced his eyes on the road. All Trace had to do was breathe and he was turned on. If he didn't concentrate, he'd never make the hour. "Okay, tell me about your childhood, Marshal." When she was silent, he started talking about every dumb, crazy, wild thing he did from kindergarten to sixth grade. If he went any older, they'd be talking about his adolescent dreams and every stupid thing he said to a girl.

He kept the conversation going until they were inside his apartment. With great care he managed to keep several feet between them. He offered her one of his old football jerseys to sleep in and tried not to fixate on how great she looked in it. She took a shower while he made sandwiches, and she cleaned up while he showered. He offered her his bed and he unrolled the sleeping bag in his empty living room. He set up tables between him and where she was sitting on a huge pillow.

Trace couldn't be still. Finally she stood and paced in front of the windows. He wasn't surprised that she went over every detail, every fact of Lizzie's case. Rick could follow the way her mind worked and knew that was the secret of her success in solving crimes.

When she disappeared with a crisp "Good-night," he stared out the window. Eleven forty-five. He'd almost made it. He wasn't even sure he'd made sense while they were talking, but he'd kept his hands off her. He'd proved that there was more to them than just sex. Lying back on his bedroll, he thought over every clue she'd lined up. Somewhere they'd missed something. He could feel it and she'd felt it, too. Tomorrow they'd both be up early, tracking down every detail, talking to Lizzie, walking the rodeo grounds, talking to anyone who might have seen anything they'd missed.

But tonight he needed sleep if he was ever going to stay awake tomorrow. Only sleep didn't come easy with Trace a room away in his bed.

Smiling, he realized he'd managed to learn a few facts

about her while they talked. She loved to read and admitted she'd like to write mysteries someday. She'd also told him she loved rainy nights and sunrises.

For a while he watched the clock with every cell in his body wanting to run to her. He had no idea how it had happened, but he knew he loved her, and if not touching her was the only way to prove it, he would torture them both.

Finally the tower clock began to strike midnight. One, two, three.

"I love you, Trace," he whispered, forcing the words out. Maybe he didn't know her favorite color or where she went on vacation as a child, but he knew her down deep to her soul. He knew what mattered to her and what drove her. He knew the good in her, and the fairness and the need she had to set things right. "I love you," he whispered again a little louder.

The clock chimed. Four, five, six.

"I know," she answered.

He turned and saw her in the doorway. For a moment he just stared, letting her beauty wash over him.

Seven, eight, nine.

Slowly, he lifted the blanket. "Come to bed," he said as calmly as if they'd slept together for years.

Ten, eleven, twelve. He'd made it to midnight.

Her face was in shadows, but he saw her hands were balled and her body turned soldier-straight.

"Time won't change a thing, Trace. Whether I touch you or make love to you or stay a room away forever, I'll still love you. I love the you who worries about people. I love the way you don't buy into any of my bull. I love the way you smile at me when you think I'm not looking. I love all of you—the soft curves, the hard edges. I love you."

She jerked a quick nod and ran to him across the empty room.

When she crawled in beside him, a cry slipped from her. Pulling her close, he cupped her face and felt the tears, though he hadn't heard her crying. He kissed her gently and whispered, "Say the words."

To his surprise, his Trace answered simply, "I love you, too."

As the midnight hour passed, their loving grew far deeper

than either of them ever dreamed it could be. A silent promise of forever blended with passion and need.

When the night grew silent, he held her as she slept and he whispered, "Now we've got the loving part settled, we'll talk about the marrying part tomorrow."

NINE

COTTON-CANDY-PINK LIGHT SPREAD across her hospital room as the sun rose, waking Lizzie. Every part of her body ached from the fall she'd taken, but surprisingly her side no longer hurt. It felt as if someone were tickling her again where she'd been shot, which made her smile. A wound shouldn't tickle, must be the pain medicine.

McCall looked sound asleep in the recliner next to her bed. A nurse had covered him with a blanket during the night, but his worn boots were still on his feet and sticking out as if blocking anyone trying to get close to her. The low rumble of his snoring whispered through the silent room.

The doctor from the emergency room the night before walked in. "Morning, Lizzie. How did you sleep?" Dr. Turner looked exhausted. Her white coat was wrinkled and tiny brown curls had escaped from her tight bun.

"I'm fine, but you look tired."

"All I need is sleep. You're my last stop before heading home." The very proper doctor looked at the big man sleeping in the recliner. "This yours? You do know we don't allow bears in the hospital."

Lizzie laughed. "He's not mine, but last night I dreamed I

was hibernating in a cave, all cuddled up with one of the bears. It was delightful."

Both women giggled as Dr. Turner moved to Lizzie's side and began examining her stitches. When she turned on the light the snoring stopped, but the bear of a man looked to be still asleep.

"If he wakes, he'll have to leave," she said.

Lizzie shook her head. "He says he's staying. Besides, he's already seen my stitches." When she looked over at McCall, his sleepy brown eyes were staring back at her, but he didn't move. She saw something she'd never seen in a man's eyes before, caring.

"You're fine. No sign of infection." Dr. Turner closed the chart. "But this time go home and take it easy for a few days. No running with the bulls. Stay in bed or on the couch and have one of your cousins deliver meals."

Lizzie nodded. "I promise. Aunt Fat has already called and plans to bring over a few meals if the road to my house isn't too muddy."

Dr. Turner turned out the overhead light. "Try to get some sleep. It'll be another two hours before they get around to checking you out of here."

Lizzie waited for her to leave, then tiptoed over to the recliner. On the way, she noticed the vet's old sweater and put it on to cover the gap in her hospital gown. It felt grand and almost went to her knees. "McCall." She poked his shoulder. "I want to sleep in the cave with my bear. Would you mind?"

He opened his arms and she slowly moved into the chair with him. To her surprise, he kissed the top of her head. "I shouldn't have taken you with me yesterday. I shouldn't have believed you when you said all was fine. I shouldn't have . . ."

She rubbed the rough line of his jaw, wondering why all the single women in town didn't see how handsome he was. "If you ask me, you did everything right yesterday. You made me laugh all day, and you worried about me the minute you thought I was hurt."

When he would have argued, she touched his lips, surprised at how soft they were next to his whiskers. "*Shhhh,* bear. I just want to sleep inside my perfect dream for a while."

He held her a bit tighter and didn't say another word.

Two hours later when they left the hospital, he still wasn't talking, but his gentle touch never left her. He loaded her in his old pickup and drove to the clinic, then carried her through the mud to her house. The rain of the night before had left her dirt road a river. After she changed into clean pajamas and put his old sweater back on as her robe, she found him in her kitchen cooking breakfast.

"I thought you'd be gone. I know you've got a full day of work waiting." She'd seen his calendar yesterday and knew he was already late for his first call.

"You want me to go?" he asked without looking up.

"No." The one word was the most honest thing she'd ever said.

He glanced at her then and smiled. "You planning to give me back that sweater?"

"I'm thinking no."

"I'm thinking I like looking at you wearing it."

She moved a foot closer. "It makes me feel like you're hugging me, even when you're not around."

"Then that's a reason to keep it, partner. If you're up for it, I think we'd better talk. I got some things I have to say, and I might as well say them before you change your mind and push me out the door." His words sounded rehearsed, as if he'd been waiting for a chance to say them.

Lizzie sat at the little kitchen table and waited. He put a plate of burned eggs and bacon on the table, folded into the extra chair, then stood up to get the toast. He sat down again, bounced up to get the jelly. Before he finished spreading jelly, he started to jump up again.

She put her hand on his shoulder. "Stop."

"But I forgot the napkins." He looked like a man solving world peace, not setting the table.

She pulled the tea towel from his shoulder and placed it between them. "We'll share this. Tell me what you have to tell me."

He nodded and they both forgot about the food.

His words were low at first. "I know most folks think my wife is dead and I never have said she wasn't, but she's alive. Or at least she was the last time I saw her four years ago. She just left me one day like it was no big deal. Like tossing away the life we planned was easy."

"You loved her deeply?" Lizzie asked.

He shook his head. "That's just it. I thought I did. I thought I'd die without her, but I didn't. I think her simply saying that she didn't want me hurt more than her leaving. She just didn't want *me*.

"I told her I'd change, but she shook her head and said, 'Into what?' She said people are what they are. A person has to take another like they are or leave."

Lizzie fought to keep from touching him. She'd known a lifetime of not being wanted; somehow knowing that someone else had also felt such pain cut hers in half.

He met her stare. "I thought I loved her. I thought we'd grow old together, but all I felt was relief when she walked away. I tried to remember when we were happy, when I'd measured up, when she'd loved me, but it was hard. I never lived up to her plans, and I don't remember her saying she loved me after our honeymoon. We were always trying to make the marriage work when we didn't fit with each other after all."

"What happened to her?"

"She divorced me and married our next-door neighbor four months later. I didn't fight over a thing she wanted. Turned out she wanted everything we had, except me. She wanted to stay at her job, live in the same town, even keep the same friends. So that left me with moving on."

Lizzie couldn't understand why his wife left him. How could a woman not love a man who loved animals as much as Doc did? "Why are you telling me this, McCall?" It crossed her mind that he was about to say he didn't want her now, so he knew how his wife must have felt about him.

Only McCall just stood. "I wanted you to know how it is with me. I'm not much with conversation and I've never been the life of any party. I'm working my way from broke to poor, but I'm honest. You're way out of my league, but I'm good with animals and you seem to like them, too."

"Are you saying you'd like to date me?" She wasn't sure if he was trying to tell her he didn't want to see her again or he wanted to make more of the friendship they had.

He laughed without smiling. "I'm no good with dating. Don't have the time or energy after I work twelve hours a day. I was thinking more something like we get married, or move in together if I'm rushing you. After four years in the same little town living next to each other, we probably know one another pretty well."

This was the strangest proposal she'd ever heard of. She couldn't tell if McCall was trying to talk her out of it while still asking, or if he was simply so shy he couldn't line up the words right.

"What are you saying?" she asked again.

He stood and moved to the door. "I'm making a mess of this whole thing. We should have just eaten the breakfast. That's another thing I can't do. I can't cook. Half the time the dogs won't even eat my cooking."

Lizzie noticed Sam had jumped on the doc's chair, but didn't look interested in sampling their breakfast.

"What do you want, McCall?" she said again, needing to know what he was thinking.

"I'm saying I had more fun yesterday than I've ever had. I liked being with you and holding you and worrying about you. I want to hold you every night while we watch a movie, and I want to take care of you when you're hurt. You're a kind person, Lizzie. Your whole family loves you. I can tell by the way they talk about you. They say you're a terrible driver, but you've got a heart as big as Texas." He reached for the door and opened it. "You think about the possibility of me and you, and if you'd be willing to take a chance on me, I'd be much obliged."

The door slammed so hard it shook the house. For a moment she just stared at the breakfast as his footsteps thundered across her porch and down her steps. He was running. Storming away from her. Not because he was mad, but because he was afraid she'd turn him down.

Only a fool would turn him down. She had to do something fast.

She rushed to the door, pulled on her boots, and hurried outside, but he was already to the gate of his corral by the time she hit the mud of her yard. Following him didn't seem logical. She needed to think. Someone was trying to kill her. She was wounded. A man had just asked her to marry him and she didn't even know his first name.

Tugging her feet from the mud-covered boots, she ran barefooted toward him.

He turned to close the gate and saw her a moment before she heard an explosion behind her. The rush of air on her back seemed to push her forward as the sound rumbled in her ears like a freight train. Instinct took over, and she covered her head and began to crumble a moment before McCall reached her.

He lifted her and held her close against him. "Don't look back," he ordered, holding the back of her head with one hand, and carried her to the porch of his clinic.

The smell of smoke filled the air. Lizzie didn't move. Something had happened. Something bad.

He set her down just inside his place. "Call 911, then lock the doors and stay inside until I get back."

His hard tone left no room for questions. She did exactly as he said as the smell of fire polluted the morning air. She couldn't look back, wouldn't look back. If she didn't see what had happened behind her, it wasn't real.

She darted to the old phone between the back door and the kitchen window. Her fingers jabbed at the keys—911, 911.

When the Harmony sheriff's dispatch answered on the third ring, a man's voice simply reported, "We're on our way, Doc," before she said a word.

"Who is?" Lizzie's voice and hands were shaking.

"Everyone. Fire department. Sheriff. Ambulance and some marshal who said she wanted in the loop about anything that happened. The minute the clinic number came up, I hit the speed dial. They're all being linked in as we speak. Who may I ask is reporting this call?"

"I'm Lizzie Matheson. I live . . ."

"I know where you live. Your home and cell number are on the emergency list, staring right at me."

"There's been an explosion near my house." Leaning over to the kitchen window, she corrected, "In my house."

"Is anyone hurt?"

"I don't think so." She dropped the phone. Her cats! Sam and Molly were inside.

Lizzie was off the porch and halfway to the corral gate when she spotted McCall coming around the side of her house with a cat in each arm. Neither Sam nor Molly was moving.

As she ran closer, McCall looked up. The sound of sirens

filled the air, almost drowning out McCall's shouts for her to get back inside.

"They're alive," he yelled, "but barely. Another minute and the smoke would have killed them." He handed her Sam, and they ran into his clinic.

"Tell me what to do," she pleaded and he seemed to understand.

As he worked clearing the animals' lungs of smoke, he kept talking, telling her how to hold them, how to calm them. His voice kept her from crying and his orders kept her busy. After a few minutes both cats were breathing on their own, and Lizzie felt as if she were taking her first deep breath since the explosion.

"Thank you," she whispered to McCall.

"I'm afraid I didn't save anything else. I knew you were safe, and I know how much these two worthless cats mean to you." He grinned and she knew he was kidding her. "They were probably watching the house burn. Cats are no good at protecting a house."

She kissed his cheek. "You know, Doc, much as you protest, I think you're really a cat person."

He shook his head. "Not a chance."

She petted her two old cats. In a minute she'd have to deal with the reality that part or all of her house was on fire, but somehow she knew it would be all right. Sam and Molly were with her.

Once Sam and Molly were safe and calm in their hospital cages, McCall took her hand. "Whatever's out that back door, Lizzie, we'll deal with it. Right?"

"Right."

Ten

RICK FLOORED THE gas pedal and raced toward Lizzie's place. He could hear the ambulance and fire truck behind him.

"She's all right," Trace announced. "She made the 911 call. She's safe at the doc's place."

Rick didn't want to talk. They'd been working leads since dawn. Trace's contacts had learned that two men had rented a hotel room near Bailee two weeks ago. One paid cash while the other signed in. The hotel was a dump off the interstate thirty miles away, and the manager couldn't read the signature well enough to get more than a last name of Rogers. He did say they looked enough alike to be twins, but one did all the talking. Kind of a nervous guy. The other didn't say a word, but he was the one who always drove the tan pickup.

There were probably a dozen tan pickups at the rodeo last night and maybe thirty more in town. All had Texas tags. The cowboy who'd given the orders to move the bulls didn't stand out, either. Medium to short in height, slim build, white hat. Lizzie had talked to a man matching that description, but the sun had been in her eyes and she only remembered his hat.

Rick guessed the two men at the hotel was just a lead. Probably wouldn't go anywhere. But the pieces seemed to fit with what Lizzie had told them last night. If he and Trace were getting close to the truth, the bad guys might be getting too close to Lizzie.

As they crossed the railroad tracks, Rick saw smoke billowing from behind the clinic. It hadn't been five minutes since she'd called, and Lizzie's house already looked like a skeleton fighting flames that danced on the roof.

"Park at the clinic," Trace shouted. "She called from the doc's phone. If you'll check on her, I'll check on the house."

Rick nodded. "Be careful." There were a hundred things he wanted to tell her, wanted to promise her, but he knew she had to do her job. If he really loved her and they were going to ever have any kind of future, he'd have to accept that.

When he cut the engine, she was gone before he even unbuckled his seat belt. He ran for the clinic door as the sheriff pulled up beside his car.

"Stay with Lizzie," Alex yelled as she climbed out.

Rick just nodded. He'd heard those same words in the same bossy tone one minute earlier.

He watched Sheriff Alex Matheson run toward the fire as Harmony's volunteer fire department began unloading their gear. Without bothering to knock, Rick crossed the clinic's foyer and walked into the vet's office.

Lizzie was sitting on a desk with her back to him while the vet pulled off her top. For the first time Rick saw all of his cousin's tattoo. Ivy running over one shoulder and brushing along her neck. His first thought was how pretty it was, then embarrassment took over and he backed away.

Lizzie looked over her shoulder. "It's all right, Rick. Brandon was just checking my stitches."

Rick didn't move for fear he'd see more of his cousin than he should.

McCall glanced up at Rick as she pulled an old sweater over her.

"She's fine." The vet's voice was low. "All stitches in place."

Rick didn't miss the fact that Dr. McCall was brushing his fingers along his cousin's shoulders, touching the tattoo. He thought of telling him to stop, but she must know the man well if she'd learned his first name when no one else in town knew it. Maybe his fingers had played along the ivy before?

Rick thought of hitting himself in the head for worrying about that, when she could have died in the blaze burning out of control yards away. Before he could ask any questions, the side door of the office, big enough to haul a horse through, opened.

Trace and Alex pulled a cowboy, shorter than either of them, through the opening. The little man looked terrified and somehow guilty at the same time. Rick had a sickening feeling he'd be appointed to defend him any minute.

"Lizzie, do you know this man?" Alex asked calmly.

"No. Who is he?"

"We don't know, yet, but Trace found him running along the inside of your back fence. With the fire, she might not have seen him right away if he hadn't been screaming for somebody named Fred."

Trace looked at Rick. "We found an old Colt and bomb-making material in his backpack, along with maps of everywhere Lizzie's been the past two weeks, including the Matheson ranch."

The man was shaking. "This isn't my fault. Fred was supposed to wait for me, but he wasn't there to pick me up."

"Is Fred your brother?" Lizzie asked. "That'd make you Johnny, my cousin. Your mother left me a message last week that if I was ever in trouble I need to get in touch with her. She said her sons Fred and Johnny would help me out. I didn't think my granny would have wanted me to call, so I ignored her message."

The little man cracked. They knew his name. "We didn't want to kill you, Lizzie. I just wanted you hurt so you'd need us. We're family. We'd come help you if you needed us."

To everyone's surprise, Lizzie jumped off the desk and walked to stand in front of the little man. "But why?"

"Mom said you ain't got no relatives. No one who cares about you. If you was hurt, you'd come to us for help. She says the oil money you get belongs to all us, not just you, and you'd see that once you got to know us."

"You're wrong," Rick snapped. "She has the whole Matheson family who cares about her and most of the people in town."

The little man looked scared. He'd said too much, but he couldn't stop. "I didn't mean to burn down her house. I was just going to bomb the shed out back. Only this fat cat ran out of the bushes and frightened me. When I fell, the bomb hit her porch and went off." He gulped down air and cried. "It's not my fault. Fred was supposed to wait for me. He said we'd never get caught."

"As a lawyer, I'd advise you to stop talking, Mr. Rogers." Rick thought of adding that everyone in the room, except Lizzie, was probably thinking of beating the guy to a pulp. Lizzie, on the other hand, looked like she felt sorry for her brainless relative.

Alex cuffed Rogers while he asked Rick, "How much trouble am I in?"

"Ten years, maybe five if you have no priors." Rick wanted to say something, like a dozen Mathesons would be waiting for him when he got out, but Rogers looked like he was already on fire with fear. There was no need to toss matches.

Alex and Trace ushered Rogers out. As Trace passed Rick, she whispered, "See you tonight. I want in on this case."

He saw the excitement in her eyes. She loved her job and if he was going to love her, he'd have to understand. "Tonight," he whispered back, wishing he could touch her just once before they were pulled apart. But there was no time.

A dozen things seemed to be happening at once. Firemen put out the house fire, but the place looked like a total loss. Rick, Lizzie, and the vet watched it all from the porch of his clinic. To his surprise, his cousin took it all with only a few tears.

When the vet went in to answer the phone, he hugged her. "You all right, Lizzie Lee?"

She nodded. "I learned a long time ago not to get too attached to things."

"You want me to take you over to the Matheson ranch? I'm sure the aunts will take you in for as long as you want to stay."

Lizzie shook her head. "I got an offer to stay here, and I think I'll take Brandon up on it."

"How'd you get him to tell you his first name?"

She giggled. "I asked him."

Rick left her in good hands as he drove back to his apartment. Trace had called in saying they'd picked up the other Rogers brother, and both were claiming the other was the mastermind of the plot to frighten Lizzie.

To Rick's way of thinking, there was no mastermind. The Rogers boys didn't have enough brain cells between them to think up this plan. He'd bet that because their address was still their mother's home, she'd thought it up. Dear old invisible Aunt Alice was probably at home in Dallas, waiting for her sons to call in with good news.

By the time he finished taking a shower, Trace was crawling through the window. "Evening, dear," he said as he handed her his cup of coffee. "Have a good day at the office?"

She kissed his cheek. "I had a great day."

They sat down on the two end tables that had been left in his living room and talked. Then, like an old married couple, he went to bed while she took a shower. When she cuddled beside him, he turned to face her.

"Somehow, Trace, we have to make this work. I can't do without a heart, and it leaves every time you do."

"I know. After today I think Harmony might be a fascinating place to live."

He pulled her closer. "After tonight, you'll know it for certain."

ELEVEN

AS THE WESTERN ended, Lizzie clicked off the TV and glanced over at McCall's two dogs sleeping on the kitchen rug; her two cats were two feet away in the kitchen chairs. McCall had been asleep since the middle of the movie they'd both already seen. She'd spent the time thinking of all the ways she'd color his world.

They'd spent an hour eating pizza, planning how she could fit into his already small space. Since she had no clothes or furniture, it wouldn't be too hard.

There were so many things yet to talk about. So many days to share. She thought it strange that he'd been right in front of her, waiting for her to see him. Now that she had, she couldn't imagine a day in the future without him.

As he slept, she snuggled close and saw their future. They'd build a house in the pasture beside his clinic. They'd work together most days. She'd always cook supper, and he'd always fret over her. He'd try to boss her around and she wouldn't listen. They'd have a big wedding and maybe children. They'd grow old together. They would never stop loving each other.

She poked his side. "Come to bed, dear."

"Why?" he said, still half asleep.

"Because I want you, Brandon McCall. And I need you to know that I'm going to want you close to me every day for the rest of my life."

"I'll be here," he answered. "It sure did take you a long time to find me."

"I know. Funny how love was right in front of me. I just had to open my eyes."

He leaned down and kissed her tenderly with just the right kind of kiss she'd been waiting for all her life. "Marry me," he whispered against her lips.

She whispered back. "I don't know you well enough yet, Doc, but maybe I will by morning."

You'll Be Mine

Marie Force

Along with their parents,
Patrick Murphy & Lincoln and Molly Abbott,

Cameron Murphy and Will Abbott

invite you to attend their wedding
on Saturday, October 24, at 2 P.M.
at their home in Butler, Vermont.

Reception to follow immediately.

ONE

TWO DAYS BEFORE her wedding to Will Abbott, Cameron Murphy shut off her laptop at exactly one forty-five in the afternoon and left it in the office she shared with her fiancé. She wouldn't need the computer for two weeks. The next time she returned to the office, he'd be her husband and they'd be back from their honeymoon.

Filled with giddy excitement, Cameron turned off the office light and closed the door behind her. Will was already gone for the day, running last-minute wedding errands while she finished up at work.

Their office manager, Mary, stood up and came around her desk to give Cameron a hug. "Enjoy every minute of this special time," she said, nearly reducing Cameron to tears.

"Thank you so much, Mary. I'll see you tomorrow night, right?" She was one of a few special friends invited to join the family for the rehearsal dinner Will's parents were throwing at the big red barn where Will and his siblings had been raised.

"Wouldn't miss it for the world."

"I'll see you then."

Cameron skipped down the stairs and into the store where she was greeted with more hugs and good wishes from the employees. While no one would mistake her little old nuptials for the royal wedding, it sort of had that feel to it. In Butler, Vermont, the Abbotts were royalty. With a family of ten children and businesses that employed numerous members of the local community, an Abbott wedding was big news.

She accepted a hug, a kiss, best wishes and a cider doughnut from Dottie, who ran the doughnut counter. After talking wedding plans with Dottie and the other ladies for a couple of minutes, Cameron took her doughnut to the store's front porch to enjoy it in relative peace. With only two days to go, she was no longer worried about fitting into her dress, so she took a seat on one of the rockers and ate her treat in guilt-free heaven.

She'd no sooner begun to relax than who should appear on a leisurely stroll down Elm Street but her very own stalker, Fred the Moose. Cameron sank deeper into the rocker, hoping Fred wouldn't notice her. In all her years of living in New York City and after scores of first dates, she'd never had an actual stalker— until she came to Vermont and slammed her MINI Cooper into Fred, the Butler town moose. Since then he'd taken such a keen interest in her that Will's dad, Lincoln, had recently concluded that Fred had a crush on her.

Fantastic. A moose with a crush. With her dad due at two, and Patrick Murphy always on time, the last thing she needed was yet another mooseastrophy. Fortunately, Fred didn't see her sitting on the porch and continued on his merry way, leaving Cameron to breathe easier about Fred but not about her dad's impending arrival.

The thought of her billionaire businessman father in tiny Butler had provoked more nerves than anything else about the upcoming weekend. Marrying Will? No worries at all. Getting through the wedding? Who cared if it all went wrong? At the end of the day, she'd be married to Will. That was all that mattered. But bringing Patrick here to this place she now called home?

Cameron drew in a deep breath and blew it out. She hoped he wouldn't do or say something to make her feel less at home here, because she loved everything about Butler and her life with Will in Vermont. She'd experienced mud season—along with a late-season blast of snow—spring, summer and now the glorious autumn, which was, without a doubt, her favorite season so far.

How could she adequately describe the russet glow of the trees, the vivid blue skies, the bright sunny days and the chilly autumn nights spent snuggled up with Will in front of the wood-stove? The apples, pumpkins, chrysanthemums, corn husks tied to porch rails, hay bales and cider. She loved it all, but she especially loved the scent of wood smoke in the air.

Cameron couldn't have asked for a better time of year to pitch a tent in their enormous yard and throw a great big party. All her favorite autumn touches would be incorporated into the wedding, and she couldn't wait to see it all come together on Saturday. At Will's suggestion, they'd hired a wedding planner to see to the myriad details because they were both so busy at work.

At first, Cameron had balked at the idea of hiring a stranger to plan the most important day of her life, but Regan had won her over at their first meeting and had quickly become essential to her. No way could Cameron have focused on the website she was building for the store and planned a wedding at the same time.

She glanced at her watch. Three minutes until two. Patrick would be here any second, probably in the town car he used to get around the city. Under no circumstances could she picture her dad driving himself six hours north to Vermont. Not when there were deals to be struck and money to be made. Time, he always said, was money.

He'd shocked the hell out of her when he told her he wanted to come up on Thursday so he could spend some time with her and Will before the madness began in earnest. Her dad would be sleeping in their loft tonight, and Will had already put her on notice that he would *not* have sex with her while her dad was in the house. She couldn't wait to break his resolve.

The thought of how she planned to accomplish that had her in giggles that died on her lips at the familiar *thump, thump, thump* sound that suddenly invaded the peaceful afternoon.

No way. No freaking way. He did not!

If this was what she thought it was, she'd have no choice but to kill him. Warily, she got up from her chair and ventured down the stairs to look up at the sky just as her father's big, black Sikorsky helicopter came swooping in on tiny Butler, bringing cars and people to a halt on Elm Street.

One woman let out an ear-piercing scream and dove for some nearby bushes.

Equal parts amused and aggravated, Cameron took off jogging toward the town common, the one space nearby where the bird could land unencumbered. As she went, she realized she should've expected him to make an entrance. Didn't he always?

Nolan and Skeeter were outside the garage looking up when she went by.

"What the hell was that?" asked Nolan, who would be her brother-in-law after the wedding. He was married to Will's sister Hannah, who'd become Cameron's close friend since she had moved to Butler.

"Just my dad coming to town."

"Jumping Jehoshaphat!" Skeeter said. "Thought it was the end of the world."

"Nope, just Patrick Murphy coming to what he considers the end of the earth. Gotta run. See you later."

"Bye, Cam," Nolan said.

"I assume that's with you," Lucas Abbott said, gesturing toward the town common with his thumb, as Cameron trotted past his woodworking barn.

"You'd be correct."

"That thing is righteous. Does he give rides?"

"I'll be sure to ask him."

"Nice."

Cameron sort of hated that everyone in town would know her pedigree after her father's auspicious arrival. Maybe they already knew. In fact, they probably did. The Butler gossip grapevine was nothing short of astonishing. If the people in town knew who she was, or who her father was, no one made a thing of it. After this, they probably would, which saddened her. She loved her low-key, under-the-radar life in Butler and wouldn't change a thing about it.

But she also loved her dad, and after thirty years as his daughter, she should certainly be accustomed to the grandiose way he did things. She got to the field just as he was emerging from the gigantic black bird with the gold PME lettering on the side: Patrick Murphy Enterprises. Those initials were as familiar to Cameron as her own because they'd always been part of her life.

Hoping to regain her breath and her composure, she came to a stop about twenty yards from the landing site and waited for him to come to her—by himself. That was interesting, as she'd expected his girlfriend-slash-housekeeper Lena to be with him.

With her hands on her hips, Cameron watched him exchange a few words with the pilot before shaking his hand, grabbing a suitcase and garment bag as well as his ever-present messenger bag, which he slung over his shoulder. Wait until he experienced Butler Wi-Fi, or the lack thereof.

He was tall with dark blond hair, piercing blue eyes and a smile on his handsome face, and as he walked to Cameron, her heart softened toward him, as it always did, no matter how outrageous he might be.

She took the garment bag from him and lifted her cheek to receive his kiss. "Always gotta make an entrance, don't you?"

"What's that supposed to mean?"

"The *bird*, Dad. You scared the hell out of everyone. They thought we were being attacked."

He looked completely baffled. "I told you I'd be here at two."

"I was watching for a car, not a chopper."

Recoiling from the very idea, he said, "I didn't have six hours to sit in traffic on the Taconic. As it is, my ass is numb after ninety minutes in the chopper."

"We do have airports in Vermont, you know."

"We checked on that. Closest one that could take the Lear is in Burlington, which is more than two hours from here. Time—"

"Is money," she said with a sigh. "I know."

"Besides, you're taking the Lear to Fiji, and for the record, I'd like to point out it wasn't my idea to move you out to the bumfuck of nowhere."

Cameron laughed at his colorful wording. "This is *not* the bumfuck of nowhere. This," she said, with a dramatic sweep of her arm, "is the lovely, magnificent town of Butler, Vermont."

"It's as charming as I recall from the last time I was here for Linc's wedding."

"Are you being sarcastic?"

"Me? Sarcastic?"

"I thought Lena was coming with you."

"Yeah, about that . . . We've kind of cooled it."

"Is she still working for you?" Cameron had spoken to her recently and hadn't heard that she was no longer in Patrick's employ.

"Oh, yeah. It's all good."

Cameron was certainly used to the way women came and went in her father's life. She'd learned not to get attached to any of them. They didn't stick around long enough to make it worth her while. "Well, it's great to see you and to have you here. I know it's not what you're used to, but I think you'll enjoy it."

He stopped walking and turned to her. "You're here. That's all I need to enjoy myself, honey."

Cameron let the garment bag flop over her arm so she could hug him. "Thank you so much for coming, Dad."

He wrapped his arms around her. "Happy to be anywhere you are."

THEY stashed Patrick's bags in Cameron's black SUV. "Where'd you get this beast?"

"Will insisted I trade the MINI for something built for Vermont winters. I don't love it, but as I haven't survived a winter here yet, I'll take his word for it."

"So this is the store, huh?"

"Yep."

"Show me around."

"You really want to see it?"

"I really do."

She took Patrick's hand, eager to introduce him to all her new friends. "Right this way."

He followed her up the stairs to the porch and into the Green Mountain Country Store in all its glory.

"Wow." Patrick took a look around and glanced up at the vintage bicycle fastened to one of the wooden beams above the store. "I feel like I just stepped into an episode of *Little House on the Prairie*."

"Isn't it amazing? I'll never forget the first time I came in here. It was like I'd been transported or something." She looked up at him as he took in the barrels full of peanuts and iced bottles of Coke and products from a bygone era, a simpler time, hoping he'd see the magic she saw every time she came through the doors to the store. "That's dumb, right?"

"Not at all. It's quite something. I'm wondering, though, how in the name of hell you build a website for a place like this."

Cameron laughed. "Slowly and painstakingly."

"I can't wait to see how you've captured it."

She tugged on his hand. "Come meet Dottie and have a cider doughnut."

"Oh, I don't think—"

"You have to! Your visit won't be complete without one." She led him back to the doughnut counter where Dottie was pulling a fresh batch from the oven. "Perfect timing. Dottie, this is my dad, Patrick, and he's in bad need of a doughnut."

Dottie wiped her hands on a towel before reaching across the counter to shake Patrick's hand. "So nice to meet you, Patrick. We're all very big fans of your daughter."

"As am I."

"Can I get one of those for him?"

"Of course! Another for you, sweetie?"

"Absolutely not! I've got a dress to fit into on Saturday, so don't tempt me." To Patrick, Cameron added, "Dottie is the devil when it comes to these doughnuts."

"Why, thank you," Dottie said with a proud smile as she handed over a piping-hot doughnut to Patrick.

Both women watched expectantly as he took a bite.

His blue eyes lit up. "Holy Moses, that's good."

"*Right?*" Cameron said, pleased by his obvious pleasure. "I limit myself to two a week, or I wouldn't fit through the doors around here. Come on upstairs and check out the office. See you later, Dottie."

"Bye, Cam. Nice to meet you, Patrick."

"You, too."

He followed her through the store, stopping to look at various items as they went.

"That's Hannah's jewelry," Cameron said of the pieces that had stopped him for a closer look. "She's Will's older sister, twin to Hunter, who's the company CFO."

"She does beautiful work."

"I know! I'm a huge fan. I have a couple of her bracelets. Helps to have friends in high places."

"I'm glad you're making friends here."

They proceeded up the stairs to the offices on the second floor. "So many friends. And now Lucy's here a lot, too, which makes it even better."

"Back so soon?" Mary asked when they arrived in the reception area. "I didn't think I'd see you here again for at least two weeks."

"I wanted you to meet my dad, Patrick."

Mary came around her desk to shake his hand. "So nice to meet Cameron's dad. We adore her here."

"So I'm hearing. Nice to meet you, too."

"This is our office." Cameron opened the door and turned on the lights so her dad could see her workspace.

"*Our* office?"

"Mine and Will's."

"You two *share* an office? They didn't give you one of your own?"

"We tried," Mary said. "Those kids are inseparable."

Cameron blushed and shrugged. "What she said. Besides, if I'm in another office, how am I supposed to play footsie with him during the day?"

"Ugh," Patrick said with a grunt of laughter. "TMI. I'd go crazy sharing office space with anyone, especially such a small one."

"Not everyone can have an acre in the sky to call their own," Cameron said disdainfully.

He tweaked her nose. "It's not a full acre, and I do need my elbow room."

"You're a spoiled, pampered brat, and we all know it."

Mary laughed at their sparring.

"Don't listen to her, Mary," Patrick said with a wink, which had Mary blushing to the roots of her brown hair. "We all know who the spoiled brat is here."

"Yeah, and it's not me."

"I'm afraid I have to side with your daughter, Patrick. There's nothing spoiled about her. She works harder than all of us put together."

"Thank you, Mary. I'll make sure Hunter hears about your fifty percent raise."

They left Mary laughing as they went back downstairs.

"What's her story?" Patrick asked.

"Who, Mary?"

"Yeah. She's adorable."

"Dad . . . Don't. She's a really nice person. Leave her alone. She wouldn't stand a chance against your brand of charm."

"Why can't I have a little fun while I'm in town?"

Cameron stopped on the landing and turned to him. "She's off-limits. I mean that."

"Don't be so touchy, Cam." He kissed her cheek and proceeded ahead of her into the store.

She watched him go with a growing sense of unease. She'd be watching him this weekend and keeping him far, far away from Mary—and all the other single women in Butler.

Two

AFTER A WINDSHIELD tour of Butler and the surrounding area, Cameron took her dad home to their cabin in the woods. "I want to make sure you know it's kind of rustic," she said, biting her lip nervously. "You might find it primitive compared to what you're used to."

"Believe it or not, I wasn't always a billionaire with a Park Avenue penthouse. You forget I grew up in a six-room ranch house in New Jersey with a single bathroom shared by five people. I can do rustic."

"It's just . . . I know you'll be tempted, but don't make fun of the cabin. Will loves that place, and he built it himself."

"Not sure what you take me for, sweetheart, but I'm not about to poke fun at my future son-in-law's home."

"Okay," Cameron said on a deep sigh of relief.

"I wish you'd relax. I've got no plans to rain on your parade. I know you're happy here, and that's all I've ever wanted for you, believe it or not."

Cameron tried to do as he requested. What did she care, really, if he hated everything about her new home? It wouldn't change how she felt about it. Except . . . she wanted him to understand why she'd chosen to live here. His approval had always mattered more than it should have. That was just a fact of her life.

"Right here is where I first met Fred the Moose," she said, pointing to the spot on the road where her life had changed forever.

"He's the one who crushed the MINI, right?"

"Yep, only he'd tell you the MINI crushed *him*, not the other way around."

"And you have conversations regularly with this moose?"

"More often than I'd like to. Lincoln says he has a crush on me."

Patrick laughed. "Is that right? Well, I hope to meet this fellow while I'm here so I can gauge his intentions toward my daughter."

"I hope none of us lay eyes on him this weekend," Cameron said hopefully. By now, she knew better than to expect a day completely free of Fred. He seemed to turn up with alarming regularity wherever she was. The thought of Fred crashing the wedding was one that Cameron refused to entertain.

"And here we are at home sweet home." Cameron took the right turn onto the dirt road that also served as their driveway. "When I first came here last spring, it was mud season and this road was full of potholes." Why was she telling him that? What did he care?

"It's nice and smooth now. Does Will have to fix it every year?"

"*Every* year."

"Sure is pretty out here."

"We think so, too."

"But remote. Seriously, Cam. What do you do when you need milk?"

"We wait until the morning and get it when we're in town."

Patrick shuddered dramatically. "I'd go crazy."

"I thought I would, too, but it's amazing how quickly I adapted to life without everything at the tip of my fingers. Being way out here is an adventure, and I love it."

"Will you still love it when you have babies and need diapers in the midst of a blizzard?"

Cameron laughed. Leave it to him to come up with a worst-case scenario. "I'll send my mountain man out to get them for me. A blizzard is nothing new to him."

"Better him than me."

"Definitely better him than you. As I recall, you've never changed a diaper in your life."

"Touché," he said, chuckling.

They drove around the final bend in the road before the cabin came into view with a huge white tent off to the left side of the house. The autumn foliage was now past peak but had retained a breathtakingly beautiful golden hue that would perfectly match the dark gold silk dresses her bridesmaids would wear on Saturday.

As she brought her car to a halt outside the cabin, she was relieved to park next to Will's big truck. She was glad he was here to help her welcome her dad to their home. At the sound of Cameron's car arriving, their yellow Labs, Tanner and Trevor, came running around the cabin to greet her.

"There're my boys," she said to Patrick. "Come meet them." She got out of the SUV and was immediately accosted by the dogs, who were now hers as much as they were Will's. "Hi, guys! How was your day?" Cameron gave them both an equal amount of love and attention, which was richly rewarded with wet dog kisses that she absolutely adored.

"Boys, this is your grandpa, Patrick. Dad, meet your grand-dogs, Trevor and Tanner. Trevor has the black collar and Tanner's is red. That's how we tell them apart. And Tanner has this sweet white patch on the top of his head."

"Nice to meet you, boys."

"Sit." Both rear ends dropped at Cameron's command. "Now shake a paw and say hello properly." Two left paws were extended to Patrick, who played along, laughing as he shook each one.

"They're adorable."

"I know, right?"

"They only do that for her," Will said as he joined them, extending his hand to Patrick.

Her dad surprised them both when he bypassed Will's hand to hug him. "Good to see you again."

"You, too." Will seemed pleased by Patrick's warm greeting. "Welcome to our humble home."

"It's beautiful." Patrick took a long look around at the towering evergreens and Butler Mountain in the distance. "I can see why you love it here."

"It's our own little slice of heaven." Cameron leaned into Will's one-armed embrace, closing her eyes when he kissed her temple. She opened her eyes to find her dad watching them with a smile on his face. "Come on in and see the rest."

"I'll get your bags," Will said.

"Thank you." Patrick offered his arm to Cameron. "We need to practice for Saturday. I've heard I'm supposed to give you away or some such nonsense?"

Cameron laughed. "It's not nonsense, Dad. It's *tradition*."

"What if I give you away and then decide I want you back? Does this arrangement come with any sort of return policy?"

"Absolutely not," Will said from behind them.

"I had a feeling he would say that," Patrick replied glumly. "A girl owns your heart and soul for thirty years, and then you have to *give* her to another guy? It's wrong, I tell you. Wrong, wrong, *wrong*."

Cameron and Will laughed at his running commentary as they led him into the tiny cabin they called home. Will had lit the woodstove, so the space was warm and cozy and immaculate, thanks to the hours they'd spent the night before cleaning in preparation for her dad's arrival.

She'd been a nervous wreck about making everything perfect, working until well past midnight when Will declared that it was as good as it was going to get. He'd picked her up and carried her to bed over her vociferous objections.

"This is great, you guys," Patrick said as he looked around at their home. "I love it."

Will took Patrick's bag up the ladder to the loft.

"That's your penthouse for the evening," Cameron said, pointing.

"Looks good to me."

Cameron went to him and hugged him. "Thanks for being such a good sport about everything."

He returned her embrace. "I have no idea what you were expecting."

She looked up at him and rolled her eyes dramatically, making him laugh. "Are you hungry?"

"Starving."

"Molly and Lincoln are coming for dinner."

"I can't wait to see them," Patrick said of his Yale University classmate. It had been Lincoln's idea to hire his old friend's daughter to build a website for the store, which is what had brought her to Butler in the first place.

"Dinner is already in the oven," Will said of the lasagna they'd made themselves.

"Smells amazing," Patrick said.

"How about a beer?" Will asked.

"I'd never say no to that."

While they waited for Will's parents to arrive, they sat on the sofa with beers and the crackers and cheese Cameron put out to hold them over until dinner.

"So talk to me about the wedding plans," Patrick said.

Cameron glanced at Will, who gestured for her to have at it. "Everything starts tomorrow afternoon with a rehearsal here followed by the rehearsal dinner at Lincoln and Molly's."

"Who's coming to that?"

"The wedding party and a few friends."

"Tell me again who's in the wedding party. I know Lucy is your maid of honor."

"Right, the others are Emma, Will's sisters Hannah, Ella and Charley, and Simone is the flower girl."

"What about you?" Patrick asked Will.

"I asked Colton to be my best man since we're practically marrying sisters," he said, referring to Lucy, Cameron's best friend from the city and now Colton's fiancée. "My other five brothers will be groomsmen along with Troy."

"That's a big wedding party," Patrick said.

"I know," Cameron said, "but we couldn't narrow it down, so we decided to have everyone we wanted." She shrugged. "This is what happens when you marry into a family of ten kids. Everything is big!"

"Ten kids." Patrick shook his head. "I still can't believe my old college buddy has *ten* kids."

"Neither can he," Will said. "They joke that by the time they figured out what was causing all these kids to arrive, they had ten of them."

"I can hear him saying that," Patrick said, chuckling.

"He also likes to talk about the long, cold winter in Vermont and the lack of things to do," Cameron added.

"Does that mean you're going to have ten kids, too?" Patrick asked.

"Oh, hell no!"

"We've agreed to stop at eight," Will said.

"He lies."

Patrick cringed at the thought. "I sure hope so."

"I've agreed to two, and then we'll see," Cameron assured her father.

"I can live with that." Patrick put down his beer and shifted on the sofa to face them. "So there's something I wanted to talk to you guys about, but I didn't want to do it over the phone."

Cameron was immediately on alert for bad news. "What's wrong?"

"Oh, honey, absolutely nothing. I swear. It's just kind of a sticky issue where you're concerned."

"What is?"

"Money."

"Dad—"

"Hear me out and then you can do whatever you want with no hard feelings. I promise."

"Okay   "

"I didn't bring this up before now, because I know how fiercely independent you are, and I didn't want to step on any toes as you were planning your wedding. I had a feeling you wouldn't let me pay for anything, so I didn't offer. That said, I'd still like to do something for you—anything you want if you'll let me."

"You did do something," Will said. "You made the plane available to us for our honeymoon. That's huge."

"That's nothing," Patrick said with the wave of his hand.

"It's not nothing to us, Dad. You made it possible for us to go to Fiji. We never would've been able to afford that otherwise."

"Well, um, you should know that your stay there has also been covered."

Cameron couldn't believe her ears. *"What?"*

"You heard me. It's all set. And you've been upgraded, too."

"Dad . . ."

"Don't 'Dad' me. You're my only child, and you're getting married. Let me have my fun, will you?"

Cameron glanced at Will, who seemed equally stunned.

"You didn't have to do that, Patrick." Will took Cameron's hand and gave it a squeeze. "But it was very nice of you just the same."

Following Will's lead, she decided to be gracious about her dad's grand gesture. "Yes, it was."

"You're not mad?" Patrick asked warily.

"No," Cameron said, laughing at his obvious concern, "we're not mad. How could we be when you're being so generous?"

"I know you, and I know how annoyed you get when I interfere."

She affected a stern expression. "I'll let it slide this time, but don't make a habit of it."

"Yes, ma'am."

"And that's more than enough of a wedding gift," Cameron said. "We have everything we could want or need."

"You're sure?"

"Positive." Cameron hugged him and kissed his cheek. "Having you here with us is the best gift of all."

Molly and Lincoln arrived a short time later, preceded into the house by their dogs, George and Ringo. They frolicked with Trevor and Tanner, who were George's puppies. Yes, George was a girl, but that didn't matter to the Beatles-obsessed Lincoln Abbott, who named all his dogs after the Fab Four.

Patrick stood to hug Linc and Molly.

"Never thought I'd see you here again," Lincoln said.

"Never thought I'd be here again, but who could've seen this coming?" He gestured to Will and Cameron, who stood arm in arm as they watched their parents say hello.

"We're so happy to have you here for such a wonderful occasion," Molly said. "We couldn't love Cameron any more if she were one of our own."

Patrick directed a warm smile at his daughter. "She turned out pretty good, despite me."

"You probably had something to do with it," Molly said.

"Not as much as I should have."

With no desire to dwell on the past during such a happy occasion, Cameron said, "Is anyone hungry?"

"Famished," Lincoln said, "and my mouth is watering at whatever smells so amazing."

"Our very own lasagna with garlic bread and salad," Cameron said.

"Sounds delightful, honey," Molly said. "What can I do to help?"

"Absolutely nothing. It's your night off."

The five of them enjoyed the meal and a conversation full of laughter and stories about Lincoln and Patrick's years at Yale.

"Before this weekend gets away from us," Patrick said, raising his glass of cabernet, "I'd like to propose a toast to Will, Lincoln, and Molly, who have made my daughter feel so at home here and welcomed her into the family she always dreamed of having, even if she thinks I didn't know that. I miss her in the city, but I sleep much better at night these days knowing she is here with you, that she is happy and well loved and has all the things I ever wanted for her, even if I didn't always do a very good job of telling her that. And to you, my beautiful, amazing, accomplished daughter, may you always be as happy as you are right now, and may your lives together be filled with all the joy and happiness the world has to offer."

"I'll drink to that," Lincoln said as Cameron and Molly mopped up their tears.

Will leaned in to kiss Cameron. "Me, too."

THREE

WITH HER DAD tucked into the loft, Cameron stepped into the room she shared with Will and shut the door, leaning back against it for a second to reflect on the evening they'd spent with their parents. Her dad had shocked the hell out of her with the toast, the laughter and his relaxed demeanor, not to mention the generous gift of paying for their honeymoon.

Will came out of the bathroom wearing flannel pajama pants she'd never seen before and a long-sleeve T-shirt.

Cameron started laughing the minute she set eyes on him. He always slept in the nude, no matter the season or the temperature. Once the laughter began, it overtook her in a fit of giggles unlike anything she'd experienced in recent memory.

"What is so funny?"

"You are." She wiped the tears from her face and crossed the room to him. "If you think all these clothes are going to keep you safe tonight, you're sadly mistaken."

"I don't know what you're talking about. We have a guest. Of course I'm wearing clothes to bed."

"No, you're not."

"Yes, I am."

Cameron tugged at his T-shirt, trying to get it off him.

He fought back, pulling it down. "Knock it off."

Sensing his determination, Cameron decided to fight fire with fire. "Fine. Be that way."

"Fine, I will."

While he got into bed, she went to the closet where she'd stashed the lingerie she'd gotten at the shower Lucy and Will's sisters had recently thrown for her. She sifted through the silky, frothy fabrics until she found the one that Will's sister Charley had given her "as a joke." Except this was not a joking matter, and since she'd be spending tomorrow night with her bridesmaids while he camped with the guys on Colton's mountain, Cameron was determined to break his resolve tonight.

With the outfit bunched into a ball in her hand, she scooted into the bathroom and shut the door. How to adequately describe the sluttiest thing she'd ever seen? Thinking about the laughter at the shower when she'd pulled this one out of the gift bag had Cameron giggling all over again. She'd had no intention of ever wearing it, but desperate times called for desperate measures.

It was black and entirely see-through with open holes over her nipples, a single snap at the crotch, a thong in the back and not much of anything else, except for the matching garter belt and sheer thigh-high hose that attached to the belt. Cameron had never before donned a garter belt, so it took some doing to get it just right. All she needed was a whip and five-inch spike heels to complete the ensemble, but she only wanted to seduce Will, not give him a heart attack.

She brushed her teeth and hair, put on the darkest red lipstick she owned and dabbed perfume in a few critical places. Once the giggles stopped, the nerves set in and she was reminded of the night they first made love. This felt like that all over again, and she tried to forget her dad was sleeping in the loft above them. She turned off the bathroom light and stepped into the bedroom where Will was engrossed in a thriller he'd been enjoying the past few days.

She cleared her throat.

He glanced at her, and she would never—for the rest of her life—forget the look on his face when he saw what she was wearing. His eyes nearly popped out of his skull, his mouth fell open, and the book dropped into his lap and then onto the floor with a dull thud. "What. The. *Hell*." His rough, sexy whisper did away with any remaining nerves, reminding her of all the many ways she loved him and couldn't wait to spend the rest of her life with him.

With that in mind, she moved toward the bed, crawling across the mattress to him.

"Cameron . . . I don't know what you're up to, but this is not going to happen with your dad sleeping ten feet from us."

As if he hadn't said a word, she straddled him and was gratified to feel the hard press of his erection between her legs. Despite what he said, at least one part of him was fully on board with her plan.

"Cameron . . . come on. I told you—"

She didn't wait to hear how that sentence was going to end. Rather, she leaned forward and kissed him, using every trick in her arsenal to persuade him. She bit his bottom lip and then soothed the sting with her tongue, drawing a deep groan from him.

"Shhh," she said, reminding him they had to be quiet.

When he cupped her breasts and ran his thumbs over her protruding nipples, she knew she had him. "You're the devil, you know that?"

She smiled. "You love me."

"Desperately."

"Show me."

"Not with him here. I can't."

She rotated her hips over the obvious proof to the contrary. "Yes, you can," she whispered in his ear. "I need you tonight. I've got to sleep a whole night without you. How will I survive if you don't make love to me tonight?"

"You're evil, *and* you're the devil. And where in the name of God did you get this outfit?"

"Your sister gave it to me at my shower."

"I don't even have to ask which sister."

"No, you don't. I believe she intended it to be a joke gift, but I'm not joking right now."

"Does knowing your dad is in the house turn you on or something?"

"*No!* Knowing you think nothing is going to happen *because* he's here is what turns me on."

"Evil."

"Guilty as charged." She tugged again at his T-shirt, and this time he let her remove it. "There's my favorite chest in the whole wide world."

"I'm always powerless where you're concerned, and then you come in here looking like a vixen . . ."

"Ohhh, a 'vixen'! I love that word."

"What else did you get at this shower of yours?"

"You'll find out in Fiji."

"God, I can't wait. How much longer till we get there?"

"About seventy-two hours."

"I don't know if I can make it that long."

"Then you'd better make tonight count." She kissed him again, and this time he participated fully, his tongue tangling with hers, arousing her to the fevered state of need she'd only ever experienced with him. His hands were everywhere, caressing and stroking her, feeding the fire inside. "Will," she said, gasping as she broke the intense kiss. "Please . . . I want you so badly."

"You have me. Hook." Kiss. "Line." Kiss. "And sinker."

Cameron smiled as she kissed him, loving him more than she'd ever known it was possible to love anyone. She tugged on the flannel pants she hadn't even known he owned. "Lose 'em."

"Are you secretly a dominatrix?"

"I might be. I'm rather enjoying this."

His eyes heated with lust that only added to the desire beating through her. "I can see that." He reached between her legs and gave a tug to the snap holding her outfit in place. And then his fingers were inside her, bending and curling to find the spot that always drove her wild. Tonight was no exception.

She would've cried out if his mouth hadn't found hers in time to muffle a sound her father surely would've heard if he were still awake.

"Shhh," Will said, laughing softly. "If you're determined to have your way with me, we have to be quiet. I'll never be able to look him in the eye again."

With her lips pressed against his ear, she said, *"Pssst."*

"What?"

"He knows we have sex."

"Not with him ten feet from us, we don't!"

Cameron rotated her hips, which drove his fingers deeper into her. She let her head fall back in bliss that she endured silently when she'd usually be letting him know how much she liked everything he did to her. Then his teeth were clamping down on her nipple and she had to bite her lip—hard—to keep from crying out again.

"So hot," he whispered. "So beautiful, so smart and talented and loving and sweet and all mine. Mine, mine, *mine*. How'd I get so lucky?" His thumb circled her clit, which was all it took to detonate the orgasm that had been brewing since the minute she'd donned the outfit.

He collected her moans and gasps in another searing kiss that, combined with what he continued to do with his fingers, had her climbing again before the first one had even ended.

She opened her eyes to find him on top of her, looking down at her with the beautiful golden eyes that had held her captive since the memorable night she met him, the night that had changed both their lives forever.

Cameron raised her legs and wrapped them around his hips, encouraging him to take what she offered.

Never one to need an engraved invitation, Will entered her in one long stroke that filled her to overflowing with love for him, for the life they shared, for all the days ahead they had to look forward to together.

"God," he whispered against her ear. "It just gets better and better and better all the time."

"For me, too. Don't go slow, Will. I need you so much."

"Be. Quiet. You hear me?"

She giggled softly. "I'll try."

"One sound and I'll stop."

"I'll behave. I promise."

He kissed her. "That'll be the day."

She squirmed under him while squeezing him tightly from within.

"Vixen," he said on a gasp, but her tricks did the trick. He began to move faster, giving her what she wanted in deep thrusts that made her see stars.

Her hands traveled down his back to cup his ass as he made love to her. She squeezed, and he groaned, loudly.

"Shhh," she said, teasingly.

"Stop doing stuff you know is going to make me groan."

She squeezed again, and he picked up the pace. Lost to him,

Cameron raised her hands over her head and grasped the slats in the headboard, letting him take her hard and fast, the way she loved it best. He knew exactly what she needed and gave it to her every time.

Coming silently, with Will deep inside her, was one hell of a challenge, but Cameron bit her lip and wrapped her arms around his neck, holding him close as he let go, too.

"God, that was hot," he whispered.

"Mmm, *so* hot."

"I didn't stand a chance against you and that outfit, which of course you knew."

"What was I to do when you came to bed wrapped in flannel?"

Laughing softly, he said, "You're quite proud of yourself, aren't you?"

"*Mmm hmm.* Quite proud."

"Love you, Cameron Murphy-soon-to-be-Abbott."

"I love you, too, and I can't wait to be Cameron Abbott."

FOUR

THE FESTIVITIES BEGAN late on Friday afternoon with the rehearsal at Will and Cam's house, where Regan, the cheerful, energetic wedding planner, ran things with the precision of a boot camp drill sergeant.

"She's kinda scary," Will whispered to Cameron as they watched Regan give marching orders to the wedding party. Petite and curvy with shoulder-length dark hair, her voice carried when she gave orders with the kind of authority no one dared to question.

"Scary in a good way. This would be a hot mess if we'd tried to do it ourselves."

"She's even got Lucas and Landon hanging on her every word."

Will's younger twin brothers were known for their comedic misbehavior at most family events, but he was right. Regan had them rapt with attention as she went through the sequence of events that would transpire the next afternoon.

"Where're our bride and groom?" Regan called.

Will took Cameron's hand and led her into the fray. "Here we are."

"Will, I need you up here with Colton—and Patrick, in the house with Cameron."

Before they parted company, Cameron put her arms around Will's neck and kissed him as their guests whistled and hooted at them to get a room. "See you soon."

"I'll be waiting."

Cameron released her fiancé and took the outstretched arm her father offered her. They walked together across the yard to the cabin. Outside the front door, the wedding party was being arranged according to Regan's instructions. First came Lucas and Landon, who would accompany their mother.

Then Emma and Troy, Ella and Max, Hannah and Hunter, Charley and Wade. Lucy, who would walk in with Simone, their flower girl, came next. A flower arbor and chairs would be placed on the lawn tomorrow. For now, they were left to imagine the aisle that would run between the chairs.

"Are we ready?" Regan asked.

"As ready as we'll ever be," Cameron said. "Let's do it!"

Beaming, Molly was escorted by her sons. Waiting for her at the end of the imaginary aisle were Lincoln and Elmer, who would perform the ceremony. She hugged them both and then broke loose to hug Will.

Cameron loved the way he laughed at his mother's infectious joy. When she was done with Will, she hugged and kissed Colton, too.

Emma and Troy were given the go-ahead, followed by the others in staggered pairs.

"Here we go," Lucy said, turning to smile at Cameron before she accompanied a giddy Simone with her imaginary basket of rose petals.

Patrick rested his hand over his stomach. "I feel like I'm going to be sick, and this is only the rehearsal."

Cameron laughed at the tormented expression on his face. "Stop it. This is the moment you've been preparing for all my life."

"And I've been thinking about it for thirty years that went by in a flash. How can you be all grown up and getting married when I still picture you as this itty-bitty thing in a tutu, dancing around the apartment like a tiny sprite?"

Cameron brushed at an unexpected tear. "Is that how you picture me?"

"I have a million pictures of you in my mind, but from now on, the one I'll always have in my mind is the way you look right now."

"How do I look right now?"

"Absolutely, positively beautiful."

Cameron hugged him, clinging to him long after Regan gave them the signal to proceed. "Let's do this, Daddy." She hadn't called him that in decades, but it seemed to fit the occasion.

They broke apart, and Patrick used his sleeve to wipe his face. "If I have to."

"I'm afraid you do."

He tucked her hand into his elbow and then covered it with his hand.

Cameron never took her eyes off Will as she walked through the yard on her dad's arm. If the rehearsal was this overwhelming, she couldn't imagine what tomorrow would bring. Will watched her intently, never blinking as she came toward him. As always, he gave her his full, undivided attention.

A hundred images spiraled through her mind in the few minutes it took for them to cross the yard: from the moment she first laid eyes on him, ankle-deep in the freezing Vermont mud with an angry moose standing between them, straight through to the night he proposed to her in the exact same spot with the exact same moose serving as their witness.

She almost expected Fred to come busting through the trees to make it official.

And then she was standing before Will, and he was extending his hand to her. Cameron turned to her dad, hugged him and kissed him and whispered, "I love you," in his ear.

"Love you, too, baby." He shook Will's hand and stepped back.

Will picked up Cameron and swung her around, bringing her down with a passionate kiss that had her blushing while everyone else laughed. "Thought you'd never get here."

She hugged him. "I've been right here, waiting for you to make an honest woman out of me."

Smiling, he kissed her again. "In that case, we really ought to get married."

"Best idea you've ever had."

Into her ear, he whispered, "I've got a couple other ideas I'm saving for Fiji."

Cameron's entire body heated at the thought of two weeks alone with him in the South Pacific. She wasn't one to wish her life away, but she was excited to be completely alone with him, away from work and able to spend day after day together. As much as she was looking forward to the wedding, she couldn't wait for the honeymoon.

"Let's practice the recessional," Regan said, clapping her hands to gain the attention of the rowdy wedding party.

Will and Cameron led the way. Halfway to the cabin, he scooped her up into his arms and carried her the rest of the way home.

LINCOLN and Molly served an Italian feast for the rehearsal dinner. As she loaded her plate with ziti, chicken, pasta, salad and bread, Cameron wasn't thinking about fitting into her dress. Rather, she wanted to enjoy every minute of this once-in-a-life-time weekend, surrounded by the people she loved best.

Cameron had never seen so many people at the Abbotts' home at one time, but the spacious barn in which they'd raised their ten children was more than up to the occasion.

Joining the party for dinner were Hannah's husband, Nolan, Hunter's fiancée, Megan, Mary from the store, Patrick's assistant, Maggie, who'd driven up from the city, and Lucy and Emma's dad, Ray Mulvaney.

Molly moved through the gathering refreshing drinks, taking plates and making everyone feel welcome. Cameron had loved her future mother-in-law from the first time she met her. In Molly, Cameron had found the mother she'd never had, as her own mother had died giving birth to her. As the wedding approached, Cameron had missed what she'd never had more than ever.

Molly had been right there to fill the void, doing double duty as the mother of the groom and stand-in mother of the bride.

Cameron followed Molly into the kitchen. "Everything is wonderful, Molly. Thank you so much for this."

"Oh, honey, it was completely and entirely my pleasure. Such a wonderful, happy occasion." She hugged Cameron. "Are you ready for tomorrow?"

"So ready."

"Will is, too. I've never seen him this excited about anything."

"I've never been so excited, either. I've pretty much felt that way since the night I met him. Or, well, I guess it was actually the next day when he stopped being mad at me for coming to town to build a website he didn't want."

Molly laughed. "He was instantly taken with you. Linc and I knew right away that you two were going to be something special. I've never been so happy to be right about anything."

A loud whistle came from the big great room in the middle of the barn.

"That'll be Linc looking to make a toast." Molly extended her arm to Cameron. "Shall we?"

"Absolutely."

They walked into the room full of loved ones. "There's the blushing bride," Lincoln said. "Come on up here with your future husband and let me embarrass you both for a minute."

"Do we have to?" Will asked.

"You bet."

Will's brothers pushed him forward, and Cameron caught him as he landed right where Lincoln wanted him. Will put his arms around Cameron from behind and held her against him.

Lincoln extended his hand to his wife and then put his arm around Molly when she joined him. "It's such a pleasure to welcome you all here tonight for this happy occasion. This has been an incredible year in which we welcomed Nolan, and now Cameron, to our family, as well as Lucy, and Megan, who'll join us before too much longer. When you have ten children, people think you've maxed out your capacity for love. But then someone new comes into your life, and you realize your capacity expands when the right people come along. Cameron, Molly and I couldn't be more delighted to welcome you into our family. We knew you as a little girl and thought you were adorable. You grew into an amazing, loving, caring woman who has made our son so very happy, and we love you very much." He held up his glass. "So I'd like to propose a toast to Cameron Murphy, who will become Cameron Abbott tomorrow, and to Patrick, who becomes an honorary Abbott when our kids get married. Our family is lucky to have you both. And to Will, who is the most wonderful son any parents could ever hope to have. Thank you for bringing Cameron to us."

"Wow." Cameron mopped up tears while Will did the same behind her. Then they hugged and kissed his parents. "You know how to get a girl."

"May I?" Patrick asked Lincoln, who gestured for his old friend to proceed. "Thank you for those kind words, Linc, and for this wonderful dinner and evening. I'd like to propose a toast to Will, the man who has won my little girl's heart and quite possibly the only person in this world who could make her prefer the wilderness of Vermont to the wilderness of New York City. After spending time in Butler and at their home in the woods, I can see why Cameron loves it here. And I can certainly see why she loves Will so much. Linc, I've wondered what the heck you were doing out here in the boonies all these years. But tonight, surrounded by your incredible family, I can see you've been doing something right in your barn in the boonies. You certainly did something right with Will, my son-in-law, a man most worthy of my little girl. Congratulations. To Will and Cameron."

Will dabbed at his eyes. "Cripes. The dads are on fire tonight."

"Weddings do that to parents," Elmer said. "And grandparents. I'd also like to raise a glass to my beloved William, who has been a joy to me—and his late grandmother—from the day he was born. You were always a happy little fellow, who grew up to be a man anyone would be proud of. And then Cameron came crashing into town, and we got to watch you two fall in love. I couldn't be happier to be celebrating this occasion with both of you, and I'd like to thank you for the honor you've bestowed upon me by asking me to officiate. When I became a justice of the peace, I thought it would be something fun to do in my retirement. It never occurred to me that I'd get to perform wedding ceremonies for my precious grandchildren. That has been the ultimate side benefit." He raised his glass to them. "To Will and Cameron, I love you both, and I'm looking forward to being a great-grandfather to your children."

Laughing through their tears, Will and Cameron hugged his adorable grandfather.

"Do we get to give toasts, too?" Lucas asked.

"Absolutely not," Molly said.

"Aw, come on, Mom," Landon said. "That's not fair."

"It's absolutely fair. This is a rehearsal dinner, not a roast."

"How does she always know what we've got planned?" Landon asked his twin.

"She has ESP," Will told his brothers.

"I know you guys," Molly said. "And I don't trust you for a second."

The wine continued to flow, along with the laughs and several kinds of cake. Cameron was blissed out on alcohol, sugar and happiness when Will joined her to tell her it was time to go their separate ways for the night. She hated the idea of spending even one night without him, but they'd agreed weeks ago to spend this evening apart.

The guys were camping up on Colton's mountain while the girls took over their cabin.

"So tomorrow," Will said, leaning in to kiss her. "You'll be there right?"

"Wild horses couldn't keep me away."

"Me either."

"Don't be late."

"Couldn't have dreamed this," he said, "so I wouldn't dream of being late to make it official."

She took his hand and led him into the mudroom, the one place in the house that wasn't overrun with people. With a minute to themselves, Cameron hooked her arm around his neck and drew him into a deep, passionate kiss.

"This time tomorrow," he whispered against her lips, "we'll be making our big escape."

"*Mmm*, can't wait for all of it."

"Let's go, Romeo," Colton called to his brother. "You've got two weeks in Fiji to kiss her face off."

Will pulled her in close one more time, pressing his erection into her belly as he kissed her again, telling her with every stroke of his tongue that she was loved and desired. "I gotta go."

"I gotta let you."

"See you tomorrow, baby." He kissed her lips and then lingered with a kiss to her forehead.

"Get some sleep."

"Not likely, but I'll try if you do."

"Deal." He hugged her one more time. "Love you."

"Love you, too."

Cameron released him to leave with his brothers for their campout on the mountain. Right after the guys left with much bickering and laughter, Hannah came to find her. "Ready to go?"

"Let me just say good-night to my dad and your parents." Patrick would be spending the remainder of the weekend at Lincoln and Molly's house.

Cameron hugged Molly. "Thank you so much for an incredible evening."

"I loved every minute of it." She kissed Cameron's cheek. "Try to get some sleep tonight."

"I'm too excited to sleep."

Molly smiled. "I'll be over in the morning to help."

"I'll see you then."

"Cameron?"

"Yes?"

"Thank you for making Will so happy."

"Being happy with him has been the easiest thing I've ever done."

She hugged Lincoln and Elmer and then her dad. "Molly and Lincoln will take good care of you."

He raised his glass of bourbon. "They already are. This is the good stuff."

"Nothing but the best," Lincoln chimed in.

"I'll see you tomorrow," she said to her dad.

"I'll be there."

FIVE

HANNAH DROVE CAMERON, Lucy, Ella and Charley to Cameron's house where everyone but Hannah, who was pregnant, enjoyed glasses of wine while they painted fingers and toes and talked about wedding plans. Emma and Ray had taken Simone back to the Butler Inn earlier. They would rejoin the wedding party in the morning.

After a couple of hours of pampering, drinking and gabbing, they noticed Hannah beginning to fade.

"We should get Mama home to her baby daddy," Ella said.

"I'm fine," Hannah insisted. "I don't want to break up the party."

"You'll be dragging ass tomorrow if you don't get some sleep," Charley said. "And Cameron doesn't want your dark circles messing up her wedding photos."

"That's right," Cameron said. "Get your ugly self home for some beauty rest."

"You fit right in with this family," Hannah said, rolling her eyes.

"Why, thank you. Nothing pleases me more than fitting in with the Abbotts."

Her future sisters-in-law left with hugs and kisses and

promises to be back bright and early to help her get ready for the afternoon ceremony. Cameron let the dogs out for the last time when the girls left.

"And then there were two," she said to Lucy, who was sleeping in the loft that night.

Lucy helped her clean up the kitchen and even made coffee for the morning. "One for the road?" Lucy asked, holding up a half bottle of chardonnay.

"Hit me up."

Lucy poured two glasses, which they took to the living room.

After she let the dogs in, Cameron stoked up the fire in the woodstove and joined Lucy on the sofa, curling her legs under her. "How about this, huh?"

"No kidding. What a fantastic evening. How lucky are we to be marrying into this family?"

"So lucky. I don't just get Will, but his parents and siblings and Elmer, too. I feel like I hit the jackpot."

"So do I."

"Are you guys talking about setting a date?" Cameron asked.

"Not really. We're in no particular rush. Hunter and Megan are next, so maybe in the spring." Lucy took a drink of wine and rested her head against the back of the sofa. "I can't believe how fast you guys pulled this wedding together. You've only been engaged for six weeks!"

"This is Will's favorite time of year, and it's becoming mine, too, after spending an autumn in Vermont. We didn't want to wait a full year, so we decided to go for it this year. Thank goodness for Regan. We couldn't have done it without her."

"She's amazing. I got her card for when it's my turn."

"I was worried about turning over such an important event to someone else to plan, but we told her what we wanted, and she made it happen. I can't wait to see it all put together tomorrow." Cameron yawned. "I can't believe I'm actually tired. I thought I'd be up all night."

"Let's get you to bed so you're ready for your big day."

They took their wineglasses into the kitchen and parted with a hug.

"Thanks for everything, Luce. It's been so great to have you here the last couple of weeks."

"I wouldn't have missed it for anything. I'm so happy for you and Will. You guys are an awesome couple."

"Stop before I start bawling again."

Lucy laughed and headed for the ladder to the loft.

"Let me know if you need anything."

"I'm good. Try to sleep."

"See you in the morning."

With the dogs sleeping in their usual spot by the fire, Cameron went into their room and went through her bedtime ritual before climbing into bed alone. She moved to Will's side of the bed where she found his woodsy, outdoorsy scent clinging to his pillow. How ridiculous was it that one night without him felt like an eternity?

She hadn't spent a night without him in more than six months, so naturally it felt weird to be alone at bedtime. Even though she'd see him in a few short hours, she'd give anything to feel his arms around her. Closing her eyes, she drifted off to sleep, thinking about everything tomorrow would bring and wishing he were here with her.

UP on the mountain, Will and Colton were the last ones standing after the others had passed out from the massive quantities of beer that had been consumed around the campfire, which was now down to embers.

"As your best man, it's my job to recommend you hit the hay," Colton said.

"Yeah, yeah. I'm wide awake, so there's no point."

"What're you thinking about?"

"Truth?"

"Of course."

"Remember the night of Nolan's bachelor party up here?"

"As it was only a couple of months ago, I do remember."

"Remember what we did that night?"

"Yes . . ."

"I'm thinking about a do-over."

"Isn't it bad luck to see the bride before the wedding? Since it's after midnight, technically it's your wedding day."

"I won't turn on any lights."

Colton scratched at the stubble on his jaw. "I'm not sure if I can condone this mission."

"I dare you to come with me, then."

"Oh, a dare . . . You fight dirty." Under Abbott family rules, failure to take a dare could result in years of abuse.

Will shrugged. "I fight to win. I need you to drive me. I've had a few too many, and I noticed you've been drinking only water."

"Someone's gotta make sure you're where you're supposed to be tomorrow."

"Thank you for that. And everything else, too."

"Thank you for asking me to be your best man. You shocked the shit out of me with that one. I thought for sure you'd ask Hunter."

"I don't like to be predictable. Plus, with you marrying Lucy and her being Cam's maid of honor, we thought it would be fun."

"So this means I've got to ask you to be mine, too, right?"

"Doesn't mean that at all."

"I would like you to be my best man. When the time comes. If you're willing."

"I'm more than willing, but don't ask me because I asked you. You should have who you want."

"If I have you, I have who I want."

"I'd be honored. Thank you."

"You're welcome."

"So, are you going to take the dare, or are you going to let us call you a pussy for the next century or two?"

"When you put it that way, I guess I have no choice but to take the dare." Colton dumped a bucket of dirt on the fire and stomped out the remaining embers.

They'd gotten away with this mission the last time they'd done it with no one the wiser when they'd left Nolan's bachelor party campout to go sleep with Cameron and Lucy at the cabin. Will knew he was pushing his luck to think they'd get away with it twice, but he was counting on his brothers being out cold for the night.

Colton went into his cabin to get his keys while Will waited for him on the porch. They were on their way to a clean getaway when Hunter appeared out of the darkness.

"Jesus," Colton said to their oldest brother. "You scared the shit out of me."

"Where you boys going?"

"Nowhere," Will said.

Hunter chuckled softly. "Liar. Are you going back to town?"

"Maybe . . ."

"Take me with you."

"Who'll stay with the little kids?" Will asked of their younger brothers, all of whom were full-grown men and well trained in search-and-rescue tactics. But old habits died hard when it came to leaving their younger siblings unsupervised.

"They're on their own," Hunter said bluntly.

"Let's go," Will said.

They piled into Colton's truck and headed down the mountain, turning on the headlights halfway down. "Another clean escape," Colton said, when he pulled onto the road that led into town.

"Another?" Hunter asked from the front seat.

"We might've done this once before," Will said. "The night of Nolan's party."

Laughing, Hunter said, "You got away with that one. I had no idea, but then again, I had no good reason to sneak back to town. And now I do."

"Now you do," Will said.

They dropped Hunter off first.

"Try not to scare the hell out of Megan," Colton said.

"I told her I'd be home if I could get away, so she won't be surprised to see me."

"That's premeditated," Will said. "A whole other level of p-whipped."

"Say what you will," Hunter said. "I'm happy to plead guilty. See you boys tomorrow."

"Don't be late," Will said.

"When am I ever late?" Hunter shut the door before they could pounce on that easy opening. He'd broken his on-time record repeatedly since he got together with Megan, even coming in late to work several times, which had never happened before.

They waited until he disappeared inside his dark house before they continued on through Butler to Will's house five miles outside of town. The cabin was completely dark when they pulled up outside.

"I don't want the dogs to bark, so let's sneak in through the mudroom."

They went around the back of the cabin where Will used his key in the door that he'd instructed Cameron to keep locked when she was home alone. Before she'd lived here with him, he'd never locked his doors. Now that he had someone so precious to protect, his doors were always locked.

Trevor raised his head off his dog bed, saw Will, and thankfully went right back to sleep.

"See you in the A.M.," Colton whispered as he went to the ladder to the loft where his fiancée was sleeping.

"Thanks for taking the dare," Will said.

"Like I had any choice."

Will was still smiling when he went into the bedroom and slipped into the adjoining bathroom where he stripped out of his clothes and brushed his teeth. Standing next to the bed, he could see Cameron sleeping on his side, hugging his pillow. Though he hated to disturb her sleep before their big day, he crawled in next to her and wrapped his arms around her.

She murmured in her sleep, which he took as an opportunity to kiss her. With only the faint light of the moon shining into the room, he saw her eyes fly open when she came to. "What're you doing here?" she asked breathlessly.

"I missed you."

"It's bad luck to see me before the wedding."

"I'm not looking."

"Yes, you are!"

"You want me to go?"

"Don't you dare."

Will laughed. "A dare is what brought me here."

"What do you mean?"

"I dared Colton to bring me home because I'd been drinking and he hadn't. Abbotts risk massive ridicule if they don't take a dare, so I pulled out the big guns to bend him to my will."

Laughter from the loft drifted into their room. "Doesn't sound like you had to twist his arm."

"Not really. Hunter came with us, too. We dropped him off at home."

"You guys are funny. You can't take one night away from your women."

"I can't speak for them, of course, but I'm madly in love with my woman, and one night away from her felt like forever."

Cameron snuggled up to him. "For me, too. It was so weird to go to bed without you."

"You've got way too many clothes on. What is all this?" He pulled and tugged at the T-shirt and moose pajama pants she'd worn to bed.

"Stop," she said, laughing. "It's cold and I didn't have you to keep me warm."

"Well, now you do, so let's lose all this foolishness."

"You're not supposed to be here," she reminded him as she raised her hands over her head to let him remove her shirt.

"Are you going to report me to the wedding police?"

"Not likely."

"In that case . . . Get naked, and hurry up about it."

"Is this the kind of husband you're going to be? If so, maybe I should reconsider—"

He kissed her hard and fast, thrusting his tongue into her mouth to tangle with hers. "No reconsidering allowed," he said when he came up for air.

"I was teasing."

"I wasn't." He slid his hand into the back of her pajama pants and pushed them down, taking her panties with them. "Are you really superstitious about me seeing you before the wedding?"

"I'm Irish! Of course I'm superstitious."

"Turn away from me then."

"Why? What're you going to do?"

"You'll have to wait and see." He stole one more kiss while he could and then waited for her to turn so her back was to him. Will tucked her in close to him, running his hand over her belly, which quivered under his touch.

She pressed her backside into his erection, making him groan.

"It appears you aren't *that* superstitious after all."

"I'm very superstitious," she said primly.

He moved his hand farther down, cupping her and dipping his fingers into her slick heat. "One part of you isn't. Want me to stop?"

"Absolutely not."

Laughing, Will slid two fingers into her. "I love how you're always ready for me."

"I can't get enough of you."

"I love that, too."

He alternated strokes of his fingers deep inside her with circling caresses of her clit.

"Will . . ."

"I'm here. I'm right here." Cupping her breast with his other hand, he pinched her nipple and felt her detonate. He loved the way she tightened around his fingers as she came. Removing his fingers, he raised her leg up and over his hip and slid into her from behind, going slowly at first, waiting until she was able to take him before he began to move faster. Then he pressed his fingers against her clit and kept them there as he pumped into her.

"I can't believe we get to do this any time we want for the rest of our lives," he whispered.

She took hold of his other hand and brought it to her breast. "Neither can I."

"Cam . . . I'm close . . . Need you."

With her hand over his on her breast, she encouraged him to play with her nipple. Once again, the combination set off her orgasm.

Will groaned and pressed hard into her one more time, thrusting as he came with her. Only afterward did he realize he was holding her tight enough to cause bruises. "God, you make me crazy. I didn't hurt you, did I?"

"Not at all."

He kissed her shoulder and the curve of her neck. "We can't have bruises on the bride."

"The bride has a man in her bed the night before her wedding. It's a scandal."

"It's because she's so hot he can't stand to spend even one night away from her."

"Do you think he'll always feel that way about her?"

"I know he will."

"Even after they have kids and their lives get crazy?"

"Especially then."

"She should marry a guy like that."

"She really ought to."

"I'm glad you came."

He thrust his hips to remind her he was still inside her. "I'm glad you came, too. Twice."

Laughing, she said, "That's not what I meant, as you well know.

"Get some sleep, sweetheart. Biggest day of our lives tomorrow."

"I was asleep until I was rudely and delightfully awakened by my future husband."

"I can't wait to be your husband." With Cameron tucked in tight against him, their legs intertwined and their bodies still intimately joined, Will was finally able to sleep.

Six

WILL WAS LONG gone when Cameron's alarm went off at eight o'clock the next morning. How had he managed to leave their bed without waking her when she'd slept wrapped up in his arms? She smiled thinking about their middle-of-the-night visit and everything that awaited them today.

Only a few hours now until they'd have the rest of their lives together, and she couldn't wait to get on with it. She bounded out of bed and into the shower where the scent of his bodywash was still in the air from his earlier shower. Cameron couldn't believe she'd slept through it all—or that the dogs had apparently slept through his departure, too.

With her hair wrapped in a towel and Will's robe tied twice around her waist, Cameron emerged from her bedroom to find Lucy in the kitchen, already chugging coffee. She handed a cup to Cameron, fixed just the way she liked it. The two women were silent until Cameron had consumed the first mug, just like old times when they'd worked together.

"Good morning," Lucy said.

"Morning. Sleep well?"

"Until I was rudely interrupted." This was said with a big

smile that told Cameron just how much Lucy had enjoyed her fiancé's rude interruption.

"They're too cute, huh?"

"Extremely cute, but I was told Colton only came because he was dared to."

"And I was told that Colton was a willing co-conspirator."

"Of course he was."

They shared a laugh that ended with a giddy shriek from Cameron. "I can't believe it's finally here."

"Because you've had to wait all of six weeks," Lucy said, rolling her eyes.

"I've been waiting forever for this."

"I know you have, and seeing you in the midst of Abbott mania . . . You're exactly where you belong."

"As are you."

"It's a nice place to spend a life."

"I couldn't agree more."

Molly arrived a short time later, bringing Hannah and freshly baked blueberry and chocolate chip muffins that Cameron and Lucy pounced on.

"Everyone sleep well?" Molly asked.

Cameron caught Lucy's eye when she said, "Like babies."

Lucy nearly snorted coffee out her nose. "What she said."

Molly raised a brow but didn't ask any questions. It was probably best that she didn't ask.

The hairstylists Regan had hired arrived a short time later, followed by Ella and Charley, who'd brought Emma and a very excited Simone. Cameron gave herself over to the hair and makeup people. She'd already told them what she wanted—and didn't want—so she relaxed and let them do their thing. Outside, the yard was full of workers making final preparations in the tent, and Regan was back and forth between the yard and the cabin, overseeing everything.

The cabin was almost too small for the wedding party, but they made it work, and by the time lunch was delivered at noon, they were almost ready to go. Only Emma and Simone were still in the chairs being fussed over as the others dug into the sandwiches and salads.

"I'm starving," Cameron said, choosing a turkey and

cheese wrap. "And everything looks good. I keep waiting to be nervous, but I haven't been at all."

"Nothing to be nervous about, because you know you got it right," Lucy said.

The stark simplicity of her best friend's statement brought Cameron to tears for the first time all day.

"Don't!" Regan's shriek made Cameron laugh. "Makeup! Lucy, if you're going to make her cry, *don't talk to her.*"

"Yes, ma'am," Lucy said with a smile for Cameron.

Things began to move fast after lunch. The others changed into several different styles of the gold bridesmaid gown. Cameron had told them to choose the style they liked best, and each of them looked gorgeous in the rich color.

"Ready for the bride," Regan said when the last of the girls had changed in the bedroom. "Cameron?"

"Here goes nothing." Cameron followed Regan into the bedroom and shut the door. For the first time, a flutter of nerves hit her belly as she thought about her dress. All her life, she'd seen pictures of her parents' wedding. They were among the pictures of her mother she treasured the most. So when it came time to choose her own dress, she'd gone right back to those photos.

With the help of her father's housekeeper, Lena, the dress had been located in the attic of the penthouse apartment where Cameron had grown up. Lena had shipped the dress to her in Vermont without anyone else knowing about it. She could only hope Lena had kept the secret.

After the dress had been located and shipped, Cameron had held her breath for a week waiting for it to arrive. She'd had it sent to the store, and the day it was finally delivered, she'd taken it straight home to try it on. It had fit her as if it had been made for her. Standing that day in the bedroom she shared with Will, Cameron had sobbed for her late mother, for the moment they should've been sharing with each other, for all the moments they had missed. Wearing her mother's dress, she'd never felt closer to the woman who'd been missing from her life since the day she was born.

The beaded antique-white sleeveless silk dress was simple yet elegant. It had a small train that was ideal for the vibe of their country wedding. Cameron knew she could've looked high and low for the perfect dress and not found one that suited her better than her mother's did.

All her life, her father had told her how much she resembled her mother. Standing before a full-length mirror, wearing her mother's dress, her hair swept up in a similar style to what her mother had worn the day she married Patrick, Cameron could see the resemblance. She'd wondered for weeks if her father would recognize the dress and had prepared herself for the possibility that he wouldn't. And that was all right.

"It's gorgeous," Regan said after she zipped Cameron in. She was the only person besides Lena who knew about the dress. Lucy had been badgering her for weeks for details, but Cameron had refused to share her secret with anyone. "Like it was made for you."

"It's funny . . . I feel like I've been sharing this big secret with my mom."

"I think it's wonderful that you're wearing her dress and that it fits you so perfectly. It's a great story."

"It's the first big secret I've ever shared with her."

"Don't cry."

Cameron smiled at her. "I'll try not to."

"Are you ready to let the others see you?"

"I think I might be. Will you ask Lucy to come in first?"

"Of course."

Regan left the room and Lucy came in a few minutes later, drawing in a sharp deep breath at the sight of Cameron in her dress.

"Oh wow, Cam. *Wow.*"

Cameron turned away from the mirror to face her best friend, who looked like she was about to lose her composure.

"What an amazing dress. It's so *you.*"

"It's my mother's."

Lucy's eyes widened with surprise and then filled with tears. "Cam . . ."

"Don't cry. Regan will kill us."

Lucy laughed and dabbed gently at her eyes with a tissue she produced from inside the bodice of her dress.

"You really like it?"

"It's . . . incredible. How did you get it without anyone knowing?"

"My dad's housekeeper helped me."

"Do you think he'll recognize it?"

"I don't know. You know how oblivious he can be."

"I don't think he'll be oblivious today. How could he be? You're so beautiful."

"Thank you for that and a million other things." Lucy took her outstretched hand. "Love you."

"Love you, too, and I'm so happy for you and Will."

"I'm happy for us, too," Cameron said with a smile. "Is it time yet?"

"A little eager much?"

"A lot eager. I can't wait!"

"Let me check with the boss. Is it okay to let the others in to see you?"

Cameron drew in a deep breath. "Sure." While she waited, she took one last minute alone with her mother, silently thanking her for the enormous sacrifice she'd made to bring her into this world, to give her daughter life at the expense of her own.

When she'd first learned the circumstances of her mother's death, she was nine, and a nanny blurted it out, not realizing that Cameron didn't know. The information had messed her up for a long time, but she'd made peace with it, even if she'd never truly "get over" it.

"I asked for a moment alone with the bride," Molly said when she came into the room, closing the door. "Oh, Cam, look at you!"

Pleased by Molly's reaction, Cameron held out her hand to the woman who'd welcomed her into the Abbott family with open, loving arms. "It's my mother's."

Molly took her hand and gave it a squeeze. "It's absolutely lovely, as are you. What a special way to pay tribute to your mother today. She'd be so proud of her amazing daughter."

"Do you think so? Really?"

"I know so. She was so excited when she was expecting you. She'd love to see you today, wearing her dress, looking so much like her. Does Patrick know?"

Cameron shook her head. "And I'm fully prepared for him not to notice."

"He's a guy," Molly said, laughing. "They don't pay attention to dresses the way we do."

Cameron knew Molly was helping prepare her for the possibility that her father wouldn't recognize the dress. "It's fine if he doesn't. It was more about wanting her to be present here today than anything."

"You've fully accomplished that, honey." Molly gave her a light hug. "We love you so much, and we're so thrilled to have you officially join our family."

"I can't tell you how much that means to me. I love you, too. All of you."

"Let me get the girls. Simone is about to spontaneously combust from the excitement."

Cameron laughed, filled with joy and anticipation and love for Will and his family. Despite the astounding stroke of bad luck that had marked her life at the beginning, today she felt like the luckiest girl in the world.

Ella, Charley, Hannah, Emma and Simone came into the room in one big burst of excitement and chatter.

"Beautiful," Hannah declared tearfully. "Stunningly, perfectly, incredibly beautiful."

"What she said," Charley added. "The dress is perfect."

"It was my mom's."

"That's so cool," Ella said. "It could've been made just for you."

Emma wiped away tears. "You're killing us, Cam, and the wedding hasn't even started yet."

Cameron laughed and reached for Simone, who was dancing around waiting for a moment with the bride. Cameron wrapped her arms around the eight-year-old girl who so closely resembled her aunt Lucy, they might've been mother and daughter. "Thank you all so much for being here today and wearing the dress I chose and being my friends and favorite sisters-in-law. Love you all."

"We love you, too," Ella said for all of them.

Regan poked her head into the crowded bedroom. "Cameron, your dad is here."

Cameron suddenly felt light-headed and anxious about her big surprise. While she was excited for him to see her in the dress, she had no idea what to expect.

"We'll give you a few minutes alone with him," Hannah said, ushering the others from the room.

Cameron took a series of deep breaths, trying to find some inner calm while she waited for her dad. Will had decided that the men in the wedding party would wear white shirts with khaki pants and brocade vests that matched the gold bridesmaid dresses. They'd gone round and round about ties or no ties, and in the end, Will had gone with no ties because he just wasn't a tie kind of guy.

Seeing the ensemble for the first time on her dad, Cameron had to agree that the no-tie look worked perfectly for the casual vibe they'd wanted for the wedding.

Patrick came through the bedroom door and stopped short at the sight of her. He'd been about to say something that died on his lips. "You . . . That . . . Your mother's dress," he said on a long exhale.

Until he said those words, Cameron would never have admitted how badly she wanted him to recognize the dress. "Yes."

"Ali . . . God, Cam, you look so much like her." He rested a hand over his heart, scaring her for a second until he recovered his composure.

"I wondered if you'd recognize the dress."

"Recognize it? I see her in it every day when I look at our wedding picture in my office. Yes," he said gruffly. "I recognize it. How did you get it?"

"With a little help from Lena. I hope it's okay."

"Cameron," he said with a sigh as he wiped tears from his face, "of course it's okay. It's an amazing gesture."

"I wanted her to be here today in some way, and it was the only way I could think of."

"It fits you like a dream, and you look as beautiful as she did wearing it." He withdrew a velvet box from his pocket and held it out to her. "I gave this to her on our wedding day, and I've been saving it for you."

Cameron's hands trembled as she took the box from him and opened it to reveal a diamond solitaire necklace. "It's beautiful, Dad."

"I used all the money I had in the world at that time to buy it for her, and after the wedding she said we should sell it because we needed the money more than she needed a diamond neck-lace." As he spoke, he helped Cameron put it on, securing the clasp and then resting his hands on her shoulders to look at her in the mirror. "I told her I planned to make plenty of money, and there was no way she was selling her wedding gift."

"She loved you so much. I've always known that because of the way she looked at you in the wedding pictures."

"I loved her, too. I always will."

"I'm sorry about the way you lost her."

"I'm not, and she wouldn't be either. We wanted you very much, and she'd never want you to feel guilty about something that wasn't your fault. It was a terrible tragedy, but this isn't the day for feeling bad or guilty. This is your big day, and you've honored your mother every day of your life, but never more so than today."

She hugged him. "Love you so much."

He kissed her forehead. "Love you more."

"No way."

"Yes way." He looked down at her, his blue-eyed gaze softer than she'd ever seen it. "Ready for this?"

"I'm so ready."

He held out his arm to her. "Let's go."

SEVEN

NEVER HAD A day gone by slower than this one had. Every minute had felt like an hour as Will waited for the appointed time to go home and get married. He and his groomsmen had taken over his parents' house to get ready, and Will had spent much of the day pacing from one end of the barn to the other.

He wasn't nervous at all. He was *ready*, and having to wait all day had been the purest form of torture, especially because he hadn't yet spoken to Cam. A day without Cameron was its own brand of torture, and reminded him of the time they'd spent apart after they first met. He'd hated being apart from her and had counted down the minutes until they could be together again.

He was doing the same thing today, constantly checking his watch, which moved far too slowly for his liking. Fortunately, his brothers had left him alone for the most part. A few digs here and there about the pacing and the watch-checking, but they'd gone easy on him, which he appreciated.

At the appointed time, Hunter had driven him and Colton to the cabin, the three of them unusually silent during the ride. Passing the place where he'd first met Cameron, Will smiled at the memories of that fateful night and all the days that had followed. *Thanks, Fred.*

When Hunter took the right turn onto the dirt road that led to the cabin, Will's heart began to beat faster. Never had coming home meant more than it did right now, knowing Cameron was there, waiting for him, prepared to take vows that would give them forever together.

"You okay back there?" Colton asked, breaking the long silence.

"Yep."

"Need anything?"

"Nope." That wasn't entirely true. He needed her like he'd never needed anything or anyone else. *Soon enough . . .* She'd be his wife and they'd have the rest of their lives to love each other.

The yard had been transformed in his absence. An arbor of flowers was positioned in front of rows of chairs separated by an aisle down the middle. The entrance to the tent had been artfully decorated with hay bales, corn stalks, pumpkins and chrysanthemums of every color.

They'd gotten a gorgeous sunny late autumn day that only added to the perfection of the scene before him. It was everything they'd hoped it would be, and it was right here in the place they called home. He loved that she'd wanted to do it here when she had the resources to do it anywhere in the world. He loved that she wanted what he did—their simple life in Vermont, surrounded by his big family, working for the family business.

Someday he might understand how he'd managed to find the perfect woman for him, but so far that understanding eluded him. Whatever higher power had put her in his path that night last spring deserved his undying gratitude.

His brothers and Troy poured out of trucks behind him, each of them in high spirits while Will stood off to the side, his gaze fixed on the cabin, hoping for a glimpse of his bride. As the guests arrived and took their seats, Regan handed out boutonnieres and instructed him and the other groomsmen to wait in an area away from where the ceremony would take place. Positioning the flowers on their lapels and trying not to stick pins in one another gave the guys something to do for the final few minutes.

Regan came out of the cabin, carrying a clipboard and a

handheld radio that she spoke into as she approached Will. "Ready to roll?"

"Very ready."

"Gentlemen," Regan said with authority that made his boisterous brothers go silent. "Take your places, please." She walked away talking into the radio, directing everyone to where they needed to be.

"Showtime," Colton said, clasping Will's shoulder and guiding him toward the arbor.

He felt everyone's eyes on him as he and his brother walked down the aisle, where they were greeted with hugs from their father and grandfather.

"Love you both," Elmer whispered in Will's ear.

"Love you, too, Gramps. Thanks for doing this for us."

"It is indeed an honor to have been asked."

While a guitarist Regan had hired provided music, Lucas and Landon escorted their mother down the aisle. As she had the night before, Molly came forward to hug and kiss Will and Colton before taking her place in the front row next to Lincoln.

Next came Troy and Emma, followed by Hunter and Hannah, Ella and Max, and Wade and Charley. After a long pause, Lucy and Simone appeared on the front porch, hand in hand as they proceeded toward the aisle.

Colton gasped at the sight of his fiancée, who was stunning in the gold dress that perfectly complemented her auburn hair. "Wow," he whispered, making Will chuckle.

Lucy released Simone's hand so she could drop rose petals on the runner that made up the aisle. When the little girl reached the front, she bolted for her Grandpa Ray, who held out his arms to her.

Colton stepped forward to steal a kiss from Lucy that made everyone laugh, especially when she gave him a gentle push to remind him of where he was supposed to be standing.

Still laughing at Colton's antics, Will glanced at the house, and the laughter died in one long exhale as he took in the sight of Cameron on her father's arm, waiting for Regan to give them the sign that it was time to go.

"Please rise," Elmer said to the guests, who stood and turned to watch Cameron and Patrick.

Will had never seen anything more spectacular than the sight of his bride coming toward him, her dazzling smile making her eyes light up with the kind of pure joy he knew he'd remember for the rest of his life. She fairly sparkled in the bright sunshine as she met his gaze and held it, taking his breath away with every step she took closer to him.

He only blinked when tears nearly blinded him. Not wanting to miss a second of this, he kept his eyes fixed on her until she and Patrick were standing before him, and Patrick was hugging him and then Cameron as he joined her hand with his.

"Stunning," he whispered to Cameron.

"Same to you, love."

As Elmer welcomed their guests, Will decided that this, right here, was the best moment of his entire life. Nothing could top this. Well, until Cameron was passing her bouquet of fall colors to Lucy and joining her hands with his to officially become his wife. That was better.

After they had recited traditional vows, Elmer said, "Will and Cameron have a few words they'd like to say to each other before they exchange rings. Will?"

He'd prepared for this, thought about it for weeks, planned what he wanted to say to her, but now, looking down at her looking up at him expectantly, his mind went blank. Before panic could set in, though, she squeezed his hands and smiled at him, calming him enough so he could remember what he'd planned to say.

"From the first time I laid eyes on you, bruised and battered and furious at the moose who'd nearly totaled your car, I knew you were special. I didn't know then how special you'd become to me, but I knew almost right away that if I let you get away, I'd regret it for the rest of my life. And now I get the rest of my life with you, and nothing could be better than that. I can't wait to spend every day with you, to have a family with you, to work with you and grow old with you. I look forward to every single minute with you. I love you more than anything in this world, and I always will."

Cameron leaned in to kiss him.

Elmer cleared his throat. "Not yet." When the laughter had died down, he gestured for Cameron to take her turn.

"I didn't want to come here, but my dad asked me to do it as a favor to him. And because he knows I can't say no to him, here

I am marrying the man who saved me from the wild moose, the mud and a lifetime of wishing for all the things I now have, thanks to you and your wonderful family. I've never felt more at home anywhere than I do with you and our dogs and the Abbotts all around us to keep life interesting. I had no idea how lonely I was until I found you. I love you, I love your family, I love Vermont, I love our cabin in the woods and our dogs. I love sharing an office with you and working with you and everything else we get to do together. And before Lucas or Landon can make a joke about that, I mean it in the cleanest way possible."

"Damn," Will said, sparking a new outburst of laughter.

"She beat us to it," Landon said.

"Colton, may I have the rings please?" Elmer said.

Colton gave a deer-in-the-headlights look that had Will's heart falling.

"Kidding." He handed them over to their grandfather.

"Payback is a bitch," Will whispered to his brother.

Elmer handed Cameron's ring to Will.

He slid it onto her finger. "Cameron, with this ring, I thee wed."

She did the same with his ring, adding a kiss to the back of his hand when the platinum band was in place.

"By the power vested in me by the state of Vermont, I now pronounce you husband and wife. William, you may kiss your bride."

Will put his arms around her and took a moment to look down at her gorgeous face before he drew her into a kiss. They'd agreed to keep it short and sweet, but now that it was upon them, he couldn't help but linger.

"That wasn't short," Cameron said when he finally came up for air.

"But it was sweet."

She smiled brightly at him.

He put his arms around her and held her close, wanting one minute with her before he had to share her with their guests. Close to her ear, he said, "You look so beautiful you took my breath away."

"My mother's dress."

"Oh, baby, really?"

She nodded.

"It's gorgeous."

"Ladies and gentlemen," Elmer said, "it gives me great pleasure to introduce, for the first time, Will and Cameron Abbott."

As their guests applauded, Cameron took Will's arm and walked with him down the aisle, where they were greeted by Tanner and Trevor, decked out in bow-tie collars for the occasion and supervised by Regan during the ceremony.

"Where did you boys come from?" Cameron asked as she kissed each dog on the top of his soft head.

"Dad brought them over to surprise you after the ceremony."

"I love it. I wanted them here all along."

"How about giving me some of the love you're giving them, Mrs. Abbott?"

She stood up straight and wrapped her arms around his neck to give him a deep, passionate kiss that set his blood on fire.

"I love you so much," he whispered against her lips. "You've made me so happy today—and every day since we met."

"Same to you. I love you, too. More than you'll ever know."

As their wedding party came down the aisle in pairs, Will picked her up and swung her around while their dogs ran in circles around their feet.

THEY took a thousand pictures, or so it seemed to Cameron as she tried to remain patient until the photographer had all the shots and groupings they'd asked him to get. Her favorite was of the Abbott family in all their wedding finery—first just the original twelve with Will at the center between his parents, and then Elmer, Cameron, Nolan, Megan and Lucy joined them for another photo.

The bridesmaids surrounded Will in another picture and then Cameron found herself lying across the outspread arms of the guys. As always, there was much laughter and joking and typical Abbott humor to go around.

"Landon, get your hands off my wife's rear end before I break both your arms," Will said as he watched his brothers manhandle his new wife.

"Where else am I supposed to put my hands?" Landon asked.

"Anywhere but there," Will replied in a low growl.

"Anywhere?"

"Landon!"

Cameron knew her husband wouldn't appreciate her laughter, but how was she supposed to resist when his younger brothers were so damned funny?

"Dad, tell Landon to get his hands off Cameron's rear."

"Do I have to say that?" Lincoln asked, sparking more laughter from the youngest Abbott brothers.

"Yes! They're out of control, and that's all your fault."

"They came out that way. We did what we could with them."

"Cameron's laughing!" Max said.

She slapped Lucas's hand, which was getting perilously close to her right breast. "I am not!"

"That's it," Will said, coming to claim his wife from his brothers' arms.

"Just for the record, I want the butt next time we do that," Colton said.

"Since the next time is my wedding," Hunter said, "no butt for you."

"You guys are no fun at all," Landon said.

"Are we fun?" Will asked Cameron.

"Lots and lots of fun, but of course I only speak for you. I wouldn't know if Hunter is fun."

"Lots of fun," Megan said to much laughter and a wide grin from her fiancé.

"I think I've got everything I need," the photographer said.

"Let's party!" Cameron said.

Will scooped her up into his arms and carried her to the cabin. "We'll be right back."

"No mid-wedding quickies!" Colton called after them.

"I'll remember you said that on your wedding day," Will said over his shoulder.

"Where're we going?" Cameron asked him, her arms wrapped around his neck and her head on his shoulder.

"I want one minute alone with my wife."

"Your wife is happy to comply."

"What do you think of married life so far?"

"I'm finding it agrees with me quite well, but then again I knew it would."

Will pushed open the cabin door, kicked it shut behind him

and then kissed her passionately. He devoured her lips and thrust his tongue into her mouth, groaning when she rubbed hers against it. "How many hours until we can escape?"

"Five."

"I'll never make it."

"Yes, you will. This is the only wedding we'll ever have. I want to enjoy every second of it."

"We'll enjoy it." He kissed her again. "Just give me five more minutes of this."

"I can do that."

She gave him ten minutes, until a tentative knock on the door had them pulling apart.

"Um, guys," Regan said from outside the door. "You've got a tent full of people waiting for you."

"We're coming," Cameron said.

"No, we aren't," Will whispered, "but we will be later."

Cameron laughed at his shameless comment as he finally put her down. She reached for the door, but he stopped her.

"I need one minute."

She glanced down at the obvious bulge in his pants and covered her mouth to contain her laughter.

"Keep laughing, and I'll go out there just like this. Won't that make a great photo for the wedding album?"

Despite his threats, she couldn't stop laughing.

When he was ready, he reached around her, opened the door and gave her a light swat on the butt, sending her through the door ahead of him. Outside the tent, their wedding party awaited them.

Regan lined them all up and gave orders to the DJ through her handheld radio.

"Ladies and gentlemen, it's my pleasure to introduce our wedding party," the DJ said. "First up, the father of the bride, Patrick Murphy, accompanied by the parents of the groom, Lincoln and Molly Abbott." Molly walked into the tent escorted by both fathers. "Next we have friends of the bride, Emma Mulvaney and Troy Kennedy. And now, we've got a whole bunch of the grooms' siblings, starting with Lucas and Landon Abbott." The identical twins walked into the tent holding hands and acting like the buffoons they were to hysterical laughter from the guests. "Let's see if Hannah Roberts and Hunter Abbott can top that . . ." Unlike their younger siblings, the older set of Abbott twins showed more decorum as they walked into the tent. "Next we have Ella and Max Abbott followed by Charley and Wade Abbott. Let's put our hands together for our flower girl, Simone Mulvaney!"

Simone went skipping into the tent to thunderous applause.

"She's eating it up," Lucy said.

"She's adorable," Colton said.

"She'll be playing wedding every day from now on after this," Cameron said.

"Ladies and gentlemen, please offer a round of applause for our maid of honor and best man, soon-to-be husband and wife themselves, Lucy Mulvaney, best friend of the bride, and Colton Abbott, brother of the groom!"

"Here we go," Lucy said, holding hands with Colton as they went into the tent.

EIGHT

TAKING FULL ADVANTAGE of a moment alone, Will put his arms around Cameron and leaned in for a kiss.

Cameron looked up at him. "I never told you how incredibly handsome you look today, or that you were absolutely right about the ties."

"Absolutely right, huh?"

"Don't get used to that. I don't expect it to be a regular thing."

He was still laughing when the DJ asked everyone to get on their feet to welcome their bride and groom, "Mr. and Mrs. Will Abbott!"

Mrs. Will Abbott . . . Walking into the tent on the arm of her husband, Cameron marveled at the magical atmosphere Regan had created. She'd seen sketches and heard the ideas, but seeing it all come together was nothing short of spectacular. Will's whispered "Wow" confirmed he was impressed, too.

Everything had been done in shades of gold with fall accents. Tea lights had been strung throughout the tent, which, coupled with the candles and flowers on the tables, contributed to the cozy, intimate feel. Cameron loved it.

They went directly to the dance floor, where their wedding

party waited to welcome them for their first dance as husband and wife. After much deliberation, they'd gone with "All of Me" by John Legend, even though Will had joked that every bride and groom in America was currently choosing that song. Cameron had said she didn't care what anyone else was choosing, because the song was perfect for them.

"You were absolutely right about the song," he whispered in her ear as they danced. "And PS, I love all your perfect imperfections."

"Imperfections? What imperfections?"

She loved that potent smile of his, and even more, she loved that she'd get to see it every day for the rest of their lives.

The DJ invited Colton and Lucy to join them on the dance floor, and the four of them finished out the song together. When the song ended and the applause died down, the DJ asked the rest of the wedding party to join the bride and groom on the dance floor for "All You Need Is Love."

"My dad will love you forever for choosing this song," Will said as he spun Cameron around.

"That's why I chose it."

Naturally, Lucas and Landon hammed it up and had everyone laughing hysterically. Then Landon snagged Regan's hand and dragged her onto the dance floor, leaving his twin to pout comically on the sidelines while Regan tried to keep up with Landon.

Having been howled over by an Abbott brother herself, Cameron could empathize with the wedding planner, who didn't seem to know what had hit her as Landon swung her around.

"Should we rescue her?" Will asked.

"I bet she's perfectly capable of rescuing herself if need be."

Regan was saved when the DJ asked Patrick Murphy to join his daughter on the dance floor.

Cameron had left the song choice up to her father and had no idea what he'd chosen.

Patrick approached her, bowed gallantly and extended his hand to her.

Smiling, Cameron stepped into his outstretched arms and held on to him as the first notes of Stevie Wonder's "You Are the Sunshine of My Life" played.

"How'd I do?" Patrick asked.

"I love it. It's perfect."

"It's true, you know. I may have done a shitty job of showing it at times, but you were always the sunshine in my life, Cam. I hope you know that."

"I do," she said, trying frantically not to cry.

Molly had chosen "You'll Be in My Heart" by Phil Collins for her dance with Will, and watching the two of them laughing and talking as they danced, Cameron was filled with love for both of them.

The DJ asked members of the wedding party to take their places at the head table and called Colton to the microphone, making most of the Abbotts groan.

"Don't give him a microphone," Max said.

"No kidding," Lucas replied.

"I'd rather he have it than any of the three of you," Will said to his youngest brothers.

"Good point," Landon said.

"If the peanut gallery is finished . . ." Colton pointed to his younger brothers. "On behalf of Will and Cameron, I'd like to welcome everyone to this very special occasion. Most of all, I'd like to welcome Cameron to the Abbott family, although she's been one of us pretty much since the day we met her, black eyes and all. For the rest of her life here in Butler, Cam will be known as . . . 'the girl who hit Fred.'" The entire Abbott family and everyone from town helped Colton finish that sentence, much to Cameron's pretend dismay.

"Cameron, you already know this, but you got yourself one of the good guys. It goes against everything we believe as Abbotts to say nice things about each other in public, but I'm going to risk the ridicule of my other brothers by saying a few nice things about my brother Will."

Lucas, Landon, Wade, Max and Hunter booed him and gave him the thumbs-down while Will laughed at all of them and Molly shook her head with exasperation.

"This is what happens when you raise your kids in a barn, Mom," Colton said to more laughter. "Anyway . . . Cam, there are a few things you ought to know about Will. You already know he's faithful and always willing to lend a hand to anyone who needs it, especially city girls who smack into moose during mud season. I suppose he's not hideous to look at, although opinions vary on that."

"I'm going to kill him," Lucy muttered, making Will and Cameron laugh.

"Now for the stuff you don't know . . . Will once won a hot-dog eating contest by downing thirty-four hot dogs in five minutes. Did you know that?"

"Um, *no*," Cameron said, looking at her husband in amazement and disgust.

"It was a dare," Will said, as if that explained everything.

"Gross," Cameron said.

"I thought so, too," Molly said.

"Incidentally, I came in second place with thirty-three," Colton said.

"Why am I not surprised?" Lucy said. Her fiancé's appetite was a thing of legend in the Abbott family.

"Did you know, Cameron," Colton continued, "that Will once climbed a two-hundred foot evergreen tree, again on a dare, and nearly broke his neck when the top buckled under his weight?"

"I hadn't heard that one, either."

"Wrap it up, Colton, before she changes her mind about me," Will said.

"There's so much more I could say."

"But you won't," Will said, "because you know I have more on you than you've got on me, and your wedding is coming up soon."

"This is true," Colton replied gravely, "so I'll let you find out the rest on your own, Cam. I'll close by saying you've married one of the finest guys I've ever known, and risking a lifetime of ridicule from the peanut gallery, I'll add that I love you both and wish you all the best. To Will and Cameron." After everyone had toasted, Colton called his fiancée to the microphone. "Luce? Your turn."

Lucy took the microphone from him. "Go sit down and try to behave."

"Well, that's no fun."

"I'm sorry about him," she said to laughter. "I'm doing what I can to fix him."

"Good luck with that," Lucas said, earning him a slap upside the head from Colton as he passed behind him.

"Will and Cameron, thank you so much for making us all a part of your special day. Colton talked about his brother, and it's my job to tell you about the bride, my best friend, a sister of my heart, and soon to be my sister-in-law. Funny how that worked out, right?"

"I love it!" Cameron said.

"Me, too," Colton added to more laughter.

"When Cameron first told me about this guy she'd met in Vermont, I was skeptical. Cameron's a city girl through and through, or so I thought, until I saw her here in Butler with Will, immersed in the Abbotts and captivated by the family business. That's when I realized she wasn't a city girl after all. She's a Butler girl, and now she's an Abbott. For as long as I've known Cam, she's longed for the kind of family she's now a part of, and I want to thank you all for giving her that. To you guys it's just another day in Abbott land, but for someone who never had siblings or a mother, you can't possibly know what it means to her to be a part of this incredible family. So on behalf of all the people who love her, I ask you to take good care of her. She means the world to us."

Cameron leaned into Will's one-arm embrace as she wiped away tears.

"Will, I might've been skeptical at first, but five minutes after I met you, I knew you were it for my girl. I've not had one minute of doubt on her behalf since then. I hope you will always be as happy as you are today. I love you both. To Will and Cameron."

As everyone raised their glasses once again, a disturbance at the entrance to the tent had a few people screaming and everyone else on their feet to see what was going on.

"Oh. My. God." Cameron couldn't believe it when Fred the Moose strolled into the tent like he'd been invited to the wedding.

"No way," Will said, equally stunned.

And then Hannah was on her feet and moving swiftly toward the moose, who stopped in his tracks at Hannah's command.

"Hannah!" Nolan shouted. "Don't move!" He vaulted over the table where he'd been sitting with Molly, Lincoln, Elmer, Megan and Patrick, and put himself between his petite wife and the massive moose. "What've I told you about taking on that moose?"

As if her husband hadn't spoken, Hannah stepped around him. "Fred, this is a private party, and you weren't invited. Now turn around and go on home." The wedding guests were barely breathing as they waited to see what the gigantic moose would do.

"*Moo.*"

"Fred . . ."

"*Moo.*"

Cameron had a sinking feeling that her resident moose stalker was looking for her. "Let me talk to him."

"No, Cameron," Will said. "Stay right here."

"If he's looking for me, maybe he'll go home if I say hello."

"I don't want you anywhere near him."

"He's not going to hurt me."

"You don't know that for sure."

"Yes, I do." Cameron figured he'd already had ample opportunity to hurt her, and he never had before. "Let me go."

"I'm going with you."

Hand in hand, they walked around the head table and across the dance floor to where Hannah and Nolan had stopped Fred from progressing any farther into the tent.

"Hi, Fred," Cameron said, feeling like an idiot to be actually talking to a moose.

"*Moo.*"

The loud noise from the moose had Cameron swallowing hard and forcing herself to continue. "Thanks for stopping by to wish us well, and thanks again for that night in the mud. I'm sorry if my car hurt you, but you did me a super-big favor, even if you don't realize it."

"You did me a favor, too," Will said. "We owe you big-time."

Cameron summoned the courage to reach out and stroke the moose's snout, causing him to let out a gentle *moo* that sounded more like a coo of pleasure.

"Well, I'll be damned," Lincoln said. "I was right. He does have a crush on her!"

"Sorry to say she's taken, old man," Will said.

Before their eyes, Fred sighed, deeply, and turned around, making an older woman shriek as he came a little too close to where she was sitting. He left the way he'd come. No one in the tent moved or spoke until Fred disappeared into the woods.

Nolan broke the silence. "You and I are going to have a conversation about this moose-whisperer business when we get home. Do you hear me?"

Hannah smiled sweetly at him. "Yes, dear."

"She's humoring me, isn't she?"

Cameron laughed as relief coursed through her. Fred had come, he'd seen her and he'd left without incident. "I believe you're correct about that, Nolan."

"I couldn't believe when you touched him," Will said. "I swear my heart stopped for a minute."

"Don't let that happen. I need that heart beating for the next sixty or seventy years."

"Then stay away from that moose."

"*He's* stalking *me*!"

"It's because you flirt shamelessly with him. I feel for him. You're pretty hard to resist when you let loose with those eyes of yours."

Before Cameron could work up an indignant reply to that, the DJ interrupted them when he started the music up again, urging everyone to get up and dance until dinner was served.

The dance floor quickly filled with couples—Lincoln and Molly, Nolan and Hannah, Hunter and Megan, Cameron and Lucy, Max and Chloe, and Patrick, who had asked Mary to dance.

"What's the matter?" Will asked, following her gaze to where Patrick and Mary were having an animated conversation as they danced.

"I don't like that."

"What? Your dad dancing with Mary?"

"Yeah."

"Why not?"

"I don't want him to break her heart."

"They're just dancing, Cam."

"He met her the other day at the office and said she's adorable. I told him then to leave her alone. She's a nice person, and he's a love-'em-and-leave-'em charmer."

"It's a dance, hon. I think she's safe."

"For now," Cameron said. "But I'll be watching him to make sure that's all it is."

"Isn't he leaving tomorrow?"

"That's the plan."

"I don't think you need to worry."

Cameron didn't pursue it any further with Will, but she

vowed to keep a close eye on her father for the rest of the evening to make sure he didn't step out of line with Mary.

Toward the back of the tent, she watched Gavin Guthrie approach Ella Abbott. He gestured to the dance floor. She crossed her arms and shook her head. He said something else to her, causing her to shake her head again. Gavin walked away from her, his shoulders slumped.

Ella watched him go, looking heartbroken and despondent.

Well, Cameron thought, wasn't that interesting? She'd have to get to the bottom of that situation after they returned from their honeymoon.

"Where'd you go?" Will asked against her ear, sending a cascade of goose bumps down her back.

She looked up at him. "I'm right here with you, my love."

"Then you're right where you belong."

NINE

THEY ATE, THEY drank, they danced, they laughed, they cried, they posed for a million pictures, they tossed her bouquet, which Mary caught, and they loved every minute of their wedding. The DJ ended the dancing at midnight with "In My Life" by the Beatles, a dedication from the father of the groom to the happy couple.

After one last dance, they tearfully said their good-byes to friends and family—as well as Trevor and Tanner, who were going to spend the next two weeks with Lincoln and Molly—and headed for the cabin to pick up their bags. They had hired a car service to drive them to Burlington to spend their wedding night at the family's lake house. They would fly to Fiji on Patrick's plane the next morning.

The second the door closed behind them, Will had her in his arms for a passionate kiss that had her clinging to him, responding to every stroke of his tongue with one of her own.

"God, I needed that," he whispered many minutes later.

"So did I." She drew him down for another kiss, this one sweeter and softer than the first one. "Should we get changed before we go?"

"Definitely not." He ran his hands down her back to cup her

bottom. "I want to take my time getting you out of this amazing dress."

"Well, alrighty then."

They collected the bags they'd packed for their trip, shut off the lights in the cabin and headed for the door. "I've never been away from Vermont for longer than a week," Will said.

"I promise to make it well worth the sacrifice."

"I have no doubt it'll be worth it," he said with a sexy grin.

"Are we really married, or did I dream this incredible day?"

"We're really married, and it's a dream come true."

He kissed her again, lingering in the silent darkness of their cabin until the sound of a car horn outside reminded them of their plans. "Ready to go, Mrs. Abbott?"

"So ready, Mr. Abbott."

He opened the door for her. "After you."

Cameron went outside and stopped short at the sight of a vintage Rolls-Royce with a festive *Just Married* banner sitting in the driveway. They had most definitely not hired a Rolls-Royce.

She glanced at her father, who wore a sheepish grin and shrugged. Beside him, Mary beamed with happiness—whether it was for the bride and groom or because of the attention Patrick had paid her all evening, Cameron couldn't say, and that had her worried.

"My only child." Patrick gestured toward the shiny black car. "What can I say?"

Most of the guests had left, leaving only their family members to see them off. Cameron hugged her dad. "It's beautiful. Thank you for this and everything else."

"You're welcome. Have a great time in Fiji."

"We will." She drew him down so she could whisper in his ear. "Go home to Lincoln and Molly's, and leave Mary alone. I mean it."

He laughed. "Stop meddling and go on your honeymoon."

"Dad . . ."

He kissed her forehead. "Go. I love you. I'll see you when you get back."

After she'd hugged his parents and grandfather, Will held out his hand to her, and though she had more she wanted to say to her dad about whatever he had planned for Mary, she took Will's hand and let him help her into the Rolls. The driver pointed out the chillcd bottle of champagne that awaited them before he raised a privacy window.

"Somehow I doubt this car originally came with that feature," Will said of the tinted window that sealed them off from the driver in front.

"Regardless, I'm glad to have it."

He waggled his brows suggestively. "Me, too."

The family showered them with more rose petals as they drove off.

Will put his arms around her, and Cameron snuggled into his embrace.

"Was it everything you'd hoped it would be?"

"That and so much more than I ever imagined. Regan did a wonderful job."

"She really did, but the star of the show was my lovely bride, who absolutely blew me away with how incredibly beautiful she was today."

"Aww, shucks, this old thing?"

"I love the dress, but that was only part of it. The rest of it was you and the way you positively glowed all day."

"That's because I'm so happy. I've never been so happy. I didn't even know it was possible to *be* this happy."

"I know, honey. I feel the same way. Lucky beyond measure."

"How about Fred showing up to seal the deal?"

Will grunted out a laugh. "He does like to be right in the middle of things, doesn't he?"

"As much as he scared everyone and freaked me out, I'm kind of glad he stopped by. It's sort of fitting in a way."

"He's been there for all our most important moments."

"Just for the record, there's no way he's going to be in the delivery room when we have our babies."

Laughing, Will said, "I'll make sure he's nowhere to be found."

"I do have my limits where he's concerned."

"Speaking of limits, I thought Nolan's head was going to explode when Hannah confronted Fred—again."

"I know! I bet there's some fighting going on in their house tonight."

"I can't say I blame him for getting worked up about it. The sight of tiny, pregnant Hannah staring down that gigantic moose gave me a heart attack. I can't imagine how he must feel."

"I saw Gavin ask Ella to dance, and she turned him down. Wonder what's up with them."

"No idea."

"I never heard what happened when she ran out of the meeting after she heard he'd been arrested. Did you?"

"Not a word."

"Hmm. They both looked upset tonight, so something must've happened."

"I know it's going to be really hard for you to have two full weeks without any family business to meddle in, but I don't want to talk about Fred or Hannah or Ella or anyone other than you and me."

"Is that so?" she asked, smiling up at him. "And what do you want to talk about?"

"This." He kissed her. "And this." More kisses. "And some of this." He kissed from her ear to her throat, setting her on fire with his lips and tongue before he returned to her lips.

She ended up on his lap, her arms around him as their kisses became more urgent. "We can't do this here."

"What? Make out?"

"Don't act so innocent. I know where making out leads with you."

He ran his hand from her calf under her dress to her thigh. "Where does it lead?"

"Will . . ."

"Hmm?" He was busy making her tremble with kisses to her neck as his hand crept farther up her leg.

"It's only two hours to Burlington. You have to wait."

"I don't think I can." He cupped her, letting his fingers delve between her legs, using the silk of her panties to stimulate her.

"Will!"

"Shhh. Let me have my fun with my wife."

"You'll have two weeks of 'fun.' "

He pressed and teased and caressed and kissed her senseless, making her forget all about where they were as he coaxed her to an orgasm that had her clinging to him in the aftermath.

"God, you're so hot. I can't wait to make love to my wife."

She squirmed on his lap, making him gasp from the pressure of her bottom against the hard column of his erection.

He sighed, deeply. "Whose big idea was it to go to Burlington tonight?"

"I believe it was your suggestion."

"I'm an idiot."

"No, you're not. If you were, I wouldn't have married you."

"I'm going to expire before we get to Burlington."

"We can't let that happen." She tapped on his arm and got him to release her so she could move into the seat next to him.

"Where're you going? Come back."

"I'm right here." She tugged on his belt, unbuckling it.

"Um, what're you doing?"

"This." She unbuttoned and unzipped him, freeing his erection from his pants and bending over him before he had a chance to say a word. The next thing out of his mouth was a long groan that made her smile as she sucked and stroked and licked him to an explosive release.

"Holy Christ," he whispered.

She put him away as efficiently as she'd taken him out and then patted his chest. "What do you think of married life so far?"

"I think it most definitely agrees with me."

Cameron laughed and snuggled up to him again, thrilled by everything about him and the life they had to look forward to together.

WHEN they arrived at the house in Burlington, Will kissed Cameron until she woke up. Holding her in his arms as she slept had given him time to reflect on their wedding day as they traveled across Vermont in the darkness. For the rest of his life, he'd never forget the way she'd looked coming toward him on the arm of her father. He wouldn't forget how she'd never looked away from him or the smile she'd worn or the light in her amazing hazel eyes.

He'd had no doubts at all about marrying her or committing his life to her, but seeing her so certain, so unafraid of what they were about to do, had only added to the joy for him. After his first love broke his heart, he'd never expected to fall in love again, and he'd certainly never expected the kind of love he had with Cameron.

They'd gotten lucky that night in the mud with an angry moose standing between them. He had no doubt whatsoever that their meeting had been prearranged by fate, which brought together two people who might never have met without the well-intentioned meddling of his father and grandfather and a moose named Fred.

"I can't believe I fell asleep," she said, yawning as Will helped her from the car while the driver unloaded their bags and carried them to the door.

"You wore yourself out the last couple of weeks getting ready for today and working crazy hours before you left the office."

"That's true. You'll forgive me if all I want to do is sleep for the next two weeks, right?"

"I'd never forgive you for that."

Cameron laughed at his indignant reply. "Good thing I'm only kidding then." She screamed with laughter when he suddenly lifted her over his shoulder and headed for the door, thanking the driver as he went.

The man laughed at their antics and wished them well.

"Put me down," Cameron said when they were inside the house. "You left our stuff in the driveway!"

"It'll still be there when I go back for it. Later."

"Will!"

He kept walking and didn't put her down until they were by the bed in the master bedroom, where he immediately went to work on the zipper to her dress.

"You're in a rush tonight."

"I've never been in more of a rush." He pushed the dress off her shoulders and reached for it before it hit the floor. Holding out his hand to her, he said, "Step out of it."

She held on to him and did as he directed.

He laid the priceless dress across the foot of the bed.

"Thanks for that," she said, gesturing to the dress.

"That's not something to leave on the floor, even if we're in a rush." He took a closer look at what she was wearing under it, and his mouth went dry with lust as he took in the sheer lace strapless bra that left nothing to the imagination, the barely there panties, the thigh-high hose and the three-inch heels that made her legs look endless.

She was a goddess come to life before his eyes, and that this beautiful, sexy woman belonged to him was the greatest miracle of his life. And then she smiled at him, fully aware of what she did to him, and he couldn't wait another minute to touch her.

Cameron unbuttoned his vest and then started on the buttons to his shirt, pushing both articles off his shoulders before she tugged the T-shirt free of his pants and pulled it over his head.

"Is someone else in a rush, my love?" he asked.

"Mmm hmm." She had his belt unbuckled and his pants around his ankles in record time. "Hurry."

Will didn't need to be told twice. He stripped off his boxers and unclipped her bra as her hand encircled his erection. They fell on the bed in a mess of arms and legs and lips and tongues and frantic need. He didn't even bother removing her panties. Rather, he pushed them aside and surged into her, nearly coming from the rush of desire that overtook him.

He told himself he should go slowly. He should show her some finesse this first time as husband and wife, but finesse was no match for the powerful need she aroused in him. Next time, he decided, he'd show her finesse. For now, he grasped her hands, propped them over her head and took them both on a wild ride.

She met him stroke for stroke, her legs wrapped tight around his hips and her breasts pressed against his chest. Then she tugged at the grip he had on her hands. "Want to touch you."

He released her and sighed with pleasure as her arms encircled him and her fingers burrowed into his hair. "Cameron," he whispered in her ear, "I love you so much. I love you more than I did when I woke up this morning, and that was an awful lot."

"Mmm," she said, smiling as her eyes closed when he pushed into her. "Me, too."

"Are you close, baby?"

"So close . . ."

He picked up the pace, giving her everything she needed to get there.

"Will . . . I'm . . . Oh . . . *yeah.*"

It took everything he had to hold off and ride the storm of her orgasm without giving in to his own. He watched her come back down from the high to realize he hadn't gone with her. Smiling down at her, he kissed her and then turned them over so she was on top of him.

"Is this what you want?" she asked as she rolled her hips and took him straight to heaven.

"Just like that."

She kept it up until he exploded inside her, gripping her hips so tightly there'd probably be bruises again.

He reached for her, and she came down on top of him, snuggled into his embrace as their bodies continued to twitch and pulse where they were joined. "I didn't mean to be so rough."

"Please don't apologize. I love everything we do together."

"In that case," he said, turning them over so he was once again on top, "how do you feel about more of the same, only a little slower this time."

"You're not tired?"

"I figure we can sleep on the plane."

"Have I mentioned there's a bedroom on the plane?"

"Oh . . . There is?"

"Uh-huh."

"Well, sleep is overrated anyway, especially when there's such a good reason to stay up all night."

"We can sleep on the beach in Fiji."

"I do like the way you think, Mrs Abbott."

TEN

BACK IN BUTLER, Mary Larkin drove Patrick Murphy to the Abbotts' home, where he was spending one more night before heading back to the city in the morning. Even though his hosts were heading in the same direction, Patrick had asked Mary to drive him.

She couldn't remember the last time she'd danced as much as she had at Will and Cameron's wedding—and she'd danced every song with Patrick. He'd kept her laughing and entertained all evening, and she couldn't deny that she was powerfully attracted to Cameron's handsome, gregarious father.

But Patrick's reputation as a playboy had preceded him to Butler, and as much as Mary would enjoy the opportunity to get to know him better, she was no fool. Theirs had been a one-night flirtation, and that's all it would ever be.

"Are you in a rush to go right home?" Patrick asked as they headed into town.

"What did you want to do?"

"What's there to do in these parts this time of night?"

"Not much. There's a piano bar at the inn, but it's only open for another hour or so."

"That sounds good to me. I could use a nightcap after giving away my daughter."

"That was traumatic for you, huh?"

"You have no idea." Though the comment was said lightly, Mary sensed he wasn't entirely kidding. Despite his easy humor, she'd caught him looking wistfully at Cameron more than once during the evening and had wondered what he was thinking at those moments.

Inside the Butler Inn, the piano bar was still open and several patrons were enjoying the music with their drinks.

Patrick followed her to a booth far enough from the piano that they could talk without having to shout.

Mary told herself that the hand he placed on her lower back didn't mean anything. He probably did that as naturally as he drew oxygen to his lungs. Still, she sort of wished for a second that she were the type of woman who could allow herself to get carried away with such a gesture.

When they were seated, a waitress came to take their order. "Soda water with lemon," she said because she was driving.

"I'll have the same, but add a double shot of Ketel One to mine," Patrick said.

"We have Grey Goose and Absolut, but no Ketel One," the waitress replied.

Patrick sighed deeply. "Grey Goose, please."

"Coming right up."

"No cell service and no Ketel One. How do you people function here?"

Mary laughed at the look of utter distress on his face. "Somehow we survive."

"I can't imagine how."

"You city slickers are spoiled by having everything you could want or need at your fingertips."

"I'm definitely guilty of that."

"That's one of the things I love about living here. You have to make do with what you have. It makes you appreciate the simple things in life."

The waitress arrived with their drinks, and Patrick paid with a fifty-dollar bill.

"Thank you," Mary said.

"You're most welcome."

"How's the Grey Goose?"

"It'll do in a pinch."

"You're spoiled, Patrick."

"I know," he said with a sigh. "I wasn't always, though. I grew up humbly and became spoiled much later. Money does that to people."

"I'll have to take your word for that."

"What's your story, sweet Mary from Vermont?"

She felt her face flush from the compliment as much as the way he looked at her. "Not much of a story. I grew up in Stowe and moved over here to the Northeast Kingdom to work on the mountain after college at UVM. I took a part-time job at the store that led to the office manager position about fifteen years ago."

"Never been married?"

"Nope. Never even came close."

"How's that possible? Are all the men in Vermont blind?"

"You are a charmer, Patrick," she said with a laugh. "I'll give you that."

"My daughter told me to leave you alone. She said you were too nice for the likes of me."

"The likes of you? That doesn't sound like her."

"Maybe not, but it's true. Since my wife died, I haven't exactly been Prince Charming when it comes to women."

"What happened to your wife?" Mary immediately regretted the question that caused a flash of pain to register in his eyes. "I'm sorry. I shouldn't have asked that. It's none of my business."

"It's no secret that she died having Cam."

"Oh God, Patrick. I didn't know that. I'm so sorry for both of you."

"Thanks." He used the stirrer to swirl the chunk of lemon around in his drink. "Cameron wore her mother's dress today. Surprised the hell out of me with that."

"In a good way?"

"Yeah. It was good, but it was hard, too. She looks so much like her mother. It's uncanny. The older she gets, the more she's Ali all over again." He took a sip of his drink. "Anyway, didn't mean to get maudlin."

"You didn't. It was an emotional day for you."

"Much more so than I'd expected it to be. Not sure what I

thought it would be like to see her all decked out as a bride and then have to give her away . . . Whose big idea was that nonsense, anyway? Raise this little girl her whole life and then 'give her away' to some other guy? How is that fair?"

Mary laughed at his mini diatribe.

"In fact, I really have no right to be so indignant. I was a lousy father to her."

"Don't say that."

"It's true. I traveled a lot, left her with nannies. She was always well cared for, but I was absent much of the time. It was easier that way. For me, anyway. I wish I had it to do over again."

"Would you have done it differently?"

"Oh, hell yeah. But losing Ali suddenly the way I did . . . It messed me up pretty bad. By the time I started to come out of the fog and took a look around me, Cam was ten and no longer cried when I left on business trips." He shrugged. "I screwed up every which way, and she loves me anyhow. Go figure."

"She's a wonderful person, Patrick. You can certainly be proud of her."

"I'm extremely proud of her. Everything she's accomplished she's done on her own. She could've turned into another Paris Hilton if she'd been so inclined."

Mary shook her head. "That would never be Cam. She's too ambitious."

"Always was, even when she was a kid and struggling in school. She found out later she had attention deficit disorder, which made me feel like shit because I used to ride her about her lousy grades. It never occurred to me that it could be something like that. Ali would've been all over it, and I was oblivious. I wouldn't have even known she had ADD, but I saw her take her meds one day and asked her what they were for. Talk about a slap to the face for dear old dad." He seemed to snap out of his melancholy all of a sudden and shook his head. "Anyway, didn't mean to turn this into a pity party. I never talk about this crap. What is it about you that makes me want to confess my sins to you?"

"Perhaps it's easier with a new friend who hasn't known you all these years."

"Perhaps that's it, or maybe it's just you, and you're sweet and easy to talk to."

Mary had no idea how to respond to such blatant flirting. She was woefully out of practice with such things.

"Have you ever been to New York, sweet Mary from Vermont?"

"No, I haven't."

"You should come down sometime. See the sights, take in a show."

"That would be fun."

"When do you want to come?"

"Patrick . . ."

"What?"

"I thought we were talking hypothetically."

"I wasn't. I was actually ham-handedly inviting you to come visit me in New York. In fact, I'd love it if you came to visit me so I could show you my city."

"Oh, well . . . I don't know. I'd have to think about that."

"While you do your thinking, could I possibly have your phone number so I could call you to try to persuade you to accept my invitation?"

"I suppose that would be all right."

"Excellent." He withdrew his smart phone from the inside pocket of his suit coat and began poking at it. "What's the number?"

She recited her phone number and watched him program it into his phone.

"There we go." He showed her the screen, where she was listed as *Sweet Mary from Vermont*. "I assume that's a landline in this cell-phone wasteland?"

"You assume correctly. I don't have a cell phone. No point to it around here."

Patrick shook his head in dismay. "It's like an alternate universe."

"Nope, it's just Vermont."

"Thanks for listening to me just now. It's been quite a day, and it helped to talk it out."

"I was happy to listen, and I enjoyed today very much. We've all come to love Cameron, and the two of them together are just perfect. Will is a really, really good guy, Patrick. The best of the best."

"I know," he said glumly. "She had to pick a prince among

men so I can't even hate him for taking my little girl away from me."

"You're a mess."

Laughing, he said, "Yes, I am." He reached for her hand and brushed his lips across her knuckles. "But I'm less of a mess than I would've been without you to talk to, so thank you for that."

Mary was still recovering from the zing of sensation that had traveled from her hand up her arm and couldn't seem to form a reply to that statement.

"How old are you?" he asked.

"You're not supposed to ask a woman that," she said with pretend indignation.

"All right then . . . I'm fifty-four. Are you too young for me?"

"I'm probably too old for you at forty-two."

"That is a little outside my usual range," he said with a wink. "But I've been thinking lately that it might be time to grow up and act my age."

"And when did this startling revelation take place?"

"This past Thursday afternoon. Around two o'clock. I met this sweet woman in Vermont who has me wondering what it might be like to get to know her better. What do you say to that?"

"I say," Mary began haltingly, "you're very nice and very charming and way, way, *way* out of my league."

"What's that mean?" His brows furrowed with what seemed to be genuine puzzlement. "Out of your league?"

"Your world and mine—two different planets. I wouldn't even know how to function in yours."

"I've just functioned for days in yours. Even lived without a cell-phone connection, and the world didn't end. I bet you could exist in my world just as easily. Hell, look at Colton. He's living between here and New York now and figuring it out as he goes."

Mary glanced at his handsome face and decided to level with him. "I've lived my whole life without having my heart broken. I think you, Patrick Murphy, could break my heart if I let you, so I'm not going to let you."

"If that's true, then you, Mary Larkin, are long overdue for a little adventure in your life."

"Maybe so, but I'd prefer to chalk this up to one lovely

evening spent with a new friend—the father of another new friend—and call it a night."

"We can call it a night if you'd like, but don't forget I've got your number now. So I'll be calling *you* some other night. Will you take my call?"

"I don't know."

"That's fair enough, but you won't blame a guy for trying, will you?"

"No, I won't."

He smiled at her and finished his drink in one last swallow. "Shall we head out? I have no idea what my curfew is at the barn."

"I'm sure they haven't locked you out—yet."

Mary was much more aware of that hand on her lower back leaving the bar than she'd been on the way in. Fortunately, she didn't see anyone she knew in the inn, so she wasn't worried about gossip. Besides, it might be fun to be the source of gossip for once.

Even though she was driving, he held the car door for her and waited for her to get settled before he went around to the passenger side of her nondescript sedan. Her entire life was somewhat nondescript when it came right down to it. Not that she was unhappy. Not at all. But Patrick had dangled something in front of her tonight that looked awfully good to her—adventure.

"You're thinking about whether you'll take my call, aren't you?"

"Don't flatter yourself."

His ringing laughter brought a reluctant smile to her face. "I do like you, sweet Mary from Vermont."

She drove slowly across the one-lane bridge that led to the Abbotts' home on Hells Peak Road.

"What do you do if someone is coming the other way?"

"You wait."

"Huh. Interesting."

"Not used to waiting for anything, are you?"

"Not so much."

She would've rolled her eyes at him, but it was too dark for him to see. She took the right that led to the distinctive red barn and pulled into the Abbotts' driveway a minute later. "Here you are."

"Do you live far from here?"

"A couple of miles."

"You'll be okay going home?"

"I'll be fine."

"I might call to check."

"I won't take the call."

He surprised her when he leaned over to kiss her cheek. "Take my call, Mary," he said softly. "I promise I'll make it worth your while."

Then he was gone, taking the scent of fine cologne with him when he left her car. She waited until she saw him go into the barn and turn off the outside light Molly and Lincoln had left on for him.

On the way home to her house on Butler's north side, she thought about the evening she'd spent with Patrick, as well as the magical wedding of two people she adored.

Maybe it was the romance of it all that had her thinking of the way Patrick had invited her to New York, asked for her phone number and promised to call her. Maybe it was the way he wanted to challenge her routine and staid existence with his offer of adventure. She was no closer to figuring out what to do about him when she arrived home a short time later, but she already knew one thing for certain.

If and when it happened, she would take his call.

WILL and Cameron never did sleep that night, and when the sun came up over Lake Champlain, they watched it on the deck, a comforter wrapped around their naked bodies.

"This was the best night of my life," Will said. "I hate to see it come to an end."

"This is just the beginning."

"Are you tired?"

"For some crazy reason, I'm not. I must be running on pure adrenaline by now."

"Whatever we're running on, I'm digging it."

"Me, too." When she kissed him, she realized how sore her lips were from a night of nonstop kissing—among other things. "We need to hit the shower and get ready to go. The car will be here in an hour to take us to the airport."

"Did we screw this up by deciding to go halfway around the world when we've got this right here?"

"As much as I love this house and the lake, it's freezing here. I want warm sun, sand between my toes and little paper umbrellas in my drinks. We can't get that here."

"True."

"Have you forgotten there's a bed on the plane?"

"I have *not* forgotten. I've thought of little else since you mentioned that last night."

"Then what do you say we go to Fiji?"

"I say I'd go to the ends of the earth if it meant I got to be with you."

Cameron smiled as she kissed him. One more minute wrapped up in him wouldn't matter in the grand scheme of things. Not when she had the rest of her life to spend with him.

Author's Note

Thank you for reading "You'll Be Mine." I really enjoyed writing about Will and Cam's wedding, and hope you felt like a guest on their big day. Special thanks to my beta readers Anne Woodall, Kara Conrad, Ronlyn Howe and Holly Sullivan for their quick work, as well as to everyone on my team who supports me every day. Thank you to all the readers whose enthusiasm for my books allows me to live my dream.

Join the You'll Be Mine Reader Group at facebook.com/groups/YoullBeMine/ to discuss the wedding with other fans of the series. Thanks for reading, and watch for much more from the Green Mountains, including *It's Only Love*, Gavin and Ella's story, coming in November 2015.

WRAPPED AROUND YOUR FINGER

Shirley Jump

To my running, swimming, and biking friends, near and far.
Thank you for the laughs and conversations on long runs,
for pushing me when I think I can't take another step, and
for being people who inspire me every single day.

ONE

IN THE SMALL Georgia town where Maggie McBride had grown up, beauty queens ruled and only boys hammered nails and wore boots. Girls were brought up to be ladies who paraded around in heels and never cursed, and worked respectable jobs while raising photogenic families who went to church on Sunday and said *please* and *thank you, ma'am*.

Maggie hated heels. Cursed like a trucker when the occasion warranted and had no idea how to fry chicken or stitch a pillowcase. *Conformity is for everyone else*, she'd once been told. *Don't be everyone else, Maggie dear. Be bold. Be brave. Be yourself.*

Which was exactly what Maggie had done for the past twenty-eight years. Her parents had long ago given up on her and written her off as "that incorrigible child." Fine by Maggie, who never did have much in common with the people who had raised her. Or the world she had left behind.

Until that dare arrived in the mail.

Maggie had promised Rachel Winters—the two of them best friends since that day in first grade when Maggie slugged the bully trying to steal Rachel's lunch, and Rachel later shared her sandwich with her new friend—that when Rachel got married, she would go back to Chatham Ridge, slip into an uncomfortable pink dress she would never wear again, and spend a few hours in a torturous pair of high heels. For Rachel, Maggie would do almost anything.

Except what had been asked of her in that note.

A note Rachel had slipped inside the invitation to her wedding, along with a book, and a reminder that Maggie might have moved away from the traditions of her past, but they still had a way of sneaking up on her when she least expected it.

"Hey, be careful with those. I'd like to be able to have children someday, you know."

Nick's deep voice jerked Maggie back to the present. She adjusted the stack of two-by-fours she was carrying and swung to the right, just before she collided with Nick's hip. "Sorry."

"What, no quick comeback questioning my manhood? You disappoint me." Nick grinned, reached over, took the pile of lumber from her and loaded it into the back of his battered blue pickup. The scuffed bed was filled with the detritus of a completed construction job—buckets of leftover mortar, boxes of porcelain tiles, a few bags of trash. After a month of hard work, they had finished up a remodel of an old mansion on Rescue Bay's western edge, one of those beachfront places built in the twenties. Maggie loved these old houses, with their quirky personalities and long-buried mysteries, all waiting to be brought to life again by her and Nick's handiwork.

"Earth to M.J. You okay? Not gonna faint on me, are you?" Nick put a hand on her forehead. His touch was warm, tender. Familiar.

For about five seconds, Maggie could almost believe Nick was worried about her. Then she remembered this was *Nick*, who was about as emotionally deep as a fingernail.

She and Nick had worked together, side by side, for the better part of two years now, rehabbing homes and renovating businesses all up and down the Gulf Coast. They'd sweated together on long, hot days of demo work, then, when the day was done, sat on overturned plastic buckets and cracked open cold beers together. She'd listened to Nick complain about the girlfriend du jour, and they'd debated the Steelers versus the Packers two falls in a row. They were friends, buddies, coworkers. And nothing more.

Not that she didn't find Nick Patterson attractive. A woman would have to be dead and buried not to find Nick attractive. The man could have been Ryan Gosling's twin, with his sandy brown hair and blue-green eyes, and that lopsided grin. He had a tattoo that peeked out from under one sleeve from time to time, like a mystery waiting to be unraveled, and a deep voice that rolled through her belly. But he was also a major pain in the ass, and a man who lacked a commitment gene. That kept him squarely in her Just Friends column.

She jerked away from his touch. "Don't be pretending like you've got a heart. You just don't want to be stuck with cleanup."

"Of course I care about you. You're my work wife."

"For one, I can't be your work wife unless you already have a regular wife. And for another," she hoisted a dusty pile of Sheetrock trimmings into the truck, then coughed when it caused a blowback of dust, "if this is what being married to you is like, then I want a divorce."

"Hey, I'm not so bad." He tucked a few tools into the stainless steel box behind the cab of the truck. His arms flexed, and that tattoo made an enticing, winking appearance. "You should be impressed that I'm at least feigning concern."

She snorted. "Yeah, very impressed. For a second there, I almost believed you."

"Then my evil plan is working." He smirked, then grabbed the next bag of trash before she could, and tossed it into the bed. "Let me take that before you hurt yourself. You are a hot mess today."

"Gee, thanks. You really know how to make a girl feel pretty."

He leaned in close to her, so close she could catch the dark scent of his cologne and see the faint dusting of stubble on his cheeks. "If you want me to make you feel pretty, then go on a date with me."

Nick had been asking her out almost from the minute they'd met. She'd turned him down every single time. She was here to be taken seriously, to earn her chops as a worker and, she hoped, down the road, a contractor. Doing that did not involve dating the guy who helped her frame walls. He was interested in her, all right—but not in anything that lasted longer than the time it took to paint a wall. "Date you and become notch number 422 on your bedpost?" She shook her head. "No, thank you."

"For your information, I do not make notches on my bed-post. Nor have I dated 422 women."

She rolled her eyes. "So I'm off by five or ten notches."

"Seriously, though, you're never this distracted, M.J.," Nick said, calling her by the nickname he'd given her on their first day together, when Mike Stark had hired Margaret Jean McBride as part of his construction crew. Maggie wasn't sure whether it was because Nick didn't see her as a Maggie, or whether it made it easier to work a construction site with someone whose name sounded less feminine. Either way, Maggie was glad Nick had always treated her as an equal and not as a girl.

"Yet, all day," Nick went on, "you've been walking around in a fog. If you were any other woman, I'd be asking if there was a shoe sale or something." He grinned, then tossed the last bag of trash into the back and shut the tailgate. "But you're not any other woman. You're more like . . ."

"One of the guys?" she filled in.

"Well, you do swing a sledgehammer better than anyone I know."

"I can swing a sledgehammer better than *you*," she said, pulling open the passenger's-side door and climbing into the cab.

Nick got in on the other side and settled his tall, lean frame behind the steering wheel. "You only *think* you can swing a sledgehammer better than me."

She smirked. "Keep telling yourself that, Conan. It's all in the center of gravity." She wriggled her hips in the seat.

He watched her hips, his blue-green eyes darkening, then he slipped on a pair of sunglasses and started the truck. "So, what are you going to do with your week's vacation?"

With the Fourth of July falling on a Tuesday this year, and with the lighter summer workload, Mike had decided to give everyone at Stark Construction a paid week off for the holiday. One of a million reasons why Maggie loved her job.

"I'm heading up to Georgia. My best friend is getting married." She thought of the note. The words Rachel had written. The challenge at the end.

I dare you.

A challenge—Lord knew Maggie loved a challenge. Tell Maggie that she couldn't do something or shouldn't do something, she would do it anyway, just to prove the naysayers wrong. Rachel knew that—as did the rest of the girls in the Southern Belle Book Club. No doubt, that was what had them sending her the note, and the book.

Your presence is also hereby requested at book club, because it's been an eon and a day since we saw you! Getting you started with this month's pick, Dared to Love *by J. K. Simmons. Yes, it is a romance novel, and yes, you'd better just suck it up. Want another genre? Come another month. Anyway, in keeping with the theme of the book, we're all embarking on a dare of our own. Here's yours, specially crafted by Rachel:*

I dare you to bring a hunky man to the wedding as your date. Like that hottie Nick you work with. (That's what you get for introducing me to him last summer when I visited ☺.) Give him a chance, and in the process, keep my aunt Ethel from asking when you're getting married. Flirt with the guy—and not about the size of his chain saw. Maybe even take the ultimate dare—and fall in love, you commitment-phobe, you.

Invite Nick as her date? What was Rachel thinking? It was enough that Maggie had agreed to wear a dress and heels. Rachel knew Maggie didn't do girlie. Didn't do makeup and manicures, and sure as hell didn't flirt. As for falling in love? With Nick, of all people? Emotional suicide.

Years ago, Maggie had fallen head over heels for B. J. Thompson, who'd played running back for the Chatham Ridge High Chargers. She'd followed him to Florida after graduation, promising to be the homey little woman he wanted. Then two weeks later she'd come home from the grocery store to find him in their bedroom, fondling the neighbor's breasts. Maggie had packed her bags, gotten her first job in construction, and flushed those happily-ever-after notions once and for all. Her friends could go and play Mrs. Cleaver all they wanted, but Maggie was much happier right where she was—smack-dab in the center of Tomboy.

But that argument wouldn't stop Rachel, who had to be as stubborn as Maggie. If Maggie didn't show up with Nick, or with a date, Rachel would undoubtedly find one for her. Maybe what Maggie needed was someone who could play the part and convince the girls that Maggie was taking the dare seriously. Then they wouldn't bug her about it every five minutes during the reception.

She glanced over at Nick as they drove away from the construction site and into downtown Rescue Bay. He had a nice profile with a strong jaw and an easy lopsided smile that appeared at the drop of a hat. He wasn't a troll, and he did have a few good manners—like taking that wood from her and opening her door, even though he knew damned well Maggie could take care of herself—so maybe . . .

Was she crazy? Spend a week with Nick? The same man who dated like some people dieted—in a constant binge and purge? What if it changed things between them? She liked things just as they were. Unencumbered, unattached, unsexualized. More or less.

Flirt with the guy—and not about the size of his chain saw. Maybe even take the ultimate dare—and fall in love, you commitment-phobe, you.

It was Friday. She was leaving Wednesday, to spend the week in Chatham Ridge before the wedding next Saturday afternoon. If she didn't ask Nick—where on earth Rachel got the idea that he would make a good date, Maggie had no idea—then where was she going to find a man in the next few days who would go along with this crazy plan? Maggie didn't go out, didn't date, didn't do a whole hell of a lot besides go to work and go to sleep. Her best—and pretty much only—prospect was sitting right beside her.

"So . . . uh . . . what are you doing this week?" she asked Nick.

He stopped for a red light and drummed his fingers on the steering wheel. A country song played at a low volume on his radio, something about pickup trucks and beer. "Monday, I'm planning on drinking a lot of beer on the beach with women in teeny-tiny bikinis." He tossed Maggie a grin. "Rinse and repeat for Tuesday, Wednesday, Thursday—"

"I get the picture."

"You almost sound jealous, M.J."

"For one, I am never jealous of you and the hundreds of women who parade through your bedroom—"

"Hundreds? That's an exaggeration. But a good one."

"For another, I think you can do something far more productive with your week off."

"Something far more productive? Like what?" The light turned green and Nick turned left, now moving away from downtown and toward Maggie's condo. "You have a side job lined up or something?"

"Something like that." She fidgeted in her seat. If she showed up without a man, she knew Rachel was right. Her well-meaning relatives, who had taken Maggie under their wing years ago as a sort of surrogate sister to Rachel, would find one for her. Given the debacle with Rachel's cousin Wilbur two years ago—him and his "feel my neck, see if I have the mumps" moments—she didn't want to put her destiny in anyone else's hands but her own.

"Well, if you do find a side job, let me know," Nick said. "I can always use some extra cash. Helps me pay down the Money Pit."

The Money Pit was a three-bedroom ranch house a half mile from the water, with a large backyard at the edge of one of the many walking trails in Rescue Bay. A foreclosure, it had sat empty for five years, decaying in the salty air and merciless Florida sun. Nick spent most of his free hours—and all of his free cash—on the ongoing renovations. Maggie had helped him out more than once on other projects he had done and had been impressed with Nick's design eye. He had a way of bringing everything together—from the flooring to the backsplash—to make a house feel like a home.

He'd flipped six houses in the time she'd known him, all foreclosures that became something amazing when Nick was done. He had claimed he'd bought each one with an intent toward a long-term residence, but he never held on to any of them. He seemed content with his life of impermanence, both in his relationships and his addresses.

Which was what made him perfect for Maggie's needs. Nick wouldn't expect anything more at the end of the week than a thank-you—and maybe a check. Rachel would be happy that Maggie had taken the dare, and in the end, Maggie would be no more committed to Nick than she was to her landlord. Win-win.

"I do have one option, if you're looking to make extra money," she said.

"I'm all ears. And empty wallet." Nick chuckled as he turned right onto Maggie's street and stopped the truck outside her condo. "Spent my last paycheck fixing a plumbing leak that went from one bad pipe to a strip-it-to-the walls-and-start-over-again nightmare."

"Are you ever going to let me see that house? I could give you a hand, you know." He'd let her help with all the other projects, but this one he'd been secretive about. Maybe he had some other girl with a hammer handing him nails. Either way, she wasn't jealous. At all.

"I'm good on my own." He flicked a glance at her. "I'm debating keeping this one."

She laughed. "Yeah, right. You've never kept any of your Money Pits. So I'll give you the same advice I gave you the last seven times you put a house on the market five minutes after you finished the reno. Put some flowers in pots on the front porch and in some window boxes before you hang up the For Sale sign. You want a house to say *home* the minute you see it."

"And I should make sure I have a swing on the porch, for quiet afternoons and reading. Like you had when you were a teenager."

She cast him a surprised glance. That swing had been the one bit of normalcy in her stark, cold childhood. For six months, they'd lived in that rental house, a campus home so unlike the usual no-maintenance apartments her parents preferred. Six months before her parents were offered jobs in California and the house had been packed up, leaving behind that swing and the window boxes. Rachel's home had been the closest Maggie had ever come to living in a house like that, but it wasn't the same, not really. Not when it wasn't her own, wasn't a place where she could put her own stamp. Hang her own swing. It was why she'd bought the silly thing years ago, though she still lived in a condo, no more permanent or homey than the places of her childhood. Some psychiatrist would have something to say about that, Maggie was sure. "You remember that? Heck, I bought that beat-up old porch swing like two years ago and made you store it in your garage. Someday it'll find a home."

"I pay attention more than you think, M.J." He shifted the

truck into Park, then draped his hands over the steering wheel. "Anyway, the house is not ready for you to see. It's still a . . . work in progress. An expensive one."

"Maybe if you dated a little less, you'd have more time for the Money Pit." She put a hand on the door handle, then released it. She wasn't here to lecture him. She needed a solution to her own problem, and solutions weren't exactly falling off a bachelor tree.

She looked over at Nick, his hair dusted with a fine layer of sawdust, his gray T-shirt so worn, it was practically see-through, and his hands rough with the calluses of a man who worked hard for his paycheck. It was a crazy idea, one that could easily backfire, but if she put him in a suit and tie, and got him to shave more than a couple times a week . . . "If you come with me to Georgia, I'll . . . I'll pay you. Three hundred dollars."

"What? Why?"

"Two reasons. One, I have my general contractor's exam in two weeks, and I need a study partner . . ."

"Something I've already been doing every day with you for free."

"And two . . ." She sucked in a breath and decided to just say it, fast, like ripping out a splinter. "If I show up without a date, everyone in the town of Chatham Ridge is going to try to fix me up with their toothless second cousin or newly widowed great-uncle." A believable enough reason. She sure as hell wasn't going to tell Nick that Rachel had dared her to do it. Knowing him, he would tease her for the next ten years. "I need you to pretend to be my . . . boyfriend."

"I asked you out five seconds ago and you said no."

"I didn't mean my real boyfriend. I said pretend." She shook her head and cursed. "Forget it."

Nick turned in his seat, draping an arm over the back of the crimson vinyl bench seat. His fingers rested inches from her shoulder, so close she swore she could feel the heat from his skin. He quirked that lopsided grin at her, and something in Maggie's gut flipped. "Let me get this straight. You want me to go with you to this wedding and pretend to be madly in love with you?"

"If you think you can pull that off."

"You doubt my acting skills?"

"If this was a carpentry job, I'd have no worries, but you aren't exactly . . ."

"Exactly what?"

She arched a brow and waved at his torn, faded work clothes, the Slovenly Bachelor look he'd perfected. It was how he looked when he went to work, to lunch, heck, to his grandmother's church picnic. If Nick owned a single thing with buttons, she would be shocked. "Devoted boyfriend material."

"You're worried I can't convince a bunch of Southern women that I am your one true love?"

"A little." She took a second glance at his attire and the rough stubble on his chin. "Okay, a lot."

"Really? Maybe I should prove it to you. I do, after all, love a challenge."

The way he'd said *challenge*, with a low, tempting growl, temporarily wiped her brain clean. All she could do was sit there, her heart thudding with anticipation. "Prove it? How?"

Nick's eyes met hers, intent, serious. His arm slid off the back of the bench, his hand coming up to gently cup the back of her head. His fingers tangled in her hair, and he brought his face within inches of hers. She caught the scent of his cologne, dark and woodsy, and watched his ocean-colored eyes draw closer and closer. Her heart began to race, and her breath got lost somewhere in the small cab of the pickup. His lips whispered against hers, and she found her eyes closing, her body dissolving into goo. She wanted him to kiss her, to back away, to kiss her—

Definitely to kiss her.

"You are my one true love." His voice was husky, his words hot against her cheeks.

She swallowed hard. "Very . . . uh . . . believable."

He drew back and smirked. "I told you so."

Just like that, he was back to Nick her friend, her buddy, her coworker. A part of Maggie was still simmering—which had her wondering if this plan was a good idea. But wait, this was *Nick*. The last man in the world she would ever date. There was no worry about falling for him, or believing his act, not for one minute.

Besides, she had her priorities—get her contractor's license, then build her own rehab business. Work was number one on her plate, not Nick, who couldn't plan for anything further than twenty-four hours out.

"Quit gloating. It was just a kiss, not an Oscar performance," she said. "Do you want the job or not?"

"I'll do it, but . . ." He raised a finger in warning. "It's going to cost you. My fee for hot-lover acting is seven hundred dollars. Because Daddy needs a new hot water heater, too."

She eyed him, debating. "Four hundred."

"Six."

"Five."

"Deal." He grinned and shook with her. "Do I get hazardous-duty pay?"

She blew her bangs out of her eyes. "Don't make me regret this already. Just be ready to go Wednesday morning," she said. "Eight A.M. And for the love of all that is holy, please try to have a wardrobe that doesn't look like it came out of a shredder at the Goodwill."

"Trust me, M.J. I can clean up pretty damned well. You won't even recognize me."

She pulled on the door handle and grabbed her tool belt as she climbed out of the truck. "That's exactly what I'm afraid of."

Two

NICK PATTERSON HAD made a lot of bad decisions in his life. Enough to write a list as long as his arm. But agreeing to go to Georgia as M.J.'s infatuated date had to be the worst.

On Friday, he'd thought this would be the perfect opportunity to give her a taste of what they could have together. In the light of a new day, though, he worried that he was going to screw it up and lose M.J. forever.

He and M.J. had the perfect relationship—they worked together, joked together, and didn't screw things up with sex. Not that he hadn't thought about sex about a hundred thousand times since the first time he saw her, wearing a tool belt slung low on her hips and a can-do attitude all over her face. There was something insanely sexy about a woman who could hold her own in a difficult, male-dominated arena. He'd had his doubts about a female coworker, but M.J. had proven herself just as capable and knowledgeable as anyone else. Not to mention the way she filled out those denim shorts, or how amazing she looked with a fine sheen of sweat glistening on her skin, or when—

Damn. This was a bad idea. If she was even one-tenth as sexy in a dress as she was in shorts, then there was a damned good chance he was going to screw things up one way or another. Because that almost kiss—

Treaded too close. Way too close. Even with a dusting of sawdust in her hair and a mustard stain from lunch on her sleeve, M.J. had turned him on. He'd almost—almost—kissed her for real.

Not that it wasn't something he hadn't thought about, oh, twelve million times in the last two years. He'd asked her out over and over, but M.J. had always turned him down, making it clear she wasn't looking for a one-night stand, and that she thought he was the king of love-em-and-leave-em.

Okay, so maybe it was a well-deserved reputation. But he was a changed man—

Correction. *Working* on becoming a changed man. Sort of like the Money Pit. In serious need of a major overhaul, from the ground up.

He glanced around the fixer-upper he had bought six months ago. It was getting there, one room at a time. Stacks of supplies, accumulated over the past year, lined the hallway. Losing the few days to the Georgia trip would put him behind in his plan, but he couldn't turn down the much-needed cash infusion. Renovations didn't come cheap, especially not the kind he wanted to do.

Renovations that he hoped would show M.J. he wasn't the man she thought he was. In the last two years, Nick had realized he wanted more than just a temporary girl on his arm, a temporary place to hang his hat. Most of all, he wanted M.J.

He wasn't quite sure when his interest in her had gone from friendly to something more, something deeper. It had evolved, like him, he supposed, after a hundred afternoons in the sun with her, a hundred lunches when she remembered his favorite snack because she knew he would forget to buy it, a hundred evenings when she'd stayed late at his current Money Pit to help him flip a profit. M.J. had been there, through thick and thin, as steady as a stream.

These few days might be just the chance he needed to let her see he was a changed man. New and improved, like the Money Pit would be soon. Pretending to be her boyfriend could maybe lead to the real thing . . .

Which wouldn't be so bad. At all.

Nick zipped up his suitcase, then stepped out into the hot

Florida sunshine. He'd lived in Rescue Bay all his life, yet the summers still took him by surprise. The weight of the heat and the thickness of the humidity always rolled in like a wall and took a man's breath away.

M.J.'s car came screaming into his driveway. She drove that Mazda like a demon ditching the fires of hell, careening around corners, braking too fast, parking like it was a contact sport. She rolled down the window. "You ready?"

"Only if you let me drive."

"Ha. Fat chance."

"Seriously. You drive like a . . ."

"Like a guy?"

"Exactly."

She grinned. "Which is why it shouldn't matter who drives. Besides, if we sit here debating any longer, we'll be late arriving at Rachel's grandparents' house, and you know how I hate to be late."

He tossed his bag in the back, then buckled up and held on for dear life as she zipped down the street and onto the highway. Today M.J. had her dark brown hair back in a low ponytail that exposed the graceful curves of her neck, and led his eye down to the V of her T-shirt. Her shorts rode up in the seat and exposed the pale strip of skin at the top of her thighs where her suntan stopped. Damn. She was an incredibly beautiful woman.

He shifted in the seat. Maybe not such a good idea to stare at her, or it would be one hell of an uncomfortable five-hour ride. He glanced to the backseat, where he spied a dog-eared copy of the *Contractors Business Manual* for the state of Florida. "Want me to quiz you for a while?"

"Sure."

He flipped to a random page. Took a moment to focus on the words instead of thinking about that sexy, pale strip of skin. "Okay. Uh . . . When trusses are stored horizontally, blocking should be used on what size centers? Six to eight foot, eight to ten foot, ten to—?"

"Eight to ten foot." She grinned.

"Right. Okay. Let's try something harder . . ." He flipped ahead, quizzing her about reinforcing bars for a few minutes. She sailed through every answer with confidence. They switched to questions on elevations, then a few on framework, sampling from each section of the thick book. "You know all these."

"I've been studying." She flashed him a smile. "And you ask me questions every five seconds at work every day. And every Tuesday and Thursday night at Flanagan's."

"That's my job as study partner extraordinaire."

"Extraordinaire?" She laughed. "Okay, you are pretty good."

"Pretty good? I want to be epic. I want to be so good, you never want another study partner but me."

"After I take the test and get my contractor's license, I won't need a study partner."

The thought saddened him. He didn't tell her that he'd volunteered to help her months ago because it gave him an excuse to spend more time with her. That he looked forward to their study sessions as much as he did the start of the weekend. That going to Flanagan's wouldn't be the same without M.J. across the table from him, teasing him about his choice of pizza toppings. "Oh, I'm sure there's something I could help you study for. Maybe there's a Kama Sutra quiz available."

She rolled her eyes and zipped into the next lane without signaling. "Good Lord, you always come back to sex. Do you think about anything else?"

She was right—that was his default position. It was like he couldn't figure out how to be anything other than the womanizer she thought he was. For the first time in Nick's life, he had met a woman who made him feel unbalanced, and that led to him saying the first, and sometimes the second, stupid thing that came to his mind. "Okay, more studying."

Maybe then he wouldn't be such a moron. Nick reached in the back for the second workbook. As he did, he spied a paperback. The cover sported a man holding a woman to his chest, her head thrown back in ecstasy while he kissed her neck. Holy cow. He'd never seen anything like this in M.J.'s possession before. He arched a brow and glanced over at M.J. "Is this yours?"

"Yes. No. Sort of. Why are you asking me?"

"I didn't realize you read . . . I mean, stuff like this."

"Yes, Nick, I read. Real books." She grinned. "I'm in a book club and everything."

"A book club?" That surprised him. Especially that it was

a romance novel, not the typical nonfiction he'd seen her with from time to time. "*Dared to Love*. What's it about?"

Her face reddened. "Nothing."

M.J. was embarrassed? She never got embarrassed. He glanced back at the cover. Looked like a close-up of an HBO late-night special. "Oh, I get it. It's something dirty."

"It's just a book for book club. Put it back and ask me some more questions for the contractor's exam."

"In a minute." He flipped the book over and read the back cover. Something about a woman in high society who was dared to be a millionaire's lover for a weekend. "Hmm . . . maybe I should read this. For research, of course. After all, a certain someone I know said I don't make a very convincing lover."

She reached for the paperback, but he yanked the book away. "I never said you weren't a convincing lover. Exactly."

"Then what are you saying? That I can't be as sexy as . . ." He glanced at the book. "Logan here?"

"Give it back!" She reached out again, but he held the novel out of her reach. The car swerved on the highway. "Nick!"

"Watch the road. I want to read."

"Nick, don't you dare."

He shifted his shoulder to come between them, then opened to a random page in the book and started to read. "'He was mesmerized by her eyes, her deep green emerald eyes. She had captured his heart, his soul, and he knew resisting her would be impossible. He closed the distance between them, and touched her cheek. God, he wanted her. His hand trailed along her jaw, down the valley of her neck, then slipped between—'"

"Nick, give me that back!"

"'Between her generous breasts.'" He glanced over at M.J., his gaze dropping to the V in her shirt, his imagination picturing his hand there, touching her. He jerked his gaze back to the book. "'His thumb traced a lazy circle over her pert nipple. She let out a gasp and—'"

M.J. yanked the book out of his hands and shoved it into the storage space on her door. The tires squealed against the road. "You are incorrigible."

"That's what my mother says." He grinned, then leaned in close to her ear. "So did that turn you on?"

"God, no. Not when *you're* reading it. You're my friend,

not my . . . lover." She made a face and turned back to the road. "Now, can you just go back to the contractor's exam questions for the rest of the ride? Please?"

He dug out the sample tests and went back to quizzing M.J., but his mind stayed distracted. Because a tiny part of him was disappointed that reading the love scene hadn't turned M.J. on. It sure as hell had his mind going down some dangerous paths. Not just because M.J.'s eyes were green, like the woman in the book, and not just because he had noticed M.J.'s breasts pretty much every five minutes—

He needed a drink. Something with a high alcohol content. Then he'd be ready to face the week ahead, pretending to be in love with the one woman in the world who refused to see him as anything other than a friend. A woman who was paying him to pretend to love her—something he gladly would have done for free.

THREE

MAGGIE HAD LIED.

When Nick stole her book and read those lines aloud, his deep voice whispering those things about kisses and nipples and hands and, oh my God, everything else, it had sent heat coiling through her belly. He'd ruined the book for her, she realized, when they switched seats a couple hours later and she tried to read while he took the wheel. When she'd read the same pages again, she heard them in Nick's voice, imagined Nick doing the things to her that the hero was doing to the heroine.

That whole train of thought had made the love scene as uncomfortable as hell, especially with Nick sitting about six inches away. She'd had to put the book away and concentrate on the dull, boring facts in her contractor's book instead, just so she wouldn't hyperventilate in her own car.

The rest of the drive, she'd done her best to keep the conversation on work, but she was acutely aware of Nick's arm, brushing against hers from time to time, of his legs, strong and muscled beneath his shorts, of the scent of soap and man and temptation. So close, so very, very close. Every time they touched, a little tremor of electricity zipped through her veins.

It was just the afterburn from the love scene from the book, nothing more. As soon as they were out of the close quarters of the car, this . . . effect would wear off. This was Nick, after all, and he was far from a hero in a romance novel. He was her friend, albeit a cover-model sexy friend, especially when he was wearing a pale blue golf shirt and khaki shorts. The wind had mussed his hair, and she ached to run her fingers through the sandy brown locks, set them to rights again.

Good Lord. What was wrong with her?

Five hours after they'd set out, they started winding their way through the hills of Georgia toward Chatham Ridge. The whole state was greener, lusher, richer than Florida with its flat landscape and endless parade of palm trees. She put down her window and inhaled the fresh, clean air of Chatham Ridge. "I love this place," she said.

"Then why'd you move?"

"Long story." One she didn't want to revisit. Not now, not later, not ever.

"We have time."

"We'll be there soon. Only another twenty minutes or so."

"Enough time to tell me your life story." He grinned. "Or at least the abbreviated version."

She let out a sigh. "Why? And since when do you care about anything other than what's her bra size?"

Nick winced. "Ouch. I'm not that bad."

She glanced over and saw genuine hurt on his face. That surprised her. The Nick she knew would rather talk about sex than personal history, would rather build a 10,000-square-foot house than a relationship. "Sorry."

"Don't you think people will expect me to know about your past, if we're madly in love?"

Damn it. He was right. She hated that. "Okay. But if you nod off, I won't blame you."

"I won't nod off. I want to know about you, M.J." He noted her dubious look. "Really."

She slowed the car as they entered downtown Chatham Ridge. The quaint shops attracted their fair share of locals and tourists, who lingered on the brick sidewalks and wooden benches. "I grew up in this town. My parents were Ph.D.s who worked at the University of Georgia, in the physics department. Every meal was a lesson, assuming we ate together at all, because both of them worked so much. I became a master at making frozen pizza. They hated that I didn't follow in the family business of smarts and groundbreaking discoveries."

"But you're damned good at your job and pretty damned smart, to boot. If I were your parents, I'd be proud as hell."

Nick's words warmed her. "Thanks."

"Everyone has their own kind of awesomeness, M.J. Yours happens to be with wood and spackle."

She laughed, then took a left, leaving downtown Chatham Ridge in her rearview. "When I was sixteen, my parents were offered jobs at Berkeley. In California. I didn't want to move, so I stayed here, with Rachel, at her grandparents' house."

"Wait. They left you behind?"

She shrugged, like it didn't matter. "We're not close. We never really were." She still remembered the silence of her childhood, with both parents immersed in books, and her sitting on the sidelines, feeling weirdly like an interloper. Only at Rachel's had Maggie found anything like a family.

"Still, that sucks," Nick said. "How'd you end up in Florida?"

"I followed a guy. Thought I was in love. Turned out it was just lust." She shrugged again, and slowed as she neared the turn for the house.

"And you worked for a few years with Joplin Homes before you came to work for Mike. Been living in Rescue Bay for seven years now."

"Yup. There you have it, my life story in a nutshell." She flicked on a directional and waited at the stop sign to turn onto Huckleberry Lane. "Not as interesting as yours."

"I haven't even told you mine yet."

"I already know it. You grew up in Rescue Bay, went to private school in a nearby town. Your best friend is Colt Harper, the town doctor, and you have a grandfather who you take out for lunch every Sunday afternoon. You love the beach and big dogs, and you've never driven anything other than a pickup truck."

He leaned back in his seat and gave her an appraising glance. "How do you know that much about me?"

"I listen, Nick. That's all." She shrugged it off, but realized it made her sound like she was interested in him. Which she wasn't. Except he did look amazing in that light blue shirt, and when he'd read that passage from her book, he'd sent a whole line of fantasies roaring through her brain. Okay, so maybe she was a little interested, but not insane enough to get involved with him for real. It was all pretend, nothing more. "Anyway, Chatham Ridge doesn't have any kind of a decent hotel, so we're staying at Rachel's grandparents' house. Rachel is meeting us over there."

"And expecting me to be googly-eyed for you?"

She gave him a sarcastic look. "When have you ever been googly-eyed for anyone?"

He thought a second. "Elizabeth Anne Whitford, seventh grade."

Maggie laughed. That was a story Nick had never told her, in all those days of conversations while they worked. Of course, she'd never asked him about his relationship past, either. It intrigued her to think of Nick falling in love with anyone. "Really?"

"Yup. She sat beside me in Mrs. Glaser's class, and I thought she was the most beautiful creature to ever walk God's earth. She wore dresses almost every day and always had this pink ribbon in her hair, like a . . . what do you call it? Headband."

"Oh, the sweet and innocent type, huh?" And why did a crush from middle school send a little flicker of jealousy through Maggie's gut?

Nick chuckled. "Turns out it was all a ruse. She broke my heart when I caught her kissing Davey Knoxville behind the Dumpster."

"And you've been a jaded, confirmed bachelor ever since?" She pulled into the driveway of Rachel's grandparents' house and turned off the engine. The car clicked a few times, then fell silent.

"Oh, I wouldn't say I'm jaded. Just . . . wiser."

"Wiser . . . how?"

"I'm only dating women who don't wear pink headbands." Nick grinned, then followed her out of the car and grabbed their bags from the trunk before she could. "I've learned my lesson, too."

"And what lesson is that?"

"Never give your heart to a woman who can break it."

"That's almost every woman in the world."

"Exactly." He slung his bag over his shoulder, and hefted her suitcase in his hand.

They headed up the brick walkway, between flanks of pretty pink and white annuals. The house looked the same as she remembered, and there was something comforting about that, Maggie thought. "So you're going to go through life, never falling in love, never getting married, never having a spontaneous fall-in-love relationship?"

"Is the pot calling the kettle black?"

She rolled her eyes and took her suitcase from him. "I'm just cautious."

He snorted. "Cautious? You don't date at all. That's called cloister-ous."

"That's not even a word."

"It is to the nuns who never have sex."

"Who says I never have sex?"

He arched a brow.

No way was she going to admit that he was right, and that she got her oil changed more frequently than she got laid. It wasn't for lack of wanting—more for lack of dating. "My sex life is none of your business."

"It is now," he said, leaning in close to her and stealing her bag again, "because I'm your one true love. Remember?"

Damn, she wished he would quit getting so close. Every time he did, it sent this little thrill through her veins. She was about to push him away when Rachel came bursting out of the house, her arms outstretched. "Maggie! Thank God, you're finally here. My mother and her wedding insanity are half the reason I'm staying here. I told her I had to be at Grandma's to supervise the setup, but really I needed to get away from my mother." Rachel grabbed Maggie in a tight hug, one that erased the years they'd spent mostly apart in an instant. "I swear, Mama is going to drive me to elope in the back of J.W.'s Chevy half-ton."

"If you did, it would save us all from having to wear dresses and heels," Maggie said.

Rachel drew back and cocked a grin at Maggie. "You aren't getting out of that, honey. I have paid good money to see you in heels, and by God, you're going to wear them for at least one day. It's all part of my evil plan to bring out your inner debutante."

"I've told ya, Rachel, it doesn't exist. It's like a unicorn. Mythological only."

Rachel laughed. "We will see about that come Saturday at

two." She turned to Nick and gave him a warm smile. "Nice to see you again, Nick."

"Same to you, Rachel." He doffed an imaginary hat. "Congrats on the upcoming nuptials."

"Why, thank you, kind sir." She giggled, clearly caught in the Nick spell, like half the female population of the world. "I'm glad to see you're Maggie's plus one." Rachel winked at Maggie, as if she hadn't forced the whole thing with that silly dare.

"Plus one?" Nick wrapped an arm around Maggie's waist and stared down at her. "Honey, don't you want to tell everyone that we're dating?"

Honey? And . . . dating?!

Rachel let out a shriek. "For real? I mean, I never thought—"

"We're not . . . uh . . . It's not . . ." She sent Nick a quick glare, but he ignored it.

"We've been keeping it quiet, but, yeah, I'm wild about this girl." Nick lifted Maggie's left hand to his mouth and pressed a kiss against her fingers. His eyes took on this soft, almost dreamy look, then his face morphed into the familiar lopsided grin that told her he was kidding. "Who knows? Maybe this wedding fever will catch us both."

"Now that would be an outcome I didn't see coming," Rachel said. "Well, ya'll come on in and have some lemonade. My grandma's gonna wanna meet Nick, after I've been raving about him all week." Rachel draped an arm over Maggie's shoulders and started walking her up the brick walkway and into the house. She lowered her voice to a whisper. "Golly. Maggie, when someone says I dare you, you take it all the way."

"It's just for the wedding, Rachel. Nick's not following directions. I told him just to be my date, nothing more."

"So, you gonna rein him in or let this play out? I always liked that guy, you know. And maybe this could turn into something—"

"It's not going anywhere. Trust me. I feel nothing for him. I'm just doing this to keep the well-meaning aunts from fixing me up."

Rachel laughed. "Cousin Wilbur was quite the catch. My aunt Edna still thinks you two should give it another go."

"If this thing with Nick goes south," Maggie said, sending a second glare in Nick's direction. He just kept on wearing that smug smirk, clearly not one bit sorry. "Dear old Wilbur might be a better choice."

FOUR

NICK WAS IN hell.

A quintet of chatty women surrounded him, in a devil's den of tulle and silk and flowers and all kinds of womanly whatnots. They sprayed questions at him like machine guns—*Where'd you meet? What was your first date? Are you in love?*—and Nick fumbled his way through the first answer while M.J. looked horrified.

This was what he got for being spontaneous. When M.J. had accused him of never being spontaneous, it had struck a nerve somewhere inside him, and the next thing he knew, he'd been spouting, "We're dating."

It was kind of assumed, wasn't it? A girl brought a man to a wedding, dating was one of those presupposed notions. But Maggie had reacted like he'd sprayed her with weed killer.

"We, uh, met at work," he said.

"Oooh," said one of the women, a blonde named Susie who was tying ribbons around silk flowers. Katie Ann was sitting behind M.J., doing something with pins to M.J.'s hair, after spending the first twenty minutes putting makeup on his reluctant coworker. *She looked amazing either way,* he thought, but the makeup and hair added a little extra something. Before his eyes,

M.J.'s long, dark brown locks were tumbled into a pile on top of her head, leaving little tempting whispers along her neck. It was the first time he'd seen her in something other than a ponytail, and he found himself wondering what it would be like to remove those pins one at a time, and watch those sexy waves tumble to her shoulders.

"Does that mean you get to see him in nothing but a pair of shorts and a hammer, Maggie?" Susie asked.

"Uh, well, no. I mean, if he didn't wear a shirt, he could get cut or hurt." M.J. dipped her gaze to fashion another bow out of the pink ribbon in her lap. He couldn't tell if she was glad he rarely went without a shirt or disappointed.

The women were all sitting around Rachel's grandparents' dining room table, assembling wedding favors. Nick had tried to help, but found out pretty fast that he was all thumbs when it came to tying skinny ribbons into blooming bows and attaching them to silvery bags of mints. Nick stifled a laugh when he saw M.J. mutter a curse after her second attempt at a bow failed. Seemed he wasn't the only one flunking Wedding Favors 101.

"But Maggie would be there to bandage you right up, wouldn't she?" Susie curved an arm around M.J.'s shoulders and gave her a wink.

M.J. shifted in her seat. "Uh, well . . ."

He'd never seen M.J. so discomfited or at a loss for words. She had a sharp retort for everything, and a sharper tongue that could spar with him any day of the week.

A tongue he'd wanted so badly to brush against when he'd almost kissed her. A tongue that enticed and tempted him. A tongue he wanted to feel on him right now.

Whoa. That wasn't the right train of thought. As far as M.J was concerned, this was all an act. If he came on too strong, she'd shut the whole thing down, and he'd lose his best opportunity to show her how he felt.

Uh-huh. And saying they might get caught up in the wedding fever wasn't coming on too strong?

"So you didn't answer us." Katie Ann, finished now with M.J.'s hair, turned toward Nick and propped her chin in her hands. "Where'd you go on your first date? Was it super-romantic? I hope so, because the men I've been dating think romance is saying 'Excuse me' after they fart." She sighed.

"Our first date?" He glanced at M.J., who looked like she wished the floor would open up and swallow her whole. "It's going to sound silly. Probably not romantic, either."

"Oh, tell us," Katie Ann said. "It's got to be better than the 'Hey, baby, let's get some BK and hit the sheets' proposition I got last week."

Nick caught M.J.'s gaze. She started shaking her head no, but he barreled forward anyway. "You girls know M.J. She's not exactly a hearts-and-flowers girl. So I thought our first date should be the kind that would suit her. She told me once she'd never been in a convertible, so I borrowed one from a friend of mine. One of those old sixties-style convertibles, big as a boat. I packed us a picnic, then showed up on her doorstep just before sunset."

M.J. had stopped shaking her head. She was watching him, her gaze cautious, and maybe, if he was reading her right, interested.

"Then what?" Susie asked.

"Yeah, then what?" Katie echoed.

"Should I tell them?" he asked M.J. "Or would you rather?"

M.J. hesitated, and for a second he thought it would all fall apart, then a smirk curved across her face. "Then he took me to the beach, and we set up the picnic on the sand and watched the sun set."

"Oh, that's so romantic." Katie Ann sighed.

"Until I got food poisoning the next morning from Nick's cooking." M.J.'s grin widened, as if saying, *Top that.*

"Nothing says romance like a day spent on the bathroom floor," M.J. added.

"Ah, but I was there the next day with crackers and ginger ale," he said. "And when you felt better that night, we took the convertible back to the beach and counted the stars."

That elicited more shrieks from the women in the group, who all insisted that it was the most romantic thing they'd ever heard. "Tell us more," Susie said. "What else have you two done?"

M.J. got to her feet and put up her hands to stop them. "This week is Rachel's week, not mine. And like Nick said, I'm not the hearts-and-flowers kind. All this talk of romance is making me a little nauseous."

"Then you have to at least promise to be a girlie girl this

week," Rachel said. "Because nothing turns you into Miss-Next-to-the-Altar like a little bridesmaid-immersion therapy."

Promise to be a girlie girl this week? What did that mean? The M.J. that Nick knew had never worn a single thing that couldn't be ripped or torn or painted on. Had never been in impractical shoes or painted her nails or worn more than a little lip gloss. Even today, she was wearing shorts and a V-neck T-shirt in a pale green that made her eyes seem even more emerald than usual.

If *girlie girl* meant more of this hair he wanted to unfetter, and lips he wanted to kiss, hell, yes, he was all for it. If only to tease the hell out of M.J. when they got back to Rescue Bay.

Rachel's grandmother, Hattie, entered the room with a platter of cupcakes and a bottle of wine. She was a short, thin woman with a wide smile and a generous hug for everyone she met. Her gray hair was cut short and curled tight to her head, and accented by bright red cat-eye glasses that gave her a sassy edge, much like her granddaughter, who looked like a younger and blonder version of Hattie. Rachel's grandmother had welcomed him like a long-lost member of the family, and she'd given M.J. the biggest hug he'd ever seen. It was clear to Nick that M.J. adored the woman, and for good reason.

"My Lord, what are you girls doing to this poor boy?" Hattie said. "Stop torturing him."

"We're just trying to get to know him, Grandma," Rachel said. "Before we give him our stamp of approval for Maggie."

"Well, ya'll can do that later. Let the poor boy go downstairs." Hattie ushered him out of the room and opened the door to the basement. "My husband and J.W. are down there, hiding from all things girl. You go on now and join them."

Nick thanked her and headed down the stairs, where, thank God and all that was holy, Rachel's grandfather and her fiancé were watching a baseball game. Herbert Wilson—Rachel's grandfather—got to his feet, reached into a small fridge beside his recliner and pulled out a beer, tossing it to Nick. Unlike his wife, Herbert was tall, with a military haircut and a stern jaw, but a friendly face. "You were up there with all those women all this time?"

"Almost got corralled into making wedding favors. Whatever those are."

"Take it from me," J.W. said, waving to the seat beside him, "you want to steer clear of them this entire week. I damned near got trampled like a calf at a bullfight for saying, 'Hey, maybe we don't need three million floral arrangements.'"

"Take it from an old married man," Herbert said, wagging a finger at his grandson-in-law-to-be, "you let the women pick the wedding stuff. The best marriages are the ones that are based on 'Yes, dear.'"

J.W. raised his beer. "To 'Yes, dear.'"

Herbert knocked bottles with him. Nick gave a tiny tap. "I don't know if I'll ever be a 'Yes, dear' guy."

J.W. snorted. "I used to say the same thing. But now . . ."

"Now you're marrying the second-best woman in this county. Next to my Hattie, of course." Herbert grinned.

A long, slow smile curved across J.W.'s face. "There is that."

Someone scored a home run, the guys let out a cheer, and the conversation about women was dropped in favor of a debate on the latest trade by the Red Sox. This was territory where Nick felt comfortable. Sports. Beer. Grunting among men.

Except his mind kept straying to M.J. To what she was doing, saying, drinking. How she'd looked with her hair pinned up, soft tendrils curling along her neck, as if whispering to him to come closer, to taste that soft skin along her jawline, her nape.

On a commercial break, Herbert tossed him a second beer. "I've known Maggie since she was no taller than a blade of grass. She's a good girl, and one that's almost family."

Nick shifted in his seat under Herbert's direct gaze. It felt as if the man could see the lie he had told, the fraud he was fabricating. "She's great. I've known her a long time myself. Can't imagine going a day without seeing her."

"Then you'll know that she's one of a kind, like my Hattie and my Rachel. So if you break her heart, you'll have half of Chatham Ridge comin' after you with pitchforks."

"And shotguns," J.W. added. "We take the chivalry thing seriously around here."

What if Nick told them he was only pretending to love M.J.? That the whole thing was nothing more than a paid gig? He had no doubt he'd be drawn and quartered before the day's end. "I have nothing but the best of intentions."

Which was true—even if M.J. didn't know it.

"Good to know, considering I didn't see no ring on that girl's finger," J.W. said. He exchanged a glance with Herbert, who gave a little nod. "By week's end, we'll be expecting you to prove your intentions. We take care of our own 'round here, and you best remember that."

FIVE

OH, HELL. MAGGIE hadn't expected this.

"I didn't know we'd be . . . sharing a room," Maggie said to Nick, staring at the two beds before her. The bedroom, located on the second floor of Hattie's old house, was small but neat, with blue walls and wooden floors that squeaked. A slight breeze danced in through the open windows, cast about the space by the whirring ceiling fan above them. Years ago, this had been her bedroom, but back then, it had had a single twin bed and seemed much more spacious. With Nick in the room, the space from her childhood suddenly seemed tight . . . intimate.

"I kinda like it," Nick said. "Makes me feel like I'm ten years old again."

She arched a brow. "And when did you stop acting like you were ten years old?"

Nick put a hand over his heart. "Ouch. You wound me, M.J."

She pivoted toward Nick and gave his chest a pat. It was solid and strong, like concrete right after it set. Damn. "I can't wound you, you big he-man."

He covered her hand with his own and pressed it against

the hard, solid planes. Never had the words *pectoral muscles* seemed so . . . tempting. "Au contraire."

She laughed and tried to tug her hand out, but he held firm. God, when he looked at her like that, it made something flip inside her. Since when did Nick turn her on with just a look or a few words? The second she'd started calling him her boyfriend, he'd taken on new dimensions in her silly mind. As if this whole charade was real, which it most definitely wasn't. "Since when do you speak French?"

"Since I started wooing you."

"You"—she wriggled her hand away—"are not wooing me. Not for real."

"Are you saying I couldn't woo you if I wanted to?"

"We already covered that ground the other day." When he'd almost kissed her and damned near made her heart stop. Oh, Nick could woo all right. It was the after-woo that worried her. "I'm saying you're not my type."

"Oh, really?" He leaned against the bedpost and crossed his arms over his chest. "And what is your type?"

She flipped out her index finger. "Dependable."

"I show up at work on time. Every day."

"You're getting paid to be there. That's different." She flipped out another finger. "Responsible."

"I'm responsible."

She arched a brow. "For what?"

"For providing beer at a party." He chuckled. "Seriously, I'm responsible for making sure the work gets done on time with no injuries and no cost overruns."

"Again, you're getting paid for that. Totally different from a relationship with a human being."

"How do you know what I'm like in a relationship? You've never dated me."

"I have observed from afar. Sometimes not far enough."

He leaned in, his ocean-colored eyes assessing hers. "Is that a hint of jealousy I hear in your voice?"

Instead of answering that question—because clearly, it should be obvious she wasn't a bit jealous—Maggie spun away from him and tossed her bag up onto the mattress. It landed with a solid thunk. "I call top."

A slight grin played on his lips. "And why do you assume you get to be on top?"

"Because I like to be in control." She poked a finger at his chest. "And because you're my subordinate this week."

"Subordinate, huh?" A devilish gleam lit his eyes, sent a tremor through her gut. "Sounds like things could get kinky in here."

"Don't get any ideas, Casanova. As soon as that bedroom door shuts, we're back to a hands-off policy."

"Well, given our sleeping arrangement"—he gestured toward the bunk beds flanking the southern wall—"I'd say hands-off will be pretty easy to stick to."

Maggie told herself that was a good thing, while she grabbed her nightshirt and toiletries and headed to the single bathroom on the second floor. That the last thing she wanted was to touch Nick. Except the few times he had touched her—in the truck, on the ride down here, when they'd first arrived—had awakened something inside her.

Oh my God. She needed to stop reading the romance novel the book club picked for this month. Was she seriously thinking good-time Charlie over there was going to make her take a risk on love? Hadn't she seen him, in action, one too many times? Nick made dating an Olympic sport, and Maggie was not interested in competing. She was building her career, carving out her name in the construction industry, working on getting her contractor's license. None of which involved falling for Nick Patterson.

A minute later, she was changed into an oversize Tampa Bay Rays T-shirt and had her hair loose around her shoulders, her face bare of the traces of makeup from earlier. She padded into the bedroom, stowed her toiletries inside her bag, then turned around to find Nick staring at her. He was still dressed, and damned if a part of her wasn't disappointed. It had to have been Rachel's comment about seeing him shirtless still ringing in Maggie's mind.

"What?" she said.

"Nothing. You just . . . well, you have amazing legs."

She glanced down. The T-shirt came to mid-thigh length, covering more of her body than her shorts did. "Same legs I have every day."

"Yeah, but . . ." He cleared his throat. "Uh, you said you wanted to be on top?"

The phrase flashed an image in her mind of her climbing on top of Nick, her hands on his bare chest, riding him with her head thrown back while his palms captured her breasts. She glanced at the bottom bunk and for a second, saw him there, her straddling his hips—

Whacking her head on the frame of the top bunk.

Apropos of any decision to sleep with Nick, meaning it would be stupid to even think it. The last thing she wanted to do was be one more woman spinning through the revolving door of Nick's love life. She hoisted herself into the upper bunk and slid under the blanket. "Let's just go to bed."

"You're right. It's going to be a busy day tomorrow."

She peeked over the edge of the bed. "What do you mean, it's going to be a busy day?"

"Didn't Rachel tell you? J.W. and her grandpa invited me to go fishing. Taking a boat out and bringing home dinner to the womenfolk like real he-men." He let out a little grunt.

"Womenfolk?"

Nick grinned. "Yup."

She shook her head and rolled back into her bunk. "You are a Neanderthal, Nick Patterson."

A second went by, another. She thought maybe he'd gone to sleep, then she felt a movement and there he was, his sandy hair and ocean eyes so close to her, the warmth of his skin filling the space between them. "Should I drag you off to my cave and have my way with you then?"

She rolled over and tugged the blanket up to her ears. "You wouldn't dare."

In one fell swoop, he scooped her up and hauled her off the bed, then dove into the bottom bunk, curling a leg over her burritoed body. "There. Now I've got you and I can have my way with you."

She laughed, and tried to wrangle free, but Nick's strong leg kept her in place. She arched against him, but he only held her tighter, leaning in until the distance between them erased. "Nick! What are you doing?"

"Proving I'm a Neanderthal." He shifted until he was over her. Maggie was pinned inside the envelope of the blanket, unable to wrestle free. Truth be told, Maggie wasn't trying very hard.

Nick was there, a face as familiar as the sunrise, yet in the dim light of the room, his features had a mysterious, dark edge. Her hands itched to trace the line of his jaw, the ridges of his mouth. To feel his body against hers, without the layer of blanket between them.

"Admit it," Nick said.

"Admit what?"

"That I'm an evolved man."

"You are . . ."

"What?"

Holy hell hot. Turning me on. Flipping the tables on me. "A Neanderthal," she teased, then let out a squeal when he pinned her tighter.

"Take it back."

Maggie laughed. "No. I refuse. It's the truth."

He reached a hand between them and tickled her waist. She bucked against him and laughed. "Take it back." His voice was hot and tempting.

"Never!"

He tickled her again and Maggie wriggled harder, flailing in vain against the blanket that bound her in place. She moved, Nick reached, and his hand rubbed against her breast. Electricity arced through her body and she gasped.

His eyes darkened. Even through the layer of blanket, Maggie could feel his erection, hard and insistent against her leg. That grin she knew so well toyed at the edges of his lips. "What were we arguing about?"

"Uh . . ." Her mind went blank. "I forgot."

"Me, too." He raised a hand to brush the bangs away from her face, the move so sweet, so tender, Maggie melted.

What was wrong with her? When had Nick ever affected her like this? Was it just the wedding? The close quarters? Or was she so caught up in the fantasy of being his girlfriend that her hormones were starting to believe it, too?

"Nick . . ." But her voice trailed off. The objection died in her throat.

He leaned in and kissed her, a long, slow, tender kiss, the kind that seemed to simmer on a stove all day like a good stew, sliding across her lips with a feather touch, then pressing harder, deeper. His hand tangled in her hair, and she almost sighed with the sheer pleasure of that easy, soft touch. A faint shadow of stubble scratched against her chin as he deepened the kiss, sending her hormones into a frenzy. It was rough and soft, fast and slow, and she found herself wanting to stay wrapped in this blanket underneath Nick for the next hundred years.

Wait. This was *Nick*. The man who didn't stay with a woman for a hundred hours, never mind a hundred days or a hundred years. She turned away, breaking the kiss. "Nick, we can't be doing that. Not . . . alone, meaning no one is here to see us. Doing it here just . . . confuses things."

His eyes were murky, unreadable. He drew back, and slid off of her. "You're right. I guess I took my job too seriously. I'm not earning overtime, am I?"

The truth, even as a joke, stung a little. "Not in my budget, sorry."

"We should—" he began.

"Go back to our own beds," she finished. Maggie started to wriggle out of the blanket, but Nick stepped out of the bed, scooped her into his arms like she was nothing more than a loaf of bread, and lifted her onto the top bunk.

"Sleep tight," he said, then ducked below to his own space. "Don't let the bedbugs bite. Or the Neanderthals tackle you."

"I'm trying not to," she whispered, and the warm night air caught the words and whisked them away.

Six

THE SUN BROKE over the lake, speckling the water with gold. Nick took a long gulp of coffee from the travel mug Hattie had thrust at him as he stumbled out the door behind the others this morning. He'd nearly drained the cup and was still stifling yawns. "Damn, it's early," he said.

Herbert chuckled. "Early? Boy, I thought you worked construction. Do they start working at noon down there in Florida?"

"No, sir. I'm usually on the site by seven at the latest." He took another gulp of coffee and rubbed the tired out of his eyes, then slipped his sunglasses into place. Damn, if he didn't know better, he'd think he was hungover. Jackhammers pounded in his head, the sun burned his eyes, and every inch of him longed to crawl back into bed. "Just didn't sleep so good last night."

Herbert shifted the handle on the motor and steered around some lily pads. "Cool enough up there? I know it can get pretty damned muggy on that second floor. I been meaning to switch out that ceiling fan. They got these fancy ones now with remote controls."

"The temperature was fine," Nick said. The air temp, anyway. Between himself and M.J., the temperature had risen to levels usually measured in Kelvins. Tumbling around in his bed, separated by only a thin cotton blanket, what had started as a joke quickly shifted into something that treaded on the edge of sex.

And that was why he'd barely slept the rest of the night. He'd tossed and turned, acutely aware of M.J. in the bunk above him, wearing only a T-shirt and white lacy panties. He'd only had a glimpse of those panties, but it had been a glimpse that had stayed with him all night. In the couple hours of sleep he'd managed to grab, his dreams had been filled with her.

When his alarm went off, he'd peered over the top bunk, but M.J. was already gone, her bed made, leaving nothing but the scent of her perfume on the pillow.

What had he expected? A note? A single red rose tucked into a copy of *Pride and Prejudice*? Seriously, any more of this, and he would turn into a girl.

Herbert shut off the boat and dropped the anchor. "All right, let's get this fishing trip started."

Nick reached for a pole, but Herbert put up a hand. "We aren't actually fishing, Nick. That's just so the women don't call us every five minutes with something to do for the wedding."

"Cover story," J.W. said. He reached in the cooler and pulled out a trio of beers. "If anyone asks, we were fishing all day."

"All damned day." Herbert reached into a bag by his feet. "Or at least until the beer and Cheetos are gone."

M.J. hadn't had this much girl time since she was in high school. Rachel, Katie Ann, Susie and Charlotte surrounded her like bees on a flower, pumping her for information about Nick and chattering about the wedding, dresses and flowers. The five of them had gone out for an early breakfast, then a day of errands, tidying up the last-minute details for the wedding.

Rachel looped an arm through M.J.'s as they headed out of Pancake Heaven. Rachel was nearly the same height as Maggie and wore her hair in this perfect brunet bob that accented her hazel eyes and long neck. "I am so going to regret those pancakes on Saturday."

"We'll just go for a run and burn it all off," Maggie said. "Besides, I've seen the way J.W. looks at you. You could gain four hundred pounds and grow horns on the top of your head, and he'd still be madly in love."

Rachel grinned. "He's pretty awesome, isn't he? He loves my family, lets all my nieces and nephews crawl on him like he's a human jungle gym, takes my great-aunt Daisy to church on Sundays, and still manages to slip a love note into my car while I'm sleeping." She fished a paper out of her pocket and danced it in the air. "He wrote about how he loves my smile, how he melts when I walk into a room, and how marrying me will be the best decision he ever made." She sighed. "He's a keeper."

A flicker of something a hell of a lot like jealousy—if Maggie had a jealous streak, which she didn't—ran through her. She'd dated men over the years, but never had she had that one all-consuming love, that man who made everything around him pale in comparison. A man who made her dreams and needs as important as his own.

Once, she had thought she had a love like that. Except it turned out she was the only one feeling that way. Once had been enough to teach her that if the road was going in only one direction, someone was going to go off a cliff. Someone like her.

Like last night when she'd wound up in bed with Nick. Kissing him. Arching up against him. Crossing all those nice, neat boundaries she had put in place two years ago. Thank God for the smothering blanket, because it was the only thing that stopped her from a bad decision.

Nick wasn't the kind of guy to leave her notes in her car, or think about how much he loved her smile. He was the kind of guy who would charm her pants off, show her an amazing time in bed, then be gone before the sun rose. No commitments, no relationships, nothing more than a good time.

She was tired of being nothing more than a good time. Of waking up alone. Of not being settled, having roots. She wanted . . .

More. She wanted the love notes and the flowers and the googly eyes. Good Lord, she had definitely been in Chatham Ridge too long. She was morphing into Rachel, who was the biggest romantic of them all.

"J.W. comes across as all manly with Grandpa and the guys, but underneath, he's just a big marshmallow." Rachel tucked the note back in her pocket and opened the door into the cake shop. The scent of vanilla and chocolate wafted up to greet them.

"I bet Nick is just like that, too," Katie Ann said. "Especially after that story he told about your first date. He's such a romantic."

Maggie snorted. "Nick? No." Then she remembered the story line she'd concocted and shook her head. "What I mean is, he wouldn't want anyone to know he's a big softy at heart."

Ha. Nick a big softy? Now she really was creating fairy tales out of thin air.

Katie Ann picked up a china plate and studied the back. In typical Katie Ann, she was wearing a pretty pink sundress today and low pumps, her hair curled and pinned on top of her head. Of all of them, Katie Ann was the only one who had done all the girlie things, modeling in pageants and hosting a giant debutante party. "Maybe I should move away. I swear, every single man in this town is either gay or related to me."

"Small-town America, keeping people celibate for thousands of years." Susie grinned, then tucked a strand of long blonde hair behind her ear. "Maybe the rest of us lonely hearts should go on a road trip. Head up to New York or something and come back with some hunky men."

"You make it sound like a hunting trip," Maggie said. "Big Game Bachelors."

A moment later, they all pronounced the cake, nearly finished for the wedding, the most beautiful ever seen. Then, just when Maggie thought the day was over, she was being shepherded off to a nail salon. Five minutes later, she had her feet in a swirling tub of hot water and a glass of champagne in her hand.

"I think we should have weddings more often," Rachel said, her voice rat-a-tatting from the shiatsu massage running up and down the back of the leather chair. "This is like heaven. Remind me to get pedicures every week."

"We'll do them for Maggie's wedding," Katie Ann said. "Assuming, that is, that Nick proposes. Which I totally think he will. That guy looks at you with stars in his eyes. If he proposes, do you think you'd come here to get married or get married on the beach?"

"A beach wedding would be awesome." Susie sighed. "If I ever get married, it'll be in Hawaii, while the sun is setting—"

"And the groom is lei-ing you." Charlotte giggled.

Laughter erupted from the pedicure chairs. A short Asian woman slipped into the space between the chairs and put

Maggie's free hand into a dish of warm, soapy water. "So rough." Her face twisted and her nose wrinkled. "Like rocks."

"I, uh, work with my hands."

"Uh-huh. Working rocks?" The woman pushed Maggie's hand deeper into the liquid. She wrinkled her nose again in distaste. "You soak. Long time." Another glance at Maggie's hands. "Long, long time."

"Better listen to the woman," Charlotte said. "I bet Nick will appreciate a nice, smooth hand on the job."

That caused another burst of laughter from the other bridesmaids, and a few snickers from the nail techs.

"I'm not—" Maggie cut off the words. She was supposed to be dating the man. Of course she'd be having sex with him. "He's, uh, not too picky."

"What man is when it comes to jobs?" Charlotte said, which sent up a whole new round of giggles.

Why had she thought this was a good idea? She should have just turned down the dare and let Rachel fix her up with her cousin again. Anything was better than talking jobs and hands and Nick. Because all it did was feed the constant fantasy reel running in her head, the one that began with that kiss last night and ended with them in bed.

The nail techs buzzed around the wedding party, filing and buffing, chattering in their native language beneath the chitchat of the bridesmaids. The other women sat back in the chairs, relaxed and at ease, but Maggie felt like inchworms were crawling up her back. She'd only been here for forty-five minutes and was already itching to leave. She could have spent the time studying for her exam or going over the plans for the reno they were starting after she and Nick returned to Rescue Bay. Or heck, chewing off her own hand and running away until the wedding was over.

The other girls had dropped the topic of Maggie's wedding to Nick, thank goodness. The lie seemed to grow in proportion to every minute she was here.

The pedicurist left for a second, then returned with a small electric tool. She settled herself on a stool and began to attack the calluses on Maggie's feet.

Maggie yanked her foot back. "Hey!"

"Like rocks. Need this." The motor whirred, spinning a sandpaper disc in a quick circle.

"That's for wood, not for feet." Maggie put up her hands. "No. No. Just . . . no."

A few words exchanged, then the pedicurist let out a long, frustrated sigh. "I just paint color." She wagged a finger in Maggie's face. "You, no complain about rocks for feet."

Rachel leaned over and gave Maggie a grin. "When was the last time you had a pedicure?"

"Somewhere between a century ago and never. You know me. I don't do this"—she waved her hand around, sending the bottle of nail polish flying, which made the nail tech curse under her breath—"stuff. Sorry about that."

The nail tech rolled her eyes, grabbed Maggie's hand and pressed it down on the table. "Stay." She muttered something to the pedicurist, who just nodded and rolled her eyes.

Maggie was pretty sure they'd said *high maintenance* in whatever language they were speaking.

"Can I get another glass of champagne, please?" Maggie said, waving to the manager of the shop. "A really, really big glass?"

Twenty minutes later, Maggie had a smudged manicure—which came from bumping the drying table when she tried to leave too soon—and a slight buzz. Four glasses of champagne had made the whole process . . . tolerable.

"Okay, girls, off to our next adventure!" Rachel said.

Maggie pressed a hand to her forehead. Her bangs cemented themselves in her still-wet nail polish. Of course. *Please don't say dress shopping. Please don't say dress shopping.*

"Dress shopping! We all need something awesome for the rehearsal dinner, right?"

"Come on, Maggie," Katie Ann said, slipping an arm through Maggie's. "Let's get you something that knocks Nick's socks off."

They hustled her into a dressing room at Daisy's Dress Barn and shoved dresses at her over the top of the door. Dresses of all colors, styles. Some with belts, some with zippers that slid up the side, treading too close to her armpit for comfort. By the time she had wriggled her way into the third dress, Maggie was sweaty and tired and needed another drink.

"Let's see it!" Susie called. "Come on out—do a little spin."

Maggie tromped out of the fitting room and flung out her

arms. "There. You saw it." She turned to go back for dress number 572.

"No, no, don't take it off yet." Rachel grabbed Maggie's hand and tugged her back. "Stand on the pedestal. And here, put these on with it." She slid off the wedges she was wearing and held them out to Maggie. "Go ahead, they won't bite."

The others all stared at her. All women comfortable in heels and dresses and manicures. Unlike Maggie, who would have paid them all to leave her in her work boots and T-shirts, her hair in a sloppy ponytail and nothing more than ChapStick on her lips. Maggie would have bolted, but she'd promised Rachel, and it was her job, as maid of honor, to participate in all prewedding insanity. So Maggie slipped her bare feet into the wedges, wobbling from side to side. Rachel braced her on one side, Susie on the other, and together they hoisted her up the step onto the carpeted pedestal that faced a quartet of mirrors. Rachel gasped.

"What? What?" Maggie spun, glancing down at the dress. "Did I rip it?"

"No, not at all. Look at yourself." Rachel stepped to the side and waved toward the mirrors. "Maggie, you're *beautiful*. I mean, you were always beautiful, but this just makes you look even more so."

The mirror reflected back an hourglass shape, outlined by a black dress that scooped across the front, tapered in at her waist, then flared out like a bell. The waist she normally hid beneath an untucked T-shirt was pronounced and defined, and the legs that most days were covered with paint or sawdust seemed almost . . . elegant when paired with the heels.

"You are beautiful," Susie agreed.

"You have to buy that dress," Katie Ann said. "Definitely."

"Nick will pass out when he sees you. Guaranteed." Charlotte nodded.

The thought of Nick passing out—or even passing her a compliment that wasn't based on her carpentry skills—filled Maggie with an odd longing. Just because she wanted to make the act more believable. That was all.

Then why did her mind wander to Nick the rest of the day? When she got back to Hattie and Herbert's house, she hung the garment bag on a hook in the bedroom closet, beside the white bag with her maid-of-honor dress and the row of Nick's dress shirts. She fingered the soft cotton, slipping down the sleeve, along the cuff, imagining his arms, his wrists, his hands.

God, what had happened to her? Was she overcome by the scent of acetone or something? No way was she falling for Nick Patterson. No. Way.

But he lingered in her thoughts as she changed and got ready for book club. She heard a noise in the driveway and looked out the window, feeling a stone of disappointment when she saw the white mail truck instead of J.W.'s pickup returning from fishing with Nick.

"You're looking out that window like you left a diamond on the driveway," Hattie said, coming to stand beside Maggie.

Maggie pivoted toward Rachel's grandma and gave her a quick hug. Hugging Hattie was like wrapping her arms around a fresh-baked loaf of bread. Soft, warm, comforting. Hattie was the closest thing Maggie had to a real family, the stand-in grandma who had welcomed her as one of her own all those years ago. "Just enjoying being here again, Grandma Hattie."

"Seems to me maybe you're looking for your heart's twin," Hattie said. "We all have one, you know. And yours is out there."

Out where? Maggie started to ask, then stopped herself. Good God, she was getting caught up in this wedding fever. Turning into a real-life romance novel. "Oh, I am far from falling in love. I've got a career to build, a business to start—"

Hattie put a soft hand on Maggie's cheek. "And you will. But it won't mean a thing without somebody to be the wheels beneath your engine, sweetie."

Maggie laughed. "I don't need someone else, Grandma Hattie. Besides, haven't you always told me to be bold, be myself, be strong? This car is driving itself and doing just fine."

Hattie's light blue eyes softened, and a bittersweet smile filled her face. "I'm proud of you for all that, sweetie. I really am. But one of the greatest joys in my life has been marrying Herbert. When you share your life with someone, you share your memories, and there's something . . . special about that. Because only you two, in this whole wide world, hold those memories together, like bookends on a life. Then you're strong together, which is something so mighty powerful, it can take on near anything the world hands you."

Maggie gave Hattie another hug. "I'm not quite ready to be

somebody's bookend, Grandma Hattie. All I want to do is enjoy being here with the people I love."

A little while later, Maggie and Rachel were just heading out the door with copies of *Dared to Love* under their arms, when Nick, J.W. and Herbert finally returned. Rachel let out a squeal and launched herself into J.W.'s arms. He drew her into a deep kiss, holding her against his waist with one arm, tangling his hand in her hair with the other, as if they'd been apart for years, not hours.

Maggie had to look away. Not just because they were kissing like they were setting a Guinness world record, but because the way J.W. cradled Rachel's head made her think of Nick, of that kiss last night in the bunk bed. Of how much she'd wanted it to continue.

Because she was insane like that. She'd clearly gotten all wrapped up in Grandma Hattie's words, to the point of no common sense.

Nick plucked the book out from under her arms and smirked at the cover. "Is this the discussion for the night?"

She snatched it back. "It's called book club. Remember?"

He leaned in close, his breath a warm tickle along her neck. "Sounds like an excuse to talk about sex."

"We don't talk about sex." Well, they had today, more than once. But only in the context of manicures. And cake. And that cute waiter at lunch.

"Too bad. Because I really like to talk about sex." He drew back and his eyes met hers. "With you."

Was this part of his act? Or was he being serious? Before she could decide, Nick had taken a step away. His face took on a look of apology. "As much as I'd love to kiss you like that," he nodded toward J.W. and Rachel, "it'll have to wait. I'm covered in fish guts. I should hit the shower."

The word *shower* flashed an image of a naked, soapy Nick in her mind. Her with a loofah, reaching all his hard-to-reach places. "Uh . . . good. But, uh, we're heading out. I won't be back till late."

Why was she telling him all that? Nick didn't truly care when she returned or where she was going. It wasn't like she was trying to schedule a time to have—uh, talk about—sex with Nick. No, not at all.

He lifted her chin with the edge of his hand, then leaned in and pressed a sweet, too-short kiss to her lips. "I'll miss you, honey."

Then he was gone, heading into the house and saving her from a response. A good thing, because hormones had muddled her brain. What was that? Where had Nick learned to look at a woman like that? And why did her insides dissolve at a simple touch of his hand?

"That Nick is quite the catch," Rachel said. She thumbed the remote on her car, and the women climbed in. "If I wasn't already engaged to and madly in love with J.W., I'd go after him myself."

The thought caused a fissure of jealousy in Maggie's chest. Insane. Nick had dated dozens of women since she'd met him, and she'd never been one bit jealous. Definitely an allergic reaction to acetone.

The talk shifted to the wedding plans and away from Nick and Maggie, thank goodness. Maybe she could go an entire evening without talking about the one man in the world who drove her crazy.

As soon as Maggie stepped through the door of the Happy Ending Bookstore, her heart swelled. She loved this silly old shop, with its hand-hewn wood floors and brass wall sconces. She loved the muffins in the case and the scent of fresh-brewed coffee mingling with the warm and slightly musty smell of old books. Seeing all her friends there made her feel as if she'd truly come home.

And she loved Noralee, who had owned the Happy Ending for three decades, ever since her mother died. Noralee came rushing forward, enveloping Maggie in a tight hug. "Darlin', I have missed your pretty face around here."

"I've missed being here."

"I made your favorite cookies. Chocolate cherry. And I put a pile of books on hold for you, ones I figured you'd take a shining to."

That was what Maggie loved about Noralee. The bookstore owner welcomed her customers like family, always going that extra little bit to let them know she cared. With Noralee, it wasn't about good business—it was about good person-ness. From the bun of gray hair on her head to her practical tennis shoes, Noralee Bondurant was a woman who loved those in her life.

Noralee drew back and parked a fist on her ample hip. "What's this I hear about our always-planning-to-be-single girl bringing along a date to the weddin' and keepin' it a secret? And where is this hunk-o-burnin'-love who stole your heart?"

"I'll bring him by before I head out of town," Maggie said. "We're not serious, Noralee, just dating."

"Not serious? I seen the way that man looks at you, Maggie, and he is as serious as a church pew," Susie said. "Why, I wouldn't be surprised if he got down on one knee—"

Maggie put up her hands before Susie went any farther down that crazy-idea path. "Oh, Nick is not going to do that. Believe me."

"If there's one thing I've learned about men," Noralee said, "it's that they're about as easy to predict as rattlesnakes on a hot day. Your man might just be cooking up a surprise at this very minute."

Charlotte put a hand on Maggie's shoulder. "He might get so swept up in wedding fever that the question just kind of pops on out."

"Like biscuits in a can," Katie Ann said, and the others laughed.

Good God, no, she didn't want him to just pop out with a ring. And knowing Nick, he wouldn't do it without a bonus or pay raise anyway. It was all an act, she reminded herself, all an act. Except for the times when they were alone and it felt all too real.

Crazy thoughts.

"Aren't we all here to discuss a book, not my love life?" Maggie held her copy aloft. "Besides, there are cookies over there with my name on them."

The women crossed to the back of the room, settling into a circle of wingback chairs that fronted a cozy fireplace. The flames flickered in the low light, casting soft golden shadows over the floor and wooden coffee table. Drinks and cookies were dispersed, with coffee quickly chased by glasses of wine. And then the book club got down to business.

Charlotte clapped, got their attention, then held up the book. The group took turns with leadership, and Maggie wasn't surprised that Charlotte, the die-hard romantic in the group, would

choose this one. Charlotte had been dreaming of her wedding day
since she found her first *Brides* magazine in seventh grade. As far
as Maggie knew, Charlotte still had a hope chest stuffed full of
pictures and trinkets she was saving for the big day. All she
needed to add, she always said, was a man. "All right, ladies, let's
talk about our first pick in our new Life Lessons theme."

"Life Lessons theme?" Maggie asked.

"If we were going to choose books to read, we wanted them
to have a message. You know, a takeaway. So we're each choosing a different book to share with the rest of the group." Rachel
reached for her copy of *Dared to Love*. "Which is why I picked
this one. Because daring to fall in love with J.W. was the scariest
thing I've ever done—"

"Besides that bungee jump off the Howard Bridge," Susie
cut in.

"Besides that." Rachel laughed. "And I want all of you to
know how awesome it is to take that leap and find someone
amazing at the bottom."

"Wait, you picked this book?" Maggie asked. "You, the
one who vowed she was never going to get married when we
were back in high school? The one who thought romance and
flowers was a silly idea?"

"Yup. When Mr. Right comes along, it can make even the
most die-hard single girl fall, and fall hard." Rachel grinned.

"Like you with Nick," Susie said to Maggie. "Am I right?"

The last topic Maggie wanted to discuss was her and Nick,
all wrapped in some romantic bow. "I think Rachel's got enough
romance going right now for all of us put together."

Rachel clasped the book to her heart. Her diamond reflected
the firelight and spattered sparkles on the table. "I know. It's all
because of J.W."

"If he wasn't such a great guy, I would hate you right now,"
Susie said. "All I want is a guy like Logan in this book. He's
ah-mazing."

"Oh my God, yes," Katie Ann said. "The way he takes care
of her after she has that fall—"

Susie sighed. "And how he carries her down the aisle at
the end—"

"And don't forget that kiss on page seventy-five," Maggie said.
"When he looked into her eyes and drew her close, it was . . ."

They all turned to look at her.

"What?"

"You sighed when you said that," Rachel said. "You never sigh."

"Or wax romantic," Charlotte added.

"Or get pedicures," Maggie said, her voice sharp. "People change."

"Or sexy guys in shorts change them." Susie grinned. "Seems being with Nick is having a good effect on you. You're getting all girlie."

"That girlie stuff won't last past the wedding, believe me." Maggie waved a hand over her shorts, her faded T-shirt. After a long day on the girlie side, Maggie had changed back into her comfort zone. But still she felt off, as if the clothes didn't quite fit. It had nothing to do with the way J.W.'s eyes lit up when he saw Rachel, all pretty in a summer dress and low heels, and the little bit of envy Maggie had felt at that. "You can't work in my industry and be taken seriously if you're running around in pink skirts and heels all day."

"Maybe not, but you can get a whole lot of men to do your bidding." Katie Anne laughed. "And that's always a good thing."

Susie picked up a cookie and took a bite. "Speaking of men doing a woman's bidding, what did you guys think of the heroine daring the hero to marry her in this book? That was quite the twist on marriage of convenience."

"I liked it." Katie Ann grinned. "I think women should always do the asking."

Charlotte sighed. "I don't. I like the romance and wine and flowers."

Noralee came walking over to the group with a new batch of cookies. She was the consummate hostess, which was why book club was so popular. It was like going to a favorite aunt's house—a favorite aunt who had serious baking skills. "When you get to my age, honey, you're happy just to have the wine. After you drink that, you can't stay awake long enough for the romance anyway."

They all laughed, then took turns pointing out their favorite parts. The question came round to Maggie, and when she looked down at her book, she realized she had dog-eared page seventy-five. "That first love scene. That was my favorite."

"Really? How come?"

"It was"—*read to me by Nick in that dark, husky voice of his*—"sweet. Tender."

That caused the others to let out a woo-hoo. "I think the wedding mood is rubbing off on Maggie," Katie Ann said. "She's becoming positively romantic."

It had to come from being around the other bridesmaids. Getting caught up in the wedding mood, as Katie Ann said. The romance novel in her hands, which still rang with Nick's voice whenever she looked down at the pages.

Except come Saturday night, this fairy tale—if that's what she could call it—would end, with her and Nick going back to being nothing more than coworkers. It was what she wanted—to get this over with and go back to the safety and security of the world she knew, the world she controlled. The one where she was on track with her career and not worried about snagging her manicure in her bangs.

Yet even as she told herself that was what she wanted, an acetone-addled side of her brain wanted the exact opposite. That side wanted Nick to bring that romance novel to life, and for her to be the starring heroine.

She stuffed another cookie in her mouth, but even the sugar didn't quell the nagging fear that by starting this charade with Nick, she had opened a door she was never going to be able to shut all the way.

SEVEN

NICK SAT ON the front porch of Herbert's house, sipping a beer, enjoying the night air, and thinking about M.J. It was something he did often—far more often than he'd ever told her. If someone asked M.J. what Nick Patterson did on his days off, she would say he was flipping through one-night stands faster than a blackjack dealer with a deck of cards. She had no idea the number of nights he sat in a broken wooden chair in the yard of the Money Pit and did exactly this—drink a beer and think about her.

"Thanks for your help today." J.W. came outside and handed Nick a second beer before taking a seat beside him. "When Rachel said she wanted an outdoor wedding, I thought it would be a quick, easy thing. I had no idea that I'd be spending the whole week weedwacking and setting up chairs."

Nick chuckled. "If it was up to us guys, there'd be a preacher and a thirty-second ceremony."

"And a barbecue and a case of beer."

"Amen to that." They knocked beers, then Nick leaned back on his elbows and looked up at the night sky. Few clouds filled the vast space over the state of Georgia, and the stars twinkled like a million winking eyes. "You nervous about Saturday?"

"Hell, yes, I'm nervous. I don't know a guy who isn't scared shitless about getting married. It's the whole forever thing, ya know?"

"Forever's a long time."

"But that's part of what makes it so awesome." A big smile curved across J.W.'s face. "Call me a sap, but I'm head over heels for that girl, and don't want to spend a day without her. Shit, this is gonna sound like I'm one of those guys who wears an ascot—whatever the hell that is—but when I think about waking up and not having Rachel in my life, well, it's kinda like how I felt when I watched them take Old Yeller out behind the barn. Ya know what I mean?"

Nick pictured himself framing a wall with some dude, instead of M.J. standing beside him, cracking jokes while they wrestled two-by-fours into place. Imagined finishing a long day in the hot sun with a cold beer alone, instead of beside her, sharing that sense of accomplishment. Thought of sitting on an overturned bucket, wishing for a bag of chips because he'd forgotten again and M.J. wasn't there with a knowing shake of her head and a ready bag of Ruffles.

Yeah, it was kinda like losing Old Yeller to rabies.

"So, you and Maggie," J.W. said. "Been serious a long time?"

"Not long, no," Nick said. "We work together and have been friends for a couple of years. To be honest, I'm afraid I'm going to mess that up."

"If you think dating her changes friendship, wait 'til you marry her. That changes everything in a thousand ways." J.W. grinned. "But marriage has a few perks that you don't get at work."

"True." Though Nick hadn't enjoyed any of those "perks" with M.J. The two kisses—holy shit, those had been amazing—but taking it further, well, hell, he wasn't sure that would be a good choice.

J.W. propped his elbows on his knees and let the beer dangle from his fingers. "My dad once said to me, if you meet a woman who means more to you than your truck, your dog and hunting with the boys on Saturday mornin's, then you hurry up and quit being an idiot and marry her."

"And that's what you're doing with Rachel?"

"Well, she might disagree on the stop-being-an-idiot part,

but yeah, I'd rather buy her a ring than buy a new truck. And that's sayin' something." He got to his feet. "Anyway, I better get on home. Rehearsal dinner is tomorrow."

"What, no wild bachelor party planned?"

"Nope." J.W. looked back at the house, casting his gaze toward the second story and a light that burned in the bedroom to the west, waiting for Rachel. "I already found the best woman in the world. No need to throw dollar bills at the runners-up."

J.W. said good-bye, got in his truck, and pulled out of the driveway. A four-door Mazda pulled in right after him, a stream of giggles pouring out of the open windows. M.J. and Rachel climbed out, dispensing hugs and good-byes to the others, then turned toward the porch. Rachel said something to M.J., which made her laugh, the merry sound filling the air like music.

Damn. She was beautiful when she laughed. Beautiful in the kind of way that hit a man in the gut with a one-two punch.

Rachel peeled off from M.J. "I'm going to bed. You two enjoy this beautiful night. Maybe reenact that scene from page seventy-five."

Rachel went inside. The screen door flapped shut, leaving Nick alone with M.J. The crickets chirped their night songs, and the stars sprinkled the lawn with light.

"Scene on page seventy-five?" Nick asked.

Even in the dim evening light, Nick could see crimson fill M.J.'s face. "Uh, just something from a book we're reading."

His gaze dropped to the book in her hands. The same book he'd grabbed from her a couple days ago. "What's on page seventy-five?"

"Nothing. I'm going in." She started to climb the stairs past him, but he reached out, snagged the book and started flipping pages. "Nick!"

"Sixty-five, sixty-seven, seventy-two . . . ah, here it is. Page seventy-five." He made a big production out of cracking the spine and shifting under the porch light. "Hey, wait. Isn't this the passage I read to you?"

"Yes, but that's . . . that has nothing to do with why I chose it." She let out a gust. "Give it back, please."

"Oh, really?" He tucked the book between his back and the porch post. "Then why did you tell Rachel about it?"

"Nick, I don't want to play this game again."

"What game?"

"Catch and release of my book. Just give it to me."

"Not until you tell me why you picked that passage as your favorite."

She let out a gust and tucked her hair—down and curling around her shoulders, he noticed—behind her ear. "Forget it. I'm going to bed."

He scrambled to his feet and caught her arm, spinning her toward him. She collided with his chest, her eyes wide and dark, her mouth open with surprise. Her perfume, something deep and floral, whispered between them, an enticing mystery, because M.J. never wore perfume to work. He wanted to dip his head and follow the trail of that scent, capture it along her wrists, her neck. "Tell me why."

Her mouth opened, closed. "I . . ."

"Why?"

"Because it . . . it . . . was a good scene." She shook her head and looked away. "Let me just go to bed, Nick."

But he knew, in that instant before she looked away, he knew. She'd chosen it because of the way hearing those words spoken aloud had shifted the air between them, charged it in a way that it never had been before.

Quit bein' an idiot

He'd been one for two years too long. He'd had two years to show her how he felt, two years to prove he was working on Nick 2.0, two years to open up his mouth and act on how he'd felt from that first day he saw her. Two years too damned long.

Before he could hesitate again, Nick leaned in and kissed Maggie. No preamble, no warning shot, just a searing hot kiss that detonated a roaring fury of need in his gut. She opened against him, her arms sliding around his back, her tongue darting out to play, and Nick was lost.

He scooped her into his arms and trundled down the steps and across the yard. She let out a giggle. "Where are we going?"

"It's a surprise." Then he kissed her again before she could ask any more questions. The garage door stood ajar, forgotten after their yard work earlier today, and Nick nudged it open with his knee, then carried M.J. inside and over to the black restored 1962 Lincoln convertible he'd seen there earlier today. Nick broke the kiss, then dropped her gently into the backseat and tugged open the rear suicide door.

M.J. sat up. The garage was dark, the only light from the moon outside and Maggie's wide green eyes. "What are you doing?"

"Fulfilling your fantasy." Then he shook his head and cursed. "That's not what I meant to say. I mean, you told me you'd never been in a convertible, and of course, never done it in a convertible, and I thought, since I never have either . . ." He let his voice trail off because it was still coming out all wrong. God, he was an idiot. Every time he tried to be the non-idiot he wanted to be, he went right back to sex, like a Cro-Magnon man on steroids.

"Oh, come on, Nick. You've done everything with everyone and—"

He put a finger on her lips. "I keep saying this wrong. Being here right now, in this car, isn't about who has had sex, where they did it or with whom. I brought you here because . . ." He let out a breath, prayed he was reading her right, that he wasn't about to screw up the most important relationship in his life. "I want to show you how special you are to me. And I'm saying all that stupid crap about first times and backseats because I'm scared as hell that I'm going to mess this up and lose you."

"Nick, we're friends. Good friends. We shouldn't muddle that with this." She waved between them, in that warm space infused with electricity and desire and temptation.

"I know what we have right now is pretty awesome. Hell, you're pretty much my best friend, M.J. But I want more. I've wanted more for a long time."

"I don't think I can give you more. What if—"

He put that finger on her lip again. "My grandpa always said that if you let them, *what-ifs* grow like weeds. Let one in, and another follows right behind it. I don't want to think about *what-if*. I want to think about what could be. And I think what could be is pretty damned awesome."

"Could be. Could not be."

"Always the realist." He trailed a lazy path down her cheek. He couldn't seem to stop touching her, to stop staring into those hypnotic eyes. "Do you want to know why I agreed to go with you to this wedding? To pretend to be your date?"

"Because you needed money for your renovations and a new hot water heater—"

"Because I wanted to be with you. I don't give a damn about buying a new hot water heater. I just want you. That's all. That's all I've ever wanted, M.J."

A heartbeat passed, one that seemed to last as long as a lifetime. He was so sure she would tell him to take her back to the house, that this was only a charade, that he was reading her wrong, misreading the message in her lips when they'd kissed.

"Then say my name, Nick," she whispered. "You've never said my name."

Because saying it crossed a line that he had firmly drawn in his head a long time ago. The line that kept her on the Friends divide of his life. The line that kept him from telling her what he really felt—and finally, irrevocably, change things between them. He was done waiting, done staying in the cautious lane.

He met her hypnotic eyes with his own, and thought a man could drown in those green depths. "I want *you*, Maggie. No one else."

Her lips curved in a slow, sweet smile. "I don't care if it's true. I just like hearing you say my name."

"Oh, Maggie." He leaned in closer, holding her against him, whispering the words on her lips. *Two years,* he thought. Two years too long. No more waiting. "It's true. Only you, Maggie."

She sighed, then wrapped her arms around him and pulled him down onto the black leather seat. He slid a hand beneath her shirt, up over the warm, silky skin of her belly, to cup her breast through the soft lace of her bra. The lace surprised him, like a secret side under the hard edges of Maggie. He tugged off her shirt, then tossed his own on the concrete floor, wanting her skin against his. It wasn't about sex; this was about something more. About being joined to the one woman in the world who filled in all his missing parts.

She reached up and placed a palm on his right arm. Her touch was light, curious, fingers dancing over the image. "A tiger, huh?"

It was the first time Maggie had ever touched him that wasn't for work. He felt like a middle school boy, for God's sake. "Didn't I ever tell you the story about my tattoo?"

She shook her head. "I've never seen it, either. You always wear a shirt."

"So that I don't end up, what did you say? Cut or hurt.

Because Lord knows your bandaging skills suck." But it touched him all the same that she worried and cared.

"Hey, in my defense, it was a deep cut. And you were out of everything but those little round bandages that aren't good for anything."

"Got me quite the laughs from the nurse at the emergency room at least." They shared a grin, another one of those memories that knit between them like stitches in a blanket, then he dropped his attention to the tattoo. "When I was five, my father took me to the zoo. There was a tiger there, pressed right up against the glass. He roared, and scared the devil out of me."

She laughed. "Don't be so hard on yourself. You were only five."

"My dad encouraged me to go back up to the window, to face what scared me again, and stand up to it, with the safety of the glass between us, of course. He told me that for the rest of my life, I'd always have a choice. I could run away from what scared me or face it head-on."

"And did you? Go back to the window?"

He shook his head. "That would be the Hollywood ending, wouldn't it? And then I'd become some Rocky wannabe, not afraid of anything. Nope, I ran back to my dad and begged him to take me to see the penguins instead. I didn't face that tiger again until I was fifteen, and when I went back to the zoo, with a date—"

"Of course."

"And the tiger looked so much smaller than I remembered. He was bored with me that time and just turned away and laid on a rock." Nick traced the outline of the tattoo. "But my father's lesson stayed with me, and when I turned eighteen, I got this. It's kind of my motto for going forward with things that scare me."

She waved off his words. "Oh, you're not scared of anything, Nick Patterson."

He captured her jaw with his hand and traced her bottom lip with his thumb, imagining his mouth on there, hers on his. God, she was beautiful, in a way that almost broke his heart. He wanted to protect her and hold her, all at the same time, even though he knew his tough Maggie needed neither. "I am terrified of some things. Like making love to you and ruining this great thing we have going."

"Doing this . . . it's going to change everything."

He lowered onto one arm beside her, and whisked a lock of hair off her cheek. "Are you okay with that?"

"Are you?"

He had waited two years to move forward with Maggie. Two years of telling himself that being just her friend was the best choice. Two years of wondering what it would be like to have her in his arms, in his bed, in his life. Two years of holding back because he didn't want to screw it up like he'd screwed up pretty much every other relationship in his life. "I am definitely okay with that."

Another heartbeat, her eyes wide, his breath caught in his throat. Maggie shook her head. "Me, too."

"Then let me love you, Maggie," he whispered.

"Okay," she said, the word a breath in the closed space of the car.

Maggie rose up, reaching for the hook on the back of her bra, but he put out a hand to stop her, to slow it down, to take a moment. "Don't. I've waited a long damned time to be with you, Maggie, and the last thing I want to do is rush it. I want to admire you first."

The blush returned to her cheeks, and he could see her ready a protest, but she lay back, and raised her arms over her head. "Admire away, Casanova."

"For one," he said, lowering his head to trail kisses along her neck, the valley of her shoulders, the dip between her breasts, "I'm not Casanova." His finger toyed with the white lacy edge of her bra, slipping it to one side, exposing one dark pink nipple. "And for another." He continued the trail of kisses, slower now, up the hill of her breast, and just beside the nipple, teasing, anticipating. "You are an incredibly sexy woman."

"Even in work boots?"

"Especially in work boots. And out of them." He slid his mouth along her belly, then fumbled with the snap on her shorts. He slid them down and over her hips, his gaze drinking in the flat planes of her belly, the lacy edge of her panties, the exposed breast. Seeing Maggie lying across the black leather seat like that had to be the sexiest thing he'd ever seen.

"You—"

He put a finger on her lips. "We can talk later. Right now, I want to take advantage of this backseat. And you."

She grinned and slid a hand between them to grasp his erection beneath the thick cotton of his shorts. "Then take advantage, Nick."

He lost a button tearing off his shorts, then his boxer briefs. He slid a hand beneath the lace panties and slipped a finger inside her. Maggie gasped and arched against him, all wet and warm and ready. He lowered his head to her breast, drew one nipple into his mouth and toyed with it using the tip of his tongue. She clawed at his back, wrapping one leg around his, breathing his name.

He tugged off her panties, tossing them to the floor, then braced himself with one hand on the seat, one on the floor of the low-slung convertible, and slid between her legs. When he entered her, Nick thought it felt like sliding into heaven.

Maggie met his thrusts with her own, grasping at his skin, urging him to go harder, faster. It was loud, it was hot, it was fast, but holy hell, it was good. Too soon, the tidal wave caught them both, his strokes speeding up, her moans and gasps becoming one long song, and then, he felt her contract around him and he came in one long shuddering moment that nearly killed him.

When he could breathe again, Nick curled onto the side of the bench seat and drew Maggie close. "I swear I saw stars. You are . . . incredible. I don't know how we're going to do that again in those bunk beds, but holy hell, I want you again already."

"Nick, let me up. I . . . I should get inside." Maggie slid out of his arms and sat up, reaching for her bra, her gaze averted. "I have some things to do before tomorrow."

He reached for her, but she slipped away. "Stay, Maggie. Stay for a while."

The air chilled in the garage, the moment evaporating like summer rainstorms. "I can't. I have stuff to do."

He sat up and watched her get dressed again. It was as if a switch had shifted inside her, and everything he'd said, everything they'd done, had been erased. "What aren't you telling me?"

She met his gaze, and the green in her eyes rippled like stormy water. "You were right. This . . . this changed everything."

Then she was gone and he was left in the dark.

EIGHT

MAGGIE DID A damned good job avoiding Nick for the next twenty-four hours. She'd gone straight to bed after they'd made love, feigning sleep when he'd come in the room and tried to talk to her. Then she'd gotten up early and spent the entire day with Rachel, doing last-minute wedding prep. While the guys were at the store picking up the alcohol, Maggie ran up to her room and got changed for the rehearsal dinner, then headed outside.

She just had to get through the rehearsal, the wedding, then the drive back. On Monday morning, they'd go back to normal—or a semblance of normal. Maybe if enough time passed, they would forget this ever happened.

Uh-huh. Like a Sequoia forgot about a forest fire.

A small white arbor had been set up at the back of Herbert and Hattie's yard. Tomorrow, flowers and ivy would be wound into the lattice, and a white runner would be spread in the aisle between the chairs. The wooden dance floor had been installed earlier today on the south side of the lawn, with a table for the DJ and several long buffet tables awaiting tablecloths and food. Christmas lights had been strung in the trees, casting a soft white twinkle over the space. Beautiful and romantic, like something out of a movie.

"I'm so nervous," Rachel said, twisting her hands together as she spun and took in the preparations in the yard. "I keep thinking I'm going to forget something."

"Even if you do, it won't matter. As long as you have J.W. and a preacher, you're all set."

Rachel smiled. "That's true. And my grandpa to walk me down the aisle. I sure wish my dad had lived to see me get married." Tears filled Rachel's eyes and the smile faded. "I miss him. He would have loved J.W., would have loved this whole thing. It's so unfair that he's not here."

Maggie took Rachel's hand and led her toward the center of the yard where the leafy oaks and Spanish moss yielded to one bright circle of lawn. Tomorrow, the white paper runner would start in this exact spot and lead down to where J.W. would be waiting to make Rachel his wife.

A tiny flicker of envy ran through Maggie. What would it be like to have a man like J.W.—*a man like Nick?* her mind asked—waiting for her, with a proud smile on his face and a heart filled with hope?

This was Rachel's day. Not Maggie's. And Maggie wasn't interested in becoming someone's missus. Making dinners on weekdays and keeping the laundry folded. No—she had her own dreams and goals, and they didn't involve marriage.

Maggie reached into her pocket and pulled out a smooth, flat stone, a little smaller from all the wear over the years, but still almost the same as the day she'd gotten it. She ran her thumb over the surface, as calm as glass. "Do you remember when your dad gave me this?"

Rachel nodded. "That summer we camped at the lake. We were, like, eleven."

"And not into boys yet."

Rachel laughed. "Yep. Camping lost its appeal after we got a look at Robbie Lee Cooper without a shirt on."

"He was the David Beckham of middle school, wasn't he?" Maggie put the stone in Rachel's palm and closed her friend's hand over it. Maggie loved Rachel's family, so normal, so welcoming. They'd taken her on camping trips and family vacations, taught her to play ball and make chicken salad. She'd been as close to Rach and her family as she could be without that blood connection, and even now, staying here, standing here, it felt like being home. Every good memory Maggie had of Chatham Ridge was wrapped up in Rachel's family, she realized, which was why she hadn't hesitated when Rachel asked her to come home and stand beside her for the wedding. Being there for Rachel, with high heels, a pink dress, and some last-minute support. And with Nick, abiding by that crazy dare. "Your dad gave me that stone when I got scared one night because there was a terrible storm outside the tent. He said to hold tight to it, and everything would be okay. That the storm would pass and the rock would still be there, solid and strong. I've kept it with me ever since, as silly as that sounds."

Rachel's eyes welled. "That doesn't sound silly at all."

"You, your dad, your grandparents . . . they were my family, Rachel. My rock. I know you're nervous and worried about tomorrow, but don't be because those nerves are just a storm, and they'll pass as soon as you say 'I do.' Until then, take this and hold on to it, just like I did for all those years. And when you stand here tomorrow, take a moment, look up, and know that your father is here. He's always been here, watching you and walking with you and your grandpa, proud as a peacock of his little girl."

Rachel's smile wobbled. "That's what he always used to say."

"Then just keep thinking about that tomorrow."

Rachel gave Maggie a tight hug. It was like they were ten again and saying good-bye at the end of a camping trip. Or sixteen and crying over the first boy to break Rachel's heart. Or twenty-one and Maggie was heading out of Georgia for a life unknown. "Thank you. For saying that, and for being here with me, even though I made you get pedicures and try on dresses and put your hair up," Rachel said. "You're the best friend and maid of honor I could ask for."

"Ditto. You were always here for me when I was young, and being here for you is the least I can do." Maggie grinned, and leaned in. "Truth be told, I kinda enjoyed the pedicure."

"Then we'll do it again for your wedding. Though I'd be a matron of honor, being an old married woman by then."

"My wedding?" Maggie scoffed. "I'm not getting married anytime soon."

"But Nick—"

"That was just a dare, remember? You know there's

nothing between us. Just trying to keep Aunt Edna from fixing me up." Maggie grinned.

"I know it was just a dare, but I have to say, after seeing Nick with you, that boy is in love, Maggie. He looks at you the same way J.W. looks at me. I wouldn't be surprised if the next wedding I go to is yours."

The thought of a wedding—a marriage to Nick—sent a flutter of panic through Maggie. They were just pretending, putting on an act for everyone. Except pretending didn't involve sleeping with Nick. That was taking the whole faking-it act a little too far.

Last night, she hadn't faked a thing. She had been swept up in the moment, in the sheer amazing ecstasy of being with Nick, and forgotten her rule to keep things platonic. Every moment in that car had been real and true—and terrifying as hell.

"I think he's just a very good actor," Maggie said. "I know Nick and he's not the settle-down kind."

"I said the same thing about J.W." Rachel shot Maggie a grin as they walked across the yard. She raised a hand in greeting at the minister, just arriving.

"Either way, there's only a few hours left of me and Nick 'dating.' After the wedding tomorrow afternoon, we'll go back to Rescue Bay and everything will go back to the way it used to be."

Although that was impossible. *This changes everything.*

Sleeping with him made her long for him in ways she never had before. Had her wondering what he was doing every other second. Had her replaying that incredible moment in the car, over and over again in her head.

"Maybe so. Or maybe this week with Nick will change things in a good way." Rachel smiled. "He's a good guy, Maggie. I saw that right off when I visited you last year. He'd do anything for you. Including drive all the way to Georgia to hang out with men he doesn't even know and pretend to be madly in love with you. If he does the bunny hop at the reception, then he's a total keeper."

Maggie laughed. "That's the litmus test? Doing the bunny hop?"

"Hey, there are the guys," Rachel said, putting a hand on Maggie's arm. "They look all handsome, don't they?"

And they did. Maggie didn't notice J.W. or the other groomsmen. Her eyes strayed to Nick, to his tall, lean frame, his sandy hair among a sea of dark hair. He had on a pale green shirt, and it accented his eyes, his hair, everything about him. She could see the edge of his tattoo peek out from under the edge of his sleeve, and something quickened in her belly.

"I'd say somebody already passed the litmus test," Rachel said softly. "You just gotta stop grading him so hard."

Noralee came running up to them, dragging Maggie's attention back to why she was here. "Ladies! It's time. Now let's put a bee in those bonnets and get this rehearsal started. So we can have cake, which ya'll know is the only reason I leave my house."

The other girls arrived, and the whole lot piled toward the aisle. Noralee waved them forward, pairing them, then shooing them toward the minister. "Just like ducks, yes, indeed. Off you go. Remember, walk slowly. This isn't a race for first to the preacher. Except for you, Billy Joe. I heard there's a daddy with his shotgun after you."

J.W.'s brother Leroy slipped Maggie's arm into his, talking about his truck the entire walk. Maggie barely heard him. Her gaze kept straying to Nick, who was standing to the side, his expression unreadable behind sunglasses. She noticed his shirt was open at the collar and exposing a hint of the chest she had been kissing less than twenty-four hours ago.

She was saved from face-planting in the aisle by Leroy's steady hand. *The rehearsal, focus on the rehearsal.*

The wedding rehearsal passed in a blur of laughter and jokes, and before Maggie realized it, they were setting up for dinner inside the house. Nick tried to talk to her several times, but she feigned busy-ness and dodged him. What was she going to say? *Thanks for the sex, but I really want to pretend it never happened?*

Except she couldn't pretend that, as much as she wanted to. Going back wouldn't mean a return to normal—it would mean dealing with the shift in their relationship. That was what most terrified Maggie—that the shift would be too big, and she'd have to say good-bye to Nick forever.

She picked up a giant bowl of macaroni salad and spun toward the dining room, nearly colliding with a firm, solid chest. Wearing pale green. And a grin she recognized.

"Nick!" The salad slipped forward in the bowl, dotting his shirt with mayonnaise. "Sorry. Let me get that cleaned up."

He caught her before she could turn toward the sink and put some distance between them. "Why are you avoiding me?"

"Lots to do." The lie slid off her tongue like melted butter. "Wedding here tomorrow."

"I know." He grinned. "I've been along for the ride since Wednesday."

She gestured toward his shirt again. Toward something to do other than talk about what was coming next. "Nick, that's going to stain and—"

"You look beautiful," he said. "Absolutely heart-stopping, stunningly beautiful. I hardly recognize you."

She shook her head. "Of course, you like this better, this all prettied-up girlie girl."

"I never said that." He shifted closer, taking the bowl from her hands and placing it on the counter. "Look at me, Maggie."

She swallowed hard, telling herself she wasn't affected by him, that her mind wasn't replaying that moment in the convertible, that a part of her didn't wish he'd just hoist her up on the counter and do it again, macaroni salad be damned.

He lifted her chin, just as he had before, with the edge of his hand. The move so tender, so gentle, she could have been a baby bird. She met his gaze with her own and held her breath.

"I love you when you're dressed up, and I love you when you're in dirty, muddy, sawdust-covered work clothes," he said. "I love you when you put on makeup, and I love you when your face is bare and a little sunburned because that means I can see those freckles that pepper your nose, because I love those, too."

She looked away. "Nick, you don't have to say any of that. We're alone right now. Everyone is in the other room."

"I know we're alone. And that's why I'm saying it."

"Nick . . ." And then it hit her. Why he was saying this. What he was saying. The words she had just heard three, four, five times. All he'd been dancing around when they were in the car, the way he'd been looking at her and touching her. "You . . . you love me?"

"I do indeed." His grin widened, took over his face. "I think I just said that ten times."

"But, but you don't fall in love. You don't date anyone longer than twenty minutes. You don't—"

He put a finger on her lip, silencing her protests. "I'm not what you think I am. I've only ever really loved one woman."

Nick had been in love? How had she missed that? "Who?"

He chuckled. "You, silly. I was just waiting to be ready to prove it to you."

Nick was in love with her? Had been for all this time? Even after hearing him say it, the truth refused to sink in. Was he still taking their charade too far? Trying to act out a little romantic scene before the cake was brought out? Yes, that had to be it. Or was he trying to make her feel better after they'd made love?

"What are you talking about? This is all an act, Nick. Pretend. Don't go turning it into something else." She whirled away, picked up the bowl and headed out to the dining room.

It was the dress, she told herself. The dress that Rachel and the girls had talked her into buying. All of a sudden it had Nick seeing her as one of those girls he dated and dropped. The sooner she got back to work, to her regular clothes, to her regular life, the sooner he would stop this insanity. He wasn't in love. He was caught up in the fantasy, in the aftermath of sex, like she was.

Someone turned on a radio, and in minutes, the potluck of dishes were set on the dining room table, wafting tempting scents through the room. Maggie stuck with the other bridesmaids, far from Nick. If she was lucky, Nick would forget whatever that had been back in the kitchen.

Maggie had a chicken wing halfway to her mouth when Rachel and J.W. got to their feet. J.W. put two fingers in his mouth and whistled. The room trickled into silence.

He turned to Rachel and took her hand, with so much love in his eyes, it hurt to look at them. "First off, we want to thank you all for coming out to the trial run. I wish it had been the real wedding because then I'd already be married to this amazing woman, and I wouldn't have to wait another day to make her mine forever."

A collective *awww* went through the crowd. Rachel dabbed at her eyes, then gave J.W. a gentle slug. "You promised you wouldn't make me cry today."

He pressed a quick kiss to her lips, whispered something that made her laugh, and turned back to his audience.

Across the room, Nick was watching her, his expression indiscernible. Did he find the whole thing overdone? Too mushy to believe? Or was a part of him, like Maggie, wondering if it was possible to have a relationship that warm and sweet?

For goodness' sake, Maggie was clearly still caught in that fantasy they'd perpetuated this week. The truth was, some people were mushy and romantic and meant to fall in love, and some just . . . weren't.

"Anyway," J.W. went on, "we aren't just here to celebrate my last day as a bachelor—"

The groomsmen booed. The bridesmaids whooped.

"—but also to give another man a chance to prove how he feels. Nick." J.W. flung out a hand in Maggie's direction. "I do believe you told me you wanted a moment to say something important."

Oh God. Her stomach roiled, and her face flushed. She wanted to run, but the bridesmaids pinned her in, all eyes on her and Nick, no one seeing that it was all a façade, that it was a joke, a way to get out of the dare. And then, Nick was there, smiling, and she thought, *Yes, we'll tell everyone the truth now. Thank God.*

"You're right, J.W.," Nick said. "I do have something to say. Something I should have said a long time ago."

Good. He'd be the one to drop the bomb that it was all a big joke. Rachel and Maggie would share a laugh, she'd change out of this dress and this entire insanity would end.

Nick took a step forward, and took one of her hands in his. He lowered himself to one knee, and looked up at her. "I have been in love with you since the day I met you, Maggie. And I wanted to ask you, here, in front of all the people who love you." He took in a breath, let it out. "Will you marry me?"

She was sure she was hearing things. That any second, he was going to say, *Gotcha, it was a big joke, ha ha*, until she saw the ring box in Nick's other hand and the simple solitaire winking back at her.

"You're . . . serious?"

"As a heart attack." He held the box closer. "I've been carrying this around for days. Bought it when I said I was fishing, because I knew a long time ago that I wanted nothing more than to be with you. Marry me, Maggie."

She stared at him. At the ring. Her brain short-circuited. "Marry you?"

The bridesmaids were cheering, the groomsmen were teasing Nick about settling down. Hattie came up and grabbed Maggie by the shoulders. "Say yes, dear."

"I . . ." The people seemed to close around her, like walls crushing the breath out of her chest. "I . . . can't do this. I can't."

"Maggie—"

Then she spun away and ran from the room, bursting through the door and out into the fresh, clean air of Chatham Ridge. She wanted to get away, to leave, to just go back to Rescue Bay and back to a week ago, when everything made sense. This constant whirling dervish in her gut would be silenced and she could focus on her career, not her crazy, made-up love life.

"What the hell was that?"

She turned around and faced Nick. His ocean-colored eyes were muddled with hurt and anger.

"What the hell was *that*?" She waved toward the house. "What were you thinking, bringing out a ring in front of everyone?"

"I was thinking that I was going to propose to you."

"That would be the crowning touch on this whole façade, but you didn't have to do that."

"I wasn't doing it as part of an act, Maggie. I was asking you for real."

The sun had gone down, casting the wedding tableau in a soft purple light. The white chairs and white wood altar stood bright and happy against the dark background, full of hope for the day to come. It was all surreal, and so was this whole thing with Nick and the ring. It was as if an alien had been switched for the man she had known for two years. "For real? But . . . why?"

He chuckled softly and closed the distance between them. "Because I love you, Maggie. I don't want to spend another day without you."

He loved her? Since when? And why did those words make her want to run even faster and farther? "Why can't we just go back to the way we were? Working together, sharing subs and chips at lunch—"

"Because I want more."

She shook her head and backed up, putting up her hands to ward off his argument. "This was just a dare, Nick. It wasn't supposed to be real, to turn into a real engagement. Rachel dared me to step out of my comfort zone and bring you as my date. That's all. You collect a check, we go home and go back to work. Done."

Amusement quirked a grin up one side of his face. "You are terrified."

"What are you talking about? I'm not scared."

"Yes you are. You, Maggie McBride, the woman who has proven herself in a field where most men can't even cut the mustard, the same woman who has never met a challenge she would back down from—is the same woman who is terrified of something as simple as love?"

"Love comes with expectations, Nick. To fit into this little box of conformity." She looked up at the house on the hill, with its bright lights in the windows and happy faces sitting around the table. It was like a Rockwell painting, and something she had never really been able to get a grasp on. She'd loved being there, yes, but never imagined she'd be the one hosting the gatherings, infusing the space with the warmth and love that Hattie did. "It means putting on a frilly little apron, baking chocolate chip cookies, and decorating dining rooms and all the things I don't want to do. I want to get my contractor's license and keep on restoring old houses. I don't want to be the little wife."

"First of all, neither one of us is afraid of a little dirt, so we don't need aprons. Second of all, I hear they have these great places called grocery stores where they bake the cookies for you, and third of all, I don't give a shit what the dining room looks like as long as you're part of the package. I want you to get your contractor's license and I want to go on restoring old houses. With you." He took two steps forward and cradled her jaw with his hand. "So there's all your best arguments shot down. Now, are you going to tell me what you are really afraid of?"

Falling in love with you. Realizing that the truth isn't all it's cracked up to be.

"Tell me, Maggie." His voice was gentle, but firm. "Tell me."

"Nick, it doesn't matter. This was all an act, let's just leave it at that."

"I don't believe you. I don't believe that the woman who made love to me back there," he thumbed toward the garage, "was just acting."

She didn't tell him what was in her heart. Didn't admit the fears that kept her rooted where she was. Instead, she shook her head and swallowed back the tears that threatened to undo her composure. "I'm sorry if this week gave you the wrong impression about us. But we're just friends. Nothing more."

She turned around and faced the woods and waited until she heard the screen door slap. Nick was gone. And she was either relieved or heartbroken. It was kinda hard to tell, with this rock on her chest.

Rachel found her a few minutes later, standing under the tree behind the altar, drawing in deep breaths. "Hey, you okay?" Rachel said.

"No. No, I'm not," Maggie said. She thought she was going to hyperventilate, right here on the lawn. How had this tide shifted so quickly without her noticing? "This was all going way too fast. Nick read it all wrong, and now he wants to marry me, when all I want to do is go back to the way things were so that I can concentrate on my job."

"There's more to life than work, Mag."

"Work is what I have, Rach." She shook her head. "You don't understand."

"But you have Nick." A soft smile filled Rachel's face.

Maggie blew her bangs off her forehead. "No, I don't have Nick. I never did. And then we messed it all up by sleeping together, and he says he fell in love and . . . God, it's a mess."

"Are you saying you don't love him, too?"

"I . . . I don't know how I feel. I just want to concentrate on my job—"

"And use that as an excuse to run away from love." Rachel gave Maggie a smile. "Oh, honey, I know how you feel. I ran and ran, but J.W. always ran faster. My grandma says that true love is scary as hell because it's precious as a new flower, and just as vulnerable. You can crush it without even knowing it, but if you water it and nurture it and take the time to love it up, it becomes as strong as an oak tree." Rachel let out a little laugh. "I know it doesn't make sense, heck, half the sayings I heard from my aunts and grandmas didn't make an ounce of sense, but . . ."

"In a weird way, they do." Maggie hugged Rachel to her, wrapping herself in the comfort of a lifetime friendship built on shopping trips and chocolate chip cookies and late-night sleepover chats. It was good to know Rachel was in her corner, even if Rachel was firmly in the fall-in-love camp. "Thanks. Why don't you go back and enjoy your rehearsal dinner?"

"As long as you come with me. And talk to Nick."

But it turned out there wasn't any reason to talk to Nick. He'd packed his bags, called a cab, and headed for the airport. Maggie had gone back to the house wanting answers. And that was what she got.

NINE

TWO WEEKS OF eighteen-hour workdays weren't enough to exhaust Nick. Not enough to push Maggie, or her refusal of his proposal, from his mind. As soon as he'd gotten home, he'd taken every last dime he had, poured it into the Money Pit, and finished up the house in record time. During the days, he'd worked on projects for Mike, taking on ones that didn't need Maggie as his right-hand person, and at night, he'd gone back to the Money Pit and worked until he could barely stand. But it was done, finally, and so was he. Tomorrow, he'd call his real estate agent and have it put on the market.

He set the ring box on the kitchen counter. He should sell it or pawn it or something, but right now, he figured he'd let the ring sit until staring at it didn't ache like a phantom limb.

He hoisted a pile of scrap wood and trash into his arms and headed out the open front door to the Dumpster sitting on the side of the house. The sun blinded him as soon as he hit the driveway.

"Hey! Be careful with that. I'd like to have children some-day, you know."

Nick stuttered to a stop. His heart leapt in his chest, but the warning bells in his head shut down the hope before it could gain any traction. Two weeks. A hell of a long time for a man who was nursing his wounds. Two weeks of no word, no contact. Enough to build a wall between them. "Maggie. What are you doing here?"

"Helping you." She took the trash from him and tossed it into the bin, then dusted off her hands. She was back in her normal attire—shorts, a battered T-shirt and the familiar Timberland boots she'd had for years. To Nick, she looked incredible, as always. "Now are you going to show me the latest Money Pit or not?"

So she was just here to see the house. For work. Not him. He told himself he wasn't disappointed as hell. "I was just cleaning it up to get it ready for the real estate agent. I'm putting it on the market as soon as possible."

She shot him a confused look. "But I thought you wanted to hold on to this one."

"I did." He glanced over at the roof, at the shingles he had laid himself, the porch he had rebuilt by hand, the paint color he had agonized over for a week. Two weeks ago, he'd thought he'd own this house forever. But he'd been wrong. "Yeah, well, plans change."

As in the woman you wanted to marry turned you down. Then showed up, looking beautiful and tempting and heartbreaking. He wanted to just get this business over with so he could retreat and forget the whole thing. Except he stood there in the driveway, with the long, ugly Dumpster blocking Maggie's view of the house, making small talk, because he didn't want to show her what he'd done to the house. Not until he could pretend it was all about making a profit, instead of making a life.

"How was the wedding?" he asked.

"Perfect. J.W. cried a little, which made Rachel cry. But they had a great time, and they looked insanely happy together." She toed at the sawdust littering the driveway. "I took my contractor's exam."

"Yeah? How'd it go?"

She kept her head down, staring at the half-moon she'd drawn with her toe, and for a second his heart sank. Then she lifted her gaze and a wide grin took over her face. "You're looking at Maggie McBride, general contractor."

He wanted to pick her up and swing her around and cheer from the rooftops. Instead, he clenched his hands at his sides, and said, "Congratulations. That's awesome. I knew you'd do it."

"With your help, Nick. You were the study master."

He shrugged. "I didn't do much."

"You did more than you know." She brushed her bangs off her face. "I wanted to apologize for not returning to Rescue Bay right away. I stayed in Chatham Ridge and just kinda got my head on straight."

"Aw, you were fine the way you were, Maggie."

"No, I was a hot mess, Nick. A hell of a hot mess. I guess I have been for a long time, which is why I keep running away instead of staying put and dealing with stuff." She ran a hand through her hair and let out a breath. "When I grew up, I never had the conventional family life. My parents were always at work, or reading, or talking about things they'd researched. It was like there was this family of two, and I was just a tenant, watching from afar. But when I went to Rachel's house, it was like walking into a fairy tale. Her family sat around the table at dinner, they went to the soccer games and cheered like maniacs. They pulled pranks and told jokes and made me feel as included as they could."

"But it wasn't the same."

She shook her head. "Close, but no cigar. I loved them, and they loved me, but it was like I was borrowing them when I was there. I was still an outsider, in a way. So I decided a long time ago to stand on my own. To not count on anyone else. And then you came along."

He moved closer. "And what did I do?"

"You treated me like one of the guys."

"I'm sorry, Maggie. I thought—"

"And that was exactly what I wanted." Her voice began to crack. "To be part of the group, like everyone else. You helped me study and every day at lunch, you pretended to forget your chips—"

"Actually, I never pretended. I'm a guy. I forget stuff."

She laughed and swiped at her eyes. "Damn it. I never cry."

"Sometimes you have to," he said, taking another step forward, catching a tear hanging off her lashes. "Sometimes you have to," he said again, softer.

She shook her head and stepped away. As she did, she moved past the obstructing view of the Dumpster. "You painted the house blue, Nick." Maggie turned and faced him. "Cornflower blue. With white trim and a white porch."

He shrugged. Like he hadn't gone through three sample cans of paint and damned near driven the guy at the paint counter into a nervous breakdown trying to get the color just right. "Seemed like two colors that went together well."

"And there are window boxes. And flowers."

He shrugged again. Window boxes he'd built himself. Flowers he didn't know the names of, but he'd chosen because they reminded him of someone he loved. "You said they would help the house sell."

He started to step through the door—there was a whole pile of leftover supplies he needed to get out of there so he could sweep the floors—but Maggie grabbed his arm and stopped him. Damn it. This whole thing was taking ten times longer than he wanted it to. Didn't Maggie understand that seeing her here, of all places, made him want to chew off his own leg?

"You . . . you hung up my swing," she said. "Uh . . . a swing."

He could deny it. Lie and say there had been a swing here all the time, and all he'd done was paint it a pale lime color that blended with the blue and white. But lying to Maggie hadn't gotten him anywhere. Neither had telling the truth, to be honest. "It's not *a* swing. It's *your* swing. And if you want it, you can have it."

She parked a fist on her hip. "What does that mean?"

"I can take it down, install it at your place." Burn it, throw it off the side of the road. Okay, so maybe he wasn't taking her refusal so well.

"Doesn't it come with the house?"

"It *came* with the house. Now . . . it doesn't matter."

"Why the past tense?"

"Because when I bought this house and started flipping it, I did it to show you that I had changed. That I was ready to settle down, to have more. To have us . . . here." He hoisted another pile into his arms and moved past her. She'd seen the house, why didn't she just leave and quit asking him questions? "But you're right. The leopard doesn't change his spots. So I'm just going to flip it. Move on to the next one."

She came up behind him with a pile of her own and stood on her tiptoes to let the trash shower down into a dusty pile in the Dumpster. "The next woman, too?"

"No, not the next woman. For God's sake, Maggie, there was never a next woman." He let out a gust and turned to face her. "Do you know why I kept making up dates to tell you about? Because I wanted to make you jealous. I wanted to hear you say, 'Nick, what are you doing with those women when you could go out with me?' It was ridiculous, all high school, because damn it, Maggie, every time I got around you, I felt like I couldn't possibly measure up to what you needed."

"You? Couldn't measure up to what I needed? What do you mean?"

"You are incredible, Maggie. Smart and strong and, hell, the most amazing woman I know. I'm just a contractor who took a little too long to grow up and realize what was important."

"And what do you think is important, Nick?"

He pitched the load in his arms into the Dumpster and turned to her. "You are. For me. But you made it clear we are just friends. Fine. We'll work together, nothing more."

"And just toss what we had that week away?" She held up the ring box over the edge of the Dumpster. He hadn't seen her grab it off the counter, but she must have when they got that last load.

"Is that what you want?" he asked. Seeing the box in her hands filled him with a bone-wracking combination of hope and pain. Jesus, he was a masochist. "Just toss it away?"

"Seems the most sensible thing to do. It's what anyone else in our position would do. We work together. Getting married would just make that a giant mess. Hell, we'd be together all the time. Could get ugly." She drew back and chucked the velvet box into the metal bin. It pinged off the side and settled somewhere in the trash.

If anything cemented the truth for Nick, it was the ring box sailing out of her hand and into the trash bin. Lord, he had to be delusional to think that that week in Georgia had contained one ounce of reality. He cursed and spun away.

Maggie stepped in front of him and blocked his way. "But there's a little piece of advice someone I love very much once gave me. She said conformity is for everybody else. That I should be brave, be bold, and be myself."

He looked down at her. "Isn't that what you've always done? You said you learned to stand on your own, to not want the family life that comes with a house like this."

To not want what he had proposed. God, he'd been a fool.

"I thought that's what I was doing, Nick. Until I was dared to be like the rest, and I realized that it was easier to slip into that with a lie than to face the truth of what I really wanted." She put a hand on his chest and raised on her tiptoes, bringing her lips just under his. "And that being brave, being bold, and being myself was about not being scared to say what I want. To go after it, when it runs away."

His pulse thundered in his veins, and he had to remind himself to breathe. She was wearing that perfume again, and it teased at his senses, dark and alluring. "And what do you really want, Maggie?"

"To wear my work boots and my T-shirts and my ponytails and marry the man who loves me no matter how I look. Or whether I curse. Or how I frame a wall. Who accepts me as I am, and who makes me feel like I belong just by smiling at me." She raised on her tiptoes and cupped his face in her warm hands and met his eyes with her own. "Who makes me feel like I have come home every single time I see him. I don't need a house or a swing or a garden to be home, Nick. I need you. Just you."

He blinked, confused. "Marry . . ." Then Nick's gaze dipped and he saw the sparkle of the ring on Maggie's finger. The ring that had been in the empty box that now sat in the Dumpster. The ring that was now on her left hand. "Marry me?"

She nodded. "If you still want a wife who won't bake cookies or decorate a dining room or do anything other than what she wants to do, even if it's the least conventional option. A wife who wants to build a home and a life with you."

"I don't know . . ." He covered her left hand with his own, and the ring pressed into his palm. "Getting married is a scary thing."

"You need incentive, Nick?" She grinned and pressed a kiss to his lips. A tempting, teasing kiss that promised more, much, much more, later. *I dare you.*

"Ah, Maggie McBride, you know I love a challenge." Then he scooped her up and carried her past the window boxes and the flowerpots and the porch swing, and into the house and the life together that had been meant for them from the very start.

CAROLINA HEART

Virginia Kantra

To all the girls who were ever told they weren't smart enough or good enough or deserving enough. This one's for you.

ONE

CYNTHIE LODGE COUNTED heads as the gaggle of third graders jostled their way from the aquarium's touch pool to the living shipwreck exhibit. *Two, three, four* . . And there was Hannah, her wild puff of hair glowing like a halo in the blue-green light, her small face absorbed in the silent underwater world before her.

She was so bright. Like a star.

Cynthie's heart contracted and relaxed in helpless response, swamped by a wave of fierce, maternal love.

Mama used to say girls didn't need to be smart. *The good Lord blessed you with a soft heart and willing hands*, Mama would say in her comfortable island brogue. *A pretty girl don't need more.*

But Hannah was smart. Both of Cynthie's girls were smart, even if some days it seemed like twelve-year-old Maddie had more hormones than brain cells. All they needed was encouragement and a good example.

Cynthie had never in her life been a good example. But for her girls' sake, she was trying.

"Look, a cannon!" a boy shouted.

"Sharks!"

The kids surged toward the huge aquarium wall, darting like a school of fish.

Cynthie smiled. She still remembered the excitement of going on a field trip, the thrill of escaping school for the day. Some things never changed.

And some things did. She actually *wanted* to be in school now, to make something of herself, to make a decent life for her daughters.

Now that the school year had started for all of them, she didn't often get to spend the day with her girls. Or any time at all that wasn't taken up with homework and laundry and bills. Working nights was great for tips, but it sure wouldn't win her Mother of the Year.

"Can we have quiet?" Miss Green, Hannah's teacher, asked. "Boys and girls, quiet, please."

There was some shushing, some shoving.

". . . re-created just as the divers found it," the aquarium guide was saying. "The artifacts from the Beaufort Inlet wreck have been tentatively linked to the *Queen Anne's Revenge*, the flagship of the notorious pirate Blackbeard."

"Arrrgh!" yelled Ryan Nelson.

"Shh."

"Whether the ship truly belonged to Blackbeard or not, you can see the different species of near-shore marine life that made a home in the wreck."

A sea turtle, round and pale as the moon, emerged from the gloom of an encrusted anchor. Cynthie watched, entranced, as it floated toward the glass.

"Miz Lodge, I have to use the bathroom."

Cynthie's attention snapped down to one of the girls in her group. "I took you all to the restroom fifteen minutes ago," Cynthie said.

"I didn't have to go then. I have to go now."

"She has to poop," Ryan said. "Take her to the poop deck."

"Be quiet," one of the younger boys said. Aidan Clark, a friend of Hannah's.

"Who's going to make me, squirt? You?"

Before Cynthie could intervene, Hannah turned. "Shut up, you guys. I want to hear."

The other girl in their group shifted from foot to foot. "Miz Lo-odge."

"Okay, honey, just a second." Cynthie caught the teacher's eye, pointed to the fidgeting child and then back toward the restrooms.

Miss Green nodded.

"Anybody else?" Cynthie asked cheerfully. "Hannah?"

Her daughter shook her head, engrossed by the spiny fish gliding through the watery landscape.

"Right. Aidan, you should go back to your group," Cynthie said. "The rest of you stick together, okay? We'll only be a minute."

But it was closer to five before they were done.

Cynthie hurried the girl back across the lobby, reentering the illuminated gloom of the galleries. Their school group had moved on from the pirate ship replica to the rusty wreck of a freighter. Hundreds of brilliantly colored fish flashed through the blue-green water.

Cynthie spotted Ryan's head and began to count the kids in her charge, *one, two, three . . .*

Her heart tripped. Where was Hannah?

She took a breath. Held it. *Hannah wasn't missing,* she told herself, scanning the clusters of children. She'd simply wandered off with another group. Or lingered behind at another exhibit. Or . . .

"Miss Green, have you seen Hannah?"

The teacher broke off her conversation with another mother to reply. "She went with you to the restroom."

A buzz rose in Cynthie's head like the white noise on TV when the cable went out. "No, she didn't."

"She followed you. You must have missed her."

Cynthie wanted to shake her.

Teachers needed to stay calm, she reminded herself. But she hadn't missed Hannah. She wouldn't.

"I'll go look," she said.

Miss Green's gaze fixed over her shoulder toward the lion-fish tank. "Ryan, don't bang on the glass." She glanced back at Cynthie. "I'm sure she's fine. Try to hurry."

Hurry, Cynthie's instincts screamed as she retraced her steps, scanning the galleries as she passed, pausing by the sea turtle exhibit that was Hannah's favorite. *What the hell kind of example loses her own child? Hurry, hurry, hurry.*

Another school tour clustered around the touch tanks, sticking their hands in the cool saltwater. Cynthie forced herself to slow down, to check each group for Hannah. But her heart raced.

She pushed open the door of the women's restroom.

No Hannah.

A young mother washing her toddler's hands at the sink glanced over curiously as Cynthie peered under the door of the one occupied stall, praying to see her daughter's purple-laced sneakers.

"Have you seen a little girl?" Cynthie asked. "Purple T-shirt, about this tall?" With her hands, she sketched Hannah's height, her soft puff of hair, as if she could shape her daughter out of air.

The woman's expression melted in sympathy and concern. "No, I'm sorry."

But sorry wouldn't fix this, as Mama liked to say.

Cynthie's heart pounded.

Hannah was gone. She'd lost Hannah.

THE little girl pivoted on one toe of her purple-laced sneakers, glancing up and down the corridor.

She must be lost, Max Lewis thought.

The public was rarely admitted to this part of the aquarium. And unaccompanied children were never allowed. She must have gotten separated from one of the school groups touring the galleries downstairs.

"Looking for something?" he asked as gently as he could.

She whirled to face him, her curly mane of hair dancing in a nonexistent wind. He stood still, at a distance, the way he would approach any wild thing.

She frowned at him. Her eyes were soft, clear green, startling in her mocha-colored face.

A memory, featherlight, brushed the back of his brain. Something about those eyes . . . "Are you lost?"

She stuck out her rounded chin. "No."

Max swallowed a grin. "Maybe I can help you get where you're going anyway."

"Maybe. Is this where they feed the sharks?"

She must be looking for the viewing gallery above the

shipwreck exhibit. "You're not allowed in the feeding area without a chaperone," he said. "Let me take you back to your group."

She shook her head. "I'm not supposed to go with strangers. Anyway, I want to see where they feed the sharks."

She was smart. Single-minded. He respected that. He was the same way in the pursuit of knowledge—or anything else. But someone somewhere must be missing her. Looking for her.

"You can watch from below with the rest of your class. Or," he added as her small chin set, "I can walk you down to the information desk and we can ask them to page your teacher."

She eyed him warily. "Am I in trouble?"

"Not yet."

She cocked her head, considering, regarding him with those big green eyes. Once again he was teased by that elusive sense of familiarity.

She sighed in defeat. "Okay."

He didn't smile. He remembered too well being at the mercy of adults' whims and rules and regulations, dragged in the wake of his parents' academic appointments and sabbaticals, constantly changing schools and houses, never quite fitting in.

It was tough being a kid.

He escorted her down to the gallery. Schoolchildren swarmed the exhibits, their voices bouncing off the high ceiling. Max paused, a little daunted by the noise. He liked kids, at least in principle. But his own students were quite a bit older.

"Do you see your teacher?" he asked.

The little girl shook her head.

"Hannah!"

A woman hurried toward them, cleaving through the sea of kids like the figurehead on some fantasy ship. Black hair, full breasts, wide green eyes . . .

Max blinked in disbelief, in recognition. His breathing stopped. "Cynthie?"

The most beautiful girl in high school. Hell, in the whole world.

Still.

RELIEF loosened the muscles in Cynthie's back, sent a warm flush like anger up her chest and into her face.

Be cool, she tried to tell herself. *You're the cool mom.*

She grabbed Hannah's upper arms, unsure if she should hug her or shake her. "Where have you been?" Even to her own ears, her voice was too loud.

Hannah wriggled, embarrassed.

"I found her trying to get to the viewing platform. Smart kid. Very, uh, determined. You must be proud."

Cynthie looked up at this babbling stranger standing behind Hannah. And up. He was tall, lean and tanned and boyish. His frayed and faded cargo shorts ended above big, square knees, revealing muscled calves dusted with dark hair and ratty sneakers. He met her gaze, smiling almost apologetically.

"Who are you?" she asked, her heart still pounding in fear and relief. *And what were you doing with my daughter?*

His smile faded. "Max Lewis."

Cynthie caught herself. It wasn't his fault Hannah had left her group. He was trying to help. And Cynthie, of all people, should know better than to judge somebody based on appearances. She smiled back and offered her hand. "Cynthie Lodge."

His clasp was warm and strong. "Yes, I know."

Her hand jolted in his hold. And then she relaxed. "Oh, right. Hannah. You must have been looking for me."

"Yes. Well . . ."

"I didn't tell him your name," Hannah said.

Cynthie shot him a quick, questioning glance.

Max Lewis shrugged broad shoulders. "I kind of knew you in high school."

Growing up on an island, you knew everybody. All the locals at least, the kids who didn't come for a week or the summer.

She narrowed her eyes, studying his face. Quiet, clear gray eyes, straight nose, strong jaw covered in dark stubble. *Very nice.* The kind of face a woman didn't forget.

But she didn't remember him.

"You went to Dare Island?" she asked.

"Just for a year. My sophomore year. You were a senior?"

She racked her brain. Nope, nothing. The school had six hundred students, grades K through 12. She should have known him.

But he'd obviously grown up, filled out since then. People

did change from the people they'd been in high school. Those shoulders . . . She felt a pulse of attraction, like a flutter in her belly, and hastily shunted it away. She'd changed, too. *Thank God.*

She smiled, shook her head. "Sorry. Thanks for finding my kid."

"No problem. So." He stuck his hands into his pockets, looking from Hannah to Cynthie and back again. "This is your daughter."

Cynthie's back stiffened. She curled her fingers protectively around Hannah's shoulder. "One of them."

"I should have guessed." He smiled. "She looks like you."

The starch went out of Cynthie's spine.

Most people assumed Hannah looked like her father, a U.S. Marine stationed briefly at Lejeune. She had her daddy's coffee-with-cream skin, his soft, dark, springy hair.

But she had Cynthie's name. And Cynthie's eyes.

She smiled. "Thank you."

"Well . . ." Max cleared his throat in that way nice guys did before they asked a question. *Are you married? Can I buy you a drink? Will you have sex with me?*

Her heart thrummed. She glanced at his left hand, instinctively checking for a ring or a tan line.

Nope. Not going there. Listening to her hormones had never gotten her anything but pregnant. And while her daughters were the best things that had ever happened to her, they left no room in her life for guys. Even nice guys.

Not that she met many of those.

"We have to get back to our group now," she said. "Hannah, you can't go off like that."

"But I had to see where they feed the sharks." Hannah fixed her big green eyes on Max Lewis like a carnie on the midway sizing up a mark. "Maybe you could take me."

"We can't bother Mr. Lewis anymore," Cynthie said firmly.

"Max," he said.

"But he dared me," Hannah said.

Cynthie frowned. "Who dared you?"

"Ryan," Hannah said. "Aidan said that when he came with his mom he got to feed the sharks, and Ryan called him a liar. And I said Aidan wouldn't lie. So Ryan dared him to do it again. Only Aidan was scared, so I said I'd go."

Cynthie squashed her instinctive sympathy. "Sweetie, you can't break the rules because some boy dared you to."

"But, Mom, he was picking on Aidan."

"She really does take after you," Max murmured.

Cynthie looked up, surprised by his intrusion.

He smiled, warm appreciation in his eyes, and something in her brain turned and clicked like the tumblers in a lock. *Max Lewis . . .*

"You tell your friend—Ryan, is it?—that the aquarium gives behind-the-scene tours on weekends. But children have to be accompanied by an adult. You really should come," he said.

To her? Cynthie wondered. *To both of them?*

"That would be cool," Hannah said. "Mom?"

Cynthie shook her head regretfully. "Thanks for the tip. But I'm usually busy on weekends."

"Oh. Sure." Color stained the high ridge of his cheekbones, the points of his well-shaped ears. "You're, uh, married."

"Divorced. I work weekends."

She needed the tips, especially now, in the off-season.

He took his hands out of his pockets. "So I could check the aquarium schedule and call you."

Was he . . . ? He was *hitting* on her, she realized. In a totally respectful, awkward sort of way. It was sweet, a welcome change from the usual grab-ass come-ons at the bar.

Well, it would be welcome if she was looking for a hookup. Which she wasn't.

"You don't need to do that. I'm sure the aquarium has the schedule online." She smiled again to soften her refusal. Well, and because the combination of those broad shoulders and pink-tinged ears was kind of adorable. She glanced down the length of the darkened gallery, searching for the rest of her group. "I've gotta go wrangle my kids. But thanks."

"Right." Max thrust his hands back into his pockets, that clear gray gaze intent on her face. "It was . . . It was really great seeing you again, Cynthie."

She sighed. He was cute. But she was trying hard these days to listen to her head and not her other parts. Guys didn't want a woman with two kids for anything other than a one-night stand, anyway.

"You, too." She left without looking back.

But she felt his gaze following her, a tickle between her shoulder blades, as she waded back into the current of kids. They eddied and swirled around her, carrying her away.

Two

CYNTHIE SCANNED THE Fish House dining room, calculating how much longer before she could clock out and go home. Table six, table four, three guys at the bar, a couple in the back booth holding hands. A quiet Thursday. The restaurant emptied early now that the season was over and the tourists were gone.

The old fish house on Dare Island had always been the heart of the community, the place where local fishermen brought their catch and talked about their neighbors and the weather.

Ten years ago the property owner had razed the building where fish were cleaned and packed, and replaced it with a restaurant. Now dark wood tables and long plank floors stretched to the back of the room. Rows of bottles glinted in the light of the flat screens over the bar.

Nothing was left of the original fish house but the name and the view of the harbor.

Yet the place still survived as a hub for the locals to gather and gossip.

Cynthie closed out table four, leaving them with the check and a smile, and made her way to the couple in the booth: Sam Grady, the owner's son, and his fiancée, Meg Fletcher, who'd gone to school with Cynthie.

As she walked through the narrow aisle, one of the guys at the bar patted her ass.

She evaded his hand expertly, jabbing him—not hard—with her elbow.

He raised his palms in token surrender. "You had something on your butt."

Cynthie laughed. "Yeah. Your eyes."

Sam Grady lifted an eyebrow as she approached the booth. "Trouble?"

"Nothing I can't handle," Cynthie said cheerfully. Nothing she wasn't used to.

"You're too nice," Meg said.

Not nice, Cynthie thought. *Pragmatic.* It didn't pay to piss off customers in the off-season. The biggest jerks were sometimes the biggest tippers. And she needed the tips to pay her bills. "He doesn't mean anything by it," she said.

"You should have dumped a drink on him."

Cynthie shrugged. She didn't want the cost taken out of her wages. "Waste of good booze. Speaking of which . . . Can I get you folks anything else? Another beer? Another . . ." She looked at Meg's drink, trying to remember her order. Something weird, something a girl who'd been to Harvard and lived in New York would know about. Something Cynthie had never in her life heard of before. "Another Aperol Ricky?"

"We're fine, thanks," Sam said.

"Unless you're trying to get out of here," Meg said. "Do you want to bring us the check?"

"Only if you all are set," Cynthie said.

Sam raised another eyebrow. "Hot date?"

Cynthie didn't resent the question. There was a time when she'd lurched from relationship to relationship, bed to bed, trying to find love and secure some kind of future. But she was trying to be an example now. The girls' lives were crazy enough with her going back to school. They didn't need a mama who was still writing her phone number on cocktail napkins.

She shook her head. "My mom's watching the girls tonight. I want to make sure they do their homework before bed."

"How's school going?" Meg asked.

Cynthie warmed, as always, at the chance to talk about her

kids. "All right. Maddie's getting used to changing classes, finally. And Hannah's all excited about her aquarium report."

"She's a smart girl," Sam said.

Smart kid. Max Lewis's voice intruded in her head. She could almost see his tanned legs, his ankle bones protruding above his ratty sneakers. *You must be proud.*

"That's great," Meg said. "But I didn't mean the girls. How's it going for you?"

"Oh." Cynthie blinked, surprised that Meg would ask. Which was silly. Meg had encouraged Cynthie to apply to the community college, had helped her fill out all those confusing financial aid forms.

"All right, I guess."

Nice girls don't brag, Mama said.

Cynthie had never done much to brag about. But the fact was, she'd done real well in summer school. All those courses she had to take as a prerequisite for her associate's degree: algebra, biology, chemistry. Of course, she hadn't gone to Harvard like Meg.

"I start my first real dental classes this semester," she offered. "And a preclinic lab."

"How long does that take?" Meg asked.

"Twenty-two class hours, six lab hours a week. Mostly when the girls are in school."

While they chatted about her schedule, Sam slipped a credit card from his wallet and laid it on the table.

"You want me to ring you up first?" Cynthie asked.

Sam smiled. "I trust you."

She carried the card away. When she returned with the check for his signature, the cell phone in her pocket hollered the chorus of "Redneck Woman."

"Great ringtone," Meg said.

Cynthie grinned and slapped her pocket. "Sorry."

"Go ahead and take it," Sam said.

"We-ell . . ." Cynthie's hand hovered. "Just in case it's the girls," she said apologetically.

She slid the phone from her pocket and glanced at the display.

She recognized the number with equal parts attraction and annoyance. Max Lewis.

He'd called her last night, too. She had listened to his voice mail right before bed, the deep, well-educated tones, disarming, diffident.

"Um, hi, Cynthie? It's Max. Max Lewis. I got your number from Gilbert Fry. You know Gil."

Of course she knew Gil, a regular at the bar, a soft-spoken waterman trying to revive oyster fishing on Dare Island. She knew everybody on Dare Island.

And lots of guys—including Gil Fry—had her number.

"Anyway . . ." She'd heard Max take a breath.

"I thought you'd like to know there's a behind-the-scenes aquarium tour this Sunday at two if you'd like to go with Hannah. And me. Or without me. I mean, you should feel free to . . . But I'd be happy to reserve tickets for you. Or us. Whatever. If you're interested, that is. You could call me."

He'd rattled off his number while her heart beat a little faster.

"Well." Another breath. *"It was great to see you again. Uh, bye."*

Of course she hadn't called him back.

She hadn't expected him to call again.

And she still didn't remember who he was. Couldn't picture him in high school, despite his bare knees and boyish smile.

With a little shake of her head, she tucked the phone away.

"Everything all right?" Sam asked.

Sam was one of the good guys. Meg was lucky. Although Meg—brainy, ambitious, determined—had always insisted on making her own luck. No stupid choices for Meg.

Cynthie flashed them both a smile. "Just fine."

"Who was it?" Meg asked.

Nobody, she should have said. Nobody she ought to be thinking about, anyway. But what actually came out of her mouth was, "Do you remember a guy named Max Lewis? From high school?"

"I don't really . . . Sam?"

"It was our senior year," Cynthie said. "Sam wasn't around then."

"I came home for holidays," he said.

Meg exchanged a private look with Sam, intimate as a kiss. "I remember. So, what about this Max guy?"

Cynthie shrugged. "I ran into him the other day, that's all."

"Max Lewis," Meg repeated thoughtfully. "Max . . . You don't mean *Maxwell* Lewis? Dark-haired, skinny kid? He was in my advanced biology class."

A vision of tall, dark, extremely buff Max Lewis rose in Cynthie's head. "I don't think he would have been in class with you," she said doubtfully. "He's, like, two years younger."

Meg nodded. "That's the one. The Boy Genius. It sort of pissed me off, actually, because his grades were always just a little bit better than mine. His parents were both university professors. His dad was here on some kind of research fellowship."

"Are you talking about Oscar Lewis's son?" Sam asked.

"Do you know him?" Meg asked.

"I know of him," Sam said. "At least, I've heard of his father. Oscar Lewis, big linguistics expert at Duke. He wrote a book about the effects of isolation on the island dialect."

Boy Genius? *University professors*?

"Not my type, then," Cynthie said.

Meg pulled a face. "Stop that. You're smart. Anyway, what does it matter whether he's your . . . Wait." She straightened, her eyes brightening. "Was that him? Is he texting you?"

"He called," Cynthie said. *And that was another thing,* she thought with an unfamiliar sense of grievance, remembering his warm, deep voice, his adorable hesitations. It wasn't fair for the man to be so cute. Not when she was trying so hard to resist him. "What kind of guy calls instead of texting?"

"A guy who's interested," Sam said.

Cynthie shook her head. "Interested gets me a pat on the ass. Not a phone call."

"I think it's sweet," Meg said.

"Ouch," Sam said. "Friend zone."

"Not even that," Cynthie insisted, trying to make it no big deal, ignoring the flutter in her stomach. "He just wanted to tell me about some behind-the-scenes tour at the aquarium on Sunday."

"Sounds right up Hannah's alley," Meg observed.

"Yes." Yes, it was. Unfortunately. Cynthie hated to disappoint her daughters.

"So are you going with him?"

"No." Tickets cost twenty dollars. Each. Cynthie had looked it up online. She didn't have that kind of money, especially not at the start of the school year when the girls needed new shoes and school supplies.

"Have you told him?"

"I figured he'd get the hint," Cynthie said. "When I didn't answer his calls."

"Guys are good at ignoring rejection," Sam said. "It's a defense mechanism."

"Or ego," Meg said.

He grinned at her, sharp and quick.

Maybe. Cynthie was used to guys who wouldn't take no for an answer, who got handsy or pushy or pissy when she turned them down.

But Max Lewis hadn't struck her as one of them. Something about his eyes and the way they'd actually focused on her face, or the endearing way he blushed to the tips of his ears, or those awkward phone pauses.

"I suppose I could call him back," she said.

Sam and Meg exchanged glances.

"Just to say no," she added. "I mean, I don't want to keep the poor guy hanging."

"You're such a softy," Meg said.

"Gee, thanks," Cynthie said, trying not to mind the echo of her mama's words.

A soft heart and willing hands.

And no brains.

THE student on the other side of Max's desk pleated her fingers together in the lap of her extremely brief skirt and fixed Max with wide, earnest eyes. "I really want to do well in your class, Dr. Lewis."

Max sighed. She was a senior. She probably needed the science credit to graduate. Unfortunately, doing well in his class actually required that students do their work. "You shouldn't be too discouraged by one bad test performance. Your class participation is very good."

She nodded eagerly. "It's so interesting. What you do, I mean. I just wish I could bring my grade up."

"Well," he said mildly. "You might try studying."

"Maybe I need tutoring. I could stay after class." She

smiled at him hopefully. "Or we could meet someplace. Like, for coffee?"

"I don't think that's necessary. If you would spend more time with the text—"

"Nothing else?" She dropped her gaze, peeking up at him through a fringe of stiff, mascaraed lashes.

"You mean extra credit?" He shook his head.

She blinked at him, crestfallen. "But—"

"It's early in the quarter," he said kindly. "Just keep up with the readings, and I'm sure you'll do better next time."

He explained the grading rubric again, reminded her to refer to the syllabus, and sent her on her way.

As she was leaving, Greg Stokes, the department's acknowledged expert on fish migration and women, appeared in the doorway of his office.

Greg turned to watch the departing student and her short skirt twitch down the hall. "Very nice."

"She's a nice girl. Terrible student, though." Max frowned. "I don't understand why she's struggling. She seems to be paying attention in class."

Greg shook his head pityingly. "Max, you idiot, of course she's paying attention. All your female students pay attention. Why do you think they take your class?"

Max lifted his brows. "I assume because they have an interest in biological oceanography."

"In saving the whales, maybe. Or swimming with dolphins. Not in restoring oyster habitat."

"That's incredibly sexist."

"Maybe," Greg acknowledged. He leaned against Max's desk, almost knocking a pile of reports to the floor. "But I'll bet you anything that girl is less interested in bivalve reproduction than in getting it on with teacher."

The tips of his ears heated. "Don't be a jackass. She must be ten years younger than me. She's a student."

"A very pretty one. It's like revenge of the nerds, man. All those girls who never gave you the time of day in high school are begging you for extra credit."

All those girls who never gave you the time of day in high school . . .

Girls like Cynthie Lodge.

Max felt a pressure in his chest as if he were sixteen again, horny and hopeless and stupid with lust.

She'd looked so . . . grown-up when he ran into her yesterday, the same and not the same as the girl who had blindsided him in high school, with her warm smiles and casual kindness and soft green eyes. She still resembled his adolescent fantasies, even though the smile was cooler now, the eyes more guarded.

But his rational adult mind had registered the changes, the mermaid tattoo that twined about her arm, the generous breadth at breast and hip.

The child.

He wished she had returned his calls. He really wished he could leave her another message without coming across as some crazy, creepy stalker.

He must have been silent too long, because Greg peered at him, his good-natured face creasing. "Hey, I'm kidding. I know you'd never do anything inappropriate."

"Thanks," Max said.

"You're a nice guy." Greg paused. "Clueless, but nice."

Max suppressed a wince. Julie, the last woman he'd been involved with, had said pretty much the same thing. Right before she moved out.

"You just need to get back in the saddle," Greg said encouragingly. "Plenty of fish in the sea. Don't let one bad apple spoil the bunch."

Despite the mixed metaphors, Greg's message came through loud and clear. Max was touched by his friend's concern "I'm fine."

"Yeah? When was the last time you asked a woman out? Since Julie, I mean."

"This week."

"No shit." Greg grinned. "Anybody I know?"

Max cleared his throat. "Ah . . ."

His cell phone rang. *Saved by the bell*.

He fished it from his pocket and then stared, transfixed, at the display. C LODGE.

His blood pounded, thick and low. "I should take this."

Greg settled his weight on the desk, as if preparing for a long stay. "Don't mind me."

Frustrated, Max raked his fingers through his hair. But he

couldn't risk letting the call go to voice mail. What if she hung up?

He turned away, cradling the phone to his ear, unable to control the leap of his heart or his voice. "Hi. You got my message."

"I . . . Yes. The first one."

"Right. Well, I only left one. I didn't want you to think I was stalking you. Even if I kind of . . . Um." Behind him, Greg made a strangled sound. Max took a deep breath. God, could he sound like a bigger loser? "Would you like to go? To the aquarium, I mean. Sunday?"

"I would," she said. "But—"

"That's great," he said heartily before she could tell him no. "The tour's at two. What time should I pick you up?"

"You can't."

"Right." He was an idiot. Of course she didn't want him to pick her up. She had children. She wouldn't just invite a stranger to their home. "So, I'll meet you there then."

"I have to work Sunday. My shift starts at four."

He had to keep her talking. He had to . . . "What kind of work do you do?"

"I'm a waitress." Her voice was slightly flat. Like that was the end of this discussion.

"Okay." Maybe her hours weren't flexible. Maybe her boss was a jerk. "We could go earlier."

"But the tour starts at two, you said."

His thoughts raced. "*That* tour, yes. But we could do something else. What time is good for you? Ten? Eleven?"

"I guess eleven. But—"

"Great. They're treating some sea turtles in the lab. I bet your kids—Hannah—would like to see that."

"Oh." A new note in her voice. "She really would."

He cleared his throat. "Of course you would be my guests."

"Well . . ."

His heart beat faster. "Eleven, then? I'll meet you by the front door."

"I . . ." Her breath rushed out in what might have been a laugh. "Sure, why not? Thanks."

He hardly knew what he said in reply. His blood pounded in his ears.

He ended the call.

Greg was watching him, forehead creased. "You're taking your date to the aquarium?"

Max pulled his mind from the memory of Cynthie's laugh, her lips, her eyes. Her tattoo. "Her and her kids. She has kids."

"I worry about you, pal. You're not going to score with a woman by taking her—and her kids—to look at a bunch of fish."

"You like fish."

"I'm an ichthyologist. It's my job to like fish."

Max smiled. "It's not any old trip to the aquarium. I'm giving them a behind-the-scenes tour."

"Yeah, because nothing says, 'Have screaming sex with me' like visiting the holding tanks. At least the regular exhibits would be dark."

"I'm not looking to drag her into the shadows and make out. We're not in high school anymore." She wouldn't have anything to do with him in high school. "Anyway, her kids will be with us."

"How old are they?"

He didn't know. He didn't know anything about her, really, this new, grown-up Cynthie with her open smile and guarded eyes. She was divorced. She worked as a waitress. And she still tangled him up inside like a pelican in fishing line.

"Ten?" he hazarded. Hannah had looked about ten. He shook his head. "It doesn't matter."

Greg regarded him with pity. "If you believe that, you don't know kids."

No, he didn't.

"Only child," he reminded Greg. No brothers or sisters, no nieces or nephews.

"Just make sure the kids don't take over the conversation. Ask her about herself," Greg suggested. "Women like that. They think you're interested."

"I *am* interested," Max said.

"Yeah, okay." Greg eyed him doubtfully. "I just hope you know what you're doing."

Max rolled his shoulders to relieve the tension knotting there. "It's a date. I'm sure I can figure it out," he said.

He hoped.

*   *   *

IT wasn't a date, Cynthie told herself as she parked her aging minivan in the aquarium lot two days later. She flipped down the visor to check her hair in the driver's-side mirror. A date was drinks or dinner or the movies, when a guy paid. This was more like a . . . well, like another field trip.

Maybe she should offer to pay for their tickets?

She met her gaze in the reflection. Her cheeks were awfully pink. And her eyes were shiny.

Hannah bounced in the backseat. "Come on, Mom, what are you doing?"

Good question. Cynthie knew better than to get all starry-eyed over a new guy. It never worked out. And every failure scraped away a little of her optimism along with a piece of her heart.

Besides, she had sworn off guys. For the girls' sake.

She snapped the visor shut.

Twelve-year-old Madison slumped in the passenger seat beside her, wearing earbuds and a neutral expression.

Cynthie smiled at her brightly. "Ready to have fun?"

"Are we going home?"

Cynthie suppressed a sigh. Under the veil of hair and bored façade, Madison was a good kid, eager for approval, anxious for affection. Cynthie liked to think that her recent mouthiness was normal growing-up stuff, a sign of increasing confidence and independence. But sometimes she missed the little girl who used to cling to her. "Come on, Maddie. You used to love coming to the aquarium."

"Sure. When I was, like, nine."

"I'm nine," Hannah said.

Madison spared her little sister a glance. "Exactly."

Something was wrong. Even on her bad days, Madison was good with Hannah. "What's the matter, baby?"

"I just don't understand why you brought us."

"Well, because Hannah is working on her aquarium report, and I thought it would be nice for us all to spend the day together."

"You mean, spend the day with him."

"Mr. Lewis is going to show us where they feed the sharks," Hannah said.

Madison ducked her chin, hiding behind her fall of hair. "I don't see why you have to drag us on your dates, Mom. It's not like he wants us along. It's humiliating."

Cynthie's heart squeezed. Madison was three when her father had lost his job cleaning and packing fish on the island. Cynthie had done her best to hold things together, had picked up a second shift as a cashier at the Piggly Wiggly to make ends meet. But after six months, she got tired of coming home exhausted to find Doug sitting on their couch, the house a mess and the baby crying. *You need to look for work,* she'd said.

So he had. On the other side of the state.

And he'd never looked back.

Cynthie was careful not to criticize Doug to their daughter, not to complain when the child support payments came late or not at all. But she knew Doug's silence over the years—and her own erratic search for love—had primed their daughter for rejection.

The last thing Madison needed in her life now was another round of Meet Your Uncle Larry or Buddy or Phil.

"It's not a date," Cynthie said firmly. "It's a tour."

Madison slid her a glance. "Seriously?"

"A group tour," Cynthie said. She absolutely had to pay for their tickets now. She'd find the sixty dollars somehow. If she packed all their lunches . . . If she didn't pay the minimum balance on the credit card until the twenty-third . . . "There will be other families. Probably kids your age."

"I doubt it," Madison said. But she got out of the car.

They walked up the path to the aquarium entrance, Madison almost smiling, Hannah skipping ahead past the cascading fountain of bronze fish.

"Three tickets for the eleven o'clock, please," Cynthie said to the fresh-faced girl behind the counter.

"You want admission tickets?"

"Tour tickets," Cynthie said. "The eleven o'clock behind-the-scenes tour?"

"There's a tour at two," the girl said. "You want me to see if we still have spaces available?"

"Mom?" Hannah said, her voice rising.

Cynthie took a deep breath, conscious of Madison's suddenly alert posture. "We have reservations. For the eleven o'clock tour. Cynthia Lodge?"

Unless Max had failed to make reservations. Unless he'd blown them off. It wouldn't be the first time a man had failed to follow through on his promises to her and her daughters.

"Cynthie!"

She turned.

Max Lewis was striding toward them, tall and tanned and broad-shouldered, wearing cargo shorts and a wide smile. *Boy Genius to the rescue.*

Cynthie's breath whooshed out as the tension she carried around inside her all the time—the voice that said, *You're responsible, you fix this, it's all on you*—relaxed.

He'd come. He hadn't let her down. The girls weren't going to be disappointed after all.

He loomed over them awkwardly—for one crazy moment she actually wondered if he might hug her—before he settled back and her imagination settled down.

He rocked on his heels, hands in his pockets, beaming. "Great to see you. Hi, Hannah."

"Is that him?" Madison asked.

Hannah grinned. "Hey, Mr. Lewis."

Madison looked at Cynthie. "Where's the tour group?"

"Ah, I guess that would be you. Us," Max said. "Hi, I'm Max Lewis, your tour guide."

"This is my daughter, Madison," Cynthie said.

"Nice to meet you," Madison muttered. But her eyes, seeking Cynthie's, told a different story. *You said this wasn't a date,* they accused.

Cynthie swallowed. She'd never meant to lie to Maddie. But the truth was, she was attracted to Max Lewis, his steady gaze, his strong, tanned legs, his adorably mussed hair.

Her insides contracted in yearning and dismay. Maybe she'd been lying to herself.

THREE

MAX HAD PREPARED for his date with Cynthie like a novice lecturer writing his first year's lesson plans. He'd consulted with aquarium staff. He'd devised activities with Hannah in mind, based on his observations of the girl and his own memories of what had interested him as a child.

Satellite tracking of sea turtles? Check.

Shark pup nursery? Check.

Oyster spat monitoring project? Absolutely.

He had this one chance to get this right, to let Cynthie know him, to make her see him, to get her to, well . . . *like* him, he supposed. He was a teacher as well as a researcher. He loved his subject. He could do this.

But by the time they all trooped outside to see the submerged ceramic tiles used to monitor drifting oyster larvae, he was miserably aware that this date was going to exile him permanently to the Friend Zone.

Nerds did not get the girl.

He shoved his hands deeper into his pockets, clearing his throat. "The tiles provide a hard substrate for the oysters to develop. So volunteers can collect data on spatfall, and we can use that data to track where the oysters are settling."

"And that's what you do?" Cynthie asked.

"That's part of it," he said. "My focus is more on adapting abandoned crab pots to restore our oyster reefs."

And God, could he sound like a bigger geek?

"Like recycling," Hannah said.

He looked at her gratefully. "Yes."

"Well, that explains how you know Gil," Cynthie said.

He nodded. "We're partnering with local fishermen to drop the pots in different locations and depths to test where the oysters do best."

"And then you eat them," Madison said.

Cynthie grinned. "'O Oysters, come and walk with us!' the Walrus did beseech. 'A pleasant walk, a pleasant talk, along the briny beach.'"

He stared, totally taken with her, her ease, her grace, her warmth.

She flushed. "It's from a poem."

"Alice!" Hannah said.

"I know what it's from," Max said. "Lewis Carroll. I'm just surprised . . ." He saw her blush deepen and stopped.

"I do read," Cynthie said. "To the kids."

"I'm sure you read. I just wasn't sure I was making any sense," he confessed. He smiled wryly. "I tend to go on a bit when I'm talking about my work. Not everyone is interested in saving the oysters."

In saving the whales, maybe, Greg had said. *Or swimming with dolphins. Not in restoring oyster habitat.*

"It's saving people, too," Cynthie said. "It's saving jobs, isn't it? For Gil and other fishermen. That's important."

She took his breath away. With one sentence, she put a human face on the gibberish he'd been spouting for the past forty minutes.

It was like being in high school again, anonymous, unnoticed, one geeky kid swimming against the tide of shoving strangers, totally out of his element, at sea. And then Cynthie would sail into view, a goddess, a senior, the one bright spot in his otherwise dreary year, and meet his eyes and smile. And for that one moment, he had substance, he was solid, he existed again.

She made him feel visible.

Before she moved on.

They began to stroll up the boardwalk toward the aquarium building, Madison hanging back, Hannah running ahead.

"Oysters have an incredible impact on both the environment and the economy," Max said. "They're not simply a source of food for humans and marine animals. Oysters clean our water. Their reefs provide protection for fish and stabilize against erosion."

Cynthie tilted her head, smiling. "So when you were growing up, did you know you were destined to become Oyster Man, Savior of the Planet?"

He laughed, suddenly at ease. "No, when I was a kid I was mostly interested in splashing in puddles and poking things with sticks."

"I have a kid like that." She glanced at Hannah, who was hanging over the rail to peer at something in the water, and then back at him, that smile still teasing the corners of her mouth. "Your parents must be very proud."

He shrugged. "I assume so."

"You don't know?"

They never said. He had given up trying to win their notice or approval years ago.

He held open the door to the building. "They're very busy with their own research," he explained. "We're not a particularly demonstrative family."

Cynthie walked past his outstretched arm. She smelled the same, like cloves and, very faintly, of cigarettes.

"But your dad . . ." She glanced up at him sideways, making his heart pound. "He's a teacher, too, right? He must be happy you're following his example."

Max laughed ruefully. "Not according to my parents. As far as they're concerned, I'm still playing in the mud and bringing tadpoles home in jars."

Those soft green eyes held his. "Ouch."

"No, it's fine." He swallowed. Bad enough he'd dragged her outside to inspect the oyster spats. He was not whining about his childhood. "Ah, here's the kitchen."

"It stinks," Madison announced.

He looked at her, startled, and then realized she was speaking literally. The food preparation area did smell. He was too accustomed to lab smells and salt marsh smells to have noticed.

"No worse than the bait shop or the fish market," Cynthie said cheerfully, rescuing the moment.

Rescuing him. She'd always been good at that. She'd saved his ass in high school.

And hurt his pride.

For a moment, the pain came back, a blur of blood and beer and humiliation.

She said something else. He barely heard, trapped by a memory.

"What?" he asked stupidly.

Her full lips quirked. "Are we going to feed the fish? Hannah was hoping we might get to see where they feed the sharks."

"The viewing platform." He nodded. "Absolutely. But first I thought we'd help prepare a meal."

On cue, the door opened, admitting a blond-haired surfer dude with a big metal tray.

"Hi, Ben."

"Hey, Dr. Lewis," Ben said, which made Max feel about a hundred years old.

"Call me Max. We're not in the classroom now."

"Sure thing, Doctor . . . er, Max." He smiled at Cynthie and her daughters. Maybe he smiled a little longer at Cynthie.

"Ben works here," Max explained after he introduced them. "He's going to show us what to do."

Ben set them up at one of the long stainless steel tables, taking over the girls' instruction with an ease Max envied.

Max looked over at Cynthie, her long hair tied back, little pieces escaping to slide down her neck. He was excruciatingly aware of the soft pale skin at the back of her neck, the siren tattoo curling around her arm, the rise and fall of her breath under the ugly lab apron. She was humming softly as she cut raw shrimp into neat, regular pieces, making the task look easy, making it fun, as if she had nothing better to do with her day off than chop bloody bits of chum.

"I'm sorry," he said. "I didn't think about how messy this would be."

And smelly. He winced. She would never go out with him again.

"It's okay." She smiled at him, revealing a single dimple in her right cheek. "I'm used to it."

"The mess?"

"The gloves."

He stared, uncomprehending.

"I'm training to become a dental hygienist. We have to wear these"—she waggled blue fingers at him—"to work on patients."

Greg's words drummed in his head. *Ask her about herself. Women like that. They think you're interested.*

I am *interested.*

Max cleared his throat. "How long is your training?"

"Two years."

He raised his brows. "Big commitment."

"I can do it."

"Of course you can. It's great that you're going back to school. It just seems like a lot of work with everything else you've got going on."

"My mama thinks I'm out of my mind. But . . ." She stopped. "You don't want to hear all this."

"Yeah, I do." He'd never met her mother. But he understood parents being disappointed in their children's choices. "Is she giving you a hard time?"

"Oh, no, Mama's been a big help with the girls. She just can't figure out why I want to clean teeth for a living when I could be bringing home a couple hundred in tips on the weekends."

"Why do you?"

The dimple reappeared. "It wasn't the uniforms, that's for sure."

He wanted to make her smile again. "I bet you look great in scrubs."

"At least I won't have any trouble picking out my clothes in the morning."

He watched her carefully. "That's one reason."

"I just . . . I want to help people, I guess. I thought about maybe being a nurse, but I've had enough of working nights and holidays. In a dentist's office, you get regular hours. Regular salary. Plus, you work in an office, people treat you with respect. Like that kid treats you."

"You mean Ben? He was a student of mine. I recommended him for the internship here. And you just changed the subject back to me," Max said on a note of discovery.

Cynthie bent her head over the cutting board. A corner of her mouth indented in a smirk.

"You can't get away with that forever, you know," he said. "Not in your job. Sooner or later, you'll need to talk."

"Are you kidding? Nobody wants to listen to their server. Mostly they want to tell you their troubles, complain about their lives, and order drinks."

"Wait until you're a hygienist," he said. "Your patients won't be able to do more than swish and spit. Or grunt. You'll be forced to talk just to drown out the awful music."

Their eyes met. Her smile escaped, wide and warm.

He grinned at her, triumphant.

CYNTHIE snuck another look at Max as they stood outside the otter enclosure.

She was used to guys who talked about themselves, about what they drove or what they drank or how much money they made or didn't make.

Max talked about the world she knew, sea and sand, mud and tides, but he invested every observation with urgency and importance, facts tumbling out of him like shells caught at the lip of the tide. She found herself smiling and nodding as he talked, conscious of every move he made, almost breathless when his arm brushed hers.

And even though she got distracted, she was caught in his passion for his subject. He kept stopping his flow to point things out, to gesture, to explain, spinning a net of words that pulled all the exhibits together somehow in a shiny, living, breathing ball.

He must be a very good teacher.

Cynthie wasn't the only one infected by his enthusiasm.

Madison and Hannah crowded close to watch as the tech Ben fed the otters through a sliding door in the back of the exhibit. Hannah was on tiptoe with excitement, her hands smudging the thick glass. Even Madison was acting like her old self again instead of a preadolescent pain in the ass.

"Thanks," Cynthie said quietly to Max. "For everything. I'm pretty sure feeding the otters wasn't on the schedule."

He looked down at her, making her aware of his height. His legs were very long. When was the last time she'd stood close enough to a man to notice his bare knees? Or the sun-warmed smell of his T-shirt, the scent of salt and man?

"Otters have a very high metabolism. They have to eat five times a day."

She shook her head. "Not their schedule. Yours. We've taken up your whole morning."

He shrugged those broad shoulders. "One of the advantages of my job is that I get to set my own hours."

"That must be nice," Cynthie said. Between work and school and the kids, she never had a moment to call her own.

"Was there something else you wanted to see?"

"No." She smiled. "This has been great. The girls are having a great time."

"What about you?"

"I'm having a good time, too," she said honestly.

"Because nothing says 'hot date' like food prep at the aquarium," he said wryly.

She smiled. This wasn't a date. But for some reason, it was important that he understand the gift he'd given them.

"It's fun just to be with them," she said. "I can't remember the last time we all hung out together without me fixing dinner or doing laundry. Without me nagging them about chores or homework." *Without worrying about shopping for groceries or paying the bills.*

One of the otters pounced on a hard-boiled egg.

Madison giggled. "Ohmigod, she's so cute."

"Ah, actually, she's a he," Max said. "All the exhibit's otters are male."

Cynthie looked at him sideways. "The aquarium doesn't like girls?"

He smiled. "They're simply following the divisions found in nature. Wild otters generally separate into two kinds of groups—mothers with their young, and small, rambunctious bands of males."

"Sort of like humans," Cynthie joked. "Growing up, it was me and my mom, and now it's me and my girls."

They strolled along the river gallery toward the swamp.

Max cleared his throat. "The girls don't see their fathers much?"

Cynthie shook her head. "Doug—that's Maddie's dad—"

"I remember Doug," Max said a little grimly.

"He lives in Charlotte. I think there's another woman now. Another family, maybe. Doug doesn't really keep in touch. Well, it's been ten years," she added, trying to be fair.

"But you have a child together."

She sighed. "Yeah. He keeps saying it's too expensive to come visit, but I wish he would invite Maddie to stay sometimes. Not that I'd feel great about her going, but he's still her dad."

"What about Hannah's father?"

She didn't look at him, focusing her attention on the pond turtles on the other side of the glass. "Not in the picture."

"Ever?" He sounded surprised.

He was a nice guy. She'd probably shocked him. Hell, she'd shocked herself, ten years ago.

"It was right after the divorce," Cynthie said. "I was drinking too much and feeling kind of low, and some Marine came into the bar and, well . . . Nine months later, I had Hannah. He's never seen her."

Max frowned. "He still has a responsibility to pay child support."

"Maybe he would. If I'd asked him." Deliberately, she turned from the glass and met his gaze, refusing to hide, hating to lie. "If I'd known his name."

Their eyes held. Her heart beat faster in defiance and something else.

There. Now he knew.

And now, she knew from experience, he would run.

Or maybe he'd run later.

Guys like him—attractive guys in their early thirties, smart, employed, well-educated guys—they didn't hit on women like her. Unless they planned on nailing an easy target.

"I told Hannah her daddy is a war hero who's away serving his country." Cynthie smiled lopsidedly. "It might even be true. My point is, I have a history of making bad decisions. I'm not looking to repeat myself."

Hannah and Madison were on the other side of the room, peering at the alligators lurking in the shadows of the man-made cypress swamp.

Max cleared his throat again, the sound rasping against the softly falling water.

Here it comes, Cynthie thought.

"You've got wonderful kids," he said. "You've done a great job with them. You should be proud."

Her breath caught in her throat. She stared at him wide-eyed, her mouth opening and closing like she was a fish.

All her life, Cynthie had been judged. By her mother, her teachers, her customers, herself. And here was this man telling her she'd done good.

Was he for real?

"Mo-om." Madison's voice jerked Cynthie out of wherever she'd been drifting and into the air. "It's almost one o'clock. I told Taylor I'd come over at two. We're going to be late."

Cynthie pulled herself together. Of course, Madison wanted to go to her friend Taylor's. Taylor was good for Maddie. And her home was perfect. Her family was perfect. Her grandmother baked cookies every day.

"No, we're not," Cynthie said. She smiled at Max. "We should go. We need to let you get back to . . ."

Your life.

And let me get back to mine.

The thought left her oddly bereft.

"Your work," she finished.

His light, intent eyes focused on her face. "It's Sunday," he said.

"Yes." She swallowed. "My shift starts at four. But this was great. We really did have a good time. Hannah especially. Thank you so much."

The girls, reminded of their manners, said all the appropriate things. Even Madison blushed and stammered thanks.

"I'll walk you to your car," Max said.

His manners, Cynthie noted, were excellent. "You don't have to do that."

"I want to."

She could argue. But she didn't want to lose his company. Not yet. Anyway, it was good for the girls to see an example of a guy treating a woman politely.

They all trooped out to the lobby, Madison walking ahead, gradually establishing a proper teenage distance.

They emerged from the building into a flood of sunshine.

"I want to see you again," Max said.

Cynthie blinked in the sudden brightness. "Why?"

His jaw squared a little. "Because . . . I like you. I always have."

His earnest voice tickled at her brain, teased at her memory. Almost, almost, as if she'd heard those words before. From him.

She stared at him, wondering. And then shook the thought away.

"I like you, too," she said. "But we're not in high school anymore."

He grinned. "Thank God."

An answering smile tugged her mouth. "Yeah, okay. But the thing is, I have kids. Bad enough I have to dump them on my mom on the nights I work. I can't ditch them to go out with you."

"So we can bring them along sometimes. Do things together. Like today."

Like a family.

For a moment, longing flooded her chest. Her eyes blurred. It would be so nice to have a man around. She didn't miss Doug. She didn't balk at hard work. She didn't mind cutting the grass and paying the bills and figuring out how to replace the washer under the kitchen sink when the pipes leaked all over the peeling vinyl floor. But the loneliness, the sheer weight of being the Only One Responsible, got to her sometimes.

What would it be like to have an ally? Another grown-up to answer Hannah's questions, to coax a smile to Madison's face.

Girls need a masculine role model, Cynthie thought wistfully. Maybe her own life would have been different if her father had stuck around.

And then reality reared its ugly head. Reality and regret. That was old Cynthie thinking. New Cynthie knew better.

Maybe Hannah was too young to remember or care about her mother's string of boyfriends, the Men Who Couldn't Commit and Did Not Stay. But Madison was more fragile. God knew what kind of damage Cynthie had already done to Madison.

She looked at them standing, waiting by the car. Madison had put aside her impatience to get home and was leaning over, teasing Hannah to make her laugh.

Love for her daughters swelled Cynthie's heart, pushing out everything else.

She was all they had.

She needed to be enough for them. Good enough. Strong enough.

"Thanks, but I don't think that's a good idea. I'm trying to get my life in order," she said. "I don't bring guys home anymore. My girls need me to put them first. They need to be able to count on me."

"Of course they do. But what about what you need?" Max asked quietly.

Her throat constricted. She swallowed hard. "I need to be the person they can count on."

He held her gaze for long moments. And then he nodded. "Right."

She blew out her breath, relieved and deflated.

"So it will have to be lunch then," he said. "Or coffee."

Her pulse leaped, but she shook her head. "You're not listening. I can't go out with you."

"You do occasionally stop to eat, right? During the day, when the kids are at school?"

"Sometimes," she said cautiously. "If I have a break between classes."

"Me, too." His gray eyes gleamed, or maybe that was a trick of the sunlight. "Say, Wednesday? One o'clock?"

She felt herself softening, weakening, giving in. "Were you this pushy in high school?"

"Nope." He smiled crookedly. "If I had been, maybe you'd remember me."

Her face got hot.

"Just lunch," he coaxed. "Just friends. Everybody needs a friend."

What about what you need? he'd asked.

Her heart quivered. Maybe she could do this. Maybe she could let herself have this much. As long as she wasn't taking anything away from the girls . . .

"Wednesday," she said.

FOUR

FIVE WEEKS LATER, Max tore his gaze from the entrance to the student union and forced himself to focus on the papers in his lap. Cynthie was late.

He wasn't worried, exactly. She had his cell phone number. She would have called if she wasn't coming.

Unless she was blowing him off.

His fingers tapped the pages. He was not going to overreact. She was running a few minutes behind schedule, that's all.

Okay, fifteen minutes. He couldn't help the quick glance at his phone. Almost twenty. But he could wait. He was good at waiting. He'd had plenty of practice, standing around on the steps after school, waiting for one of his parents to remember to pick him up. Even Julie, when they'd lived together, had never been on time for anything.

Female prerogative, darling, she would explain breezily, dismissing his concern and irritation.

Power trip, Greg had said the last time she'd canceled dinner plans at the last minute.

But Cynthie wasn't like that. *Single moms are good at time management,* she'd informed him once with a brilliant smile. *We have to be.*

She'd never been late for one of their dates before.

Max frowned, unseeing, at the neatly typed pages. Not that she would call this a date. He wasn't sure he could call it a date, either. She wouldn't let him pay for her lunch, not after the first time. But he'd bought drinks, bottled water for him, Diet Mountain Dew for her. He'd had time to learn her habits. For the last five weeks, they'd been meeting for lunch three days a week, squeezing in an hour between classes, snatching coffee and conversation in the well-lit, noisy, very public student center.

Cynthie had made it clear she wasn't ready to take their relationship outside this building. Max wanted more. But if he pushed for more, he might lose even this.

"Sorry I'm late."

Cynthie stood beside "their" table, her face flushed and smiling, her dark hair sliding from its messy ponytail, and all Max's frustration dissolved in simple happiness.

"No problem. It's good to see you." He started to his feet, spilling papers to the floor.

"Oops." She bent to pick them up, her head more or less level with his lap.

His body tightened at the attention.

"I've got that," he said, embarrassed, stooping.

She glanced at a page before handing it to him. " 'Insufficient contribution of sink habitats to spawning stock,' " she read aloud. "Sexy stuff. Did you write this?"

She was so pretty, smiling on her knees before him, her green eyes alight with humor. Need balled in his gut.

He cleared his throat. "Ah, no. It's a dissertation draft for one of my grad students. I promised I'd get it back to him this week."

"I don't want to interrupt your work."

"You're not. I just brought it along so I'd have something to do." He shoved the pages into his backpack.

"Max . . ." Cynthie straightened slowly, her expression troubled. "You've got better things to do than hanging around wasting your time with me."

It was an apology.

Or maybe a warning.

"I'm not wasting anything," he said firmly. Certainly not this chance to see her, to be with her, again. "I like spending time with you."

Her face glowed.

"Anyway, I've got to eat," he added. "Have a soda. How was your class?"

"Thanks." She slid into her usual seat across the table. "It was good. Better than good. We had a guest speaker today. An oral surgeon. That's why I'm late."

"Lecture run long?"

"No, I stayed after class." She rummaged in her monster-size purse for her brown-bag lunch. "That's the exciting part."

She always brought her lunch from home. To save money, Max suspected. He'd taken to doing the same so that she wouldn't feel awkward about the relative state of their finances.

Pulling out two squishy plastic packages, she laid one in front of him.

He looked from the package to her bright, expectant face. "What's this?"

"Lunch."

"I brought my lunch."

She sniffed. "Hard-boiled eggs again, I bet, and an apple. I've seen what you pack. I made you a proper sandwich."

Warmth suffused his chest as he stared down at her offering. "That was really nice of you."

He peeled back plastic wrap, revealing a white, moist, lumpy, unappetizing square. He was pretty sure his eggs had more nutritional value. But he didn't say a word.

"I hope you like chicken salad," she said.

"Love it." Anyway, he would love this chicken salad. Because she'd made it for him.

He took a hearty bite, and flavor exploded in his mouth, tangy, creamy, sweet. *Wow.* He swallowed. "Okay, I owe you one. This is really good."

She grinned. "You don't have to sound so surprised. It's Mama's recipe—Duke's Mayonnaise and a touch of pickle relish."

"Your mother is amazing."

She tipped her head. "Your mom never made you chicken salad?"

He shook his head. Dr. Dorothea Bell-Lewis did not cook. She opened cans. And bottles of wine. And he was not so pathetic that he was going to discuss the imagined shortcomings of his privileged childhood with Cynthie, who grew up with nothing and never complained about anything. "Tell me about your class. What happened?"

"Well." Cynthie swallowed a bite of sandwich. "This doctor came in today, Dr. Rice. He does a lot of implants, bone grafts, wisdom tooth extractions, stuff like that. Anyway, I asked some questions in class about postoperative care. So later, when I was leaving, he stopped me and asked if I was interested in a part-time job."

"That's great," Max said. "You obviously impressed him."

She blinked. "You think?"

"You don't have to sound so surprised," Max said, echoing her words to him, and was rewarded when she laughed.

"It would be like a receptionist job, answering phones, making appointments. But he'd pay. And he said I'd have a chance to observe him."

Max nodded. "Job shadowing."

"Yeah." Cynthie smiled her lopsided smile, revealing her dimple. "Not that I have time to pick up a second job."

Max frowned. He didn't like to see her dismiss an opportunity so easily. "What are the hours?"

"He said he could be flexible. He mostly wants somebody in the office when his regular staff takes lunch. Twelve to one-thirty, Monday through Friday."

Max set down his sandwich, his appetite suddenly gone. "You could do that. You don't have classes then."

You have lunch with me.

"I don't know." She crumpled her napkin. "I probably wouldn't be any good. I don't have any experience."

He didn't want to lose her company. But he couldn't sit here and listen to her denigrate herself. "You're a quick learner. Look at how well you're doing in class. Anyway, the whole point of the job is that you'd get experience. Training."

She collected her trash and his, stuffing it in her lunch bag to throw away. "I have to think about it. My schedule's crazy enough already."

"The job pays, you said. If you took it, you could cut back your hours at the restaurant. Maybe take a night off now and then to be home with your girls and do your homework."

Her busy hands stilled. Her gaze fixed on his face, her eyes wide and shining.

Max shifted, uncomfortable. "What?"

"Thank you."

"For what?"

"For making me feel like I can do this."

Heat crept up his neck to his ears. He didn't deserve her thanks. "I didn't do anything."

Except wonder, selfishly, how he was going to get through his days without her.

She shook her head, smiling. "Maybe it comes naturally for you. Maybe teachers have to be encouraging or something. But all my life, nobody's ever looked at me the way you do. Made me believe in myself the way you do. It's like I see this future for myself that nobody else sees. Except my friend Meg. And now you."

She was killing him here.

"Glad to help," he said gruffly. "Anytime."

She stood with him to bus their table. "You're a nice guy, Max Lewis," she said softly.

She stepped in, standing on tiptoe to brush her lips across his.

Shock held him still. Her lips were so soft. Her breath was so warm. Her body was round and lush against his and he forgot where they were and what he was doing and kissed her back hard, sliding his hand up into her hair, taking her mouth with his.

He heard a rushing in his ears like the sound of the sea. He was drowning in her, so warm, so close, trembling in his arms, kissing him back, making him dizzy. His blood roared.

A sound intruded, hard, percussive.

Someone clapping, Max thought dimly. Some wise-ass student applauding them.

He raised his head. "I have to see you again."

Cynthie licked her lips, her eyes dark and unfocused, so beautiful he almost lunged for her again. "When?"

"We could go out. Friday night. Dinner."

"I . . ." Her pulse beat in her throat. He wanted to kiss her there, in the fragrant hollow below her jaw. He wanted to lick her skin. "I have to be home with the girls."

"Then let me come over."

She took a step back, folding her arms across her breasts. "You can't. I can't." There was a shaky note in her voice almost like panic. "I don't do that now. I won't risk them getting attached to some random guy I'm dating."

The words stung. *Some random guy* . . . She meant him. After five weeks, that's all he was. Whatever she said about his belief in her, she still didn't trust in him.

"Are you sure it's the girls you're worried about?" he asked slowly.

Color flooded her face. She didn't answer him directly. "It's not that I don't want to see you."

"Right."

"We can still . . ." Her voice trailed off.

"Have coffee," he suggested.

"If that's what you want."

"You know what I want."

She raised her eyebrows.

Because, he realized with blinding clarity, all her life guys had been wanting things from her. Her smiles. Her attention. Sex.

And, yeah, he wanted those things from her, too. But that didn't automatically make him an asshole. There were other reasons a guy could want her, more reasons than she could imagine or was ready to hear. He loved her optimism and her grit. He admired her cheerful determination to make the best of things.

And he needed her to want him, too.

"I want to spend time with you," he said firmly. "When's your first class on Monday?"

"Nine o'clock."

"We meet at eight-thirty, that gives us half an hour for coffee," he said.

Her smile bloomed. "I guess it does." She met his gaze hopefully. "Friends?"

His heart squeezed like a fist. She asked for so little. He wanted to give her so much.

All my life, nobody's ever looked at me the way you do. Made me believe in myself the way you do . . . Except my friend Meg. And now you.

Cynthie needed friends. She needed him, even if it was only for this.

"Friends," he promised.

FIVE

"STUPID TURTLE," CYNTHIE muttered, staring at the ditch where the turtle had disappeared after she'd rescued it.

Except the turtle was smarter than Cynthie.

If she hadn't stopped to save it from crossing the road, she'd be home by now. Not stalled by the side of the highway with darkness coming on.

Dumb, dumb, dumb.

She tried Meg's number again without success, and then, with a little sigh, called her mother.

"If you'd just stay home," Mama said, "instead of running around like some eighteen-year-old college girl—"

Cynthie gripped the unresponsive steering wheel. "I know. I'm sorry. I'll be there as quick as I can. It's probably just the battery. Somebody will stop and give me a jump."

She tried not to imagine a truckful of drunk, rowdy yahoos pulling up behind her on this deserted stretch of road.

At least the girls weren't in the car with her.

"Do you need me to come get you?" Wanda asked.

Cynthie's muscles relaxed. That was the thing about Mama. She might fuss, but she always came through in a pinch.

"Thanks, Mama, but I'm forty minutes away. I need you to wait for Hannah. Jane's bringing her home after soccer."

"Madison can watch her."

"For a little while. But I don't know yet when I'll be home. Maddie's not old enough to babysit yet."

"You were younger than that when I left you."

That's how I know she's not old enough, Cynthie thought. "Times are different now," she said. "Please, Mama."

And Mama, being Mama, agreed.

Cynthie thanked her and ended the call and tried the ignition again. *Click*, and then nothing.

She resisted the urge to bang her head on the steering wheel. The whole evening was turning into some kind of horrible math problem: *If x = the probability of a helpful stranger happening by with jumper cables, and y = the groceries in the trunk, how long will it take for the milk to spoil?*

Another call to Meg went straight through to voice mail. Jane was already helping Cynthie out by taking Hannah to soccer practice.

Cynthie bit her lip, doing more mental calculations. She barely had money for a new battery. No way could she afford ninety dollars for a tow.

She needed a jump. Or a friend who didn't live forty minutes away. Or a man she could count on. Not that she'd had a lot of those in her life.

Until—maybe—recently.

Before she could talk herself out of it, she reached for her phone again.

HEADLIGHTS swung in a blinding arc across the highway. Cynthie shielded her eyes as the vehicle U-turned to face her car, pulling onto the grassy verge ahead.

Max.

She got out to meet him, her heart skipping, her flat black shoes sinking in the sandy soil.

He looked very tall walking toward her along the shoulder. The light splintered behind him, casting long shadows. She felt a jump in her belly like nerves.

"I'm so sorry to bother you. But I really appreciate this," she said when he was close enough to hear. "I stopped at the grocery store after class tonight, it's a lot cheaper than the one on the island, and—" She was babbling.

"No bother." His face emerged in the fading light, all lean planes and sharp angles. His gaze sought hers, a smile tugging the corners of his mouth. "What are friends for?"

The thing that was wound tight inside her all the time suddenly relaxed like the broken coil of a watch. She stared at him, speechless.

His eyes narrowed. "You okay?"

She nodded. Now that he was here, she was safe. Everything was fine. But a slight quiver remained in the pit of her stomach like the premonition of danger.

Help.

He nodded toward the car. "What happened?"

She'd already explained on the phone. "My car died."

"While you were driving?"

"Uh, no. I had to stop, and then the engine wouldn't start again."

He glanced at the empty road, the quiet ditch. "You stopped. Here?"

"Yeah." She sighed. "Okay, see, there was this turtle crossing the road . . ."

"You stopped for a turtle," he repeated in that expressionless voice men used when they thought you were an idiot.

"Look, I know it was dumb."

"Probably a box turtle."

"Whatever. It was going to be a flat turtle if I didn't stop."

"Turtle conservation," he said. "I like it. Good for you."

She hunched her shoulders, embarrassed by his praise. Grateful he wasn't yelling at her for her stupidity. "Good for the turtle, anyway."

He smiled and strolled toward her car, propping open the hood. "Let's see what you've got here."

She peered past his shoulder at the tangle of dirty pipes and wires. "I think it's the battery." She hoped. She didn't know how she was going to pay for anything else.

"No cracks. That's good. When was the last time you replaced it?"

She shrugged. "Three years?"

"Uh-huh. Your connections are corroded."

"How can you tell?"

He pointed. His sleeves were rolled halfway to his elbows, revealing corded muscle and fine dark hair. "See that white stuff around the terminals?"

"Um . . . Yes?"

He grinned and turned his head. His eyes were warm and amused, his face close enough to kiss. He smelled amazing, like salty ocean and musky male. If she leaned forward just a tiny bit, she could bury her nose in his shirt.

Tension arced between them, sparking a jolt in her tummy strong enough to power a hundred batteries.

Her lips parted.

He cleared his throat. "I'll get the jumper cables."

She blinked, watching him walk away. It had been two weeks since she told him she wanted to be friends, two weeks of hastily gulped coffee and snatches of conversation, exchanging status updates that had gradually become more intimate, like Facebook posts. *What are you up to? What's on your mind? How are you feeling today?*

Just friends. Most of the time, she could make herself believe it.

But not at night, when loneliness lay beside her like a restive bed partner, when she woke aching and empty in the long stretch between two and four A.M., when the memory of his smile drifted with her into sleep and was the first thing she looked forward to in her day.

And not now.

She watched him pull jumper cables from his trunk and pop his hood with the unself-conscious assurance of a guy who didn't need to read instructions. She was used to doing things for herself and her girls. But there was a certain shameful relief in letting him take care of things, in letting him take over.

She took a deep breath of evening air, filling her lungs with the scents of salt marsh and exhaust.

He pulled a handkerchief from his pocket—wow, you didn't see a lot of younger guys with those—to wipe the posts before connecting a clamp to her battery. His hands on the tools were blunt-tipped and tanned, broad across the palm and callused. Not what she'd imagined a professor's hands to look like at all. She imagined the feel of them on her skin and swallowed.

To distract herself, she said, "I thought you would drive one of those hybrid thingies. Like a Prius or something."

He shot her a smile as he fixed clamps to his own battery, red and then black. "Not much room to haul things in a Prius."

She glanced at his car, a Volvo SUV, sleek and muscular, safe and unassuming, more than she could ever afford. There was no place in her life for a car like that.

Or for a man like Max, no matter how grateful she was.

He connected the final clamp to a protruding bolt under the hood of her rusting minivan.

"My old car was a Thunderbird," she said out of nowhere. Like she had something to prove.

He cocked an eyebrow. "Sexy."

"Yeah."

"Not very reliable, though."

She sighed. "No."

"Okay, we're all hooked up. I'm going to start my engine, let it run for a few minutes. Then, when I give you the signal, I want you to try to start yours."

"I know how hookups work," she said dryly.

He laughed.

In the car, Cynthie waited, watched. When he gave the thumbs-up, she held her breath and turned the key. The engine coughed and caught. The van shuddered to life.

She rolled down her window and grinned as Max approached. "Success!"

"For now. I'll follow you home."

"You don't need to do that."

"Yeah, I do. In case you stall out again."

She wanted to argue. He'd gone to enough trouble already. She couldn't ask him to drive almost an hour and a half round-trip when they weren't even sleeping together.

But the truth was, her girls were waiting for her. She couldn't risk stalling again. So she thanked him and watched his SUV pull out behind her.

His headlights shone in her rearview mirror, a steady, reassuring presence all along the dark roads toward home.

* * *

AS he drove, Max kept an eye out for someplace open in the off-season, somewhere he could grab dinner on the way back. The Fish House. Wasn't that where Cynthie said she worked?

Her rear lights blinked, signaling a turn. He followed her van as she turned away from the harbor down an increasingly dark and narrow road that ended under the trees. PARADISE SHOALS, the weathered sign read.

Max looked around. Definitely not paradise. And no shoals, either, only a haphazard cluster of trailer homes up on cinder blocks, out of sight of the water, out of mind for the people who summered in the overblown beachfront McMansions slowly eroding the dunes.

People like Max's parents.

Cynthie parked the van under a listing metal carport beside one of the trailers. Weeds sprouted through holes in the wooden lattice. But he spotted a pot of yellow chrysanthemums decorating the sagging porch and striped curtains in the rusting slatted windows.

A second car sat in the driveway. Max angled the Volvo to avoid it, pulling in under a narrow stand of pines.

Cynthie got out of the van.

Probably expecting him to flash his lights and drive away.

"I can stick around," he said. "If you need a ride to work."

He was going that way anyway, right? He wasn't really desperate enough that he'd grasp any excuse to spend more time in her company.

She shook her head. "Thanks, but I'm not working tonight. I did what you said and cut back my hours at the restaurant. Do you—"

The front door banged. "There you are." The woman on the porch was an older version of Cynthie. Or a drawing of Cynthie that had been submerged under water for years, her brightness blurred and faded, her outlines softened by age. Only the woman's hair, an improbable yellow, glowed in the light spilling from the trailer. "Girls are getting hungry. I put your casserole in the oven."

"Thanks, Mama. You want to stay for dinner?"

"No, honey, I want to go home, put on my shows, put up my feet, and have a cigarette." Her gaze fixed on Max. "Who's this?"

"Max Lewis. I'm a friend of Cynthie's."

Her eyes were sharp, her handshake soft. "I'm Wanda. Nice to meet you."

"You, too. You make good chicken salad."

She dimpled. "Well, aren't you sweet."

"Max gave me a jump," Cynthie explained.

"Did he?" Wanda surveyed him, up and down. "You can jump me anytime."

Max felt his ears heat. "Er . . . Thank you."

Cynthie rolled her eyes. "Bye, Mama," she said pointedly.

"Bye, baby girl." Wanda hitched her purse over one shoulder and descended the rickety trailer steps. "Don't do anything I wouldn't do."

Cynthie grinned. "Well, that gives me lots of options."

Wanda's laugh rasped as she got into her car. She waved and drove away.

Cynthie smiled at him ruefully. "Well, now you've met the whole family."

Her mother and her daughters. No fathers in her girls' lives. Or in Cynthie's, apparently.

"I like your mother," Max said.

"Mama's great. She wasn't a big fan of me going back to school, but every time I need her, she comes through. I couldn't make it without her." Cynthie hesitated. "You want to come in before you head back? I can give you dinner. Or at least a cup of coffee or something."

He hadn't followed her home to beg a free meal. He was all too aware of the limits she'd set on their relationship.

"I've had enough coffee recently to last a lifetime," he joked, and then could have kicked himself at the flash of hurt in her eyes. She was offering him *friendship*. He felt like a heel for rejecting her. "But I'd love to have dinner with you," he added hastily. "If it's not too much trouble."

"No trouble." Her smile shot straight to his heart. "Let me just grab the groceries."

"I can help with that."

He filled his hands with grocery bags and followed her inside.

Cynthie's daughters sprawled on the couch, watching the old tube television in the corner.

At their entrance, Hannah danced over, throwing her arms around her mother's waist. "Hey, Mom. Hiya, Mr. Lewis."

Cynthie smoothed back her daughter's wild puff of hair. "Hey, yourself. How was school today?"

"Good. I got an A on my science report."

"That is awesome. Can you take this into the kitchen for me, sweetie? Madison, how was your day?"

The older girl didn't take her eyes off the TV. "All right."

"You remember Mr. Lewis."

She glanced over her shoulder. "Hi."

"It's nice to see you again," he said.

"Are you done with your homework?" Cynthie asked.

"Grandma said I could watch *Modern Family*."

Cynthie made a humming noise in her throat. "After you've done your homework."

Max went outside to get the final bag of groceries.

"I'll do it after dinner," Madison said.

The television shut off. In the silence, Max could hear Cynthie. "You need to do it now. We're eating late tonight."

"That's not my fault."

He pushed open the door. Madison was on her feet, glowering at Cynthie. Hannah swiveled her head like an observer at a tennis match, her small face creased with worry.

"I don't want to do it," Madison said. "Algebra's stupid. Anyway, Meemaw says boys don't like girls who are too smart."

Cynthie opened her mouth. Shut it.

"Smart boys do," Max said.

Three faces turned to him with nearly identical expressions of surprise.

Madison recovered first. "You mean dorks."

Max shrugged. "If you like."

"I'm a dork," Hannah said.

Max bit back a grin.

Madison's face softened as she regarded her little sister. "It's okay for you to be smart, Hannah Banana. But I'm not. I can't do it. I don't get it."

"Have you asked for help?" Max asked.

Madison's shoulders rose to her ears, an automatic defensive gesture that made him twinge in sympathy. "Who's going to help me? You?"

"It's been years since I took algebra. I thought you could ask your mom." He met Cynthie's wide green eyes. "Didn't you take algebra this summer?"

"I—"

"Mom's too busy," Madison said. "She's always too busy."

Max's mom had been too busy. She had no time to volunteer at his various schools or attend his track meets. It would never have occurred to her to monitor his homework. In Dorothea's view, his parents had provided Max with superior genetic material and an excellent example of academic rigor. If he failed to live up to them, he had only himself to blame.

Cynthie was a great mom.

And Madison was clearly trying to jerk her chain.

Cynthie broke Max's gaze, her face flushing. "Not too busy to help you, baby."

"You have to make dinner."

"It's a casserole," Cynthie said cheerfully. "All I need is a minute to throw together a salad."

Max shook his head in admiration. After the lousy day she'd had, after dealing with school and work and a crappy battery, she was still holding it together. Still all-in where her daughters were concerned.

He wanted to hug her. He wanted to help.

"Hannah and I can make salad," he said. "You two do homework."

AFTER dinner, Cynthie watched Max tease a half smile from Madison across the kitchen table and felt her heart expand to bursting point. This evening had turned into everything she'd once longed for.

And everything she feared. A guy who could appreciate her mama's chicken salad and praise her daughter's science report. Who would be there when her car broke down or Madison was acting up. Who made her feel special and smart.

If Cynthie wasn't careful, she could let herself want this. Want him. And that would never do.

Max was being nice to them now because he was a really nice guy. But nice guys didn't stay with women like her, a single mom with two kids and no money and a twelve-year-old minivan. And when he figured that out and left, Cynthie wasn't the only one who would be hurt and disappointed.

She took a deep breath and stood to clear the table.

Max got up with his plate.

She smiled and took it from him. "I've got this. I'm sure you want to get on the road."

"I want to help."

Hannah piped up. "The rule is, whoever cooks doesn't have to clean up."

Max kept his gaze on Cynthie. "Will you be okay now?"

The question tugged at her heart. She made herself answer lightly, which was a lot better than throwing herself on his chest and begging him to stay. "I think I can handle loading the dishwasher on my own."

He frowned a little. "I meant in the morning with the car."

"I'll work something out," she said. That's what she did. Worked things out. She wasn't going to burden him anymore. "Thanks for the rescue."

"I owed you one."

"It was just a sandwich."

"What are you . . . Oh, the chicken salad. I was talking about you saving my ass back in high school."

Cynthie glanced around automatically for the girls, but they were already gone, taking advantage of her distraction to turn on the TV. Anyway, they probably heard worse in school every day.

Max cleared his throat. "Cynthie."

His low tone made her shiver. She was achingly aware of him, standing close, those steady eyes, that earnest voice. His heat. His scent. She trembled, as if she were seventeen again, teetering on the brink of her first love.

Except even at seventeen, he wouldn't have been her first. She wouldn't have been his type.

"Hey, I was watching that." Hannah's voice rose the way it did when she got tired.

"It was a commercial," Madison said.

"It was almost over. Change it back."

Cynthie pulled herself together. "Well." She smiled at Max, taking a step back. "It's been fun. Thanks for helping me out."

"My pleasure. Thanks for dinner," Max said, which was

polite of him, considering that the casserole was mostly noodles and canned soup and he'd made the salad.

Men liked meat. Doug had always complained when their
budget didn't stretch to hamburger every day. It was another
depressing reminder, if Cynthie had needed one, of how little
she had to offer a man like Max.

He left soon after, leaving her to referee the girls' squabble
over the remote.

A piece of her heart trailed after him.

Stupid, stupid. She was not standing around feeling sorry
for herself. She had too much to do.

She supervised the girls as they showered and packed their
lunches for tomorrow, listened to Hannah's spelling words
while they brushed their teeth, found Madison's gym shorts in
the dirty laundry and a permission slip for Health crumpled at
the bottom of her book bag.

"I can't find my book! We have library tomorrow," Hannah
said.

So after tossing the first load of clothes into the washer, Cynthie searched for the missing library book. By the time their
backpacks were ready by the door and the girls were in bed,
Cynthie was ready to fall flat herself. Or follow Mama's example
and curl up on the couch with her shows and cigarettes. She'd
given up smoking last winter when Hannah caught that cough.
But after her crappy day, she deserved something. A glass of
wine. A cigarette. Sex.

Sex with Max, she thought, and shivered deep inside with
longing and regret.

With a little sigh, she pulled out her biochemistry textbook.

She was taking notes on the effects of phosphate concen-
trations on tooth enamel when a noise penetrated her concen-
tration. A car, outside. Cynthie frowned. The residents of
Paradise Shoals, the ones who weren't unemployed or retired,
worked whatever hours they could get. So it wasn't unusual to
hear somebody coming or going at this hour.

She heard the beep of a key lock and then a muffled metal-
lic thump right by the house.

She wasn't worried. Not exactly. Not on Dare Island. But a
single woman with two little girls had to be careful.

She twitched aside the curtains. A car was parked behind hers on the drive, a looming shape in the dark. Her heart beating wildly, she flipped on the outside light. Yanked open the door.

Max smiled on her front porch. "Oh, good, you're still up. I need your keys to pop the hood and change your battery."

Six

MAX SEATED THE heavy battery in the hold-down tray, taking care to line up the charges.

Cynthie sat in a mildewed plastic garden chair, watching him. She'd tugged a hoodie over her dress, but her legs, curled around the chair, were smooth and bare.

He was glad for her company. From the corner of his eye, he could see her feet in flip-flops, her toenails painted sparkly silver. The image of her glittery toenails burned the back of his eyeballs like fireworks against the autumn sky.

He stuck his head back under the hood before he got any ideas.

She sighed contentedly, cradling a longneck bottle in her hands. "This is nice."

Max's beer stood untouched on the table beside her. From the darkness around them, a few late tree frogs, joined by a backup insect chorus, sang their mating song. *Let's get it on . . .*

Like he needed encouragement.

He cleared his throat, ratcheting the clamp that held the battery in place. "Yes."

She took a pull of her beer. "Nice of you, I mean. I was

afraid we'd scared you off. A lot of guys—single guys—don't like kids."

"I haven't been around them much. I like yours," he said simply. "I had a good time tonight."

"So did I. I get so used to listening to the girls, I sometimes forget what it's like to have an adult conversation at the dinner table."

"You're good at getting them to open up. My parents—" he said and stopped.

"Your parents," she prompted softly after a pause.

It wasn't only the kids she could get to spill their guts, Max reflected. But he was a grown man, long past the point of complaining about his parents' absorption in their own pursuits. As he got older, their lack of interest in how he, their only child, spent his days was actually something of a relief.

He looked at Cynthie, her cloudy dark hair, her soft green eyes, her glittering toes. Besides, he didn't want her pity. A pity fuck, maybe . . .

He shook his head, reattaching the battery cables to the terminal posts. Red, then black.

"Anyway, you're good with the girls, too," Cynthie said. "That was cool what you said to Maddie. About boys liking smart girls."

"It's true." The battery in place, he risked another glance at her. "She certainly speaks her mind."

"She doesn't mean to be rude," Cynthie said. *Mama Bear,* he thought, touched and amused by her immediate defense of her cub. "She's at a difficult age."

He tested the clamps. "You don't have to explain to me. I went through a difficult stage myself."

"And you turned out all right. How long did it last? The stage, I mean."

"Most of middle school. Well, and high school," he admitted. "So, basically, my entire adolescence, give or take a couple years."

A soft huff of laughter escaped her. "I can't see you as a problem teenager."

"I wasn't a problem student. More wildly awkward."

"And I was plain wild."

"You were beautiful. Bright. Kind."

"Was I?" Her voice was wistful.

He nodded. "You are beautiful."

Her eyes were huge and dark and slightly unfocused, tempting him to thoughts he was better off not thinking. She was wiped out after her lousy day and, he suspected, more than a little drunk. He was not taking advantage of her car troubles to make his move while her defenses were down.

He gave the battery a final wiggle, making sure it was tight. "Let's see if she'll start."

The engine turned over on the first try.

Max climbed out of the van and smiled at Cynthie. "You're all set. I'll go wash up."

"I'll come with you."

She wobbled a little on the steps. He put a hand on the small of her back to steady her.

They crept into the kitchen like teenagers sneaking in after curfew.

"Be right back," Cynthie whispered.

He washed his hands at the kitchen sink, prepared to say good-bye and go.

Cynthie returned, still wearing her dress and hooded sweatshirt. She pulled two more beers from the fridge, holding them up in his direction. "Another round?"

He'd barely touched his first. She was on her . . . second? Third? But he didn't want to leave her. "Thanks."

She tiptoed back outside, swaying as the cold air hit her. *"Brr."* She wrapped her arms at her waist, still holding a beer in each hand. "Let's sit in your car."

"My car," he repeated.

She nodded. "Big backseat. And no candy wrappers."

Max's blood pounded. Cynthie Lodge, the girl known in high school as Body of Sin, wanted to climb into his backseat.

He was trying hard not to make assumptions, not to misread her invitation. Just how much had she had to drink? "Sure."

Once they were inside, she seemed content to stay on her side of the seat, bottle in hand.

The car wrapped them in a bubble of glass, magnifying the sound of their breathing. Max inhaled the commingled smells of leather and car wash, the warm clove scent of Cynthie. Her long, pretty feet were pale in the gloom, one bare foot swinging idly back and forth.

"You like my nail polish?" Her voice swam out of the dark.

"Er . . ." Had he been staring? "Yes. Very much."

"Thanks." She twisted her foot, so that the silver sparkles caught the light. "It's Maddie's."

"It's very . . . shiny."

Her low, warm chuckle stirred him deep inside. "That was the idea. You ever notice a server's shoes? They have to be close-toed, to protect from spills, and nonskid, to protect from slipping, and flat, because you're on your feet all day. Which is fine, except I've been wearing those shoes all my working life. So I paint my toenails. It gives me a lift, wearing something pretty where nobody can see." She rolled her head against the seat back to smile at him. "Like really good underwear."

All the blood deserted his head, replaced by images of underwear. Cynthie's underwear. Cynthie without underwear. His mouth dried.

He took a swig of beer he did not want. "Boy, this takes me back."

Her full lips quirked. "Cheap beer?"

"Talking to you like this in the dark. Feeling inadequate."

She laughed, which actually made him feel better. "You're a college professor. You love your work, you make a difference in people's lives, and you can change a car battery. You are definitely not inadequate."

"I was in high school," he admitted ruefully. "The one time I talked to you—really talked, more than mumbling 'Hi' in the hall—was a disaster."

"You never . . . Wait. You're that boy. The guy in glasses. Doug punched you."

He winced. She remembered. "And you were the most beautiful girl at the party. I couldn't believe you'd even speak to me."

"Of course I spoke to you. You looked so . . ."

"Out of place?" he suggested wryly when she paused. "Awkward? Inept?"

"I was going to say 'nice.' "

"That might be worse."

"Well, but you *were* nice. Sweet."

He shook his head. "Definitely worse."

She laughed, the sound warm and husky in the dark. "I liked it."

He didn't remember. The particulars of their conversation that night were lost in the mists of time, in a blur of beer and wonder and lust. Until Cynthie's boyfriend had shambled over. He'd shot one squinty-eyed glance from beneath his ball cap before dismissing Max as of no importance. *"Come on,"* he'd said to Cynthie, jerking his chin toward the door. *"Out back. I got us a bottle of Jack."*

She had tossed her head. *"I'm not done here, Doug."*

"Yeah, you are." He'd snapped his fingers at her, like she was his dog.

Something inside Max went hard and bright. *"Don't talk to her like that."*

Doug's head lowered like a bull's. *"Who's gonna stop me, dingbatter? You?"*

"Dingbatter"—the island term for idiot outsiders. One of Doug's buddies guffawed.

"Quit it, Doug," Cynthie said.

"You shut your mouth."

Max's hands clenched. *"I said, don't talk to her like that."*

He'd stood then, the room tilting around him. But before he found his feet, before he saw it coming, Doug swung. His fist plowed into Max's face.

And Max went down in an explosion of pain and beer.

"Max?" Cynthie's voice, soft and urgent. "Are you okay?"

He blinked, recalled to the present. "Fine. You stopped your boyfriend from kicking my ass."

"He should never have hit you. You weren't doing anything."

"I wanted to," Max admitted. "I had a crush on you."

"That's . . ."

"Please don't say 'sweet.'"

Her smile broke. "All right, I won't. But Max . . . I'm not that girl anymore."

"I don't want that girl," he said. "I want you."

Then. Now. Always.

Cynthie tilted her head against the back of the seat to look at him, her eyes wide and gleaming. A smile curled her mouth. "So what are you doing over there?"

Max went still. "Exactly how much have you had to drink?"

She held up two fingers, her eyes laughing at him. "I said you were nice."

"I just don't want you to regret this."

"The only thing I'm going to regret is if you don't kiss me right now."

A jolt of arousal shot straight through him. He looked at her smiling and glowing in the dim light, her sleepy eyes and mussed-up hair and pretty, naked feet. "I can do that," he said and reached for her.

CYNTHIE moistened her lips in anticipation as Max shifted on the leather seat, looming over her, caging her in his heat. He stretched one arm along the seat behind her and raised his other hand to cup her cheek. His scent wrapped around her, salt and laundry, sweat and grease. Max smells. Man smells. Her skin hummed.

She parted her lips on a sigh, a barely audible invitation, and he lowered his head and kissed her, his breath warm, his touch light. He tasted like Max and very faintly of the beer they'd both been drinking. She swallowed, intoxicated by his nearness, by the fact that he was kissing her again. *At last.* His hand slid from her face to her throat, his fingers curling around the back of her neck, his touch warm and coaxing. They kissed and kissed, deeper, wetter kisses, until she gasped and his breath rasped in the darkness, in and out. Oh, God, she wanted . . . she wanted . . .

"Come here," he said, his hands sliding from her waist to her hips, tugging her closer, dragging her deeper, pulling her into the dark. She gave herself up to the urging of his hands and her heart and climbed onto his lap, straddling his thighs, loving the feel of him, hot and solid against her.

He broke their kiss. "Cynthie . . ."

She twined her arms around his neck, answering without words, buoyant with confidence and desire. She was ready for this, ready to take this next step with him. She kissed the corner of his eye, where the skin was soft and fine, and the hollow under his ear, where his pulse beat fast and strong. Her heart overflowed with tenderness.

His hands moved, sliding up her thighs, encountering bare

skin. No panties. He jolted and groaned her name against her mouth.

"Yes," she said. To this, to him, to everything.

She unbuttoned the first button of his shirt and then the second, exposing the line of his collarbone, the beginning of coarse, dark hair. Her fingers trembled with eagerness. His skin was warm and firm, denser than hers, a feast of textures. She wanted to bury her nose in his chest, wanted to lose herself in him and never come out.

She reached for his belt, yanking at the buckle.

His hands caught hers. "Sweetheart."

She ignored him, intent on uncovering her prize.

"Cynthie." His touch, his voice firmed. "We can't. I don't have a condom."

So he hadn't taken this for granted. He wasn't taking her for granted. She melted a little more. "I do. I got it from my bedroom when I ditched my underwear." She shrugged. "Not very romantic."

His gaze met hers. His eyes were deep and dark and hot. "I get to be with you. That's all the romance I need."

His words shot straight to her heart and quivered there. She had never felt so cherished. So vulnerable. She hid her face in his neck.

His large, clever hands stroked her hair, tilted her head. "You are so beautiful."

She trembled as his mouth found hers. They kissed, long, greedy kisses, until her body flushed and shuddered and her heart ached and yearned and her mind emptied of everything but this, Max making love to her in the near dark.

He nuzzled her breasts as she kneeled above him, his breath searing, his mouth searching through her soft cotton dress. She shoved his jeans open and down, the rough denim abrading her thighs. His fingers stroked her, opened her, as she wrapped herself around him, desperate to feel him, flooded with heat and need. She lifted up. He pulled her down, pushing hard inside her. The shock rocked them both. Pleasure filled her, thick and hot, rushing along her veins. She bit her lip to keep from crying out, and then he drove into her again and she did cry out, the sound spilling from her like joy. She rocked to his rhythm, feeling him slick and hot inside her, taking her pleasure, absorbing his.

Her butt clenched. Her breath sobbed in relief and gratitude. *This. Yes. And this. Now.* He thrust up, his hands hard, stroking her inside and out, and she clutched his shoulders, shaking, quaking, coming again and again.

Until he turned his lips into her throat, his fingers gripping her butt, and followed her.

THEY sprawled, tangled, skin to skin, glued together by sweat and satisfaction, until their breathing calmed and their heartbeats matched and slowed.

Cynthie released a long, shuddery sigh. "Wow."

He stroked her hair back from her face, a faint tremor in his hand, the aftershocks of desire. "That good? Or that bad?"

"Good. But . . ." His shoulder tensed under her cheek. She pushed herself up to meet his gaze, dark and steady in the uneven moonlight. "It's like chocolate ice cream." Or a bottle of wine that cost more than six dollars. Like something she'd done only for herself, a selfish indulgence she couldn't afford every day.

"Let's say you're on a diet. You want chocolate ice cream," she explained earnestly. "So you tell yourself, *It's just this once, you'll only have a little.* You know, to treat yourself after a lousy day. But then you start eating, and, ohmigod, it's like the best ice cream ever, and you can't stop eating."

He grinned up at her, his lean face suddenly relaxing. "You can have as much as you want, sweetheart. Though I might need a couple minutes here. We're not in high school anymore."

She struggled to sit, to find her balance against the tide of temptation. "That's the point. I have the girls to think about now. I have responsibilities. I can't go around—"

He raised his brows. "Eating ice cream?"

"—whenever I want."

He rearranged her weight on top of him, coaxing her head down onto his shoulder. "That's okay. I get it. Your kids have to be your first priority."

He held her a long, wordless time, his breath at her temple, the steady thud of his heartbeat under her palms. Gradually, she relaxed, melting into his lap. He felt so good, so solid against her, his body supporting her weight, his arms holding her secure. Maybe it was only temporary, but it was very sweet.

"Still friends?" she asked finally in a small voice.

His arms tightened around her. "If that's what you want."

"I want you," she confessed. "I want this. But I've got to put my kids first. I haven't been able to give them everything they need. But I can show them every day that they matter more than anything to me. They'll have that."

"Then that's everything."

"You must have really good parents."

He was silent.

Uh-oh. She raised her head, seeking his expression in the dark. "Or really bad ones," she guessed.

His throat moved as he swallowed. "This isn't about me. I'll take whatever is right for the kids. Whatever you're comfortable with."

She snuggled closer, grateful for his understanding. But the pinch at her heart would not go away. Max was such a good guy. He deserved more. Better. *Who put him first?* she wondered.

"I'm sorry," she mumbled into his chest.

He kissed the top of her head. "I'm not sorry. About anything. As long as I get to see you sometimes, that's enough for me."

SEVEN

CYNTHIE HELD ON to the refrigerator door for support. *Get a grip,* she ordered herself. This morning, she'd had some dream of impressing Max with a real family dinner, a home-cooked meal of fried chicken and mashed potatoes and Mama's biscuits. It made her happy to feed him something besides takeout. The man didn't eat properly. But now . . .

She stared sightlessly at the refrigerator's contents. All she could see was the image of Dr. Rick Rice's hand on her breast. A light touch, over her blouse, as Cynthie sat beside him this afternoon observing a procedure on a sedated patient. Hardly a grope at all.

But the memory of his splayed fingers crawled like a spider across her mind.

"Are you okay, Mom?" Hannah asked.

Her pulse hammered. She felt sick. Powerless. If some guy had tried anything at the bar, she would have known what to expect. How to react. Her turf, her terms. But she hadn't been braced to defend herself against her mentor. Dr. Rice had said, with a white, perfect smile that did not mask his lack of real apology, that he'd only been reaching for the instrument tray. It was possible, Cynthie supposed, that her boob got in his way. Anything was possible.

Including that she could jeopardize her job-shadowing experience by calling the oral surgeon a lying sack of shit.

"Mom?"

Cynthie shut the fridge without taking anything out. "I'm fine, honey."

Madison wandered into the kitchen. "What's that smell?"

Crap. The biscuits were burning. Cynthie whirled back to the oven and yanked open the door, reaching for a pot holder with her other hand.

"What time is Max coming over?" Hannah asked.

Cynthie threw a distracted glance at the clock, dumping the biscuits onto the counter. "Soon."

The bottoms were only a little charred. Maybe she could salvage dinner after all. She turned to the chicken sizzling in the skillet. She really wanted to make this work. Not just the meal. Everything. When she was with Max, she could almost believe they could be more than friends. When he touched her, her hair or her arm, or smiled at her a certain way, her insides tingled. Her world glowed. She felt . . . not confident. But hopeful.

"I thought he was supposed to be here at six," Madison said.

So she had noticed he was late. Was that a good sign? Was her daughter actually looking forward to seeing him again?

"He must have gotten held up," Cynthie said.

Madison shrugged. "That's okay. I just wondered what he thought of the picture I sent him."

Cynthie blinked, tongs suspended. "You sent Max a picture?"

"Of Taylor's dog. I sent it from Taylor's phone."

"How did you get his number?"

"Your contacts list. Max says I have a good eye for photography."

Cynthie focused on turning a thigh, her mind seething like the fat in the pan. She was glad Maddie was taking an interest in something other than hair clips and boy bands. She wanted Max and her children to get along. But . . .

"Honey, I don't think you should be using your friend's phone to message Max."

"I could get my own phone. I'm old enough," Madison said.

"Too expensive," Cynthie answered automatically.

"How about a dog?" Madison asked.

"Yeah! A dog!" Hannah said.

Cynthie closed her eyes, her head pounding. She so did not have the energy for this now. Not after the craptastic Dr. Rice.

The doorbell clunked its broken two-note chime.

"Max!" Hannah skipped to the door.

But it was Wanda, come to pick up some of Hannah's hand-me-downs to give to a neighbor's child.

"I'll get them!" Hannah ran to her room and back, carrying a trash bag full of outgrown clothes. "Max is coming over for dinner," she told her grandmother.

Wanda made the Universal Mom sound, shooting an interested glance at Cynthie. "Hm. Isn't that nice. He came last week, too, didn't he?"

"He's late," Madison said.

Cynthie flushed. She transferred the chicken to a plate, hoping Mama would attribute her heightened color to the heat of the stove. "He must have gotten hung up at school." She wiped her hands on a dish towel before reaching for her phone. "I'll just call him."

But he didn't pick up. Not the first time. Or the second.

Cynthie supervised the setting of the table, trying to ignore the unsettled feeling in her stomach, the tightness in her chest. Trying not to catch her mother's sympathetic eyes.

She and Max hadn't made plans to meet up at school today. Knowing she would see him tonight, Cynthie hadn't given the change from their usual routine a second thought. But now, as she waited, she wondered.

And worried.

She thought about him all the time, his steady eyes and careful, sure touch and fantastic body. But in the three weeks since he'd had her half-naked and gasping in the backseat of his Volvo, he'd never once behaved inappropriately in front of her kids, never pushed to spend the night, never complained about their lack of sex life. Only the occasional measuring look in his eyes, the tension in his muscles when he kissed her good night, suggested he wasn't satisfied.

The minutes ticked by.

Cynthie took a deep breath. She was better than this. She was stronger than this. She wasn't teaching her girls to live their lives waiting on a man who didn't call.

She removed the foil from the chicken. "Time to eat," she announced brightly.

"Where's Max?" Hannah asked.

"He isn't coming," Madison said.

"You want me to stay?" Wanda asked.

Cynthie looked at the table set for four, at Hannah's confused face, at Madison's scowl, and smiled gratefully at her mother. "I'd love for you to stay." She gave a broken half laugh. "There's plenty of chicken."

Wanda didn't say anything. But after the meal, as Cynthie stood to clear the dirty plates, Wanda reached over and squeezed her hand.

Her eyes stung at her mama's unspoken support. Nobody understood disappointment like Mama. She'd been let down all her life and still kept going.

Cynthie cleared the lump from her throat. "Who wants ice cream?"

"Me!" Hannah said.

"You want chocolate ice cream." The words played in a dismal loop in Cynthie's head as she scooped dessert into bowls. *"So you tell yourself,* 'It's just this once, you'll only have a little.' *You know, to treat yourself after a lousy day. But then you start eating, and, ohmigod, it's like the best ice cream ever, and you can't stop eating."*

Cynthie bowed her head over the bowls, her eyes and nose stinging, her heart aching. She'd thought she was being so smart, protecting her girls, guarding her heart, taking her time to be sure.

She didn't trust herself.

But she had believed in Max. *"As long as I get to see you sometimes, that's enough for me."*

And now their time was up. He was fed up with her, frustrated with the limits she'd set on their relationship.

She couldn't even blame him.

"He's still not answering his phone," Madison said, hanging up the landline as Cynthie returned to the table.

"Maddie . . . You can't call him again."

Hannah's eyes widened. "Why not?"

"Because . . ." *I screwed up. I couldn't give him what he wanted, and now he's gone.* "He's very busy."

Madison's chin stuck out at a familiar angle. "Or maybe he's sick. He lives all alone. Maybe he hurt himself. He could have been in an accident, even."

Cynthie's chest squeezed as she regarded Madison's stubborn, concerned face. Her precious daughter, who—despite all Cynthie's mistakes— still believed there were nice guys in the world who didn't walk away.

He could have been in an accident, even.

She owed it to Madison to call.

She owed it to Max.

He'd never been late before, never willingly disappointed the girls or failed to keep his word. When Cynthie was late, he had waited. When her car battery died, he had been there.

She pulled out her cell phone. No messages. No voice mail. Her heart quailed. She might not have a degree from Harvard, but she knew what it meant when a man stopped calling, when he didn't bother to return a text.

She looked at her daughters' expectant faces. Held her mother's resigned gaze. Three generations of women on their own. They didn't need anybody else. But if Max needed them . . .

Cynthie swallowed and pressed Call. One ring, two, three . . .

"Cynthie?" He sounded terrible.

"Hi."

"What time is it?" His voice was raspy, slurred, like a man coming off a three-day bender.

"Um."

"Oh, God, I'm sorry. I must have dropped off."

Dropped off what? The face of the planet? she thought, and was instantly ashamed. "Are you all right?"

"I'm . . . I was throwing up most of the night. And today. But that's no excuse."

She clutched the phone, giddy with relief and concern. "You're sick."

"Food poisoning. Grad student potluck last night." He groaned. "I thought I'd be better by tonight. God, I'm so sorry."

"It's okay," Cynthie said. "Is there anybody with you?"

"What?" He sounded dazed. "No. Cynthie, about dinner . . ."

"Don't worry about it." He was sick and alone. Poor guy.

"I'm really sorry," he repeated. "I should have called. I would have called, but—"

"You fell asleep," she finished for him. "You probably didn't hear the phone."

"The phone?" A pause, while she imagined him checking his messages, and then a clunk. *Max, beating his head against the wall?* "Shit."

"It's okay," she said again. "Try to get some rest. I'll talk to you soon."

"Wait. Cynthie—"

"Rest," she ordered.

She ended the call to find Mama and the girls watching her with varying degrees of fascination.

Cynthie took a breath. Straightened her shoulders. "Mama, I need a favor."

NOT okay. Max dropped his head in his hands with a groan. Not okay at all, no matter how reassuring Cynthie tried to sound. He was trying to prove to her that he wasn't like all the other guys in her life, that she could trust him enough to take their relationship to the next level, and then he blew off dinner with her daughters.

At least he'd stopped heaving.

He pressed the heels of his palms to his eyeballs, as if he could push his brain back into his skull. He needed to think. To move. He could fix this. All he had to do was . . . All he had to do . . .

A shudder shook him. His muscles, already stiff from spending the night on the cold tile floor, seized.

Hot shower, he thought when the spasm had passed. He stank like a corpse dragged from a swamp.

The doorbell rang while he was getting dressed. He yanked his gray T-shirt over his head and padded barefoot to the door.

Cynthie.

His heart leaped.

He blinked, half-afraid she would vanish, a vision concocted of too little sleep and the lingering effects of the graduate student potluck dinner.

But, nope, she was still there, on his doorstep, carrying one of those reusable grocery bags.

"Hi." She smiled and stepped over his threshold. "You should shut the door. It's cold outside."

He complied automatically. "What are you doing here?"

"Somebody has to take care of you."

He couldn't remember anybody saying that to him before. Julie? Never. Maybe his mother, years ago. "I'm fine."

"Mm." Her soft green eyes widened as she took him in, from his bare feet to his wet hair. "You look . . ."

He smiled wryly. "Like the walking dead?"

Her mouth quirked. "Like you just got out of the shower," she said tactfully. "How are you feeling?"

"Better."

Much better, now that she was here. He couldn't believe she was here.

She stepped in close, smelling like cloves and Cynthie, and laid a quick, cool hand on his forehead before cupping his jaw. He turned his face into her hand, pressing his dry lips to her palm in gratitude.

Her cheeks were pink as she moved away. "No fever," she announced. "Is your kitchen this way?"

"I'm not sick. It's just food poisoning. I really am better now."

She tipped her head. "When did you last eat?"

He winced.

She made another of those soft, judicious noises. "All right, what have you had to drink?"

"I can't keep anything down."

"Not even water?"

"I haven't tried." Not since the last disastrous attempt. "I brushed my teeth," he added defensively.

"That's not going to stop you from getting dehydrated." She carried the grocery bag to the kitchen. "That's okay. I brought you something."

"I really don't want anything." *Except for you to stay.* To make her stay, he was even willing to force food on his protesting stomach.

She set the groceries on his immaculate granite counter. "Sit down before you fall down. I'm making you ramen. You don't have to eat the noodles, but the broth will replace salt and fluids."

It was a relief to fold himself into a chair. "Yes, ma'am."

She looked around as she removed things from the bag—soup, ginger ale, crackers. "This is a nice big kitchen."

"Um, thank you."

He had considered the house a good investment when he bought it, new construction in a relatively featureless development, close enough to campus that he could bike to work. It was not a *home* like Cynthie's trailer. But there was certainly more counter space.

Cynthie opened and closed cupboards. "You don't have a lot to cook with."

"Julie took most of it," he said, and bit his tongue. Probably not the best time to bring up his former house partner. Was there a good time?

Cynthie poured ginger ale into a glass, no ice, and set it in front of him. "Julie?"

"My, ah, ex-girlfriend."

Cynthie nodded. "How long?"

"Did we live together? About a year."

"Since she left."

"Oh." He sipped the soda, grateful for something to do with his hands. "Six months."

Cynthie raised her brows. "Plenty of time to buy a pot."

"It's easier to eat out."

"Cheaper to eat in. Better for you, too." She wrinkled her nose. "And now I sound like your mother."

Not *his* mother. His mother's favorite thing to make for dinner was reservations. "No, you're right. I should pick up some pans and stuff."

Cynthie set a pot of water on the stove. "Unless you're hoping your ex is coming back with all your cookware."

"God, no," Max said without thinking and was relieved when she laughed.

She arranged three crackers on a plate and set them on the table. "Tylenol?"

"In the bathroom."

Cynthie dimpled. "I meant, have you taken any?"

"Oh. No."

She took a little white bottle from her bag and shook two tablets into her palm. "How's your stomach feel?"

He thought. "Not bad," he admitted.

"Good. Now that you've kept some soda down, these will help with your body aches."

She poured his soup, refilled his soda, handed him a spoon and a napkin. "Eat slowly. Don't push it."

He had often admired Cynthie with her daughters, her easy caring, her casual hugs, the nurturing she exuded as readily as air. Her fussing over him was another kind of pleasure, a secret, half-shameful comfort to the child he'd once been.

"This is great," he said as she sat down opposite him. "Thank you."

Her eyes met his shyly, pleased, before she looked away. "Packaged soup and ginger ale. Yeah, I really knocked myself out."

He didn't have the words to tell her how much her kindness meant to him. "Aren't you having anything?"

"I already ate."

Right. The dinner he'd blown off. "This isn't how I imagined your first visit to my place," he admitted ruefully.

Cynthie smiled. "It's fine," she said.

Like she really meant it.

He dug into the broth, surprised by how good it suddenly tasted.

"So why did you and your ex break up?" Cynthie asked.

Max swallowed. "It wasn't anything big or dramatic. No bad guys, just . . . She decided I wasn't capable of giving her what she needed."

She cocked her head. "Marriage?"

"Fun."

"You stopped having sex?"

"Ah . . ." Toward the end, definitely. Because Julie had moved on to another relationship before she'd moved out of his house. "I don't think sex was her definition of fun."

Cynthie sent him a slow, sizzling smile. "Then she definitely wasn't having sex with you."

He inhaled sharply.

She shrugged. "Anyway, that was Doug's excuse. He felt

bad enough, what with losing his job and all. And I was worn out from work and trying to keep up the house and taking care of Maddie. I guess at the end of the day, I didn't have much left over for him. Can't blame him for going elsewhere to find it."

Anger at her ex spilled through Max, corrosive as battery acid. "You mean, you supported him and he cheated on you."

"I mean, we both got married too young, thinking things were going to be one way, and they turned out another. After Maddie came along, I wasn't that wild girl he fell for in high school anymore."

"You were never that girl," Max said. "You were always more."

THOSE clear gray eyes looked into hers.

Cynthie's breath clogged. "More what?"

"Braver. Kinder. More intelligent," he said simply. "More . . . you."

A warm, liquid flush swept her face and flooded her chest. Hoo boy. It was quite possibly the nicest thing anybody had ever said to her in her life. Her eyes flooded, too.

Which was stupid. He was sick. He didn't need her weeping all over him.

Though his color was better, she noted with a mom's experienced eye, the death-warmed-over pallor replaced by actual skin tones. With his two-day scruff and damp-from-the-shower hair, he looked masculine, relaxed, and very, very sexy.

"Well." She exhaled. "I should probably get going."

He held still for a moment before he nodded. "Right. The girls."

The girls were fine. Her mama was staying with the girls tonight.

But she didn't tell Max that. She didn't want him to feel he owed her anything in return for her visit. Like a bed. Or sex. Three weeks had passed since they'd made love in the backseat of his Volvo. *Pleasure filling her, thick and hot, rushing along her veins . . .*

The memory brought a surge of blood to her face and other places lower down. If she didn't get out of here soon, she was going to melt into a formless puddle of lust on his kitchen floor.

"I need to get something first," Max said. "Be right back."

Well, okay, Cynthie thought, watching his retreating back down the hall. Clearly, *he* wasn't thinking about sex. *Because he's getting over food poisoning, idiot.*

And if he was fetching his wallet to pay for the groceries, she would just refuse, that's all.

Whatever he was doing took a while. By the time she had loaded his few dishes into the state-of-the-art dishwasher, rinsed the pan and lined up the tummy-friendly foods on the counter where he could find them, Max still hadn't returned.

She frowned, drying her hands on a paper towel. He needed dish towels. Maybe next time she came . . . If there was a next time.

Maybe his stomach wasn't ready for noodles. Maybe he was throwing up again. Or curled in a ball on the bathroom floor.

"Max?"

No answer.

She tiptoed down the hall, feeling like an intruder. He had a nice house. Too much space for a guy living alone, but that was his problem. His decorating was as bland as the soup and crackers she'd served him for dinner. White walls, beige carpet, neutral wood. No evidence of that other woman who had lived here. Or maybe she had been bland, too. The thought was vaguely cheering.

There were bookshelves everywhere, their spines bright notes of color, and some black-and-white photographs in the hall that looked like they belonged in an upscale island art gallery.

The door at the end of the hall stood open. Max's bedroom, more beige mixed with navy. A vivid seascape in oils hung opposite the bed, where he must see it when he woke every morning.

A big bed, with rumpled covers.

Maybe she should offer to tuck him in.

Max stood in front of an open closet, examining something in his hands. The soft gray knit of his T-shirt clung to his broad shoulders. His short, dark hair was adorably mussed. A rush of yearning tightened her chest and loosened her knees.

"Hey."

"Hi." He turned, his smile weakening her knees even further. "It took me a while to find this."

She stood there, dry-mouthed with longing and lust, remembering the feel of him against her. Inside her. She wanted to slide her hands under his T-shirt, over the smooth muscles of his back, along the bony indents of his spine.

To distract herself, she looked at the object in his hands. A digital camera. "You want to take dirty pictures before I go?" she joked.

"Ha. Good one." A gleam lit his eyes. "Although if you want to take off your clothes, I won't stop you."

Her heart hammered. Was he kidding?

"Here." He held out the camera. "It's an old one. For Madison."

She stared at the slim silver camera as if it were a snake in the Garden of Eden. Her fingers itched to take it from him. She tucked them behind her back, away from this new temptation. She didn't know how much a camera like that originally cost, but . . . "I can't accept this."

"I never use it. And she would."

"I didn't even know she was interested in photography."

"We talked about it. It could be a passing thing. At her age, kids should be experimenting, exploring different interests. But if she keeps it up, she could do a photography elective in high school."

"That's three years away."

Max shrugged. "Something to think about anyway."

Right. She'd simply add it to the list of, oh, five hundred other things she had to think about. "I'm not used to thinking long term. It's all I can do to make it from Saturday night to Saturday night or paycheck to paycheck."

"That's not how I see it. You're very focused on making a life for yourself and your kids. Look at the way you've gone back to school. You took on a second job so you could get some dental experience."

"And look how well that's working out," she muttered.

His dark brows twitched together. "What?"

"Nothing." *Nothing important.* But the memory of this afternoon, the image of her boss's hand on her breast, intruded on the quiet room, the intimacy wrapping them like silk.

She hadn't stopped him. Her failure dug at her. She'd sat there like a dummy and let that bastard get away with putting his hands on her because he could. The specter of her helplessness rose like a ghost to taunt her.

"I wish I'd known, that's all," she said. "I should have seen. I would have done something."

"Cynthie," Max said with controlled patience. "It's a camera."

"It's not just the camera." A sense of her own inadequacy sharpened her voice. "It's paying attention to who Maddie is, to what she wants. I feel like I'm letting her down."

"Bullshit."

She blinked, shaken from her sulks. Professor Maxwell Lewis, swearing. Imagine that.

"I'm not a parent," he said. "I don't pretend to share the kind of bond, the kind of insights, you have with your daughters. But I do know that loving somebody doesn't mean that you automatically understand everything that's going on in their lives. Or that you can fix all their problems."

"It ought to. I'm her *mother*."

Max smiled. "You're a great mother. She's a lucky kid. But you're also your own person, with your own dreams, your own abilities." He pulled her close against his warm, hard body. "Your mother had to learn that with you. And you have to accept that with your girls. You can't live their lives for them. Or through them. All you can do is love them and hope that gives them the confidence to follow their dreams to the best of their abilities."

She dropped her forehead against his chest. "That makes me sound so selfish."

"You're the least selfish person I've ever met."

She shook her head.

"It's the truth." He cupped her face, tilting it up to meet his gaze. His eyes were the color of the sea on a cloudy day, deep gray and shining. "You never complain. You never give up. You're not afraid to put yourself out there. You have the biggest, softest heart of anyone I know."

She wriggled her shoulders, uncomfortable with compliments. "The softest head, maybe," she joked.

"Stop it," he ordered quietly. "How can you see the best in everybody else and not see yourself that way? The way I see you. You are amazing." His lips, slightly dry and oh-so-tender, brushed hers. "Kind." He kissed her again. "Strong." Another kiss, like punctuation. "Smart."

She searched his gaze, her heart trembling on the brink of possibilities. Was that really what he saw when he looked at her?

He was so close, she could see herself in his eyes, two tiny reflections gazing up at him with love and longing. He kissed her again, longer, deeper, shutting her eyes, drawing out the sweetness until her whole body shimmered. She touched his jaw, rough with stubble. She wanted to touch him all over, to feel his roughness against her smoothness, his hardness against her softness. Wanted him, his mouth, his hands, all of him on all of her.

"How long do we have?" he murmured minutes later.

Forever.

She drew back, breathless. "I . . . Are you sure? You're still sick."

"Food poisoning isn't contagious."

"Yes, but . . . Are you up for this?"

He brought her closer so that she could feel him, taut and aroused against her. "What do you think?"

Her breathing hitched. Her hips arched, seeking the pressure of his. She was tired of thinking, about the future, about her job, even about her girls. She wanted to be the woman he described, loving and giving and fearless.

"I think we've got all night," she whispered. "I asked Mama to stay with the kids."

His smile broke like sunrise over his lean face. "Then let's make the most of it."

She watched, transfixed, as he reached behind his head and grabbed his collar, dragging his T-shirt over his head the way men do. But when she reached for the hem of her own shirt, his hands stopped her.

"Let me." His fingers trapped hers just above her belt. Their eyes locked. "You take care of everybody else. Let me take care of you for a change."

"WHEN I was fifteen, I used to imagine you in my bed," Max said much later. They lay as close as spoons, her smooth bare legs entwined with his, her hair across his pillow, his hand resting possessively on her hip. The sweet, heavy curve of her ass nestled warm against him.

Her head moved against his arm. He thought she was smiling. "Only when you were fifteen?"

He grinned. "Recently, too."

"And what did we do? In your imagination." Her warm, teasing tone set fire to his brain.

"Everything," he admitted. "Every raw, dirty, secret fantasy I could think of."

"Sounds good to me," she said. Definitely smiling. He could hear it in her voice.

Happiness pooled inside him. "The reality is better." He kissed the top of her head. "Thanks for coming over.".

She snuggled deeper into his heat. "What are friends for?"

Something rippled across his contentment like a disturbance on the surface of a pond. He could almost see the posted warning sign: DANGER. DEEP WATER HERE. He waded ahead anyway. "Is that what you'd call us? Friends?"

"I think so. The new, improved version maybe. You know, like the commercials?" She intoned in a fake announcer's voice, "Still friends. Now with benefits."

He didn't laugh. "And that's what you want."

She lay very still. "What I want doesn't matter. It's what I can have."

He pushed down his own disappointment, trying to read her body's cues, wishing he could see her face. He'd been inside her. He was good at observing detail, at drawing conclusions from the available evidence. But he didn't have a clue what she was thinking right now. "Forget what you can have. Tell me how you feel."

She caught his hand and pressed it to her breast, trying to recapture their earlier playfulness. "Very friendly."

Her breast was soft and heavy in his hand, the nipple a tight knot against his palm. But he would not be distracted.

"Cynthie." Gently, he turned her in the circle of his arms, waiting patiently until her gaze lifted to his. "I'm falling in love with you."

A quiver ran through her. "Don't. You're not. I'm just . . . I was your high school crush. Guys always have a thing for their high school crush."

He kept his eyes steady on hers. He was hurt. Part of him wanted to retreat behind the wall of his family's well-bred politeness. But he couldn't let her dismiss his feelings for her as the by-product of teenage hormones. "You can tell me what you want. What you're afraid of. But you can't tell me how I feel."

The quiver spread to her lips. "I can't tell you anything. I don't know what to say."

"Say yes. It's time for the next step. I don't want to wait until your car battery dies or I get food poisoning to sleep with you again." He waited for her response. When she didn't say anything, he kissed her forehead. She smelled so good, sweet and spicy, like cloves and sex. Like Cynthie. "I don't want to be the friend you have sex with sometimes. I want to be your . . . " His mind considered and discarded terms. *Boyfriend? Lover?* Neither one was big enough for his emotions. "I want us to have a regular relationship," he said finally. "Like any two rational, healthy adults who could have a future together."

"It's not only our future. I have to think about the girls," she said.

It wasn't just the girls, he thought. Something else was holding her back. But how could he reassure her fears when he didn't understand them?

He thought of pointing out to her that he could make all their lives easier. He had money. He was more than willing to spend it on her daughters. But she didn't need him to rescue them. She didn't need him at all.

"We can go as slow as you want. As slow as they need," he said. "But I'm ready to be part of your life. And I want you to be part of mine."

EIGHT

"I DON'T GET it," Meg Fletcher said to Cynthie.

The two women sat at the kitchen table of the Fletcher family's bed-and-breakfast while the girls—Hannah and Madison and Meg's niece, Taylor— played with the puppy outside.

"You've got this sweet, smart, sexy guy who's totally crazy about you," Meg continued. "He likes your kids, he has a job, he doesn't live with his mother. I don't see an issue here. Unless he's, like, I don't know, a meth addict. Or has the bodies of his six ex-wives stashed in the attic."

Cynthie smiled, wiggling her toes inside her ugly black server's shoes under the table. It was a treat to sit down in the middle of the day, to share coffee and confidences with a girlfriend. But even Meg's teasing couldn't chase away her lingering insecurities. "No drugs. One ex-girlfriend. And she's out of the picture."

"And how long have you been dating?"

"We're not exactly . . . " Cynthie met Meg's eyes and gave up the pretense. "Three months."

"So?"

"So, he invited me to this big fund-raiser for the aquarium. For the exhibit expansion he's been working on? Cocktails, dancing, semiformal, he said." Cynthie twisted her coffee cup in her hands, her stomach knotting with nerves. "All the board of directors, everybody in his department will be there. Maybe even his parents."

"Well, that's a good sign. He wants you to meet his friends. His colleagues."

"I can't go."

"For heaven's sake, why not?"

All her old self-doubt rushed in at her, all the times she'd been told she wasn't smart enough, good enough, deserving enough. "It's movie night at the kids' school."

"They can go with Taylor," Meg said promptly.

"We wouldn't be home until late."

"Then they can spend the night." Meg shook her head. "Still not seeing a problem here."

Cynthie sighed. For all her Harvard education, Meg could be really dumb sometimes. "It's like, if our lives were a high school movie, Max would be the cute nerd, you would be the brainy girl who lands the captain of the football team, and I would be the girl who gets knocked up under the stadium bleachers."

Meg laughed, but her eyes were sympathetic. "News flash for you, pal. High school was over for us a long time ago."

"In my head, I get that. But in my gut . . ." Cynthie pressed a hand to her jumpy stomach. Her gut was Jell-O, quivering between terrifying panic and an even more terrifying hope. "Max and I are from totally different worlds. He's so far out of my league, we're not even playing the same game."

"Forget your head and your gut," Meg advised. "What does your heart say?"

"My heart is a great big scaredy-cat," Cynthie admitted. "Meg, he says he's falling in love with me."

"Wow. The big *L*. And what did you say?"

"Nothing. I've got all these feelings for him churning around inside me, here." Cynthie thumped her chest with her fist. "But when I open my mouth, they get stuck. And every day I don't tell him how I feel, it's like a brick in this wall I'm building between us."

Meg pursed her lips. "You're afraid of being hurt. That's natural."

"I think I'm more afraid of letting him down," Cynthie

confessed. "He's so good to me. He deserves someone who fits into his life. Who won't embarrass him. What if I can't be the person he needs?"

"Isn't that up to him to decide?" Meg asked gently.

From the sunlit backyard drifted the sound of the girls' laughter, interspersed with the dog's happy barks.

"You can tell me what you want. What you're afraid of," Max had said, in his quiet, unyielding voice. *"But you can't tell me how I feel."*

"Look, I'm not in any position to tell you what to do," Meg said finally. "But I do know that sometimes in life you have to take risks to get what you want."

Great. Cynthie stared into her coffee mug as if it held a fortune-teller's tea leaves. She could either end up hurting Max by turning him down, by continuing to push him away.

Or she could take a risk and maybe break her heart.

She shook her head. No choice at all, really.

"I'll need to borrow a cocktail dress," she said.

Meg grinned. "That, I can help you with."

"YOU look really pretty, Mom," Hannah said from her position on Cynthie's bed.

Cynthie gave a half twirl in front of the mirror, admiring her reflection in Meg's dress. The sequined silver sheath flashed and clung, fitting like fish scales before flaring above the knee. "Thanks, sweetie. I feel pretty." She grinned and then winced as her matching rhinestone sandals rubbed her toes. "Like Cinderella, only with big feet."

Unfortunately, while she and Meg were almost the same size, their feet were not.

"You should wear your cowboy boots," Madison volunteered. "The good ones."

Cynthie shot her a doubtful look. Yes, the Lucchese boots were the most expensive footwear she'd ever owned, a one-time extravagance left over from her wild days, studded and tooled and now relegated to the back of her closet. But she was trying to fit in with Max's colleagues tonight, not stand out.

Madison shrugged. "You always tell me I should be comfortable. Better than hobbling around all night."

She did say that. Along with, *Be yourself.* And, *It's what's inside that counts.*

But was she really supposed to set an example over shoes? What would have happened to the fairy tale if Cinderella had rejected the glass slippers?

The broken doorbell thunked.

Hannah ran out of the room to answer. Cynthie heard her mother's murmur and then Max's deep voice.

Her heart beat faster as she hurried through the rest of her preparations, gave a last tug, a final tweak. Taking a deep breath to stifle the butterflies in her stomach, she smiled at Madison in the mirror. "Pumpkin time."

Madison smiled back. "You do look pretty."

A wave of love suffused Cynthie's chest. "Thanks, baby."

Max was standing by the trailer door, chatting with her mama and Hannah, his lanky athletic body in a charcoal gray suit over a black T-shirt. The unfamiliar clothes made him appear tall and lean and unattainable, like a fifties movie star. He glanced up at her entrance, his gray eyes widening, darkening, taking her in.

Her heart rioted.

"Wow," he said. "You look beautiful. Like a mermaid."

Her smile spilled, too wide to contain. She felt herself glowing. She stuck out one foot. "Not quite."

His gaze dropped to the cowboy boots beneath her sparkly hem before he laughed.

CYNTHIE had worked parties before, weddings on the beach, family reunions and corporate retreats at the golf and tennis club. She was used to white linen tablecloths and spectacular views, to men in suit jackets and women in heels staggering over the sand.

But the aquarium at night was magic, its columns wrapped in fairy lights, the glassware on the tables reflecting the green and blue glow of the tanks, fish flashing, drifting, and darting above and behind the circulating guests. Live music filled the air, floating through the gallery, a band playing covers of beach music that Cynthie's mother had danced to.

She caught her breath in wonder. "It's prom."

" 'Enchantment Under the Sea,' " Max said dryly.

"Is that from *The Little Mermaid*?"

His gray eyes glinted with humor. "*Back to the Future.*"

She took his arm, smiling at her mistake. "Okay, I am such a mom. And you are such a geek."

It took them forever to make their way through the galleries as Max stopped to introduce her to chattering knots of people. Like the marine life in the tanks behind them, the guests formed their own sort of food chain, Cynthie thought—the patrons, sleek and gray and confident as sharks; the bright, busy academics, focused on the food; the scuttling servers.

"Your friends are nice," Cynthie said as they left one group.

"They like you." Max replaced her wineglass with a fresh one from a passing waiter. "You made everyone feel comfortable."

Her grin escaped. "You mean, superior."

He shook his head. "You're a good listener. I've noticed it before. You ask questions."

"Because I don't understand what they're talking about otherwise."

He guided her through the crowd. "You understand as much as most of the donors. The difference is that they won't admit what they don't know."

Cynthie relaxed into the touch of his hand on the small of her back, basking in his approval. "Because they want to look smart to all their friends. But when you're in food service, you figure out pretty quick that nobody cares what you know as long as you get their order right."

His hand tensed on her hip. He looked over her head, his face suddenly wiped of expression.

She craned her neck, trying to follow his gaze. "What?"

"Hello, Mom. Dad." He spoke over her head, his voice perfectly neutral. "May I introduce Cynthie Lodge? Cynthie, these are my parents, Dr. Oscar Lewis, Dr. Dorothea Bell-Lewis."

His parents? Here?

She turned, giving them her best what-can-I-get-for-you smile. "Hi." They didn't look scary. A well-upholstered woman in a plain black dress covered by an embroidered shawl, a tall, lean man with grizzled gray hair. "Nice to meet you."

"I didn't expect to see you here," Max said.

His father raised unruly gray eyebrows. "We *are* patrons of the aquarium."

You're his parents, Cynthie thought. "It's so nice of you to come tonight," she said. "To support Max."

They all looked at her like she was speaking Mandarin. Unless they spoke Mandarin. Someone—Sam?—had said Max's father was a linguistics professor or something. "Because of his project," she explained. "The oyster reef expansion?"

"Ah. Yes," Oscar said. "You must be a colleague of Max's from the university."

"Um, no."

"Where did you meet?" his mother asked.

"Here, actually. At the aquarium."

Dorothea nodded. "You're involved in the exhibit installation, then."

"Cynthie is my date," Max said firmly.

"Isn't that nice." Dorothea leaned closer, lowering her voice. "He's had a terrible time since Julie left him."

"Was that her name?" Oscar asked.

"We were actually quite worried about him," Dorothea said.

Max shot her a surprised look, his brows lowered, as if their concern was news to him. He was so adorable.

"I can understand that," Cynthie said.

"I doubt it," Dorothea said grandly. "Only a mother can truly understand."

"I have two daughters," Cynthie said.

Oscar squinted at her. "You're a Dare Islander, aren't you?"

"Yes, sir."

"Thought so. I recognize the brogue."

Linguistics expert, Cynthie told herself. "And you're a dingbatter," she said.

A moment's frozen silence while she wondered if he'd understand the reference. If he'd get the joke or be horribly offended.

Max drew breath to speak.

And then Oscar barked once with laughter, and Cynthie exhaled in relief. "Ha. Very good. What did you say your name was?"

"Cynthia," said Dorothea.

"Cynthie," Max said.

"Good to meet you, Cynthie. Guess you can teach an old dog new tricks." He met her gaze, a glint in his pale gray eyes. "Maybe a young one, too."

Cynthie grinned.

Dorothea touched her husband's arm. "I see the Parsons. We should say hello."

"Right. Well, then." Oscar cleared his throat. "Congratulations," he said to Max, with another glance at Cynthie. "On the installation."

"Thank you, sir."

She bit the inside of her lip, containing her laughter until Oscar and Dorothea had moved out of earshot.

"God. I'm sorry," Max said when they were gone. "I owe you one."

"For what?"

"Subjecting you to that. Can I get you another drink? After a conversation with my parents, I usually need a drink."

"I liked your parents." And they had liked her. She hugged their unexpected approval to her like a secret. Maybe she could fit into his life. "I don't need a drink. But I'll take a shrimp if the server comes by again."

"I'll get you one." He brushed her lips with his, a brief, social kiss that still set her senses humming.

"And then I want to dance," she said, filled with an unfamiliar sense of her own power.

"You got it." Another kiss. "I'll be right back."

She could offer to go with him. But after her successful evening, she didn't want to appear clingy. She was fine here, surrounded by his friends and colleagues. Actually, she was great.

She admired his broad shoulders cutting the crowd a surfer paddling out to catch a wave—before she turned to watch the couples on the dance floor. The band launched into a cover of "Under the Boardwalk."

When a hand settled, warm and familiar, on her hip, she smiled, swaying into his touch. *Max.*

Or . . .

Her skin prickled.

Not.

The hand curved inward, slid down onto her ass. A man's

breath—not Max's—filled her ear. "I didn't know the aquarium hired cowgirls to cater these things."

She jerked, almost spilling her wine. Turned.

"Dr. Rice," she said faintly. Her boss.

SHE wanted to dance, he would dance, Max thought as he made his way to the buffet table. He only hoped the band played something slow. His dancing skills hadn't progressed beyond the standard wedding clutch-and-shuffle.

But the thought of holding Cynthie in his arms, pretty and soft and smelling of spice, was appealing.

He scored a couple of the shrimp she'd asked for and added some puff pastry thing he thought she might like.

"Not so clueless, after all," Greg Stokes said beside him.

"Pardon?"

"You. Your date." Greg nodded toward the dance floor. "Very hot. Also sweet, which makes a nice change."

Max followed his gaze to Cynthie, swaying softly by herself in her shiny dress and cowboy boots. Something swelled in his chest to the point of pain. She was more than sweet. She was . . . *More,* he thought again. She was everything. "She's good with people."

"A natural. So, are you two . . ." Greg waggled his hand. "Serious?"

"I'm going to marry her," Max heard himself say. "As soon as I can talk her into it."

"Wow. Well, congrats." Greg's good-natured face split in a grin. "Good luck with that."

Max smiled. "Thanks." He glanced again toward the dance floor.

Where some dickwad, some stranger, had his hand on her ass.

Max saw red.

"Excuse me," he said to Greg and started across the room.

As he watched, Cynthie jumped and whirled, the animation draining from her face. She looked almost stricken.

Remember where you are, he told himself. Cynthie wouldn't appreciate it if he made a scene. But he wanted to rip the offending hand off and beat the guy over the head with it.

Cynthie met his eyes. Her face went from white to red, her expression a muddle of relief and consternation.

He tried to smile reassuringly. "Hi, sweetheart."

He put a hand at her waist. Universal male body language for *Mine*. Sent the dickwad a death glare. *Back off*. "Who's this?"

Cynthie bit her lip. "Max Lewis, my boss, Rick Rice."

Her boss.

Max nodded shortly in acknowledgment, trying not to embarrass her. Cynthie could handle herself. She could handle anything. He didn't need to indulge in primate displays of aggression to defend her. No matter how much he wanted to.

The other man—mid-forties, well-groomed, expensive cologne—bared perfect white caps in a smile. "You must be Cynthie's date."

Max set the shrimp plate on a nearby table—he was pretty sure Cynthie wouldn't want to eat now anyway—and shook hands, frustrating Rice's attempt to turn his wrist up. Their eyes met.

Max smiled tightly. *Yeah, buddy, you go to the gym, but I haul crab pots out of the mud*. "That's right."

"Dr. Rice is here with his wife," Cynthie said.

Max followed her glance to a dissatisfied-looking blonde on needle-thin stilts. "Great. My dance," he said to Cynthie.

The air thickened and pulsed between them.

With a little sigh, she relaxed and moved into his arms.

CYNTHIE dropped her head against Max's chest, absorbing the steady beat of his heart, the undemanding clasp of his arms.

He wasn't a good dancer. He didn't attempt anything beyond the two-step shuffle your average twelve-year-old could do. But he held her safe, gradually restoring her sense of balance.

"Okay?" he murmured against her hair.

She nodded against his shirt. "Thanks."

He smelled so good, like laundry soap and Max. Slowly other details seeped into her consciousness, the brush of his thighs, the fine wool texture of his suit, the hint of dark hair at his collar. Being with him didn't make all her problems suddenly go away. It just made her feel better. Stronger. More able to deal with things.

His chest expanded with his breath. "Your boss . . . He's an asshole. You know you don't have to put up with that."

Had he ever in his life felt helpless? Powerless? But of course he had, she thought, remembering high school. It hadn't stopped him from standing up for her. She smiled at him. "I know."

His brows were still knit. "If he's bothering you, you could report him to your instructor. Or the dean."

"I don't want to talk about it."

Not now. She wanted to close her eyes and be with him, simply be, to stay in this magic place, this moment out of time, where she danced at the bottom of the sea with the man that she . . .

Loved.

She loved Max.

"Not here," he agreed. "When we get home."

His house. *Home.* Yearning unfurled in her heart.

"Not tonight," she said. "Tonight's about you. " *About us.*

His arms around her tensed. He wanted to argue, she knew. He kissed her forehead instead, his breath warm, his lips soft. "Whatever you need."

"I need you."

She felt him smile against her brow. "You got me, sweetheart."

She flushed all over, loving him. Wanting him. "I mean, now."

His feet stopped moving. "I'll get the car."

Thirty minutes, she calculated, until they reached his place. "I have to use the ladies' room first."

"I'll meet you out front."

He left her with a kiss and a smile. *Tonight,* she thought, she would find the words to tell him. Not falling, but fallen, fathoms deep in love.

She was still smiling a few minutes later when she left the restroom.

And ran smack into Rick Rice, lurking in the hallway outside.

She swallowed a groan. *Be cool,* she thought. *Don't make a fuss. You have to work for this guy.*

She gave him a brief, in-passing smile and started for the exit.

He shifted to intercept her. "I saw you lose the professor. Smart move."

She tilted her chin, her heart beating faster. "Actually, he's waiting for me outside."

"Let him wait." He caught a strand of her hair between two fingers, close to her breast. She flinched back, and his hold tightened, stinging her scalp. He smiled into her eyes. "He won't miss you for a few more minutes."

Cynthie's mouth dried. Creepy bastard. "What about your wife?"

"Marion?" He rubbed the strand between his fingers, making her skin crawl. "What about her?"

"Won't she notice you're gone?"

"She won't care. She gets what she wants from our relationship."

Cynthie took a deep breath. She couldn't afford to piss him off. Calm, that was the thing. "I'm sure you're very happy together."

"Oh, we are. She has my name and my money, which leaves me to pursue . . ." He raised his gaze from . . . her hair? Her breast? "Outside interests."

"Yeah? Well, all I'm interested in is my job."

"Of course. You're a student. You need references. Experience." Rice straightened, looming over her. "But I think it's time we renegotiate exactly what kind of experience you should get while you're . . . under me."

Her stomach sank. *Crap. Crappity crap.*

And then, somewhere deep under the dismay, outrage ignited.

Work hard, she always told her girls. *Do your best. Believe in yourself. Stand up to bullies.*

What kind of an example was she setting for Hannah and Madison if she let this creep ass talk to her this way? Who the hell did he think he was? Who did he think she was?

Cynthie stepped back, ripping her hair from his grasp. "That's not what you're paying me for."

Rice's expression hardened. "Don't be stupid. Why do you think I hired you? Why would anyone hire a girl like you? Not for your brains."

A girl like you. The words struck her like a slap, whipping color to her face. She stared at him, stunned.

And then Max's words, Max's voice, played in her head. *You were never that girl*, Max had said. *You were always more.*

She pulled herself up, flushed with indignation and confidence. "Anybody would be lucky to hire me. I work hard. I'm in the top five percent of my class. I don't need you, I don't need your references, and I sure as hell don't need your shit. So you can take your job and your tiny little dick and shove them."

She pushed past.

He grabbed her. *"Hey!"*

She tugged her arm. "Let go."

"You ungrateful bitch, I—"

"You heard her." Max's voice, deadly calm. "Let her go."

Rice released her elbow, his face dangerously suffused with blood.

Good. She hoped he dropped dead.

Max took his arm. "Let me help you outside."

"Take your hands off me."

"Keep your voice down." Max's gaze held Cynthie's. "Are you all right?"

She nodded. She felt . . . Okay, she was still really angry. But she felt good. Powerful. "Never better."

"Right. Here's how this is going to go," Max said to Rice. "Ms. Lodge will find your wife and tell her that you're not feeling well, and I'm going to take a walk with you outside, where security will call you a cab."

Rice sneered. "You can't tell me what to do. I'm a donor. A major donor."

Max's expression never flickered as he steered him toward the exit. "I guess for a good cause, the aquarium will take anyone's money."

When Max returned a few minutes later, Cynthie's anger had faded. But the powerful good feelings remained.

"Thank you for rescuing me," she told him as he took her in his arms.

He shook his head, his gray eyes rueful. "You rescued yourself. I told you you were amazing."

"Yes." She beamed, twining her arms around his neck. "But it took you to make me see it."

She didn't need him to save her, she realized. She needed him to believe in her. To love her.

She held on to him with both hands, absorbing his strength, breathing him in. "I love you, Max."

His quiet eyes kindled. "I love you, Cynthie."

He kissed her then, deeply, sweetly, while her heart turned over in her chest.

"Me and Maxwell Lewis," she said in wonder when at last he raised his head. "Who would have thought?"

His lips curved. "I guess we did."

"Yeah." She grinned at him, giddy with joy. "I always was a smart one."

NINE

ON A SATURDAY afternoon in February, the aquarium was full of young families, toddlers in the arms of their mothers, fathers pushing strollers. Their voices bounced off the high ceilings and echoed back like dolphin cries.

Watching a father grab the back of his daughter's overalls before she nosedived into the tidal touch pool, Cynthie melted a little inside. She was working for a family dentist two afternoons a week, but even regular contact with his pediatric patients didn't quell the surge of nostalgic longing. "I miss that stage."

Max slanted a look down at her as they entered the ocean gallery. "I'll remind you of that when Madison starts driver's ed in two years."

Cynthie narrowed her eyes at him.

He grinned.

Hannah danced over, her curly mane bobbing at every step. "Mom, Max, come on. We're going to be late for the dive show."

Cynthie looked at Madison, simmering with some barely suppressed excitement, her camera slung around her neck. "Maddie, do you want to come with us or go watch the otters?"

"I'll come." Madison glanced at Max. "I want to take pictures."

Cynthie's heart brimmed as they entered the gallery together. Like a family.

The past four months had been a period of adjustment for all of them. Love really didn't solve all your problems, Cynthie reflected. Sometimes it created new ones. But nothing she and Max couldn't tackle together. Hannah had accepted Max from the start. Madison was slower to warm to the idea of another adult in her life telling her what to do. But Max had been wonderful, respecting the teen's boundaries and the occasional bumps in the road, telling Cynthie not to worry, letting Madison set the pace of their relationship. Gradually, they were all learning to fit their lives together. Well, they'd already survived car repairs and food poisoning, school projects and a job change. Cynthie smiled. *Life, in other words. For better or worse, in sickness and in health.*

The aquarium guide stood in front of the living shipwreck to begin her spiel, her body outlined in eerie light. Cynthie stood back to allow the milling children a better view. The divers were already moving slowly through the giant tank, churning up tiny puffs of sand, releasing silver clouds of bubbles. One of them gestured her closer.

She turned around to look at Max. He shrugged.

"Go on, Mom," Hannah said.

Cynthie let herself be prodded to the front of the crowd. The guide smiled, her body blocking Cynthie's view of the tank. "Are you Cynthie?"

"Ye-es."

What was going on? Hannah was almost hopping in excitement. Madison stood a few feet away, her camera aimed at the vast sunken wreck behind her.

"Good. One of our divers has a message for you," the guide said, and stepped away from the glass.

Cynthie blinked.

He was holding a sign. A large white sign with two blue kissing fish below the words CYNTHIE, WILL YOU MARRY ME? MAX

Her stomach dropped. Her heart soared. Phones lit up the gallery like a rock concert.

She whirled to find Max and almost stumbled. He knelt at her feet, a ring box in his hand and love in his eyes.

He rose to his feet, his fingers sliding beneath her chin to tilt her face for his kiss. A slow smile curved his lips. "What do you say, sweetheart?"

This time the words came easily, flowing from her heart. "Yes. Oh, yes."

Yes to marriage, to building a family with this man and Madison and Hannah.

Yes to life.

Yes to love.

BETTING THE RAINBOW

by Jodi Thomas

Available now from Berkley Books

New York Times *bestselling author Jodi Thomas returns to the town of Harmony, Texas, where life has a way of making better plans than anyone ever imagined . . .*

Sisters Abby and Dusti Delaney have spent their entire lives on Rainbow Lane, but they dream of something bigger. So when a poker tournament comes to town, Dusti is determined to win enough money to leave. Enlisting expert Kieron O'Brian to teach her the game, sparks begin to fly as they play their hands. But Kieron refuses to stand in the way of her dream, even if it means losing her forever . . .

After a year of traveling, Ronny Logan is settling into a home on Rainbow Lane, but that's all the settling she'll be doing. Ronny refuses to fall for anyone, regardless of the chemistry she has with her neighbor, Austin Hawk. Yet something undeniable begins to grow between the two loners—if only they can let their barriers fall and open their hearts . . .

It's Only Love

by Marie Force

Coming November 2015 from Berkley Sensation

The new Green Mountain Romance from Marie Force—the New York Times *bestselling author of* And I Love Her.

Ella Abbott has long been secretly in love with Gavin Guthrie. A few recent encounters have only added to her infatuation, especially the kiss they shared at her sister's wedding. It doesn't matter to Ella that Gavin is in a bad place. He says there's no hope for a future with him, that he has nothing to offer her. But all Ella cares about is the love she feels.

It's been seven long years since Gavin lost his brother. He'd kept himself under control and moving forward until his brother's beloved dog died and his brother's widow remarried. Since then, he's been drinking, fighting, and even getting arrested. It seems the only time his demons leave him alone is when Ella is around.

Gavin knows it wouldn't be fair to drag Ella into his darkness, but when she inserts herself into his life, what choice does he have but to allow her to soothe his aching heart?

WHEN SOMEBODY LOVES YOU

by Shirley Jump
Coming October 2015 from Berkley

First in a new series from the New York Times *bestselling author of the hugely popular Sweetheart Sisters novels!*

At heart, Elizabeth Palmer is a practical Jersey girl. And her life reflects that—until everything suddenly falls apart. In a bid to change her luck, the intrepid reporter accepts a job to write a story on a reclusive quarterhorse breeder in Chatham Ridge, Georgia. To her surprise, she finds herself settling into the warm, inviting town—even joining the Southern Belle Book Club—and craving the company of the rancher she's there to interview . . .

Hunter McCoy has good reason to keep his distance from the determined reporter. Tragedy has taught him to stick to things that don't require his heart. But he can't seem to resist the vulnerability he detects beneath Elizabeth's tough demeanor.

But when tragedy strikes the ranch again and Hunter shuts her out, Elizabeth will have to prove to Hunter that having somebody love you can heal all wounds . . .

CAROLINA DREAMING

by Virginia Kantra

Coming February 2016 from Berkley Sensation

Virginia Kantra continues her beloved Dare Island series about family bonds and the power of love. From the New York Times *bestselling author of* Carolina Blues.

Bakery owner Jane Clark learned the hard way that life isn't all sugar and spice and everything nice. Divorced from her abusive ex and determined to protect her young son, Jane has convinced herself that the life she has—with a healthy child, a thriving business, and a home on beautiful Dare Island—is all that she can handle and maybe more than she deserves. Until the arrival of a stranger tempts her to dream of the woman she could be . . .

Former Marine Gabe Murphy is struggling to rebuild his life after his protective instincts landed him in jail. He has enough baggage of his own without taking on a vulnerable woman and her child. Yet Jane's hesitant smiles and soft strength impel the sexy loner to imagine a home and a family of his own for the first time. He is determined to prove to Jane that he's worthy of her trust—and her love.

Loving Gabe is dangerous for a woman afraid of taking chances, but their attraction proves too powerful for Jane to resist. Until a ghost from her past appears, threatening their chance at happiness.

Now, Jane and Gabe must believe in themselves—and in each other—to make their dreams come true.